Road's End Series—Book Three

Misjudge

Road's End

Everyplace Else

Deborah Dee
Harper

Misjudge
© 2022 Deborah Dee Harper

ISBN-13 Paperback: 978-1-7368419-4-5
ISBN-13 Digital: 978-1-7368419-5-2

Published by 11:11 Publishing.

Printed in the United States of America.

Dedication:

To my publisher and dear, dear friend, Tracy Ruckman, without whom this book or the ones before and those that follow would ever have seen the light of day.

Acknowledgements:

My God, my family, my colleagues, my friends.

Praise be to my Lord and Savior Jesus Christ, the Maker and Sustainer of all creation and the One responsible for any talent or skill I possess. Thank You for this opportunity to serve You. May my words honor You and Your Kingdom.

A big thank you goes to my family—my three children and their spouses, and my seven wonderful grandchildren. Each one of you helped me along the way and I'm so blessed you're a part of my life.

My deep appreciation also goes to Tracy Ruckman, publisher extraordinaire and sweet, loyal, and talented friend. Without you, Tracy, this book wouldn't have happened.

The path of the righteous is like the morning sun,
shining ever brighter till the full light of day.

Proverbs 4:18 NIV

Prologue

They say your life flashes before your eyes when you think you're going to die. Must be I had a pretty boring life to that point because nothing flashed before my eyes except a red haze that accompanied a steely determination I've never felt before. I remember it because Shiny looked a lot like that old caricature of the devil. I guess, too, that I was fed up with people messing with the folks of Road's End. We are some of the gentlest, most generous, and earnest, Christ-loving people you can find on the planet, yet we're constantly in the middle of some kind of war—and I don't mean spiritually, although that's no doubt behind all our troubles. The devil (the real one, not Shiny) likes to target the virtuous because he's a cowardly loser who doesn't know when he's defeated. He takes his rage out on the innocents of this world. He knows he can never have us, so he sows seeds of danger and any other disruptive, evil, and cruel thing he can think of to make us miserable, create doubt about ourselves, and limit the good we can do for the Kingdom.

But not on my watch, buddy. Not on my watch.

As if I didn't have enough on my plate with Del hiding in the root cellar, Bristol doing something … dangerous, and all the women scattered around who-knew-where so I had no idea how to protect them, and a bad guy staring down his gun barrel at me, it started to rain. I don't mean drizzle, sprinkle, or even pour. I mean it *rained*—buckets, dump trucks-full, heck, even those planes that drop water on forest fires couldn't compare to the volume of water pouring down from above. Tons upon tons of water droplets in clouds sneaked their way across the sky to surprise us with the mother of all rainstorms.

At first, I was annoyed but a split-second later I realized what a blessing it was. Talk about a diversion. If I was soaked that meant Shiny was too. And no doubt distracted. Before I had a chance to think, I aimed my gun and stalked toward him with a determination I can't describe. God was giving me super-courage. No doubt about that. I hoped He'd also endowed me with a bullet-proof force field. Even as I stepped closer and closer, I thought to myself, "Hugh, what on earth do you think you're doing? You'll die here in the rain, all wet and shot to pieces." But it didn't matter what my brain was telling me. My heart was saying, "I've had it, devil. I'm sick and tired of you interfering with our lives. From now on, I'm the new sheriff in town and you can just get the heck out of Dodge."

At the moment I would've had to make my decision to shoot or be shot, I detected movement in the trees behind Shiny. While we stood facing one another on a very wet playing field, whatever I'd detected exploded from the woods. Ten seconds later I was standing and Shiny wasn't. Something arrayed with tree branches, mud, leaves, and a nasty attitude stood staring at me in the rain.

I'll bet you're confused. Let me start from the beginning and set the stage. We'll get to the fight-to-the-death part soon enough.

It had been a while since our last catastrophe during our daughter Mandy's wedding when a tornado aimed itself straight at Road's End. Since then, things had been fairly quiet but peace and quiet never last in this town and the problems never come with a warning. Nope. Not this time either. All I did was open the front door. Granted, it was 4:00 AM, but the knocking woke me and since we run an inn, the logical thing for me to do was find out who was on our front porch.

But logic doesn't work in Road's End. No matter how hard I try to avoid problems, they find us just as surely as the biggest magnet on earth will find that nail that rolled under your bed last year.

Read on ...

Chapter One

It was all I could do to keep from screaming like a little girl when I saw who was standing on the other side of the door. If you know me, you'll understand why I often *think* about doing that, but seldom act on my impulse.

But this time was different. This wasn't one of my crazy neighbors and parishioners, the president of the United States (who's been known to visit Road's End), or even Sophie the camel. No, this was worse than all that put together and quadrupled. And from the look on the face of the person standing behind and apparently accompanying my scream-inducing visitor, he too knew what I felt. The odds of them arriving separately were slim, at best. They must be together, although the last I knew, the man in front of me had sworn to never darken our door again.

And yet here he was. Not a man of his word, I guess.

During the blizzard of last year when as a town we manhandled, shot, witnessed to (vigorously and without mercy), and generally misused a gang of drug dealers bent on killing our good friend and church handyman, Bristol Diggs, another unsavory character showed up in the form of Delbert T. Jackson.

And that's who was standing in front of me, looking none too pleased to be back in Road's End. Behind him stood my friend, Ross McElroy, the POTUS's Special Agent of the U.S. Secret Service. Counting Ross, there were two very unhappy people on that porch and one standing just inside the house pondering slamming the door in their faces.

I was speechless. I imagine I hardly looked like the retired Air Force chaplain and current pastor of the Christ is Lord Church with my mouth and eyes opened as wide as God, my eye sockets, and my jaw allowed.

"Uh ... hello there, Delbert. What brings you here today?"

Nothing. Delbert is not the friendly type.

I looked to my friend. "Hey, Mack. Good to see you. Why are you and Delbert standing on my front porch? Is the president here?" I peeked out the door, but thankfully, the Commander-in-Chief wasn't bringing up the rear. I wiggled my finger between the two of them. "Are you guys together?"

Nothing from Delbert. A growl from Mack. Yep, they were.

Mel was going to kill me for this. I stepped back, and said, "Well, come on in. I'm sure you'd like some coffee this early in the morning." I checked my watch. "By the way, just why *are* you here at 4:00 AM?"

Mack finally spoke while giving Delbert a not-so-gentle nudge. Coming from Mack, it was more like a punch in the back that propelled the grumpy man in front of him into our foyer like a charging bull. "I need that coffee, Hugh. Now." When an armed giant tells you to get him some coffee, you scurry as fast as you can to the kitchen. They followed.

"Have a ..." I heard two chairs screeching across our brick floor. "... seat."

Mack growled, "Sit, Jackson. Not a word out of your mouth. Got that? Not a word. Don't even breathe loud. If I so much as hear your heart pumping, I'll take you out. Understand?"

Apparently, Delbert understood because he didn't answer. He scowled, sneered, and looked generally ugly, but he didn't talk.

Mack looked up at me with that "where-is-my-coffee?" scowl and I mouthed, "Can I talk?" Mack nodded.

"Okay, then, guys. Coffee's on and should be ready soon. Sorry I don't have any of Sadie's baked goods. We did, but I ate them last night. If I'd have known you were coming, I'd have saved some for you." I know I wouldn't have because I've never been able to resist anything Sadie bakes, but I felt I should at least pretend I would.

It was awkward sitting in my kitchen at 4:00 AM with the president's chief Secret Service agent sitting next to a man the residents of Road's End would just as soon lynch as poison, shoot, stab, or drag face-down across the snow, but that paled in comparison to the awkwardness that followed.

Because just then my wife, Melanie, entered the room.

Chapter Two

Chances are you haven't met my wife—in person at least—but I can tell you she is one of the gentlest, most God-fearing, loving, generous persons the Lord has put on this Earth. But there are times … like now …

"Whoa … (Translated, that meant "You mean to tell me you let that disgusting man back into our house after all he did the last time he was here and what is Mack doing here and oh, my gosh, I sure hope it doesn't mean what I think it means. Are you absolutely *insane*?") Isn't she eloquent? She's always been able to express displeasure with a glare that would melt cement.

She quickly pulled herself together, but I've seen happier looks on her face during a marathon childbirth session with our oldest son. I don't think she's ever really forgiven him (or me, for that matter).

"Well, gentlemen, what brings you here before sunrise? Hugh, where are those doughnuts we had last night? I'm sure Mr. Jackson and Mack would like one to go with their coffee."

I had the smarts to keep my mouth shut and thank goodness Mack had the presence of mind to fix the problem. "Thanks, Mel, but Hugh already offered. We don't need anything right now."

I wanted so badly to sigh with relief, but Mel's so smart she can tell when I'm fibbing just by my ratio of oxygen to carbon dioxide. And it's always about what I gobble up behind her back. I'm sure she didn't believe a word of Mack's comment and I'll be in the doghouse until I run over to Sadie's and replace those doughnuts. On the other hand, that's not a bad idea. Life was looking up.

Then I remembered who we had sitting at our kitchen table—the biggest man in the world right beside the ugliest man in the world. What are the chances we'd have two Guinness world record holders right here in Road's End, Virginia? At that moment, the odds were pretty good.

"So," I said, as I stood to pour coffee refills, "just what does this visit mean?"

Jackson started to cough, but one look from Mack and he choked it back. He nearly strangled to death before he got it under control. Mack said, "Remember when Jackson was here this past winter?"

I looked at Mack as if he had the brain of a chipmunk with a skull fracture. I nodded slowly and gripped Mel's hand to keep her from smacking Jackson across the nose with the napkin holder. "Yes, Mack, I think we do remember. Very well, in fact. But what's that have to do with this visit?"

"Well, he's back."

I almost broke Mel's hand squeezing it, but I couldn't squeeze her mouth shut. "No, Mack. No. That's not happening. No. Just ... *no!*"

Mack looked at her with as sympathetic a look an armed giant escorting the ugliest and shadiest man on Earth can muster. "I'm sorry, Mel, but it's true." He held his hand up to stop her rebuttal. "Please, just listen, okay? I know I'm asking an awful lot of you and I wouldn't do it to you if it weren't absolutely imperative."

"In what way?"

"His life depends on it."

My mind kicked into high gear. *So? He almost died the last time he was here. Can't you take him someplace else where they might have better luck?* I admit I'm not the most sympathetic or gracious man at four in the morning, but I'm a pastor and I should act, think, and speak like one. *I'm sorry, Lord. Forgive me and please give me the strength and brains to hear Mack out.*

"How's that, Mack?"

"Jackson here got himself in deep water with a big drug cartel. And not just any cartel. No, he had to choose the most powerful one in the northern hemisphere, and tee off the head honcho. I'd say he had about forty-five minutes to live if I hadn't grabbed him and brought him here."

Mel spoke up. "Mack, I'm sorry I was so upset earlier. You too, Mr. Jackson. You and I will talk later, okay?" She looked back at Mack and said, "Is there a chance you brought the mob with you to Road's End?"

"I took every precaution possible, Mel. We left at night from an undisclosed location, flew in the wrong direction, then flew under the radar from wherever we ended up after flying so far out of the way."

"I didn't hear anything land out there, Mack."

"Yeah, well, that's because Mr. Intestinal Distress here got airsick and we had to land about seven miles out of town." He glared at Jackson, who had the good sense not to glare back.

Mel stared at Mack. "You walked seven miles? Seven *miles*?"

Mack nodded. He looked as tired as he should have, considering his busy night. "Yep. With Prince Charming here."

Well, that explains a lot.

"You mean you meant to be here earlier?"

Mack looked at me sideways. "Yes, Hugh, I meant to be here earlier." It sounded a lot like "Yes, simpleton, I'd rather be sleeping at the moment, instead of marching Jackson all over Virginia, but you know how plans sometimes go awry."

I chose to ignore the sarcasm. After all, if anyone deserved to be sarcastic, it was Mack. "So, what's your next move?"

Mel spoke up with her usual hospitality. "Why, they'll sleep here tonight before they head out again after breakfast. Right, Mack?"

"Wish I could agree, Mel, but I can't. Jackson's here for a while."

"Define a while, Mack." That was Mel, getting more nervous, aggravated, and shrill by the minute.

"Quite a while, I'm afraid."

I choked back a gasp and nearly asphyxiated myself in the process. "But why here? Aren't there safe houses everywhere? Couldn't you have dropped him off there until the danger is past?"

"That's just it, Mack. The danger is never going anywhere. Not today. Not tomorrow. Not for the rest of his life, unless we're able to bring down the whole cartel."

Well, we can take care of that right here and now, Mack. Let's just leave Delbert alone with Mel for five minutes. The rest of his life might not be as long as you expected.

Again, I asked for forgiveness. It was hard to believe, but I know the Lord loves Delbert T. Jackson as much as He loves anyone else in the world. That left me with a conundrum. Either God loves everyone in the world, including Del, with a love so deep and wide that we will never comprehend it, or He loves us all equally, including Jackson and his ugly face and attitude, but doesn't care all that much for *any* of us. I chose the first option because as hard as it was to believe, it was the truth. I was stuck with it. Delbert is—or soon would be if the ladies in this town ever had a chance to witness to him—a child of God. Now that is something I'd love to see. God doesn't play favorites, so Del is as loved as anyone else on Earth. I hoped he was saved, but I highly doubted it.

"How long is he going to live, Mack?" I stopped for a minute and rephrased that. "Sorry, Del, that didn't come out right. What I meant to say was how long will he be here … In Road's End … with … (big sigh) us?"

"That depends, Hugh. Might be just a few days. Might be forever."

By now, Mel was in the throes of a panic attack.

I swallowed. Hard. "Why's that?"

"Because Mr. Jackson is the newest member of the Witness Protection Program."

Chapter Three

"Uh ... witness protection? Isn't that for people who implicate others in crimes or testify against them?"

Mack nodded. "Sure is. We had to rush him out of Richmond tonight, well last night, I guess, even though his new identity information hasn't been completed. It'll be finished soon, but in the meantime, it was imperative we get him out of there in a hurry. Don't ask, Hugh," he said, holding his hand up to stop my words. "I can't give you any more details, but I would if I could." He stopped, thought for a moment, then continued. "Normally, Homeland Security wouldn't get involved in witness protection, and believe me, I've mangled some rules by bringing him to your house. I'm doing a favor, a big favor, for a friend by bringing him here. I'll have to ask you to swear you won't release the reason why he's here to anyone else, especially the crazy people in *this* town. *Nobody.* Not anyone in town, not your kids, your parents, your best friend. *Nobody.*"

"What about Bristol? Can I tell him? I'm going to need some back-up if Mr. Jackson is here for any length of time." *Let's try twenty minutes. Thirty, tops.*

"Yes. But tell him to keep his mouth shut."

"Will do."

I could tell Mel wasn't a happy camper, but she held it in and said, "But why here, Mack? Aren't there other places he could stay in safety?"

"Mel, to be perfectly honest, you two—well, Bristol too—are the only people in the world I'd ever trust to do this."

Back to Mel. "You mean you trust us enough to put the entire town in danger and ask us to house, secretly, no less, a man who antagonized everyone he came into contact with here in Road's End the last time, not to mention he swore, made snide remarks, and misused the bedroom we gave him to stay in during the blizzard? Is that what you mean by trust?" She took a breath, and believe me, she needed it. She turned to Jackson, who, if he had the intelligence of a tree stump would've dived under the table. "Mr. Jackson, I'm not normally a person who would judge anyone, but I make an exception for you. We, and the other people in this town, gave you every opportunity to enjoy yourself, eat good food, and stay in warm, clean, and safe surroundings. Forget about the ladies dragging you around in the snow. You had that coming. I've forgiven you, but it's hard to forget. Can you tell me how you'll behave differently this time around?"

Del opened his mouth, but no words came out because Mack had his hand around the back of his neck in a squeeze only Mack could generate. "Didn't I tell you to clam up, Jackson? I'll answer Mel, and you'll abide by what I tell her. To the letter. Got that?" Del didn't nod fast enough, so Mack tightened his grip and shook Del's head up and down." Needless to say, Jackson nodded his head (on his own) as soon as physically possible.

Mack released Jackson's neck and turned to Mel. "That's a fair question, Mel. He was a moron last time. I know that. From what you told me I'd have let him sleep out in that blizzard in his jammies. But this time will be different." He scowled at Del, and said, "Won't it, Jackson?" This time Del nodded before Mack could throttle him again. "There will be no swearing, no nasty remarks, no complaining, and no messing up the bedroom. Got that? Because these folks are saving your life. If those gangsters ever found you, you'd be out of luck all by your lonesome, so you'd better behave like a perfect gentleman around Hugh and Mel and even those crazies out there." He jerked his head toward the window.

I exchanged a glance with Mel. She shrugged, smiled, and said, "Okay then. Mr. Jackson, you're going to be a new man when you leave The Inn at Road's End. The Lord tells us to take in strangers, feed them, clothe them. We'll do it because our Heavenly Father tells us to, and we obey our Heavenly Father. Besides, He tells us we might entertain angels." *I wouldn't count on that, Mel.* She ended with "And I like a challenge. Okay?"

This time Del nodded so hard I thought he'd fracture his skull on the table.

Mel pushed her chair back and stood. "Come on, Mr. Jackson, let's get you settled. Hugh, maybe you could ask Mack a little more about the situation and what to expect while I'm making our guest comfortable?" I nodded. "Okay, then, I'll be back in a few minutes. Let's go, Mr. Jackson. Do you have any luggage with you?"

Jackson jerked his head in the direction of the dining room. Mel waited with her arms crossed. "I'm not your bellboy. You can grab that and follow me upstairs, okay?" Jackson stalked over to the bag and jerked it upward so violently the handle broke off in his hand and the clasps gave up the ghost. Clothes that looked as though they hadn't been washed or ironed in six months tumbled out across our dining room floor. I could sense Mel's horror as she turned to me with a look that said, "We'll talk later." I smiled as encouragingly as I could under the circumstances.

"Delbert, maybe you'd like to make use of our laundry facilities for the guests. Wouldn't want to mess up Mel's beautiful bed wearing dirty clothes. You get settled and bring your clothes back down and I'll show you where you can wash and dry them."

Mel blew me a kiss and walked to the dining room and around the corner to the staircase. Del followed after, looking furious, humiliated, and just plain grumpy.

I glanced at Mack just as he looked up. "I know, Hugh. I'm sorry. This is such a mess. We, or rather my friend, got word that some enforcers of that top kingpin in the organization were in Richmond looking for Jackson. Somehow or other, they got word that he was going to testify against their boss, and the boss ordered them to get him out of the picture. As luck would have it, my friend, who is at the moment undercover, overheard the conversation and asked me to get Jackson out of Dodge. Pronto. He'd have blown his cover if he—my friend, that is—had anything to do with removing Jackson from harm, so he called me. I told him I knew the perfect place. By the way, I shouldn't have told even *you* this, so keep quiet about it."

"Bristol?"

"Yes, you can tell Bristol and Melanie, but no one else."

"Okay, you've got my word, but you know how news spreads around here. They're going to see Del eventually."

"I know. I'll tell Del and you two what he's to tell others in town. I've gotta think this through."

"So, Road's End is perfect? I don't believe I've ever heard that before."

"Yeah, me neither. But for keeping Jackson alive, it's the best place aside from maybe an underwater cave in Europe or somewhere like the Andromeda Galaxy. Even that's too close. Funny thing, though. I never figured he was the same Jackson who gave you and Mel grief last winter. He just happened to mention he'd been up the road, if you can call it that, that brought us here. He started to tell me about the idiots who lived in the hokey little town he got stranded in, and suddenly I knew it was the same guy, same town, same idiots. Quite a coincidence, right?"

"Not so fast, Mack. God must have wanted Del to be here for some reason or other."

"Or He's punishing you for something—probably that dragging across the snow episode the ladies gave him. Boy, what I wouldn't give to have seen that." He started to laugh, and I thought he'd choke before he could get himself under control.

I brought him back from the brink of death by asking if he wanted more coffee. He nodded, wiping tears from his eyes (something I never thought I'd see), and settled back in his chair. "I'd love some more coffee, Hugh. Too bad about those doughnuts, though."

I grinned. "I owe you, don't I?"

"You sure do, my friend. You sure do." He smiled with a glint in his eye. "But I'm curious, Hugh …"

"Yeah?"

He pointed to the floor. "What's with the chickens?"

After I shooed Sadie's chickens out of the inn, I hit the hay. Despite knowing Delbert T. Jackson slept a few doors down from us, I awoke in a good mood, although Mel kept me awake for most of the rest of the night asking why on earth Road's End, for all its insignificance, kept attracting catastrophes. I had no answers, so eventually she fell into an uneasy sleep. Maybe it was the sunshine, maybe it was my wife, all warm and cozy beside me, maybe it was because I knew Sadie would have some fresh doughnuts at her place. Whatever the reason, I was in great spirits.

That is, I was until I left through the front door to cross Gloucester Street, a fancy name for our teensy little road that separates Sadie Simms' Bake House and Egg Plant from The Inn at Road's End and leads to the cul-de-sac that comprises our bustling four-business downtown area. Mel and I and the other residents live in the suburbs, a distance of 40 feet or so from downtown. I could hear George and Dewey from down the street where Dewey lives with his wife, Winnie, in a house nearly as old as the town itself. George and Martha live a mile or so out in the country.

"I say it should be 'Washington and Wyandotte.' Just sounds better. It flows, don'tcha think, Dewey?" I have no idea what George was thinking by asking Dewey if his name should come last in ... let's see now ... oh, right ... *anything*.

"Oh, no you don't, George Washington. I've been bringing up the rear ever since forever."

"Ever since forever? That doesn't make sense, you big dope. Forever hasn't happened yet, so 'since forever' can't be."

"Can too. And don't call me a big dope, George. They don't come no dopier'n you, Mr. I've Always Had My Name First."

By that time, they were nearly on top of me, and if I hadn't spoken they'd have plowed right over me and not missed a beat. George and Dewey can argue themselves to just about anywhere and not remember how they got there.

"Morning, George. Morning, Dewey."

"It's Dewey and George, Hugh."

"'Tis not."

"'Tis too."

"Not."

"Too."

I said nothing further. This could've gone on forever and I didn't have all day to get a hot cup of coffee and a fresh doughnut in me. A pastor needs his morning kickstart, and nothing fills the bill better than Sadie's coffee and baked goods. So, I headed toward Sadie's door and didn't even bother to intervene. I knew I'd be involved soon enough, anyway (I always am), which meant I'd soon be in hot water with one or other of them and eventually both. Those two revel in alternately loving and hating one another, sometimes in the span of thirty seconds. It makes me dizzy just thinking about it.

I held the door for them. They walked past me, still squabbling, until Sadie brought it to a halt. "Shut the door, Hugh. Yer lettin' the flies in. And shut your mouths, you old coots. Sit down and just shut up."

I thought that was pretty clear, but apparently Washington and Wyandotte, or the other way around, didn't. They sniped back and forth until Sadie walked from behind her counter, towel in hand, and smacked both on the back of the head.

"Hey, Sadie, cut that out!"

"Yeah, that hurt, Sadie. Why'dja do that?"

"'Cause yer both idiots, that's why. And ya didn't shut yer traps."

They must have agreed because they shut right up. They were lucky. She had a rolling pin in her other hand, and I have no doubt that if they didn't shut up, she'd knock them senseless.

They sat at their usual table and waited for their cohorts, Leo, Frank, Joe, Rudy, and Pastor Parry. I sat at a table closer to the coffee pot and waited for Bristol. We met here most mornings to enjoy what little peace and quiet Road's End ever has during a 24-hour period.

He walked in a minute or so later. "Hey, Hugh. Coffee hot and fresh?"

"Just like always," I said, toasting him with my mug.

Sadie walked over with a scowl. "You gonna have coffee and doughnuts, too, Bristol?"

"Yep, I sure am, Sadie. Hey, why the long face?"

Now I wouldn't have asked Sadie about her mood, which always hovers somewhere between fuming and homicidal, but that's just me. She surprised me, though, by not smacking him or pouring a pot of hot coffee all over his pants. Instead, after she poured his coffee and set the fresh doughnuts on the table between us, and said, "You know, Bristol. I don't really know just what's wrong with me. Normally, I'm happy, cheerful, you know, kind and considerate to others. But I'm not in a good mood today. Confuses me. I guess I'm just stressed."

Aside from the fact that she appeared to have lost her mind, Sadie looked perfectly normal to me. I couldn't look Bristol in the eye or both of us would've burst out laughing, so I used my time wisely by eating my first doughnut in three bites and getting ready to tackle my second. No sense letting hot, fresh doughnuts go to waste just because the woman who baked them had gone insane overnight. It'd be a loss of great food and a travesty against backed goods the world over.

Sadie left the table, and I chanced a glance in Bristol's direction. He was hiding his grin by trying to drink his coffee, but his upturned mouth made it impossible. His shoulders shook with the effort of keeping his laughter to himself. Only when Sadie went back to the kitchen did he stop drinking, put down his mug, and wipe his mouth.

"Sad, isn't it?" I said.

"You mean poor Sadie losing her mind? Yeah, it's sad, all right. Besides, what stress is she talking about? She's always the stressor, not the stressee. Is that a word? Stressee?" He took a sip of coffee. "By the way, I saw lights at your place real early this morning. What's that about? Insomnia?"

"No. Worse than that."

"Were you sick? Or Mel?"

"Well, no, not physically. Lots of mental anguish, though."

"Good grief, man, just tell me!"

"I'll tell you after we leave the gossip factory here."

"You're gonna make me wait?"

"Yep, but it's worth waiting for. You'll understand when I tell you."

After two more cups of coffee and a promise to Bristol that I'd hook up with him later that morning, I wandered over to the Inn to find out what I could from Mack. He was sitting at the table in the kitchen with Mr. Sunshine and my lovely wife.

"Hey, everyone. Nice morning, isn't it? What's new?" I looked over the table and despite having two doughnuts and three cups of coffee just five minutes earlier, my stomach growled. "Nice-looking breakfast, Mel. Got any extra?"

"Yes, dear. Sit down. Coffee's fresh and I saved a plate for you."

That's my girl. I pulled out a chair just as Mel set the plate of eggs, bacon, and toast in front of me. Next came the coffee. She refilled Del's cup, then Mack's, and eventually sat down.

So far, neither of the men had spoken a word to me. I threw a "what's going on?" look at Mack. He swallowed, took a gulp of coffee, and said, "Okay. I've already told this to Jackson, but I'll let you two know what I've told him, so he won't screw everything up and get himself killed."

Not to mention us.

"Now listen up, Jackson. After I tell them what I told you earlier, you'll have no excuse to go off-script, will you? *Will you?*" Jackson's eyes bulged and he nodded. Maybe Mack told him never to say a word to anyone, anywhere, at any time. That in itself would be an improvement.

"Mr. Jackson here is going to present himself as a gentleman to the residents of this town. I know they'll have a tough time believing him, but here's the deal. I'll let him stay here under one condition: he acts and says exactly the opposite of what he would normally do or say."

Notice Mack didn't ask us if he could stay? Yeah, me too.

"Uh, Mack, don't Mel and I have a say in whether or not he stays?"

Mack cleared his throat. "I wondered if you'd notice that part. I'm really sorry—both of you—but this guy's going to get himself killed if they find him. And you can bet your bottom dollar the big boss has dozens of his minions looking for Jackson right this minute. No doubt there's a big, fat reward to the one who kills him, so they have even more incentive to find and eliminate him." He looked at Jackson, who looked terrified. "Do you thoroughly understand what a mess you're in, Jackson? If you don't do precisely as I say, I'm giving Melanie and Hugh the authority to call me and have you removed from their home. Got that?"

"Mack, to be blunt, I don't think Jackson has even the slightest chance of following through on your rules. You know how aggravating the people around here can be. Who's to say he won't crack under the pressure? Then Mel and I have to make the tough decision whether or not to let Jackson take his chances with the mob." I was more than a little upset over the whole thing.

"I get it, Hugh. I really do. But I won't just take him and drop him off at the first stop sign I see. We'll see to it he goes somewhere else— maybe not as safe, but at least out of their eyesight. If he truly realizes he's one wrong word from death, I'm pretty darned sure he'll toe the line. Am I right, Jackson?"

Jackson nodded. I looked at Mel; she looked resigned. "Hugh, you're a pastor and I'm a pastor's wife. We have an obligation to Mr. Jackson and to our Lord to take him in. I prayed about this last night. Hard and long. I think we, well, the Lord, can do wonders with Mr. Jackson if he allows it. And being so close to death might just do the trick. God will be with us. He always is."

I have a very smart wife. I bowed to her superior thoughts on the matter. "Mel, you're right. I prayed last night, too, but I admit I was asking God to find some other way. That was selfish and un-Christian of me." I turned to Mack. "We'll take him in, Mack. But don't blame me if the ladies of this town witness to him day and night. Or the men pester him 'til he wants to tear his hair out, or theirs—those who have any."

"Hugh, I know. But all that's Jackson's problem. Not yours, not mine. Besides a little witnessing and pestering is the least he can put up with in exchange for a sanctuary against the men who want him dead. So, do we have a deal?"

I looked at Mel and she nodded her head. That was good enough for me. "Okay then, deal."

"It's a deal for me, too," Mel said. "But I think Mr. Jackson needs to agree to it, as well, don't you think? After all, it's his life and his eternity. Coming to Road's End might end up being the best thing that ever happened to him."

That was my brilliant wife. She never ceases to surprise me.

The three of us turned toward Del, who sat there looking like a puppy who'd been caught stealing a prime rib off the kitchen counter and rubbing it all over the white couch. He nodded. Probably afraid to use his voice in front of Mack. I almost—almost, mind you—felt sorry for him. We waited for his response.

Finally, with a look of dread on his face, he said, "Deal." He might as well have said, "Go ahead and kill me now."

It was official. Our lives had just become more complicated. But why shouldn't they? After all, we live in Road's End, Virginia— "Home to Weird Happenings and Even Weirder Citizenry Since the Beginning of Time." I should ask Bristol to make a sign to put under the "Welcome to Road's End" sign at the village limits. An "Enter at Your Own Risk" sign might be in order, as well.

We sat around the table talking and moping (guess who moped) for another ten minutes. Just as we were about to get on with our day, Mack looked down again and said, "Are you two keeping chickens now? In the house?"

Mel was mortified and I was disgusted. "What on earth are you doing here, Francine? How do you keep getting out of your pen? For that matter, how do you get into our house?"

No answer. Chickens are like that.

Chapter Four

After seeing Mack off, I went back inside to make sure Mel was doing okay with Del. She had him clearing the table. I couldn't help but smile as I remembered the days when she made sure our kids helped in the kitchen. She was ruthless, and eventually they figured out that being part of a family meant pulling their share of the load appropriate to their age. Each one grumbled and mumbled under their breath about the unfairness of it all. Mel pretended she didn't hear them and after a few weeks they quit altogether. I doubt Del will dare grumble or mumble while Mel and I have Mack's number on speed dial.

"You guys doing okay here?"

Mel looked up and grinned. "We sure are, hon. Mr. Jackson is an amazingly good kitchen helper. Says he's never done it before, but he's taken to it quickly."

Del tried to hide his glare, but it was about as difficult as hiding Godzilla in a cookie jar. He wiped it off his face immediately, leaving just his usual sneer. I wondered what he looked like as a baby. I shuddered and decided not to travel back into his childhood. At least not now. There was certainly something that made him what he is today, though. He couldn't have been born with that sneer on his face. Could he? Naw, he'd have scared his mother off.

"Way to go, Del," I said. I thought about giving him a pat on the back. Unlike Mack, I could reach his shoulder, but decided it was too much, too soon.

"Listen, Mel, I've got to go to the church to finish up some correspondence. Will you two be okay here alone?" Del probably thought I considered him a threat against Mel. Truth be known, I was fearful for *his* safety. Mel was doing her best, but I knew she was still teed off because she kept me up most of the night telling me she was still teed off. I'm intuitive that way. It's a gift.

"Don't worry, hon," she said with a smile that looked as if she were being strangled by a boa constrictor and didn't want to worry anyone.

"Okay then. I'll be back for lunch. Where'd the chickens go?"

Mel waved her hand and said, "Who knows. I'll call Sadie in a few minutes. They won't listen to me, so she'll have to be the one who wrangles them back home."

I walked out the back door and turned to my left to cross Rivermanse Lane. I arrived at the church's front door about three minutes later.

"Hi, Grace."

Silence.

"Grace? Are you here?"

"'Course I'm here. Hold your horses. I'm making coffee." She stomped to the doorway of our miniscule coat-closet-turned-smallest-kitchen-in-the-world, with her hands on her hips. "Give a girl a chance."

"Sorry. Coffee smells good. How are you this morning?"

"I'm good. Great day to work for the Lord. You?"

"Truthfully?"

"No, Pastorman, I want you to lie. Look around. You are, after all, in the Lord's house."

I looked around, and sure enough I was in the church. "Yep. You're right. Sorry, Grace. I would never lie to you. You know that. It's just that we had a rough morning."

She grinned that sly grin she has whenever she already knows what I'm about to tell her.

"'Bout your early mornin' visitor, right?"

My mouth dropped open. "How on earth …"

"Did you forget where you live? This is an odd town, Pastorman." Grace has an uncanny way of reading my mind and knows what I'm thinking about long before *I* know.

"Odd people, Grace. Please …"

"Don't worry. I won't go tellin' Ruby Mae. She'll get on that phone so fast it'll melt in her hand."

"Then how did you know?"

"A little bird told me."

"From one of your mother's hats?" Ruby Mae has an outlandish hat for every occasion—from colonoscopy day to her arrival in Heaven.

"Good one, Colonel. No, I just had a feeling." Grace has feelings about a lot of stuff, none of which I know. It seems everyone in Road's End knows something—make that everything— before I do.

"You haven't said anything to anyone, have you?"

"No. I figure they'll know soon enough. What on earth made him come back here? I thought he hated the town and everyone in it."

"I can't say, Grace. Sorry. But I think you'll see a different man than the one who came here before."

"I sure hope so, Colonel. For a while there, I thought we were bein' visited by the devil himself. That man has a way of repellin' everyone in sight. Maybe he'll keep the mosquitoes away."

"Don't I wish. He'll be staying with Mel and me for a while. Hard to say how long."

She laughed out loud. "I'll bet Mel is fit to be tied. He made a mess of the bedroom she put in him during the blizzard and acted all kinds of nasty. I'm surprised the ladies didn't drown him draggin' him around in the snow, but I gotta say it was fun to watch. Pure joy, in fact. 'Course after that, Ruby Mae put her funeral hat on the chair in your living room and George thought it was Mothman and shot it to smithereens. That was a good night, all right. Really good."

Yes, Grace, chasing men who want to kill Bristol and kidnapped our wives in the middle of the granddaddy of all blizzards is my kinda fun, too.

She stopped long enough to draw a breath. "Don't worry, I won't tell her he was here. That would put her over the edge, not to say she isn't already teeterin'."

"Thanks, Grace. I don't know how you know, but I won't ask again. It's enough to know that you know and leave it at that. I think we might be in for some excitement around here once the word gets out that Jackson's here."

"Excitement? 'Bout the only excitement we have around here is blizzards, tornadoes, and havin' the president visit for Mandy's wedding. Wonder what natural disaster Mr. Jackson brought with him this time."

I groaned but brightened up when Grace handed me a fresh mug of coffee. "I haven't even thought about that. I probably figured *he* was the disaster."

"Speaking of disasters, have you heard about the latest project George and Dewey have cooked up?"

"No, but I'll bet it has something to do with Dewey wanting his name first and George's second."

"Yeah, that too. But they're opening up a detective agency. Callin' it either Washington and Wyandotte or other way around. Either way it's gonna be a disaster."

Oh good. First Jackson and now these two. My very own Three Stooges. "I'd ask if you were pulling my leg, but the look of horror on your face says otherwise. What on earth are they going to investigate? Nothing happens around here."

"You mean aside from natural disasters, visits from the president, and Jackson showing up again?"

I slapped my forehead and said, "Oh no, if they find out about Jackson, sure as shootin' that'll be their first case, and they'll get him killed. Maybe all the rest of us, too."

"Hope not. Nobody would know for years. We'd just lie around— dead—until someone came to the inn."

"That's a pleasant thought, Grace. Thank you for that uplifting message." I turned toward my office. "I think I'll just sit down and pray. Yep, pray. Like crazy."

Chapter Five

I did exactly as I told Grace I would. I prayed for Jackson and his safety and hopefully, salvation. I prayed for Mel and me that we would have patience and compassion toward him no matter how grumpy he was. I prayed for the town and the safety of everyone in it. And lastly, I prayed that George and Dewey or the other way around would forget all about their detective agency. As a P.S., I prayed that if the town residents were killed, we'd be found before the next guest arrived in town. Not a good first impression, you know.

I know God has things under control, but I couldn't help but wonder why on God's green earth Jackson ended up back here. The last thing I remember hearing from him was that he'd never return even if he ended up in the Witness Protection Program. I didn't take him seriously. I was so happy he wasn't going to press charges or sue the town, he could've told me he was an interstellar visitor bent on Earth's domination. I wouldn't have cared. All I wanted was to get him out of town as quickly as I could; I'd worry about the alien invasion later. Besides, we had our hands full with the men who wanted to kill Bristol last winter. We were housing them in the church, and even though they were tied hand and foot, they still had to have 24-hour supervision and it wore on all of us.

But looking back on Jackson's last words, it was beginning to make sense. Apparently, he was in deep trouble even back then.

I finished up my work, said goodbye to Grace, and walked outside smack-dab into the middle of an argument between George and Dewey. Surprise, surprise. Why am I *always* right where they happen to be?

"Hi there, guys," I said, holding out my hand for a handshake. "How's it going today?"

They both looked at me as if to say, "Where'd you come from?" Then they battled to be first to shake my hand. Reminded me a bit of a couple of balding, very large first graders vying for the chance to erase the chalk board. George elbowed Dewey in the stomach and shook my hand first. Dewey glared at him. "Hey, George, what was that for? No need to go hurtin' me just 'cause you want to be greedy—like always."

And then they were off and running. I could hear them arguing all the way to my house. Then I noticed that instead of going to Sadie's place across the street from the inn, they were heading for my back door.

I hung my head in despair. They were going to run into Delbert and there wasn't a single thing I could do about it. I picked up the pace and did my best impression of an Olympic sprinter as I headed to the inn. Maybe I could distract them. But no such luck; they were already opening the back door.

I reached the back porch in record time. The next thing I heard was a yelp from Dewey and a shout from George.

"What the heck are *you* doing *here*? And *how'd* ya git here? There's no car out there." That was George. "I know my ve-hickles, and I know every single one of 'em here in Road's End. I'd know if a strange one was in town."

Yes, George. You would. There are probably seven cars in the whole town. You'd no doubt notice an eighth.

Then Dewey got into the act. "We did it, George! We did it. We have our first case! And it's a mystery! How did Delbert T. Jackson get here?"

I opened the screen door. "Guys, guys. Let's calm down, okay? George, Dewey …"

"That's Dewey and George, Hugh …"

"Whatever you say, Dewey, but please quiet down and greet Mr. Jackson in a civil manner. He's a guest here, and I think you'll be pleasantly surprised by his demeanor. Don't you agree, Mel?"

"I sure do. But aside from that, did you come to visit or is there a problem of some kind?" She pointed to two vacant chairs. "Would you gentlemen like to sit down and have a cup of coffee?"

"Are you kiddin', Mel? PVs don't have time to lollygag around drinkin' coffee when there's a mystery foot." That was Dewey, the one who was just about to be ridiculed.

And then he was.

"Not a mystery foot, you fool," George barked. "It's 'afoot'. And it's not PV, it's PI."

"That's what I said, George. It's a foot. A mystery foot. And PV is *too* right. It's short for private 'vestigator." He shook his head in disgust so hard I thought he'd displace one of the three hairs he still had atop his shiny bald skull.

"Are you mocking me, old man?"

"Mocking? Am I mocking you? Did you just say I was mocking you?" That was Dewey, stuck on the word 'mocking.' He turned to me. "Hugh, did you just hear George asking me if I was mockin' him?" I knew he didn't want my opinion, so I ignored him, and Dewey continued. "Listen, you nincompoop, I'm not mockin' you. I'm just makin' fun of you. Big difference there, right?"

"It's afoot, Dewey. *Afoot!*"

"That's what I just said, George. How many times do I gotta tell you, man?"

George did the only thing he could under the circumstances. "I give up, Dewey. You win. You're wrong, but you win. Let's go git some coffee at Sadie's. Working PIs need their nourishment more than the average Joe."

"That's PVs, George."

They wandered through the kitchen, into the dining room, and out the foyer to the front porch, forgetting us—and Del, thank goodness. From there they walked across the street, presumably to Sadie's. I guess our coffee can't hold a candle to hers.

I watched out the dining room window to make sure they'd left and stayed that way. I never did figure out what they wanted in the first place. It was a beautiful fall day and Mel had the windows open. They were almost out of earshot and out of our hair when I turned from the window and heard …

"Who's Joe?"

Deborah Dee Harper

Chapter Six

Well, one problem was solved, temporarily, at least. But I knew that wouldn't be true in fifteen seconds, just long enough for George and Dewey to argue who was going to be the one to blurt out that Delbert T. Jackson was back in town. I don't know who was more nervous—me or Delbert. I have to live with these people, but he might get himself whacked, so maybe Mr. Congeniality was in worse condition than I was. I wouldn't blame him for being nervous.

I walked back into the kitchen and sat down with Del and my wife. They were just finishing up the last of the coffee. I thought about making a pot, but realized any more caffeine, mixed in with George and Dewey, the new PVs in town, would put me over the edge. I had to keep it together and then find Bristol to tell him what was up.

I found him perched precariously on the east slope of the church roof, one foot low, the other higher, holding a broom-like instrument he was using to clean out the gutters.

"Hey, up there. How's it going?"

He looked up. "Gosh, Hugh, you nearly scared me to death!"

I chuckled. "You can stand like that on a roof, but my voice scares you?"

He made his way toward me and scrambled down the ladder with the agility of a spider monkey. "Well, Hugh, I really didn't want you to find out like this, but yes, your voice scares me."

"More than Sadie's?"

"Gosh, no. But more than, say, Hazel Parry's."

"Okay then," I said, "what about Ruby Mae's?"

He pretended to shudder. "You've got a point there. I don't mean to speak ill of the hatmakers in town, but Ruby Mae's voice is definitely one of the scarier ones around."

"I thought so." I slapped him on the back and said, "Coffee? Grace always has a hot, fresh pot for me when I come in."

We walked up the steps and opened the heavy oak doors and stepped inside. "Grace? Are you here?"

I could hear stomping—well, Grace doesn't stomp, but she does wear heels every day because she always dresses for work just as she would if she were coming to a church service on Sundays. She always says, "No reason not to. After all, we're still in the Lord's house." She has a point. I looked down at my shirt and pants. Casual, but neat and professional. I was good to go.

"What *is* it with you asking me if I'm here all the time?" She appeared around the corner of another set of huge and heavy doors that led to and from the sanctuary. "You stalkin' me? Oh, hi there, Bristol. Want some coffee? I'll put on a fresh pot for you." *So much for always having a fresh pot for me.* She stabbed her finger in my direction. "There might be a cup for you if you stop with the stalkin'."

"Deal."

Bristol added, "Sounds good, Grace. Looks like you manage to keep the pastor here in line."

"Sure do. Can't have just any run-of-the mill character leadin' our worship, now can we?" She walked toward the kitchen, and we followed. "I think with a few more years of trainin', I might just have him up to speed with bein' a good example for the young'uns in town."

"Young'uns? I think Bristol here is the youngest person in town and he doesn't need any training. Does he?" I turned to Bristol. "Are you positioning yourself to be the next pastor? Tryin' to drive me out?"

Grace smirked. "Bristol? He don't need trainin'. But I think Ruby Mae wouldn't mind takin' a shot at it." She shook her finger at me. "You'd better be watchin' yerself, Pastorman, or you'll find Ruby Mae in the pulpit and yer scrawny rear-end in the pews."

"Yow! Well, I mean Ruby Mae would be a fine preacher …"

Grace snorted. "You don't mean that and you know it. Ruby Mae would be up in that pulpit for one thing and one thing only—to show off those ridiculous hats she makes. Oh, she'd preach, all right, but it'd all be about how thrilled the Lord and all His angels will be when they behold her and her hat in Heaven."

It was all I could do to keep from laughing out loud. I must admit, Ruby Mae is awfully proud of those idio… those big hats she makes.

Grace turned to pour our coffee and said, "Go ahead and laugh. Yer right. The only thing she'd be up there for would be primpin' and showin' off those idiotic—yep, I said idiotic, Pastorman, 'cause you couldn't bring yerself to think it—hats she insists on making."

"Grace, how do you *do* that?"

"Do what?"

"You know what," I said while she handed me a mug of coffee, "that mind-reading stuff. That's downright scary."

"Well, don't mean to scare you, Colonel Pastor, but it's a known fact that most men don't know what they're talkin' 'bout, so women have to pick up the slack and do it for 'em."

I waited until I'd swallowed a first sip of coffee; I like to savor that first taste no matter how many cups I've had in a day. "Well, whatever your reason, it's downright fr …"

"Freaky?" She burst out laughing.

"Don't you have something to do other than mock me?"

"Don't forget the mind-readin'. Well, I better get back to my desk. Someone's gotta do the work around here."

At that she turned and walked into her office. Bristol and I stared at one another for a second, afraid to say a word. I whispered to Bristol, "That woman scares me sometimes." We turned in the direction of my office. It was time I let Bristol in on my dilemma.

Just before I sat down, I heard her say, "I heard that."

Deborah Dee Harper

Chapter Seven

Bristol looked shell-shocked. "Can she really do that?"

"You mean the mind-reading and knowing everything before I know it, even if it's in my own home?"

"Yeah, that."

"Seems to be able to, or else she's real good at guessing."

"Geesh, how do you stand it? Isn't it aggravating to think she can read what you're saying before you even say it?"

Another sip. Man, that's good coffee. "Used to. Freaked me out if you want my honest opinion. But then I started to notice that she wasn't doing it with everything we talked about—just the stuff we've talked about before. She's just real good at picking up on how I feel about certain things and when we talk about one of those topics again, she has a head start. It doesn't hurt that she's brilliant on top of being beautiful and kind. That probably plays a part in it."

"Does she know about what you're gonna tell me?"

From out in the hall, we heard, "Yep!"

I hung my head—I seem to be doing that a lot lately. "Bristol, there is absolutely *no way* Grace could know what I'm about to tell you. *No way.* And yet she does."

Grace appeared in the doorway with that sly grin that always signals defeat for me—no matter the topic. If she's grinning like that, I've already lost.

"All right, Kreskin," Bristol said, "spill it. Just what is it you think you know?"

"Oh, you mean Delbert T. Jackson bein' back in town 'cause he's in the Witness Protection Program, so Ross MacElroy brought him here real early this mornin'? That thing I know?"

I put my face in my hands preparing to cry. I couldn't believe Mack hadn't been gone for two hours yet, and now most of the town already knew what Ross told me *no one*—aside from Bristol, Mel, and I—could know. He's going to hang me by my thumbs.

"Oh, Pastorman, don't cry now. That wasn't a feat of magic on my part. 'Member that little bird I told you about earlier? Well, I happened to be in Sadie's place getting doughnuts—for you, I might add. They're in the kitchen on top of the fridge—when George and Dewey were blabbin' all over the place. Is it true you hired them to find out how Mr. Jackson got here?"

I took my head out of my hands and stared at her. "What do you think, Grace? Do you think I'd do something to encourage *anything* those two gentlemen do? Do you really think I'd hire them to do anything at *all*, let alone blab a federal secret all around town?"

She stood there with her forefinger tapping her lips. "Let me think, Hugh." She snapped her fingers. "Aha! What about that time you hired them to rake your leaves? Or the time you hired them to wash your car or vacuum the entryway here in the church. Oh, and wait, what about that time you hired them try to prop up old Roscoe or ..."

"Okay, okay. But I hired them to let them feel useful. They were pity hirings because they looked so bored, and they begged me, and I was afraid they'd start thinking on their own about something to do—and nobody wants that. Or else I hired them to get them out of my hair so *I* could get some work done. They got a little spending money and I have some peace and quiet. I love those old guys, but I don't trust 'em with anything remotely dainty or breakable or top secret or that has sharp edges. Come to think of it, I probably shouldn't have given each of them a rake. They might have used them on one another."

"They did," Bristol said. "I bandaged Dewey up when George 'accidentally' whacked him across the rear end. He was afraid to go home. Said Winnie would ground him."

"I wish she would. Maybe we can get Martha to ground George, too, and we'd have a few accident-free days around here."

Bristol cleared his throat. "Aren't we forgetting what you're going to talk to me about?"

"I think you already know it, thanks to Miss Mind Reader here.

Grace turned to go. "You go on ahead, Pastorman. I'll just get out of your hair."

"Thanks, Grace."

I was just about to launch into my story when I heard her say, "If you had any."

"See what I have to live with? She's brutal. Truthful, but brutal, nonetheless."

Bristol laughed and added, "At least it's not boring around here."

"True, true, but why am *I* always the butt of the jokes?"

"I guess you're just so good at it she can't help herself."

I rolled my eyes. "Thanks, friend. Now I'm not gonna tell you anything more about you-know-what."

"Aw, come on. I'll quit with the teasing."

"Okay, then, but I'm holding you to your word."

I launched into my tragic story, while Bristol alternately smiled, frowned, or looked like he was in the throes of a gall bladder attack.

"Good grief, man. How much more punishment can this town take?"

"Well, it's not really the town that suffers, you know. It's usually yours truly who always—in some way or another—gets the blame. And then you and Mel get caught up in it, too. The others just have fun messing up what we're trying to do to clean up the mess *they* made. They never taught this in seminary."

"Well, they've probably never run across a town like Road's End. I'd sue 'em."

"You can say that again."

"I'd sue ..."

"Cut it out, smart aleck. I need some ideas. He's being given a new identity, of course, but it wasn't ready when Mack snatched him and got him out of town. Even if it came and we used it, that would give away the fact that he's in the WPP because they all know him by Delbert T. Jackson, and then, of course, everyone would want to know why it's changed. We have to figure out a reason why he's returned to a town he hates—and that hates him in return."

"Geesh, Hugh, have you made it complicated enough?"

"I tried, Bristol. Believe me, I tried." I leaned back in my chair, closed my eyes, and pretended I was four years old again and getting ready to twirl the chair until I got dizzy and my mom had to pick me up from the floor when I walked like a tiny, drunken sailor. But when I opened my eyes, I was, sadly, still in the present.

"Okay, Hugh. I've got it."

"Spit it out, the faster, the better."

"Well, since everyone at Sadie's this morning—which is most of the town—already knows, and the rest will know in, oh, say … thirty seconds, why don't we call a town meeting …"

"With refreshments, right?"

"Ya got that right, friend. Anyway, let's call a town meeting, let them in on as much as you feel comfortable telling them, and let them think they're in on it—which they will be, come to think of it—and tell them it's up to them and us to make sure Delbert T. Jackson doesn't bite the dust."

"Sounds good, Bristol, but first of all, I'm not comfortable with telling them anything at *all*, and keep in mind this crowd would not only enjoy watching him bite the dust, but they'd gladly shovel more down his throat. Remember, they don't have fluffy-kitten-and-cute-puppy-dog memories of him. I'm not sure one of them wouldn't go home, dial the mob's number, and snitch on him."

"True. But who in Road's End would have the mob's number?"

"Bristol, Bristol, Bristol. Of all the people in this town who would have the mob's number, who's the most likely?"

He thought for a moment, then simultaneously, we said, "Sadie."

"It's a sad thing when the town's best baker and coffee-brewer—no offense to Mel or Grace—has ties to the mob." Bristol looked stricken. First Grace, now Sadie.

"Friend, I don't think she has ties to the mob. I think she keeps the mob under control—not as the boss, but as an enforcer. Our enforcer, not theirs. Tell me this, would you rather have Sadie on your side or the enemy's?"

"Ours, of course, Hugh. But if I had my druthers, I guess I'd want her to be a double agent. You know, pretend to the mob she's on their side, and double-cross them by snitching to the Feds every little thing she knows."

I shook my head. "Can't have it both ways."

Just then a voice that sounded suspiciously like Grace's yelled out. "Cut it out, you guys. If you don't call a meeting, I will. It's the only solution that has as ghost of a chance at workin'. Right?"

Bristol and I looked at each other.

"Well, *right*?"

I hollered. "You're right, Grace."

I turned to Bristol. "As much as I hate to do it, I'll call one for tonight at the Inn at 7:00 PM." I raised my voice again. "Grace, I know you can hear me, for real or telepathically, so will you give your mom a call?" Our church is blessed with a one-woman communication system. While other churches use calling trees, ours uses Ruby Mae. I call it our "one and done" system. Grace calls her mom, and within five minutes, every living soul in Road's End knows what Ruby Mae knows. I wouldn't be surprised if a few residents lying in the cemetery next to the church might even get the news. Ruby Mae is known to have a heart for including anybody who will listen to her. Even some who won't.

"Already did, Pastorman, while you and Bristol gabbed 'bout foolishness in there."

Mel rolled her eyes when I told her about the meeting of the minds at our place that night, because she knew it was mostly about the refreshments we served, thanks to Sadie, and not about the actual reason for calling one. But being the sweet, accommodating person she is, she said, "Are you kidding me, Hugh? Isn't it enough that I have one nut here? I have to have the entire town of nuts in the same room with the nut all the other nuts want to lynch?"

I marveled at her ability to use the word "nut" so many times in one sentence. I shrugged my shoulders because she had a valid point, but other than letting the town nuts take whatever story their batty brains could conjure up and run with it, we had no choice. She knew that, I knew that. She gave me a look that said, "Okay, hon, I know we're called to be hospitable and not call our guests or townspeople nuts even when they obviously are, so I'll do it without grumbling, but the first person who gets out of line is going to have to babysit Mr. Jackson for the length of time he's here. By 'anyone,' I mean you." Mel can say a lot with a look.

I didn't remind her that by making that statement she was already grumbling (and I knew she hadn't really made the statement even though she knows I know perfectly well what she means by *that look*), and instead decided to take what she offered. She'd allow the meeting, but hold me responsible for everyone's behavior lest Mr. Jackson get himself killed by someone denied the doughnut they had their eye on. Happens every day all across America.

I looked around the kitchen. "Where's Del?"

"In the oven, Hugh." Apparently, she was still testy. "I'm sorry, hon. I'm just a little riled up right now. He's upstairs cleaning his room. His mother sure didn't do a very good job of teaching him to keep his room clean, but then this is Del we're talking about. She was probably afraid of him."

I smiled, gave her a hug and a kiss on her forehead, and hightailed it out the back door. I'm smarter than I look most days. I took the list of baked goods Mel wanted Sadie to prepare, along with a nice pile of money for her services, across the street to the Bake House and Egg Plant.

"Shut that door!"

Felt good to be back inside Sadie's. I always know where I stand with Sadie—at the bottom of the heap. But I didn't take offense because everyone else in town, with the exception of Mel and Emma, are lingering down there along with me.

"Hi, Sadie, I'm back."

"Got that list?"

Good grief, another mind reader in town. "Yep, got it right here. Looks like we're going to have a wonderful meeting—at least the refreshments." Whenever I could, I tried to get on Sadie's good side. Sadly, it was so hard to find her good side I seldom made it there, but that didn't stop me. I hoped I could love her into being a more cheerful person.

"Coffee?" That was Sadie barking at me.

"You bet." I smiled and she scowled; then she did something so out of character for the lady I knew as Sadie Simms, I nearly fled the scene. But of course, there were cookies involved.

"I'm sorry, Hugh." Sadie Simms apologizing? What's next? An end to hunger? Lower gas prices? Maybe an end to robocalls?

"For what, Sadie?"

"For being so grumpy this morning. I didn't mean to be, but somethin' came over me and I can't figure out what."

"Do you want to talk about it, Sadie?"

"Are you nuts?" That told me two things: regular Sadie was still in there somewhere, and I must be one of the nuts around here. "Aw, rats, I did it again."

I took a sip of about the fifth cup of coffee I'd had that morning and it was only 9:30. Might be a jittery day. "Let's talk a bit, okay? Do you remember ever feeling like this before?"

"Once."

Silence.

"That's it? Can you tell me why it happened and what you did to address it?"

She folded her hands. The only times I've ever see Sadie's hands folded are when they're in a fist and she's getting ready to pop someone in the face.

"Near as I can remember, it was back in the forties or fifties. Maybe the early sixties." *Well, that narrows it down a bit.*

"What happened to cause it? Can you recall?"

"Musta been closer to the late fifties 'cause I was full-grown and the world hadn't gone crazy with all that free love."

"Well, that's a start. Anything else come to mind?"

She stood and turned toward the kitchen, walked over to the coffee pot, plated some fresh cookies, and grabbed a mug. After returning, she set the plate of the best-smelling peanut butter cookies in the known universe between us, refilled my mug, and poured one for herself. She sat down. She sat *down.*

Am I imagining things now? Sadie never sits down with her customers, and frankly most of them are comfortable with being as far away from her as they can get and still drink her coffee and plow through a plate of anything she bakes. *She's in worse condition than I thought.*

Silence. I ate a cookie. More silence. I drank some coffee, added a little cream. Even more silence. This was nerve-wracking—except for the cookie-eating part.

Finally, she opened her mouth and said, "Promise to not tell a soul? Well, Mel's okay, but no one else. *No one.* Deal?"

"Sadie, I'm a pastor, and I promise you I will never divulge your secret to anyone but Mel and only if I think she can help. We've got a deal."

She looked at her folded hands, and for a moment I wondered if she was thinking about popping me in the nose for ...well, anything she wanted.

She glanced at me and said, "I was lonely."

"Oh, Sadie, I'm sorry. But you're the most visited person in this whole town. Why do you think you're lonely?"

"Because people come in to eat what I bake, drink my coffee, and use my bake house for their gathering spot every day."

"Doesn't it make you happy to know that your friends come to the Bake House to have your wonderful food and drink?"

"That's just it, Hugh. They come here because I can provide them with something they like."

I was getting confused. "And ...?"

She looked up at me. There were tears in her eyes. "Because they don't come to see *me*."

Chapter Eight

I had to admit she had a point. Dealing with Sadie was a lot like walking through a mine field or using a rickety bridge to cross over a blazing caldera of lava. Most folks were either afraid she'd tell them to shut up, or worse, knock their lights out. So, yes, I could see how Sadie could be lonely.

But I couldn't tell her that. "Well, Sadie, I can understand what you're saying, but I think folks just like your baked goods and wonderful coffee so much, they dig right in and forget all about socializing."

"Good try, Hugh, but they have time ta yak with each other for hours on end. Only time they bother ta talk to me is if the extra coffee pot's empty and they need me for a refill or to bring the idiots more doughnuts."

"Sadie, we're going to take care of that. Give me some time to mull this over and I'll get back to you. Maybe Mel will have a solution. You know how she's always coming up with something that nobody else knows about, so ..."

"You mean that *you* don't know about? 'Cause I gotta tell ya, Hugh, you're not too quick on the draw."

"I'm not?"

"Nope, you're not. Hurts me to tell ya this, Pastor, but you're usually the last one to know about anything around here."

I knew that, but it still stung to hear it from someone else. My mouth dropped open. "But ... but Sadie ... why is that?"

She whacked me on the arm (which was pretty darned intimate for Sadie) and cackled, "'Cause I'm pullin' yer leg, ya numbskull."

For a moment I thought the real Sadie was back. Folks don't often call their pastors numbskulls, but if it would make her happy and bring her out of her loneliness, I'd deal with it. "You are?" I leaned back in my chair with a big sigh and said, "You have no idea how glad I am to hear you say that, Sadie."

"But don't go gettin' a big head, Hugh. You're near as bald as one of Francine's eggs now, and gettin' a bigger head is only gonna spread those hairs out."

Well, that's one problem taken care of. No getting a big head for me. "Well, Sadie, I'll try not to get a big head, and you try to understand how much you're loved—not only by the folks here in Road's End, but by God."

She nodded, got up, grabbed up the two mugs and the empty cookie plate, and headed for the kitchen. I don't know if the good Sadie still reigned or if the grumpy one had returned. Complicated lady.

I took the hint and left, relieved to find my head still fit through the door.

I walked in the direction of the church. I still had some work to do and my talking with Grace and Bristol and Sadie had gobbled up a sizeable chunk of my morning. I realized I had to come up with something to tell the residents about Delbert T. Jackson before the meeting tonight; I didn't want to talk off the top of my head.

And speaking of heads, I noticed one bobbing toward the church from a different direction. It looked familiar, but I couldn't put my finger on just who it was. It was a woman, and she had her back to me. That's all I could figure out on my own.

I made a beeline toward the stranger and said, "Can I help you?"

The head looked up and I was staring at the face of Ruby Mae Headley, sans the orchard atop her head. "Why, Ruby Mae, I didn't recognize you without your gard … hat."

"Pastor, I jest didn't feel like wearin' one of my superb hats—I make 'em myself, you know—this morning. Don't know what came over me. Just didn't feel like it. I'm going to ask Grace what she thinks."

Oh, dear. That's not such a good idea, Ruby Mae. I knew precisely what Grace thinks. She hates those hats as much as just about anyone in town and won't be afraid to tell her mother how awful they are. Grace can be rather … uh, truthful at times. Make that *all* the time.

If Ruby Mae was looking for sympathy, she sure wasn't going to get it from Grace—daughter or not. She'd be better off going to Sadie's place. As cranky as Sadie is, Grace can be worse.

I thought about redirecting Ruby Mae, but realized she was going to hear Grace's thoughts one way or the other. After all, they live in the same house, along with about 200 hats, so hearing it now wouldn't be any more painful than hearing it later. I decided to keep my nose out of it.

I held the church door open for Ruby Mae, who turned right towards Grace's office and then I turned left and skeedaddled straight to my office. I shut the door. This was one conversation I wasn't eager to be a part of.

I didn't have much to do, so after I finished some small items, I grabbed my Bible and verified Scripture I was using this coming Sunday. I'm not sure, but I might have been staying hidden until Ruby Mae left and the coast was clear. Oh, let's be honest. That's exactly what I was doing. I didn't want to get involved in another squabble, so I played chicken, which reminded me of Sadie's lament earlier and now Ruby Mae's. Maybe we have a bug going around town that's just bringing them down. On the other hand, no bug, microscopic or not, voluntarily comes to Road's End, and seldom do any of the residents leave town to go find them. So that left me with the conclusion that nothing could be blamed for their dismay. They were both telling the truth and both not acting like themselves. Odd, I know, but then this is Road's End. But as far as Ruby Mae's problem went, I decided to leave that to Grace to handle. She'll never forgive me, but I'm deliberately making the conscious effort to distance myself from some of the … let's say craz … *unique* people in town when there's no real need for me to be involved.

That lasted about 27 seconds when two things happened. Mack called and George and Dewey walked in.

"Mack, can you hold for just a second? George and Dewey are here and I'm going to ask them to have a seat in the sanctuary while we talk. Thanks … be right back."

"Hi there, fellas. Come to see me?" Before they could answer, I asked them to wait for a moment in the sanctuary. They grumbled and mumbled but did as I asked them to do.

"Okay, I'm back. Sorry about that, but I don't dare let those two overhear anything. They can take a sneeze and turn it into a threat from the Russians. What can I do for you?"

I instantly regretted asking. He told me, apologetically, that things were heating up in the cartel and there was renewed talk of finding Del. They know he's north of Florida, he said, but then we knew that when he brought Del to our house. Some way or another, though, they know approximately where he's located.

"This is great, Mack. He's been here one day and already they know he's here?" I waited with my eyes closed to ward off the bad news. Didn't work. "Listen, I know you can't help any of this and would change circumstances if you could. But he's here and unless you move him, here is where he'll be until the government makes other arrangements for him. Are we in any danger?"

I closed my eyes again. Still didn't work. "Well, when will anyone know if they're leaving Florida and when we should abandon ship or get Del out of here?"

This time I didn't even bother to close my eyes. "Okay, I'll wait, and I promise I won't say a word, even to Mel. Maybe Bristol. I don't want Mel worrying and I don't want the town to get crazier than it already is. Bristol is level-headed and better at this kind of stuff than I am. In the meantime, I'll just wait for your call, okay?"

Two minutes later, we hung up. Suddenly my problems went from idiotic to galactic war proportions. *Lord, are You testing me or just having fun watching this all unfold? Please be with us.*

I sat there, brooding, and was just about to head for home when I remembered George and Dewey. Rats.

Talk about unique characters. I'd forgotten about the Discouraging Duo. I plastered on a smile and said, "Guys, how's it going?"

"Not too good," George said.

Not to be outdone, Dewey chimed in at the same moment with, "Couldn't be better."

Combined, all I heard was "Cobenottoobet-good-er." I could tell by their faces who was happy at the moment and who wasn't. George looked glum, so Dewey must have scored some kind of victory in the last 30 seconds. Wait for a minute, and they'll have switched moods two times.

"Well, have a seat." I gestured toward the chairs in front of my desk. They both chose the one nearest them and a kindergarten wrestling match took place until George finally won out, squeezing his behind in the chair before Dewey had time to elbow him aside.

"Coffee?" I couldn't bear the thought of the two of them with caffeine in them, although they'd already had plenty of it at Sadie's. But I was a pastor, after all, and I had an obligation to be generous and giving.

They yelped, "Nope" and "Yep" simultaneously, and again, all I heard was "Yenopep."

I pushed back from my desk, stood, and said, "Be right back, okay?" I walked to the kitchen and poured two cups of coffee. I knew if I brought just one cup, the one who didn't want it a moment ago, would've changed his mind. The thought of another grade school tussle was just too much. It was 10:30 AM and I already had my daily headache.

On the way out, I nearly mowed over Ruby Mae, a sobbing, soggy mess of a woman who had clearly not heard what she expected. I took a step to the left and peeked into Grace's office.

She looked up at me and said, "What's up, Pastorman? You finished with your meeting with two of the other crazies in this town? I just finished up with mine."

"How'd she take it?"

"How do you know what we talked about, Mr. Snoopy Pants?"

Mr. Snoopy Pants? "I ran into her outside. Almost didn't recognize her without her hat. She told me she was going to talk to you about not wanting to wear her hat today. I just figured you'd have to tell her the truth."

"And what would that be?"

"You're going to push this as far as you can, aren't you?"

"Yep."

"Okay, then, I know you don't care for her hats and I know you don't lie. Somewhere in that conversation, you probably had to tell her something she didn't want to hear."

"Well, ya got that right, Pastorman." *Good. Snoopy Pants was gone.* "She asked me why she didn't want to wear one of those monstrosities this mornin' and I told her I didn't know why, but it was the right decision nevertheless. She looked at me as though I'd thrown a spear through her." She took a breath, looked away for a moment— probably wondering if a Molotov cocktail was heading toward her window at that very moment—then continued, "I know she was hurt— mostly because I didn't encourage her to march home and put one of her flower beds on her head that very moment. But I've told her repeatedly over the years that those hats are ugly, and I wish she'd just stop makin' 'em. It's not as though she doesn't have enough of 'em. There's hats everywhere. On the tables, on the nightstands, in the closet, the kitchen cupboards, and I had to move five of 'em from the bathtub 'fore I could shower this mornin'!"

I could tell she was getting a head of steam up, so I tried to de-escalate things by changing the subject. "Well, my guys are still in my office, so …"

"Don't go changin' the subject on me, Mr. Smarty Pants." *Smarty pants? Guess it could be worse.*

And then it was.

She stood up and walked to her door. "Hey! Hey, you two in there… George and Dewey—and Dewey, shut up. I'm not changin' how I've been sayin' yer names ever since I could talk. Just hold yer horses for a minute, will ya? Pastor and me got somethin' more important to discuss. Whatever it is you two want can just wait a minute."

Okay then.

"Well, what's up? Has your mother been acting strange lately?"

"You mean stranger than usual?"

"Well, yes, but I didn't want to say it that way."

"Don't worry 'bout hurtin' my feelin's, Pastor. I live with that woman. I know she's nuttier'n a can of peanuts and a jar of peanut butter stirred together, but I love her, and I try to accommodate her strange desire to build—and I do mean *build*—those ugly hats. But I just can't bring myself to coddle her when she asks me something about them. Take this mornin', for instance. I know she was lookin' for sympathy. She wanted me to say her hats were too beautiful to keep from the public, but for cryin' old loud, I couldn't. For one thing, you know how I tend to be … uh, truthful at times." *Is she reading my mind again?* "Next, I want to protect her from hearing her hats are atrocious by someone other than me. And last, I'm sick to death to waking up with another hat—or five—somewhere in the house. It has to stop. Either she doesn't make another one for the rest of her life, or she gets rid of some of them she already has."

"You might have just hit on the solution, Grace! Why don't we have a hat sale? She could make some money and you'd get rid of some hats. What do you think?"

"That's just about the dumbest thing I've ever heard you say. Who in their right mind—which is pretty rare around here, to begin with— would buy one of them? If they did, she'd pester them about why they weren't wearin' them, when in truth, they've got them buried in the back yard. Sorry to be so blunt, Hugh, but selling them isn't going to work. At least not around here."

I sighed. "You're right. Too bad there isn't a way to get them to buyers in other parts of the country, or the world, for that matter. Maybe there are other people as hat-crazy as Ruby Mae."

"Well, I hope there aren't too many of 'em. But you might have a point. I could look up some stuff online if our internet doesn't go down—again—and maybe get her a website. She could take orders. That'd keep her busy and I don't mind her makin' more if she's not gonna keep the darned things."

"It's a deal," I said. "Better get this coffee to them before they come looking for me."

But no, they were still in their chairs playing rock, paper, scissors.

"No-o-o, George. Paper doesn't cover rock. The rock smashes the paper."

"You old coot!" That was George, the non-coot, I guess. "Listen. I'm gonna tell you this one more time. Rock smashes scissors, but rock is covered by paper. Paper covers rock, but is cut by scissors, and scissors cut paper, but are smashed by rock. Got that?"

"I've never seen a paper coverin' a rock. Why on earth would anybody bother to do that? But I can see rock squashin' paper. But … heck, George, the rock wins every single time 'cause a rock can smash paper *and* scissors. Nothin' can bother a rock. See that, George?"

"I give up, you old fool. Fine, have it your way. Rock smashes everything. Then what's the point of even playin'?"

Dewey sighed. "So you can smash the paper and scissors. Didn't your mother teach you anythin'?"

"You leave my mother out of this, Dewey Wyandotte. It wasn't her fault no one taught her how to play Rock Smashes Everything. But she *did* teach me to poke my fist into your nose."

"Guys, guys, let's talk about what you came here for. Just what was it?"

George frowned and Dewey looked confused. Apparently, they'd argued themselves into amnesia. They thought for a minute, and it finally dawned on George. "The PI office!"

Dewey brightened. "Yep, that's it, all right. But it's PV, George. How many times I gotta tell ya?"

"It's *in*vestigators, Dewey."

"No, George, it's *ves*tigators. Don't you never watch those Perry Mason shows yer wife gotcha? Why would a person be *in* a vestigator? Seems kinda weird, if you ask me."

George shook his head. After a moment, he said, "Weird is right, Dewey. Weird is *exactly* right."

I leaned forward, elbows on my desk, and said, "Well, you can iron all that out later. You fellows have a question for me?"

"Yep, Hugh, we do. Me and Dewey …"

"Dewey and me …"

"Shut up, Dewey. *We*—is that better, Dewey? *We* wanna use the church for our PI office."

I gulped. "But why?"

"Why? *Why?* Did you jest hear Hugh say 'why,' George?"

George nodded. "Well, Pastor, we got to thinkin' 'bout gettin' our office situated and all slicked up …"

"It's gonna be a beauty," Dewey interrupted gleefully, at his peril.

"Shut up, Dewey. I ain't tellin' you again."

"So, Pastor," George said, "when we got to wonderin' where we oughta put our office, we thought of the church right off the bat." He sat back in his chair and looked as though he'd just won a Supreme Court case.

I didn't quite know how to put this delicately, but I tried. "*No! No! A million times no!*"

The two of them looked at one another, stupefied.

"No?" That was Dewey, man of few words.

George, a man of even fewer words, just looked at me in disappointment, anger, and pleading.

"Listen, guys," I said. "A church is no place for a PI—I know, I know, Dewey—a PV office. It just isn't. Why would you even consider the church?"

"'Cause we'd get free rent and heat and air conditioning and water and coffee and a bathroom! It's just perfect for us, Hugh." Dewey was nothing if not truthful.

"He's right, Pastor. You know Dewey and me can't afford to build an office anywhere in town, so we thought you'd *have* to let us have it here. After all, yer a pastor, and just last Sunday you were talkin' 'bout hospitality. Ya gotta let us. It's in the Bible." He nodded his head, folded his arms over his generous belly, and waited for my agreement and approval.

He wasn't getting either one—not from me, at least.

"Listen, George, Dewey—don't say it, Dewey—yes, I spoke of serving Jesus by showing hospitality to strangers. But it also says in the Bible that Jesus drove out those who were buying and selling and upended the tables of money changers from the Temple courts. The Lord's house isn't a marketplace. Besides, George, why can't you have it in your antique store?"

"His wife won't let him," Dewey blurted out.

"How about in one of your homes?"

"Gee, Pastor, if she won't let us use the store, she sure as shootin' isn't gonna let me use our house. And Winnie 'bout threw a fit when we asked her."

Smart wives.

"Well, I'm sorry, fellas, but a church is no place to run a business. And that includes your office. I'm sure you'll find another place to put it."

George thought about that. "Okay, then. How 'bout the inn?"

I couldn't speak for a moment because I'd swallowed my tongue. I dragged it up from the depths of my esophagus and replied, "No, George. Mel would kill *me* if I agreed to that. I'm sorry, but that's my final answer. No to both the church and the inn."

"How are we supposed to solve crimes if we don't have a place for folks to visit demanding justice be served?" Apparently, he *had* been watching those old Perry Mason shows.

"I'm not sure, George. In fact, I'm not sure you're going to find anyone at all who will patronize your business. Nothing goes on here that needs investigating." I turned to Dewey. "Or 'vestigating.'"

"Hmph-ph!" Dewey was either showing his disgust for me or grunting while he got out of his chair. I'm sure they both thought they were jumping to their feet, when in reality they were clawing their way out of their chairs by grabbing onto the edge of my desk, finally getting to their feet, all stooped over, and then helping one another stand straight and find the energy to walk away. This took five minutes.

While I watched them, I realized that must be how I looked some mornings. I sure would tomorrow morning. It was still morning, and I'd already talked to half of the town's residents. I needed to get back to Mel to see if she had any problems with Mr. Sunshine. I thought about going to bed around 11:00—AM, not PM—and forgetting this town and everybody in it. But then I'd miss lunch, and I thought I heard Mel say she was fixing chicken salad sandwiches. I'd have to soldier on.

Chapter Nine

George and Dewey left disgruntled and at odds with one another over something they managed to disagree on in the time it took to move from their chairs and walk to the front door. About ten seconds and maybe 15 feet. So getting a "no" from me hadn't daunted them into getting along. Life in Road's End was back on track.

I yelled goodbye to Grace.

"Enjoy your chicken salad sandwich!"

I groaned, opened my mouth to reply, then gave up and walked out the door. I walked home slowly going over all the conversations I'd had before lunch. Sadie was sad, Ruby Mae was devastated, and George and Dewey were furious. And to make everything even worse than I could imagine, Mack tells me the cartel might be making a move. Not bad for a morning's work. I decided that as soon as Delbert was in another part of the house, I'd ask Mel for advice.

It was a beautiful fall day, warm and breezy, and the leaves drifted down like colorful snowflakes from the trees above. Fall in Virginia is glorious. The relief from summer's heat and humidity is a lifesaver to begin with, but the sight of thousands upon thousands of trees decked out in the colors of gemstones, the smell of damp earth and burning leaves, the brisk air, the impossibly blue skies, and that feeling of being safe inside your home when the cool nights turned colder made this a wonderful season. I'm sure Mel was looking forward to a day of soft breezes and fresh air. Too bad she wasn't getting it. I could hear Del before I opened the screen door.

"Listen, lady. I'm not your slave. I'm your guest."

Ever the gracious one, Mel answered, "Yes. Yes, you are, Mr. Jackson. A guest under house arrest, whose life, at the moment, hangs in the balance of my mood. And right now, I wouldn't give two cents for you living until ...well, this afternoon."

Good for you, honey.

"But don't I have any rights at all?" Delbert was whining.

"You have the right to be quiet, sit down, eat your lunch, and await further instructions. Listen, Del, I don't want to argue with you over every single thing. I didn't ask you to rake leaves to punish you. I honestly thought you'd enjoy getting outside in this beautiful weather and doing some man stuff for a change of pace. But if you want to stay inside and vacuum and dust the inn, I'll be more than happy to hire George or Dewey—who don't have a price on their heads—to do it for me. Your choice."

I walked in the back door nonchalantly, but inside I was screaming, "Way to go, Mel!"

"Hey there, you two. What's new? Beautiful day, isn't it? The leaves are getting pretty deep out there. Wish I could rake them, but I have to prepare some remarks to tell the residents tonight at our meeting."

"What stinkin' meeting?" That was Del, our personal bluebird of happiness.

"Well, Del, it's about you, actually," I said, as I pulled out a chair and sat down at the table. "And please don't refer to our business with the townspeople as stinkin', okay? To be honest, we're holding this meeting so we can protect you. We don't want any of our neighbors calling their kids or grandkids and having them find out you're here. Who knows what innocent links they might have to the mob? Maybe someone's daughter's hairdresser's nephew's first girlfriend from fourth grade went to school with one of the mob big-wigs and puts it on Facebook that we're hosting a man wanted by North America's biggest and most powerful drug cartel. I'd say it would reduce your life span to about thirty minutes."

Delbert glared, and boy, could he glare. It was all I could do to stop myself from throwing my glass of iced tea in my face to put out the flames. But I held my ground until he muttered, "Got it."

"Good. Now let's eat. Honey, this looks great. I've been thinking about this sandwich all morning. Del, you're in for a treat. Melanie makes the best chicken salad in the free world—and quite possibly beyond."

He looked at me as if I'd just launched a missile from my head. Maybe that's what he was thinking during that glare.

After a prayer followed by a few sandwich-eating minutes, I turned to Mr. Jackson and said, "Okay, Del, about tonight. As you no doubt recall, during your last visit to Road's End you met a good share of the residents of this town." I held my hand up and said, "Don't say it, Del. I know they're weird, but their hearts are in the right places, and they're devout Christians. But as you'll also recall, you didn't leave under the best of circumstances. You didn't like them, and the feeling was mutual."

Mel stood to reach the pitcher of iced tea and poured a refill for us all. "Thanks, Mel," I said, and then stared at Del until he took the hint and grunted. I guess in thug-land that's the equivalent of a heartfelt thank you.

"Okay, back to tonight. I didn't think much of it at the time, but as you were leaving last winter, I clearly remember you saying something about never returning to this town even if they *did* put you into the Witness Protection Program. I assume you were in some trouble even back then. Am I correct?"

He merely nodded, but then he had a mouthful of sandwich, so I didn't throttle any words out of him. "Okay, then. Was it the same group?"

Another grunt.

"I'll take that as a yes."

"How did you manage to elude them back then?"

Shrug. *This guy is eloquent.*

"I'll take that as an 'I have no idea,' but fair warning, Del, from now on I want you to use your voice. Just answer my questions. Is it that hard?"

Stall … stall … "No."

"Thanks, Del. Much better. So, if I'm correct, up to now you've been able to elude them on your own, but something changed, and you needed the government to help you out."

"Yeah."

"Can you tell Mel and me? I promise it'll go no further—aside from Bristol, that is, but I need him if trouble comes. If we're able to protect you and keep the details away from the other residents as much as possible, I think your stay here will be much more enjoyable."

He looked incredulous.

"Okay, not enjoyable, maybe endurable? Is that better?"

"Inside man."

"You mean *you* were an inside man? As in working-for-the-government 'inside man'?"

A few seconds passed while Del took a drink of iced tea, probably trying to find another silent, surly, snarky mode of communication. He must have drawn a blank, so he used his words and said, "Yeah. The feds were willing to drop my racketeering charges if I turned on the cartel and reported what their plans were to them—the feds—so they could catch 'em in the act."

"Wow," Mel said, "that took guts." She was genuinely amazed, and I have to admit I was too. No doubt there was a lucrative aspect to it (maybe letting him live and getting out of a long stretch in prison?), but as cranky as Mr. Jackson was, that was still a bold move on his part. Out of character, even unbelievable, but bold nonetheless.

"I agree, hon." I turned to Del. "See? We would never have known how brave you can be if you hadn't confided in us. That shows us a whole different side of you."

"Yeah, well, I was headed to prison for most of the rest of my life, so I didn't have much choice. Not like I *wanted* to snitch."

"Lesser of two evils then. You get to stay out of prison, live the rest of your life, continue doing what you've been doing with the mob, but reporting their activities to the correct agency so they'd get caught."

"That's about it," Del said.

"Well, Del, I can't say I'm proud of you for racketeering, but turning to the good side was the right thing to do, and that took courage."

For a split second I thought he was getting ready to say something nice, like "I appreciate that," or "Thanks," but that thought passed when he burped. Loudly. I looked at him until he said, "Pardon me, Mrs. Foster."

Mel nodded. "Please call me Mel."

He averted his eyes and nodded once. Clearly, being appreciative or having nice things said about him weren't everyday events for him. I wondered about his parents. Were they alive? Was he abandoned? Or did he just get in with the wrong crowd years ago and never found his way out?

"Well, let's get our story straight for tonight. I don't want to outright lie to my parishioners, but I think we all agree that giving them the whole truth isn't going to work either." I turned from Del to Melanie. "Any ideas?"

Mel spoke up. "How about telling them Del is here for his health? I mean, that's not exactly the whole truth, but it touches on it, and frankly, I think the residents would be okay with that. Suspicious, maybe, since his last visit was disastrous, but they're good-hearted people and if Del is friendlier to them while he's here, I think they'll return the favor."

I thought about that. It was brilliant. You couldn't find anything worse for your health than being dead, so in truth, he *was* here for his health. "Sounds good, Mel. Maybe we could even say it was tension and stress from his job that caused it, and he couldn't find any place more out of the way and quiet than Road's End." I looked at Del. I couldn't gauge his full reaction, but at least he wasn't snarling. "How's that sound to you, Del?"

He blinked his eyes as if he'd zoned out, then said, "Yeah, that's fine. That'll work."

I slapped the palms of my hands on the table and said, "Good. We have a plan. Del, I'll try to shield you from their questions, and you just try to look a little … (*What? More human?*) "… tired and happy to be here with them. If you feel like it, you can even say something like 'It's as tiny and pretty as I remembered.' No, forget the pretty part. That doesn't sound like you."

"How about 'it's as quaint as I remembered'?" That was my brilliant wife.

Del nodded, I grabbed Mel's hand and kissed it, and we spent the next fifteen minutes smoothing out our plan for later that night.

As always when we have a meeting scheduled, the hours flew by and before I knew it, I was standing in front of our beloved residents. They had all taken their usual seats—Ruby Mae, still hatless, in the back row with Grace, Emma next to Melanie in the front row, George and Dewey butted up against the buffet table as close as they could without crawling into the drawers, and their wives within slapping distance. The rest of our merry men, with Frank snoring, were in a group about midway to the back. Bristol sat nonchalantly in a chair leaned against the wall between the dining room and kitchen looking all content with that "even-though-I-know-we're-all-about-to-die-I'm-not-going-to-let-it-get-to-me" look, even though I'd talked to him a little earlier about the call from Mack. I've got to get him to teach me that look.

Sadie was still fussing in the kitchen and when she ambled in and set a plate of brownies as far away from George and Dewey as she could without putting it on the back porch, I thought they were going to cheer.

"Ready, everyone? Thanks, Sadie. Those smell wonderful. Okay, folks, I know you all remember Mr. Jackson from our fight with the drug dealers last winter." I turned to Del seated slightly behind me, facing the crowd. As we rehearsed earlier, he gave them a little salute and a smile so anemic I was tempted to arrange a blood transfusion following the meeting.

Just as I expected, the room erupted into a bunch of jeers.

"What's he doin' here?"

"Never could stand that fella."

"Where'd he stash the drug guys?"

"Is the president coming again?"

"Can we have a brownie?" That was George and Dewey's question, followed closely by two distinct slaps from their wives.

I raised my arms and asked for order. "Listen, guys, I know you and Delbert didn't get along all that well last time, but let's face it. We were all under a lot of pressure and stress. I don't think any of us acted normally that night. Let's just give Del the benefit of the doubt and do the right thing. Let's welcome him to Road's End as Christians do."

Silence. It always amazes me how little influence I have on the behavior of these people. Most of the time I can't shut 'em up, but when I really want them to speak, they clam up tighter than a bank vault.

"Folks? Did anyone hear me?"

Emma stood in the front row and turned to address the crowd. "Folks, listen. We didn't get along well with Mr. Jackson when he was here last time, but if you recall, we didn't treat him as well as we should have either, considering we're Christians. None of us, including Mr. Jackson, were at our best during that stressful time, so why don't we let bygones be bygones and give him another chance? You did for me, you know, and I treated you all badly long before Mr. Jackson was even born."

I smiled at her candor. "Thanks, Emma. Friends, Emma's right. It's our Christian duty to welcome him to our town. I know that Mr. Jackson was sent here for his health. He was suffering stress and tension, and if he didn't take some time off in a remote location, someplace peaceful and beautiful, his health would suffer. I think you'll agree that Road's End, for the most part, is about as peaceful and out of the way as any town in the whole country. I don't suppose he ever imagined returning to this town, but when Mack—you remember Mack, the Secret Service agent? —was told by a colleague that he'd heard Delbert needed a quiet place to regain his health, he brought him here. Some of you may have seen Mack here early yesterday morning. He brought him in the middle of the night because Mack had some important things to do back in Washington very early in the morning." I assumed, given his job description, that I was truthful in telling them that.

I looked around at the residents looking around at the other residents. No one wanted to incur the wrath of their neighbors by welcoming Del back into the fold, even temporarily, so they stalled hoping someone else would take the lead.

Melanie jumped up just then. "I say we do what Hugh and Emma suggested. We forget the past and start over again." She turned her attention to Del and said, "Welcome to Road's End, Mr. Jackson."

Bristol, Grace, Pastor Parry, and Leo all stood and said, "Good idea," "Welcome," "God bless you, Mr. Jackson." Leo contributed a pipe squiggle, and Frank snored in a welcoming way.

"Okay then, everyone. It's official. Mr. Jackson will be living among us for a while until the danger of ill health passes and he is able to get back into the world-at-large. I'm proud of you, friends. Let's enjoy Sadie's refreshments."

Surprisingly, it was Emma who jumped up first and walked to the buffet. George and Dewey looked on in dismay as she picked the best of the goodies. She poured a cup of coffee and put a doughnut, cookie, and brownie on a plate, grabbed a fork and napkin, and marched them over to Del. "Here you go, Del. Can I call you Del, or do you prefer Mr. Jackson? I'm Emma, by the way."

I smiled at Emma and mouthed, "Thank you," but could just as well have screamed it. No one was paying attention, anyway, as they migrated (or stampeded, in some cases) to get their refreshments.

The hard part was over. At least I hoped it was the hard part. Little did I know this was a stroll through the daisies compared to the next few days. Just as well, though. I hate eating brownies when I'm nauseous.

Chapter Ten

After the others went home, I helped Melanie bring the dishes in from the dining room to the kitchen. It surprised me to see Delbert bringing in a load of them too.

"Thank you, Del," Mel said with a smile. "But you've had a hard day and I think you've earned some time to yourself and a good night's sleep. We'll get this. Set your alarm, though, because breakfast is at 7:00. I hope you like pancakes and bacon."

He set the platters on the counter and turned to Mel and me. "Uh, I'm not usually one to say thanks, but …well, thanks." Then he turned and left the kitchen before my wife and I had a chance to close our mouths. Mel reached over and put her fingers under my chin and lifted it.

"You'll attract flies, dear."

"Wow. Never thought I'd see the day, but I'm thrilled," I said.

Melanie looked up from the dishwasher and said, "Del doesn't look half-bad when he's being agreeable, does he?"

I'm not much for commenting on men's looks, but I agreed. "Tell you what, Mel. If you'll leave those dishes until tomorrow morning, I'll let you do them then." I got a particularly stinging towel-smack across my behind for that.

"Just for that, buster, I *will* leave them until tomorrow and you can get up early just to finish them for me before breakfast. How's that sound?"

"Why, Melanie, you've cut me to the quick. I never thought you'd make me do domestic chores."

"Since when? You've helped out our entire marriage. What's changed?"

"Nothing, but I thought I'd give it a try."

"Well, good try, smarty pants, but nothin' doing." *Smarty pants? Has she been talking to Grace again?*

We walked upstairs, tired, but relieved that the meeting was over and everyone was on-board (as much as could be expected considering the players), changed into pajamas, pulled back the covers, and crawled into bed.

Morning broke and we gathered around the kitchen table to enjoy the pancakes and bacon Mel had promised the night before. Coupled with orange juice and coffee, it was a feast. Both Del and I dug in with enthusiasm, while Mel ate with a little more decorum—okay, a *lot* more decorum. Fortunately, she'd forgotten all about the dishwashing I was to do before breakfast, so I skedaddled out the front door to meet Bristol at Sadie's a few minutes later. A man can't go too long without coffee, I always say. Well, not always, or I'd never say anything else. But at that time every morning, that's what I say.

I reached Sadie's Bake House and opened the door. Ah! I was back in the land of peanut butter cookies and fresh coffee. The little bell on Sadie's front door dinged and I braced myself for the usual, "Shut that door! Yer lettin' in the flies!"

Nothing. Quiet. *Very* quiet. And weird.

I walked toward the counter. I could smell fresh-baked cookies, hot coffee, and a hint of cinnamon and brown sugar. But no sign of Sadie. No smart remarks, no yelping, no complaining. I cleared my throat, scuffed my feet, whistled a few notes, the usual stuff people do when they're trying to get someone's attention without appearing to do that very thing. Still nothing. I don't think I've ever gone into Sadie's Bake House and Egg Plant without being yelled at upon arrival. There was only one conclusion to be drawn.

Sadie Simms was dead.

Odd how your mind goes to the worst-case scenario right off the bat. She could've been in the bathroom, had her mouth full of cookie, listening to music and didn't hear me—any of those simple explanations would account for her lack of greeting ... well, in Sadie's

case, snarling. But no, my thoughts went straight to "She's dead."
That's what happens when you live in a town like Road's End.

Happily, I was dead wrong.

"Hugh! Good morning. How are you this morning? Gorgeous day,
huh?"

"Uh ..." That was me, the one who's always ready to address any
topic, except this one.

It was worse than I thought.

Sadie Simms had lost her mind.

Or ... on the bright side, maybe God was calling us home.

While I stood waiting for an apocalyptic event, Sadie bustled
around the kitchen, clattered some cups and saucers, checked her oven,
and finally pulled out a pan of fresh-baked cookies, all the while
whistling. *Whistling?*

I finally sat at one of the tables—more out of being weak in the
knees than getting ready to eat. She walked out from behind the counter
and set my coffee mug and a plate of cookies in front of me. "Here you
go, Hugh. Let me get the coffeepot and some nice cream for your
coffee." Cream for my coffee? I've been in here every day since we
arrived last fall and she's never once remembered I use cream in my
coffee. When I remind her, she sighs, thumps back into the kitchen, and
brings me .0000054% milk, so pale it could pass for fog. And now
she's bringing me some *nice cream*?

Where are those crazy senior citizen men who plague me night
and day except when I need them to witness something?

Well, speak of the you-know-who.

Chapter Eleven

I won't go so far as to say the men of Road's End, Virginia, are for the most part, insane—wait, yes, I will. Past experience with these well-meaning, inventive, hardworking, irritable octogenarians proves (to me, at least) that they're one-part normal senior citizens and 4000-parts nuts.

Now I don't say this lightly. I don't want you to think I'm belittling the worth of America's older generation, nor the roles they played in the past, nor as part of today's society. We would not be the country we are today without their sacrifices and hard work. Let's face it—the rest of us are products of the generations above us—and we owe them a debt we can never repay.

But this particular group of older men have cornered the market on eccentricity. Perhaps it's living in Road's End that causes it. It is, after all, a weird little town. Maybe it's the ladies they live with (sorry about that, ladies). Maybe Road's End was the site of some government tests—bizarre, experimental, atmospheric tests back in the 50s—whereby gaseous, noxious chemicals spewed out over the land and settled (wouldn't you know it?) right here. Who knows for sure? Well, God does, but none of us humans do.

At any rate, they showed up when I needed them, which is a first. In the door they tumbled, one after another, jostling one another like second graders in the lunch line. George and Dewey scrunched shoulders against the doorframe, but in the end, Dewey won out, spurting into the room like a balloon losing its air. George followed hot on his heels, trailed by Leo Walling, Perry Parry, Frank Wiley, Rudy Wallenberg, and Joe Rich. Bristol Diggs, smart man that he is, hadn't arrived yet, but it was just as well. Being part of a stampede is never a good way to start the day. Most of them hollered their "good mornings" to Sadie, then waved at me. Frank sat, dropped his head to his chest and initiated his snoring sequence, while Leo puffed out a smoke ring.

Nobody seemed to notice the lack of a venomous retort by Sadie to their cheerful greetings. Irritating, but not particularly unusual. They often concentrated on themselves rather than on what's going on around them. We could be in the eye of a hurricane and one of them would remark, "You know, we could use a little rain one of these days."

I could hear George and Dewey still bemoaning the demise of their latest venture—harnessing the electrical power of lightning bugs.

"It coulda worked, George," Dewey said, shaking his head and pounding his fist on the table. "I just know it coulda. We just didn't think it through far enough."

George leaned on his elbows and stared Dewey in the face. "What more could we do, man? We just couldn't train 'em to fly into those slots. We tried, Dewey," (he too pounded the table in frustration) "but it just couldn't be done. Even if they did line up like we wanted 'em to, how were we gonna convince 'em to plug in?" He shook his head as if bemoaning the loss of Microsoft to that pesky Bill Gates. "We did what we could, Dewey. No one can ask any more'n that."

I was just happy they weren't talking about their PI/PV office. Whoa, not so fast, Hugh, my ears said. Listen up.

"But we got this new case to work on, Dewey," George said. "Let's just ferget about the past and concentrate on our PI office."

"PV." That was Dewey, of course, the one who never knows when to keep his trap shut.

"Yer not startin' that up again, are ya, nincompoop?" That was George.

"I'll start it up 'til ya git it right, ya ninny!"

Pastor Parry, bless his sweet heart, spoke up. "Why not just call yourselves private investigators and bypass the whole abbreviated stuff? Wouldn't that be easier?"

George and Dewey looked at one another, shrugged and said, "Okay."

George continued, "Yeah, Pastor, that works. We'll call it Washington and Wyandotte, Private Investigators."

"Nope. Wyandotte and Washington, Private Vestigators."

Perry added, "Wait up, gentlemen. Let's not get into that 'whose name is first' thing again. Have you thought of combining the two names?"

Joe Rich, who had been silent so far, threw his hat into the ring. "How 'bout 'Washingdotte'?

Next came Rudy. "Naw, how 'bout 'Wyanwash'?"

All heck broke loose.

"How 'bout Georey?"

"That's just stupid."

"I got it! 'Deworge!'"

"Sno-o-r-re ..." That was Frank. "Sno-o-r-re ..." Frank again.

Smoke squiggle. Leo.

I couldn't take it any longer. "Hey guys, how about 'Road's End Private Investigators'?"

Silence. I could almost hear the gears turning in those brains of theirs. Some sounded a little rustier than others. Finally, George spoke up, "That's brilliant! Great idea, Frank!"

Frank? He hasn't spoken a word in the past decade. Didn't they just hear me speak that suggestion?

Apparently not. There were back slaps all the around the table. They had to be careful with Frank the hero lest he topple over in his chair to the linoleum below. "Road's End Private Vestigators, it is!" Dewey crowed.

"Investigators."

Thank goodness the troops (or troop, in this case) arrived in the form of Bristol, although I wouldn't have minded a whole battalion of soldiers right about then. Bristol looked at me with a question on his face as he passed their table on his way to mine.

He pulled out a chair next to me and sat down with a thud. "Those guys couldn't get any weirder if we paid 'em."

Sadie hollered from the kitchen, "Hey, Bristol! Good morning. The usual?"

He stared at her for a few seconds, nodded, then leaned toward me. "What's gotten into Sadie? Is it just me or is Sadie acting different this morning? Sort of ... I don't know. Human? Kinda scary if you ask me."

I lifted my mug and saluted him. "Very good, Bristol. You'd make a good detective." I felt safe in saying that since he'd been a big city detective for many years before changing his life and settling down in Road's End. In my mind, that wasn't the most the most logical way to get away from the stress and strain of fighting crime, as this town seems to attract drug thugs and presidential assassin wannabes like crab grass to my front lawn. But to give him his due, Bristol probably didn't know that when he moved to town. He does now, though.

"Very funny, Hugh. Seriously, though, what's up with her? Is that a dress she's wearing? And her hair looks different."

"Not sure what's up. And yes, that's a dress, and I think she combed her hair this morning," I said. I took a big bite of cookie, chewed it slowly, savoring every morsel, and followed it up with another sip of coffee.

I watched Sadie as she walked—sashayed is more like it—past our table to where George and Dewey and the rest of the men sat snoring, smoking, talking over one another, plotting a galactic takeover—you know, the usual early morning coffee house banter.

I shook my head. "Not sure what's up yet, but I'm forming a theory." I cocked my head toward the table behind Bristol. "Notice anything?"

Bristol did his best to appear inconspicuous by making a 180-degree turn, dragging his chair with him, its legs screeching across the linoleum floor, leaning forward with his elbows on his knees, and gawking at the folks behind him. The only reason nobody noticed his slick black-op surveillance technique was because his targets were too incapacitated by their tongues hanging out of their heads to do anything but stare and drool at Sadie.

Sadie loved every second of it. She made cow eyes at Leo; he puffed out a smoke squiggle. She giggled. He squiggled. Giggle, squiggle, giggle, squiggle. I grew nauseous.

I looked at Bristol. Still busy gawking. I smacked him on the arm, and he turned in my direction. He couldn't have looked any more shocked if he'd written the word in big black letters across his forehead.

"Uh ..."

"Well said, Bristol. My sentiments exactly."

Sadie Simms wasn't dead, or playing games, or even temporarily insane. No, it was worse than all that combined. Well, for Leo Walling at least.

Sadie Simms was flirting.

Chapter Twelve

After my coffee with Bristol, I walked over to the church. Grace either hadn't come in yet, was hiding, or this was her day off. It varies from week to week, but when she isn't coming in, she always leaves a note on my desk. Five seconds later I found the note. It read: Working on what we discussed yesterday. Don't mess up everything while I'm gone. I *mean* it. Don't. Mess. It. Up." Grace is such a softie. And subtle.

I sat down and realized I didn't have a cup of coffee in front of me, but figured things were weird enough around this town without the pastor getting all jittery and going bonkers. One by one, I ticked off the situations (read: problems) I was involved in, including, but not limited to (after all, it was not yet noon; anything could, and probably would, happen as the day progressed), harboring a man with a price on his head and already hated by the residents of our tiny town, Ruby Mae was down in the dumps, George and Dewey were starting up a useless business which would, somehow or other, cause me grief, and finally, Sadic Simms had lost her mind. Exactly the agenda of all small-town pastors.

I bowed my head and started to ask, "Why, God?" but remembered I've asked this question of our Heavenly Father almost every day since Mel and I bought The Inn at Road's End and have yet to receive a definitive answer. Either the Lord delights in watching me squirm, or He's trying to teach me something I'll need for … what? Refereeing old men's wrestling matches? Judging "The Most Beautiful Hat in the World" pageants? (Shudder.) Leading the war against drugs? Sad to say, but that last one makes the most sense because twice now Road's End has become embroiled in problems involving drugs. Whatever His reason, though, I am more than happy to await further instructions from our Heavenly Father. In the meantime, I'll limp by the best I know how.

I didn't really have any reason to come to the church this morning but chose this little part of the world to hide from my problems. I don't know why I bother. They always find me anyway. Since our arrival, we've had one incredible thing after another happen inside the village limits—a record-breaking blizzard, drug thugs, an outdoor Nativity which should go down in history as the strangest of its kind ever to grace Earth, a visit from the president of the United States (yes, you read that correctly), a tornado, and a host of other smaller situations that I'm pretty sure most people, let alone pastors, have never endured.

But that was neither here nor there. Since I didn't have any control over these zany people and the problems that inevitably land in my lap, I might as well spend my time praying rather than complaining. I know God has things under control. All I have to do is listen to His leading and let Him take the reins. So, I spent my time in my office praying for wisdom, patience (lots and lots of patience), discernment, and strength. Tons of strength. Somehow, most of the fiascoes I become involved in wear me out in every way possible. I vowed, as I always do, to lay my burdens at the foot of the Cross.

After a few minutes of heartfelt prayer, I left the church invigorated and ready to face the rest of the day.

And immediately ran into George and Dewey (as always), but also Ruby Mae Headley, still hatless and sobbing. I didn't know if this was a new episode of sobbing or left over from yesterday's weeping, but she remained a very unhappy without-a-hat woman.

"Gentlemen, Ruby Mae, how's your day going?" I knew that was a stupid greeting since George and Dewey were fighting and Ruby Mae was in the throes of a meltdown. Instead of waiting for an answer, I approached them with my hand extended for a handshake with George and Dewey, and a comforting look toward Ruby. "Were you on your way to the church to talk to me?"

George and Dewey finally quit arguing over who would shake my hand first and Ruby Mae had to stop sobbing long enough to take a breath.

For once, the two octogenarians agreed, and both nodded at me. Ruby Mae began to wail.

"Why don't we go back into my office and we'll talk about it."

I asked the men to sit in the sanctuary for a minute until I had a chance to talk to Ruby Mae. She sat in the chair across from me and dabbed her eyes.

"Do you have something you want to talk to me about, Ruby?"

Sniff, sniff, snort, sniffle, snort. "Yes, Pastor, I do. It seems that I have lost my desire to make my splendid hats—I make them myself, you know—and I don't think Grace wants me to, even if I find the strength to carry on. How can she betray me so?"

"Ruby Mae, I can't speak for Grace, or whether or not she wants you to make hats. That's between you and her. What I *do* know is that she loves you very much and wants only the best for you. That might not help much, but I hope it relieves your mind of any worries in that area. Ideally, what you and Grace decide to do will be a good blend of the wishes of each of you."

"But bein' God's special project brings so many responsibilities with it. You have no idea"—sniff, sniff, snort—"what a body goes through day after day jest tryin' to be the beautiful person God made me to be. It's a burden some days, Pastor, but up 'til now I've been able to rise above it all and show those 'round me the real meanin' of beauty. But now," … sniff, sniff, lo-o-ng snort … "I jest don't know if I can do it anymore."

I grabbed a box of tissues from my desk drawer and extended it to Ruby Mae, then reached down to grab the small wastepaper basket beside my desk, which had apparently escaped her notice as evidenced by the growing mound of tissues in the middle of my desk. "Here you go, Ruby." She accepted the box of tissues, but ignored the basket. I'd need a shovel to remove them at the rate she was using them. "Have you prayed about this, Ruby Mae? Perhaps the Lord would rather you showed your beauty as one of His children by … well, just being you. No worrying about the latest hat, no gathering supplies from the yards in town, no sending Grace to Richmond to bring home a trunkful of artificial flowers for you to use. Why don't you pray that God will lead you down the path He has planned for you? Perhaps you have another skill or hobby you could take up that wouldn't require so much … well, space on your head ... I meant to say space in your home."

She looked up, her eyes swollen and her nose red from blowing it so much, and said, "My path?"

I nodded. "Yep. The path the Lord has planned for you."

"But I'm God's special project. I don't think I can just up and abandon my calling. He'd be crushed." *Frankly, Ruby Mae, I think your abandoning hat-making might just make His day. And no, you won't be crushing the Creator of all there is, was, and ever will be. You can count on that.*

Oh boy. "Okay, maybe He has a new role for you in today's world. Something more like leading a Bible study in your home every week or working on your flower garden, or ... I don't know ... (I was fresh out of ideas, so I threw up my hand and said), "becoming a YouTube star." *Anything but hat-making. And where did YouTube come from?*

"Oh, Pastor, I have the most beautiful Bible study hat at home—I make them myself, you know. I'll have to make a new one for my gardening. What's Yoo-Hoo™?"

Me and my big mouth. "Nothing, Ruby Mae. Really, it's just something on computers where people make videos to show someone how to make something, for instance. But don't even give that a thought. It just popped off the top of my head."

"Hallelujah, bein' a star fits right in with my hat-making! I have so many hats I could show people! And I'd be the finest star that Yoo-Hoo™ has ever seen!"

"I'm sure you would, Ruby Mae, but how many hats does one woman really need?"

You'd have thought I'd morphed into a reptilian creature and told her I was a being from ... I don't know... a galaxy far, far away and as soon as I finished her off, I'd tackle the rest of the world.

"Why, Pastor, I don't think I've ever been so insulted. It's a well-known fact that a woman can never have too many hats."

"Please forgive me, Ruby Mae. Being a man, I didn't know that. But God might have other plans for you at the moment. Why don't you just go on home, get something you like to drink, sit down, and pray? That always works for me." *And believe me, Ruby Mae, I'll be praying tonight.*

A determined look crossed her face, and I felt faintly threatened. Was this going to blow up in my face? Oh, who did I think I fooling? Of course, it was. I don't know when, and I don't know how, but it will.

She threw her shoulders back, blew her nose for the last time, thank goodness, then tossed it toward the small mountain in the middle of my desk. I was afraid my desk would collapse under the weight if she continued to sob. "I'll jest do that, Pastor. Yes, I will. I get your message loud and clear, and now I'm happy to do what God has asked of me."

I felt a cold chill run up my spine. I've learned from experience that whenever I get that feeling, trouble—usually lots of it—finds me one way or the other.

Chapter Thirteen

After seeing Ruby Mae out the door I turned back to my office, but just as I reached the door I heard, "Told ya, George! I told ya!" That was quickly followed by "No, you didn't, Dewey. You said 477 and I said 190."

Criminy sakes, I'd forgotten all about George and Dewey. No telling what they were arguing about, but I'm sure it wouldn't make sense to anyone but them.

"Hi, guys! How's it going?"

Silence. They were busy glaring at one another, their chests (chests that had long ago descended to their belt buckles) the only things that kept them from touching nose-to-nose.

"What's up?" Me again. More silence from them.

"Well, I'm going into the kitchen to brew another pot of coffee and grab some brownies I brought back from Sadie's. You're welcome to join me if you want to."

They morphed from tall gnomes into high school sprinters and blew past me out the door and into the kitchen before the "to" in my sentence was fully spoken. I'll have to remember this trick.

I thought about asking them what they were arguing about but realized I didn't give a rip. Maybe a brownie would give me some silence before we met.

Nope.

"Hey, Hugh, thought you said you had fresh coffee."

"No, he didn't, Dewey. He said he was going to brew a fresh pot."

I stepped in before this could escalate to heights greater than the Hubble Telescope. "Hey, guys, let me get in here and I'll brew us some coffee. In the meantime, why don't you go into the office. Take the ..."

And they were gone. And so were the brownies. Maybe Grace isn't the only one who can read my mind.

A few minutes later, I carried, slowly and carefully, three mugs of coffee to my office and set them down on my desk. I strategically placed coasters in front of the men, but of course, neither one used them. I ran back to the kitchen to grab some napkins and cream and sugar. I was back in fifteen seconds, tops.

And the brownies were gone.

I sat down, said a quick prayer that this meeting would go well, whatever it was about, then looked at them and said, "Okay, men, what's on your minds?"

"Plenty," George said, as he hunted for a brownie crumb in his lap. I assumed it was a brownie crumb; could have been a grenade for all I knew.

"Yep, plenty," Dewey said, successfully corroborating George's story.

I waited until George demolished a crumb the size of a grain of salt.

"Well, Hugh, it's about this Jackson guy."

I nodded. "Okay, what about him?"

"Well, since we've opened up our Road's End Private Investigators, Premiere PI/V Office in Road's End—that's our logo. Sounds good, don't it? Proud, but not obnoxious, I think. Don't you?"

I moved my lips, and he took that as a yes.

"Anyway, we've been hired to do the dangerous job of finding out more about this Jackson, so we're here to interrogate you."

"Interrogate me? About what? And why? You know as much as I do."

"Hold on there, Hugh. We're working under some legal complaints most laymen don't understand." *You mean "constraints" against my strangling the two of you and hiding your bodies?*

"Okay then, what would those constraints be?"

Silence. Blessed silence. For five seconds.

"Well, to be honest, we haven't figured that out yet, but jest take my word fer it, okay?"

"So, what's all this about?" That was me, the befuddled pastor, the one who was close to tears—along with homicide if I'm being completely truthful.

"Jackson. Delbert T., in particular."

"All right. I'm sorry, I forgot you mentioned that. What about him?"

"Sorry. Our client won't let us divulge the nature of our business with you."

"Client? What client? And if your client won't let you divulge the nature of your business with me, why are we having this meeting?"

Dewey turned to George and said, "See? I *told* ya he'd turn difficult. Besides, you forgot to read him the Melinda rights."

Melinda?

"Cain't." George said, "He's not talkin'. Cain't ya see that?"

"'Course I can see that, George. What'll we do about it?"

"No choice, I guess." He shook his head.

"You know, guys, I have a full schedule this afternoon. Why don't you go to your office and figure out what you want to ask me, even though there's nothing to interrogate me about."

"We'll be back with a warrant."

"A warrant? For what? And where on earth would you find one?"

"Don't go gettin' mouthy, Hugh, or we'll be forced to take you in for questioning. As I see it, you're our number one suspect."

I sighed, grabbed the edge of my desk, and prayed I wouldn't jump over it and kick the two of them in their balding heads. "Number one suspect, George? Meaning you have more than one?"

He looked confused. "Uh ..."

Dewey dived in. "'Member those legal complaints, George."

George snapped his fingers. "That's right. We have complaints that most laymen don't know 'bout."

Darned tootin' you've got complaints, George. Ask anyone in town if they have a complaint about you two. They'll be lined up for ... well, considering our population, about six feet. But I couldn't say that, so I settled for ending the meeting on my terms and ignoring them if they stayed.

"Well, gentlemen, I have work to do, so if you'll excuse me, I need to get back to it." Eventually they tired of not being paid attention to and left in a huff.

I had just sighed in relief, sat back in my chair, prayed, and asked forgiveness for losing my temper with those two, when there was a knock on the door. Gee whiz, if this is another resident with a problem, I'm making a dash for Cincinatti. After I pick up Mel, that is.

"Come on in!"

There was a slight hesitation before the door opened slowly and Emma River peeked around the door. "Are you sure you aren't too busy, Pastor? I just saw George and Dewey leaving and they didn't look very happy. Do you need some time to yourself?"

A normal person! "Why, Emma, it's a pleasure to see you. Come on in and have a seat." I pulled a chair out for her. "Yes, George and Dewey wanted to interrogate me about Delbert."

Emma sat down and held up her hand. "Say no more, Pastor. Those two are the dickens, aren't they? Well-meaning, but crazier than all get-out."

For a moment I was stunned. I've never heard Emma say anything about anyone, let alone those two. "Exactly, Emma. Exactly. Now what can I do for you?"

"Actually," she said, "I'm hoping I can do something for *you*."

Take those two characters out of town and tie them to a tree for a day or so?

"Well, that sounds good, Emma. What do you have in mind? Oh, Emma, I'm so sorry. I forgot to offer you some coffee."

She shook her head. "That's quite all right, Hugh. I had about a quart over at Sadie's just now. I'll be awake for the next two days."

Emma was quiet for a moment, obviously thinking, then looked at me and said, "I know you know this already, Hugh, but Sadie and Ruby Mae aren't in the best situations right now."

I nodded, then said, "I know Ruby Mae is distraught about not wanting to wear her hats."

Emma grinned and winked. "That's just God's way of giving us a break, Hugh."

I chuckled. Felt good. "I'll bet you're right, Emma. But it's Sadie who worries me the most. One minute she's cross and sad, and the next she's flirting with Leo at the Bake House. What do you suppose she's trying to do?"

"I think she's self-medicating, Hugh. I've seen her in both of those moods lately and they're as different as night from day, aren't they? But the flirting with Leo is probably just her way of finding out if that's what she's missing. Maybe she thinks she's lonely and decided to pounce on the one bachelor in town who's even remotely her age.

Knowing Sadie, it'll pass one of these days—or maybe by this afternoon!"

I thought about that, nodded, then leaned back in my chair. It seemed nice not to have to get ready to pounce on someone. I could relax. "Could be you're right, Emma. Now, please go ahead. I interrupted you with my wondering about our ladies."

She waved her hand. "Don't worry about that, Hugh." She continued, "The whole town is wondering!" She paused for a moment, no doubt gathering her thoughts. "So, I don't know if you know this or not—perhaps no one knows it, for that matter. Maybe Sadie knows. Anyway, in my younger days I used to spend my summers at a secluded place deep in the Blue Ridge Mountains. I own about 200 acres there. Anyway, there's a cabin on it in a beautiful meadow. Now, when I say cabin, I mean no running water, one-room, tin roof, and only kerosene lanterns and God's creation above for light. I'm sure the residents of Road's End back then thought I was going on a grand tour of Europe or some such thing, but no, I just jumped on a train, and when I reached my destination, I hired a man to take me and my luggage deep into the mountains. I specified a day and time when he should return. Then I came back here at summer's end."

"Why, Emma, how adventurous of you. Is the cabin still standing?"

"Yes, it is. I sent a friend out there not so long ago to see what needed to be done to it to make it habitable. He says it was remarkably untouched, and ready to go."

"Well, I'm so glad to hear that, Emma. You never cease to amaze me."

"Well, I'm not finished yet, Hugh. Perhaps you'll think I'm a silly old woman for thinking of this, but I'll tell you anyway." She smiled at me and it lit up her face like a candle.

"Then let's hear it, Emma. You have my curiosity piqued and I'm all ears."

"Okay then. Here goes. As you know, we just talked about both Sadie's and Ruby Mae's dilemmas at the moment. I've thought for several months now about taking anyone who is interested up to the cabin. I call it Riverbluff, by the way. And as for Delbert Jackson, well,

I thought you might want to consider using Riverbluff for a mini-vacation for the ladies, and a good hiding spot for Delbert if needed."

My mouth dropped. "You know about Delbert?"

She nodded her head. "Yes. Well, I surmised it from the beginning. It just fits him, doesn't it? A man like that doesn't want to mingle with old folks like us. Makes him feel old and he's hanging on to his youth so hard. Poor man. God surely didn't bless him with good looks—or personality, for that matter, but he's one of God's children nonetheless. So, there you have it, Hugh. I thought the ladies—and I mean any of them in town—might need a change of scenery to put their lives in perspective and believe me, even a bloodhound couldn't find this place."

"You mean you're willing to take on any of the ladies who would like to accompany you, *and* Del, if needed?"

She nodded.

"That borders on either lunacy or heroism, Emma, but I'm so happy to know you and have you as a friend! You are a blessing to this town. I think it's a grand idea, and I think if you broach the topic with the ladies, you'll find they're more than ready to take a break from … well, this town. And if things get dicey with Del and his situation, I thank you sincerely for your hospitality and willingness to take on Del."

"Oh, Hugh, taking on Del is no problem. It's just putting him together with the ladies that worries me. They might just send him over the edge."

"Good point, Emma. Very good point. Perhaps if he misbehaves we can threaten him with it!"

She grinned, rose from her chair, and walked to the door. "I'll bring it up to Sadie and Ruby Mae first, and then approach the other ladies, if you think that's wise. I'll let you decide, when and if it happens, what you think is best for Del. But I have to say, Hugh, this place is really hidden. If you think Road's End is off the beaten path, wait until you see Riverbluff."

"Thank you, Emma. I'd really enjoy seeing it. Just let me know how I can be of help to you and the ladies when you're ready to take off."

"I'll do that, Hugh. Thanks so much for listening to me."

"Are you crazy? You're the only one I've talked to today, aside from Mel, who isn't off his or her rocker! I'm happy to listen to you anytime, anywhere."

She smiled and gave me a little wave before walking out the door and into the beautiful fall day.

I spoke aloud before she got to the front door. "Don't be surprised, Emma, if you end up having a pastor hiding up there with all of you. Getting out of town right now sounds mighty good."

Little did I know how close I was to doing just that. And Emma, bless her heart, had just given me a possible answer to take care of that problem Mack tossed in my lap.

Chapter Fourteen

The next few days passed with only the usual amount of drama around town. Sadie was still fluctuating between angst and flirting, Leo had no clue, Ruby Mae was down in the dumps, Grace wanted to drop her off at the dump, George and Dewey were gung-ho about the PI/V business—although to my knowledge, they still haven't found an office, let alone a client—I couldn't get Mack's phone call out of my head, and Frank was still asleep.

But things were about to change.

I arranged with Emma to speak to the congregation this past Sunday to address the ladies in town on the topic of going away for a retreat deep in the mountains. The only one who voiced any problems with the plan was Sadie. I have to admit I shared her doubts about her being out of town for any length of time.

"What're you guys gonna do without my coffee and baked goods while I'm gone? Go bonkers?"

There was much discussion on that heavy topic, but we finally came to an agreement that all the ladies going to the retreat would make meals ahead of time for their husbands with clear warming-up instructions attached (although I doubt they would ever leave their husbands alone for 30 minutes without arranging a meal ahead of time). Sadie would bake all night long, if need be, to stockpile the Bake House with cookies, doughnuts, cakes, pies, and bread for the poor souls left in town, as well as enough to take to the mountains. She was going to be one busy lady.

She gave a key to me and one to Bristol. "You're the only two bozos I trust enough to leave a key with." Made me swell with pride. Finally, I had reached the pinnacle of Sadie's bozo heap. She also gave both of us clear instructions on how to make her coffee and keep the men out of the goods marked for the next day. "Those bozos'll eat it all up the first day and starve to death before I get back," she told me after the service, so we ended up being responsible for the lives of her customers *and* the safety of her Bake House. Fair enough. It was a heavy responsibility, but one Bristol and I were willing to undertake to get first dibs on Sadie's goodies every day.

Through Mel, Grace, and Emma, I was kept updated on who was going. So far, the list included just about everybody—Sadie, Winnie Wyandotte, Martha Washington, Ruby Mae, Hazel Parry, and of course, Emma. I think Grace was trying to find a way to get out of going, as this would be a once in a lifetime opportunity to have a few days to herself. I wouldn't be surprised if some of the hats disappeared, as well. But she was still sitting on the fence. I don't think Mel was all that keen to leave home to spend time in the company of a group of "boisterous" women, as she called them (although I think she was thinking "crazy as loons"). But she knew I'd feel better about the safety of the ladies if she was there to keep them under control.

That would leave Frank, Leo, George, Dewey, Joe Rich, Rudy Wallenberg, Pastor Parry, Bristol and me at home. Well, Del, too, but I don't imagine he'd be doing much besides sleep and be messy and irritable. That's another reason Mel didn't want to leave the Inn, but I assured her I would lay down the law and it would be in pristine condition when she got back.

Emma told me she thought a week would be long enough for the ladies to relax, regroup, and face Road's End and their men again. She was also careful to let the women know what they were in for. "No indoor toilet, no water, no electricity. It's a one-room cabin with a kitchen and a stone fireplace in one corner, a living room in another, and a bedroom across the back. It'll be close quarters, ladies, so if any of you are leery of the restrictions placed upon each of us, as well as the general lack of spaciousness, please let us know as soon as possible. We probably can go again in a few months, so if you don't want to do it now, maybe we can do it another time."

Surprisingly, none of the women backed out, and they began the countdown. Three days remained in which they would pack, cook the meals for their men, and get themselves ready to face the wilds of the Blue Ridge Mountains.

The men were understandably horrified that their sources of nourishment and clean underwear were going to be absent for that length of time. "A whole week?" That was George, the one who remembered things he learned in 1st grade, while Dewey, who obviously didn't remember much of his elementary curriculum, yelped, "You mean they're going to be gone for eight days?" I didn't stick around to hear the ensuing argument, but I'm sure there was one. There always is.

I hadn't heard anything from Mack, which worried me on one hand and pleased me on the other. If there was no communication, that would imply no bad news to report. But if the lack of communication meant the WPP had yet to clear his new identity and hopefully find another dwelling for him to hide out in, that could mean Del would be here for a while. And in the meantime, I was left with the worry that drug thugs were once again coming to Road's End. What *is* it with this town that makes it continually involved in drug trafficking? Getting the ladies out of town was a bonus I hadn't counted on. If the cartel thugs happened to get to town undetected, at least we didn't have to worry about the ladies. Please don't tell any of them I said that.

It was agreed that Bristol and I would accompany the ladies to make sure they arrived safely, and to help carry their provisions, clothes, and sleeping bags to the cabin. When Emma was young, she took a train, but it was easier now to drive them. We took two cars— Mel, Emma, Sadie, and Ruby Mae rode with me. Bristol took Grace, who had grudgingly agreed she should go as sort of a combo bouncer/mediator/assassin, since no one believed the women (given who they are) would get along with one another long enough for the sound of our slamming car doors to fade away.

Along with Grace, Bristol took Martha, Winnie, and Hazel, and had the majority of the luggage and other stuff. We negotiated the seating arrangements because Grace had already threatened to pitch her mother out the window into a valley far below if she had to ride with her. So, it was agreed I'd take Ruby Mae, but that meant he had to take Winnie and Martha. The other ladies were harmless, thank goodness, so after goodbyes and begging, the ladies tore themselves from their husbands—some of whom were almost in tears at the thought of doing the laundry themselves. We jumped into our assigned cars and off we went.

It was about a two-hour drive, and I hesitated to leave the town in the hands of … well, anyone. I trusted Bristol, of course, but since I'd already commandeered him to drive one of the cars to the cabin, there were no sane men left in town to maintain control until we returned later that night. Then I remembered Pastor Parry had his head on straight. Besides, it was just a day trip, and I hoped the men would spend the whole day trying to get into Sadie's Bake House until we got back home rather than come up with some other hare-brained idea. It was a risk, but I thought Perry could handle them for a few hours.

Why do I always assume these men have the collective presence of mind to match that of *at least* a monkey peeling a banana? They don't. Individually, they're lovable and crazy, but collectively, they're as dangerous and unpredictable as a 7-year-old riding his first two-wheeled bike in your living room with Grandma's priceless glassware sitting around.

Emma was excited to share her little chunk of paradise and she spent a good part of the ride there talking about what she'd done over the years. Of course, when she was younger, she could hike, fish, and do repairs on the cabin. Age, of course, brought some slowing down with it, and now she was content to leave it as it is. I couldn't wait to see it. She talked of the silence and peace in the meadow, the scent of tall grass waving in the afternoon sun, the beauty of a water glass filled with a variety of wildflowers brought home from a walk through the meadow, the small river that gurgled its way beneath a bluff behind the cabin, the sounds of bees and other insects as they joined butterflies taking their fill from the flowers, and the adventures she'd had hiding from bears, cleaning fish, enduring thunder storms, and learning to bake bread in her primitive surroundings.

But the most important thing she did, as far as I could tell, was relax and take in the grandeur of God's creation. Even remembering her adamant denial of God's mercy just a few months ago, I found it hard to believe she didn't have a spark of faith still burning in her heart while she spent her summers at Riverbluff. The look of expectation on her face took twenty years off her face. I could tell this was a very special place for her.

There was an old firebreak, a dirt road built long ago to enable firefighters access to remote areas during a forest fire (but not yet in place when she first began vacationing at Riverbluff) that made it relatively easy to get to the nearly non-existent trail that led to the meadow. I pulled up and waited for Bristol to catch up. Ten seconds later he rounded the bend and parked behind me. We opened our trunks and hauled out suitcases, boxes of food and water, at least six sleeping bags, pillows, and extra blankets. The ladies climbed out of the vehicles, stretched, and greeted one another as though they'd been apart for a decade or two. I guess a lot happens in two hours when you're traveling in separate cars.

It was obvious it would take more than one trip to get all their stuff to the cabin, so we sent them on ahead, grabbed what we could, and followed the giggles.

"Sounds like a Girl Scout camp-out."

Bristol snickered. "What would you know about Girl Scout camp-outs?"

"Not much, but I did have a sister and a couple of cousins who told tall tales about their camping adventures. If I remember correctly, they all involved a campfire, a monster or two, and screaming."

Just then a shriek of laughter or call for help—hard to tell—broke the hush, and I apologized silently to the beautiful day for the interruption of the peace and quiet by raucous, let-free-for-seven-days (or eight, depending on whether or not you were married to Dewey) women. Unfettered by their suitcases, filled with what felt to me like assorted anvils, the women quickly out-walked us to the cabin and by the time we broke through the trees, they were alternating sniffing, twirling around, or standing around with their mouths wide open. It reminded me of a scene from *The Sound of Music*.

I looked over at Bristol and sang, "The hills are alive …"

"Shut up, Hugh. I'm already tired. Making me laugh will only make me weaker." He turned to me and grinned. "You're right, though. Which one is Julie Andrews?"

"Why, Mel, of course," I said.

He snapped his fingers. "You're right." He cocked his head toward the cabin. "Mel's also the only lady helping Emma out, and those two are the only ones with their mouths closed. Wait. I see Grace over there." He jerked his head in the direction Grace stood talking (or maybe threatening) Ruby Mae. "She's probably helping by keeping her mother away from the others. I hope the ladies aren't so star-struck they forget to help out around the place."

"Are you forgetting Sadie?"

"Whoops. No problem then."

We traipsed past the women in various stages of ecstasy at their surroundings. You'd think they'd never laid eyes on a sea of grass and flowers waving at the sun in time with the silent breeze tickling the meadow. Maybe they hadn't, come to think of it. I hadn't, so why not them? Aside from o-o-hs and a-h-hs, they were silent, something I've never before witnessed in this group of women. I knew that wouldn't last—they had to come out of their collective state of oblivion sooner or later, but it was nice while it lasted.

And it didn't last long.

"Move, move, move!"

I turned to see Sadie behind me, lugging a huge box of something that smelled out of this world. I jumped out of her way just in time to keep from getting mowed over. "Doughnuts, Sadie?"

"And cookies and bread and rolls and pies and a cake or two, bozo."

I reached for the box. "Let me take that, Sadie."

"Hands off, Clown Boy! I've got this. You go back and help Bristol."

Clown Boy?

I didn't realize Bristol left to return to the car. I hoofed it back there as quickly as I could, and grabbed a box of drinks—juice, milk, and water, from what I could see. "Good grief, this stuff's heavy. How on earth did she get this out to the car to begin with?"

"Are you forgetting who we're talking about here, Hugh? Sadie could've brought her stove with her if she'd wanted to. Carried it out to the car, too."

I would've answered, but that would require moving my lips and wasting breath, so I settled for a grunt.

"You can say that again, Hugh."

I didn't bother.

We reached the cabin in record time. I set the drinks on the floor and looked around. I was surprised. It was everything Emma said it would be, but somehow even better than I expected. Someone, Emma I supposed, had opened the windows and the blue-checked, gingham curtains fluttered in and out at the whims of the fragrant breeze, giving the cabin an earthy scent. It was a warm day, but the gusts kept the air moving in the cabin, making it refreshingly cool.

Emma walked up beside me. "Emma, this is wonderful! No wonder you wanted to spend your summers here."

"Thank you, Hugh. I love it, but I must admit it's nice to have company, too. I spent many a summer here, but if truth be told, I was lonely a good share of the time. I wouldn't admit it at the time—that would've meant admitting to myself that I needed someone—but this beauty and tranquility is meant to be shared. I hope the ladies enjoy themselves."

"Look around you, Emma," I said. "I think they are."

The women kept crowding in behind us until we were nearly inside the tall and deep fireplace.

"Well, it's gonna be close quarters, but I hope we can make the most of it and not tear one another apart over a few inches of extra space." I must have looked horrified, because she chuckled and said, "I'm just teasing you, Hugh. The ladies and I have had many discussions about the concessions we're all going to be making during this week, and I think they're all on board."

"Well, it appears so at the moment. I don't think I've ever seen Ruby Mae so quiet." I nodded to the area where Ruby Mae was standing and peering out the back window. "She's either admiring the view or struck dumb by the solitude."

"Must be the view, Hugh. I don't think I've ever seen Ruby Mae struck dumb. Just isn't in her. She can do a lot of things but staying quiet just isn't one of them."

I looked down at Emma and she winked. "Let's let that last comment be our little secret, okay?"

I laughed and nodded. Emma surprises me daily with her wisdom and sense of humor. What a treasure she is to Road's End and its residents. I think she's truly happy now that she's become reacquainted with everyone, and I know we're better for having her in our midst.

Sadie walked up just then and said, "I think we'd better hunker down, guys. Looks like a thunderstorm's gettin' ready to dump all over us."

I leaned down to peer out the window, and sure enough, the dark clouds were above us and a little to the west, billowing and moving at quite a clip. I looked around for Bristol and motioned him over when I saw him standing outside with Grace. He said something to Grace, then jogged over to me. "Thinkin' about the storm?"

I nodded. "I don't want to leave the ladies here with that storm coming in, but I don't want to leave Road's End in the hands of the men, either."

Bristol nodded. "Yep, we'd better split up. Why don't you stay with the ladies, and I'll get back home so I can make sure the men are doing okay without their wives. They might have mutinied and left poor Perry tied up somewhere while they try to break into Sadie's place."

"Yeah, no doubt it's at least crossed their minds. Okay, you head back and I'll make sure the ladies are all set to go here and the storm's over before I leave." I paused and gave it some more thought. "No, wait, I don't feel right leaving them alone this first night. I'll spend the night to make sure everything works the way it's supposed to before leaving them alone. I'll start back tomorrow morning. Do me a favor, though, will you? Give me a call when you get back so I'll know Mel will be able to get my calls? I'm not sure they'll have reception here."

"Will do."

Bristol walked away, stopped to say something to Grace, and then loped back to the car. Grace walked over to Winnie and Martha, pointed upward, and motioned that they should head for the shelter of the cabin. They did as she asked and within a minute, everyone was inside, and the first drops of rain began to fall. A flash of lightning sliced the sky and a roll of thunder deafened us as it bounced back and forth between the mountains surrounding us. The women were busy closing the windows and within two or three minutes, we were all buttoned up.

Emma was right. The cabin was tiny. The ladies seemed to take it in stride, though, as they made room for one another at the small kitchen table and on the bed. There was one upholstered rocking chair by the front door and a small couch sitting along the side wall. Surprisingly, everyone found a place to sit with the exception of Mel and me. We held hands as we listened to the rain on the tin roof and watched as the light breeze grew into heavy gusts. Before long, the clouds moved along, taking the thunder and lightning with them and blue skies followed. A fine mist rose from the warm ground and dissipated once it rose over the tall grass. It was over.

I shouldn't have worried about making sure everything was in place. Sadie had the ladies divided up into teams of two. Winnie and Martha unpacked the boxes of food, Hazel and Ruby Mae put everything on shelves along the wall, and Mel and Grace took charge of the pillows, blankets, and sleeping bags, stowing them in out-of-the-way places until they'd be needed later that night. That left Emma and Sadie who took pitchers, pails, and anything else that would hold water down to the small river that crossed through the property. After hauling them back to the cabin, they poured the water into a covered barrel Emma had along the side of the cabin nearest the kitchen. She had ingeniously located the barrel just below a small window in the kitchen, so all she had to do was lean out the window and scoop up what she needed. I helped them bring container after container to and from the river, and I don't mind admitting it was hard work. I couldn't imagine how the two older women managed to keep up, but they're from a generation accustomed to hard work, so I shouldn't have been surprised. After several trips we had the barrel filled, and it was just one more trip to bring back enough water for the kitchen.

Emma got everyone's attention by asking "Anybody for supper?" The din of all those women talking at once immediately quieted and they sprang into action. Before long, there was a feast spread out on the table and everyone grabbed a plate, silverware, and napkin, and dug in. The ladies did themselves proud with that meal, not that I'd expect any less. Before long, dessert was served, and this guy was ready for bed. Before anyone could hit the hay, though, there were dishes to wash and dry, beds to prepare, and goodnights to be said. All in all, the first day at Riverbluff was a great one.

I told Mel I'd spend the night in the car. No sense taking up space in the cabin when conditions were already tight, and I'd be comfortable enough. She gave me a kiss and said, "Thanks, honey. I don't know how you'll fare in the car, but I appreciate your staying the night. Just makes me feel better about being alone in the mountains with women who drive us nuts on a regular basis."

I hugged her tight. "Bristol should be calling to let me know if we can get calls up here. I don't know why I didn't think about this before—you might be stuck up here with no communication if we can't get a signal."

"Even if we are, Hugh, we'll be fine. Emma spent a lot of summers up here all by herself with no phone. I think we can manage."

Looking back, I wish I hadn't believed her.

Chapter Fifteen

Mel's concerns about my comfort were spot-on. In order to keep any fresh air circulating inside the car, I had to crack the window, but that allowed around 250 million mosquitoes to invade my bedroom-for-the-night. I was glad to see morning arrive. I got out, stretched, headed for the cabin for coffee, but veered off in the direction of the outhouse first. It was just as Emma described it—outdoors. I smiled as I spotted a rough-hewn, obviously homemade shelf that held extra toilet paper and a pile of decade-old *Reader's Digests*.

The ladies were bustling around the cabin, tucking their bedding back into their hidey-holes and preparing breakfast. Mel met me at the door with a cup of coffee brewed in a coffeepot just like my grandmother used to have. It was strong, but good, and I don't believe I've ever tasted a better cup of coffee. A doughnut followed, and I looked around to make sure I hadn't died overnight and landed in Heaven.

Mel drifted over to me. "Any news from Bristol?"

I shook my head. "None. Either he forgot or he wasn't able to get through. I tried to reach him before I left the car, but the call didn't go through. I'm afraid you ladies might be up here without a phone."

"We'll be all right. Honestly. Besides, who in their right mind would mess with us anyway?"

I looked around. She was right. Taking on Rambo would be tough. Taking on these ladies would be suicide. Not too many people are dumb enough to attempt that once they saw what (and who) they were up against.

I was just about ready to head out for Road's End when Emma approached me and motioned outside. I followed and found her on the other side of the rain barrel.

"What's up, Emma?"

"I thought I'd show you why I feel so confident that no one will ever find Delbert here. I haven't shown the ladies yet, and maybe I won't. Depends, I guess, on how they react under pressure."

"Well, you've got my attention, Emma." I smiled and admired the determination in her face. "You'd make a good Navy Seal or Army Ranger, you know."

Emma laughed and said, "Well, that's something I never thought of, Hugh. Not sure I could get through the training. Anyway, there's a root cellar beneath the cabin that would make a perfect hidey-hole for Del. The entrance is actually inside, but I didn't want the ladies to see what I was showing you. At least not yet. Anyway, I get to it through the floor of the living room. There's a braided rag rug between the rocking chair and that couch. Do you recall seeing it?"

"It's quite colorful, isn't it? Blues and yellows?"

"That's the one. It's an oval and braided, so when a person goes down into the cellar and closes the door behind them, the rug doesn't accidentally fall in such a way that someone else would know what was under it. I've attached the rug to the little hatch in the floor with a couple of industrial staples."

I nodded. "Okay, I get it. It's just stiff enough that it won't wrinkle. It just falls back right where it was when you lifted the door, right?"

"Right. I don't know why I thought it was important when I first made that rug, but I think I know now. Normally I wouldn't care if the door closed securely and invisibly under it, but this is the one time when it would matter. I just wanted you to know that if you bring Del up here, I'll have a spot to hide him that's practically foolproof, especially if I keep its location from the other ladies. Well, I'll tell Sadie and Mel, but I don't know if the others need to know. What do you think?"

"I think you're a genius, Emma. But what if you need to get into the root cellar any other time? Won't the ladies know then?"

Emma grinned. "This is where the genius part comes in. I also have an entrance outside the cabin. It's right over there. I'll just use that entrance if I need to go down there. And if any bad guys try to use that entrance, they still won't see Del because there's a false wall in there that, if I say so myself, looks pretty darned realistic. Took me forever to design and construct it—couple of summers, in fact, working on it a little at a time. It's not a spacious space—frankly, I think Mr. Jackson might have a tough time keeping that stomach of his tucked in back there—but it'll hide him as long as he keeps quiet."

"I have a feeling not getting killed will be incentive enough to keep his mouth shut, don't you?"

Emma smiled. "Well, if that doesn't do it, nothing will. And just so you know, I'm not claiming—or hoping, for that matter—that Del will have to be moved from Road's End, but this location just seems to have that God stamp on it. If worse comes to worst, you can bring him up here, and he won't be in danger from the men who are after him. Whether or not he's in danger from the ladies is another story and I can't make any promises there!"

"Well, if his trip around the yard last winter didn't teach him a thing or two, he's a lost cause."

We walked back to the door of the cabin, and I leaned in. "Well, ladies, I think you're all settled in. Is there anything you might have forgotten that I can bring back with me when I visit?" I didn't want them to feel abandoned, so I'd made arrangements with them that either Bristol or I would return every other day to check up on them. No one seemed to have forgotten anything, so after giving Mel a hug and kiss, I walked through the damp grass and climbed into my car.

Rats. I forgot to grab a second doughnut.

The drive home was uneventful and less than two hours later, I was pulling up to the inn. No one seemed to notice (or care) that I was back in town, so I walked inside to use the bathroom and grab something cold to drink. I found Del at the kitchen table, looking glum.

"Hey, there, Del. How's it going?"

He glanced up but said nothing.

"I'll take that as a "It's going just fine, Hugh. Thanks for asking."

He sneered at me but nodded. "Yep."

"Stay here," I said. "I'll be right back."

Five minutes later, I was at the refrigerator door hoping there was some iced tea in there. There was. *Thanks, Mel.*

I held up the pitcher. "Tea, Del?"

He nodded and I grabbed two glasses from the cupboard and set them down on the table, then grabbed some ice cubes, and poured the tea. "Mel makes great iced tea."

He didn't say anything but took a second gulp before he set the glass down in front of him.

"Feel like talking?"

He shrugged.

"Okay. Anything new around here? I didn't plan to stay the night, but I hated to leave the ladies alone up there the first night."

"Yeah," he said. "They're so helpless."

I sensed sarcasm. "I know where you're coming from, Del. They're probably the least helpless group of women in the world, but I guess the man in me wanted to feel I was making a difference."

We sat and sipped. "Anything curious go on around here?" I looked at his face and realized what a stupid question that was. "Well, aside from the usual curious stuff that goes on around here on a daily basis."

He seemed to ponder that for a moment, then said, "Those two old geezers seem to think they're detectives."

"You mean George and Dewey?" He nodded. "Come to think of it, it had better be George and Dewey. I'd hate to think there were two more old geezers around here who've opened a PI agency."

I thought I saw a smile, but it could've been a trick of the light. "Have they solved anything yet?"

Del looked at me with that "Are you nuts?" look I get so often.

"Well, at least it keeps them from coming up with something else dumb to do. I know they're weird, Del, but those two men fought in World War II and have spent long lives working hard to keep their families in food and shelter. I guess opening a harmless PI agency is the least they can expect their neighbors to put up with."

He shrugged again. Maybe it was just my imagination, but it seemed to be a friendlier shrug than the last one.

"Nothing from Mack?"

He shook his head. "Not sure if that's good or bad."

"You read my mind. I was thinking about that yesterday. Do you have any idea who the top guy would send after you?"

"Officially, he'd send a couple of guys I've worked with before, but there are always freelancers who'd love to off me for the reward."

"Are those two guys easy to spot?"

"As in noticeable characteristics?"

I'm ashamed to admit I was impressed with his language. I didn't think Del had it in him to know what "noticeable characteristics" meant, let alone use it in a sentence. "Right. Bald? Tall, short, fat, skinny, walks with a limp, you know, the usual stuff."

"Well, aside from the height and maybe the limp, the others could be disguised easily enough. One is about 5'10" and the other a couple of inches taller. They make their living by being nondescript, so I doubt you'd recognize them if you saw them on the street."

"But would you? If you've worked with them before, maybe you'd have a better chance of spotting them than I would."

"Or the detectives in town."

I hung my head. "Oh, gee, I hope they stay out of it. We're in enough trouble without worrying about two old guys trying to take down a couple of thugs. No offense meant, Del."

"None taken. I was a thug. I'm not ashamed of it."

"Seriously? You never felt any guilt over stealing or hurting innocent people?"

Del was quiet for a minute. "You'd feel differently if you'd grown up like I did."

I wanted so badly to pursue that, but Bristol walked in just then, pulled out a chair, and sat down. "I want overtime pay."

"Bristol, I hate to lay this on you, but you don't get paid … period."

"Yeah, there is that, come to think of it. These guys are driving me crazy."

"You're just now noticing that?"

His glance said it all. "You haven't been here for 24 hours, so you don't know what I'm talking about."

"You're right. Let me have it."

Bristol stood up, grabbed a glass from the cupboard, and poured himself a glass of tea. "Gee whiz, I'm sorry, Bristol. I wasn't thinking." He waved me off and sat down.

mtotocrfully now.

"Okay, we were right about Perry. He pretty much gave up at the first sign of trouble, which occurred about four minutes after we left town. The guys worked hard to get inside Sadie's Bake House, but with no key they couldn't do anything without breaking and entering. Even these guys wouldn't do that unless they thought they could lay the blame on someone else." He tipped his glass toward Del. "You're lucky they forgot you were here, Del."

I cringed. "And?"

"Just more of the same. I came home and before I even got out of the car, I had to fight off the men who knew I had a key to Sadie's. They finally went home to eat the food their wives left for them. Frankly, missing a meal or two wouldn't hurt them, but you'd think they were on the tail end of a 365-day fast the way they were moaning and groaning."

"Where are they now?"

"Last I knew, they'd gone out to Mt. Vernon to see what Martha had made for George."

"Mt. Vernon? As in George Washington's Mt. Vernon?" That was Del, looking confused.

"Yep," I said. "He and Martha, who used to be Geraldine before she changed her name to Martha, live at Mt. Vernon. It's nothing like the real Mt. Vernon, though. It's a farmhouse they named Mt. Vernon to keep up appearances at their antique store—Thirteen Colonies Antiques."

"Don't you mean hornswaggle, rather than keep up appearances?" Bristol grinned at me, and I couldn't help laughing. "Those two haven't sold an antique in their lives."

I looked at Del, who was looking from me to Bristol, back and forth. "Del, I'm sure this won't surprise you, but George and Martha Washington sell things from *their* Mt. Vernon that they bury in the ground at their house to dirty them, like burning a candle for a while, then sticking it in the ground so it'll look really old, then try to pass them off as antiques from the real Mt. Vernon. Pretty shady, huh?"

"Pretty clever, I'd say," Del said. "How do they get away with it?"

"Well, it's not that we haven't tried to convince them of the error of their ways, but as soon as we stop one scheme, they come up with another. They're stubborn, I'll give them that. But I sure wouldn't let my friends buy anything from them!"

Bristol chimed in just then. "And if you see a batch of kittens in a basket with a sign that says, "Kittens sired by descendants of George Washington's cat," don't fall for it. We have a church cat named Pewter who is evidently quite friendly with George and Martha's cat. She has kittens once in a while, and those two try to pawn them off on unsuspecting tourists."

Del looked dumbfounded. "You mean people actually fall for that?"

"Some. Not many, but some."

Del snorted. "Seems to me they deserve it if they're that dumb."

"Well, we can't be with them constantly to police their sales, so I guess you're right. At some point, the customer has to take some responsibility." I poured us all another glass of tea and put the rest of it back in the fridge. I made a mental note to remember to ask Mel how she makes it. If I keep sharing my tea with others, I'm gonna run out and I won't be any better off than the rest of the men in this town.

"Well, I'd better get back to fixing that roof," Bristol said, sliding his chair backwards and rising.

"The church roof? I thought you finished that a couple of days ago."

"I did—at one spot. Then another hole appeared. That roof is mighty old, you know." He reached over to take one last sip of tea.

I know next to nothing about making repairs, but I felt I had to offer to help. "Need any help?"

Bristol guffawed and almost spit out his iced tea. "That's a good one, Hugh. You can't get higher than the second step on a ladder, and you're offering to help me fix the church roof? Thanks, but you take care of the stuff that goes on inside the church, and I'll take care of the rest."

I gave him a little salute. "Sounds good to me. Hey, how about coming back for supper tonight? The three of us can muddle through a meal without Mel."

"I'll be here. See you guys later."

After Bristol walked out the door, I stood and took our empty glasses from the table and deposited them into the sink. "Got anything planned for this afternoon, Del?"

He looked at me and shook his head. "Well, I thought I'd rob a bank, but you don't have one. Then I thought I'd scam a few folks, but half of them are out of town, and the other half has already been scammed by the Washingtons. So, no, I don't have any plans."

"Okay, then. How about we retire to the living room and finish our talk?"

"What talk?"

"The one we were having when Bristol came in. About how you grew up. I'd really like to help if I can, Del. I know I'm a stranger and all, but I *am* a pastor and listening is what I do."

"When you're not blowing up someone's Hummer or making me shovel the snow?"

"Right." He had a point. "Not to make too much of this, but technically, the ladies blew up the Hummer, and Mel made you shovel the snow, so that leaves me ... innocent, I guess."

"Or a coward."

I nodded. "Or a coward."

Chapter Sixteen

We pushed our chairs beneath the table and walked to the living room. I couldn't help wondering if Del remembered the last time he sat in this room. Sadie gave him a dressing-down I was sure he wouldn't forget for the rest of his life.

"Have a seat." I took one of the armchairs flanking the fireplace and motioned Del to the other. I thought back to when the president of the United States sat in that chair just a few months ago while he was here to attend the wedding of his nephew, Jonathan, to our daughter, Mandy. And now a criminal hiding out from a mighty drug cartel was sitting in that same chair. God surely does work in mysterious ways.

"You said I wouldn't be surprised that you weren't ashamed of stealing from others if I knew how you grew up. Care to expand on that?"

"Not particularly," Del said, "but I guess it won't hurt anything. My days are probably numbered anyway."

I put my hand up and said, "Whoa right there, Del. What makes you think your days are numbered?"

"Already forgot why I'm here?"

"Well, no, but the government is doing all they can to protect you. I wouldn't say it's a foregone conclusion that the cartel's going to win this one."

"Wish I shared your optimism."

"Maybe some of it will rub off while you're here." I grinned and wiggled my eyebrows at him.

"That's creepy."

"Creepy? That's my Groucho Marx imitation."

"No, it isn't. It's creepy."

"Really? I wonder why no one else has ever told me that."

"Probably afraid of you."

I laughed. "Afraid of me! That's rich. I'm about the least-afraid-of person in this town."

"Well, keep up with that creepiness and you won't be."

"Okay, okay. I bow to your superior knowledge of Groucho Marx. Let's get back to the original topic."

Del looked around the room—at the couch, the fireplace, the draperies, the door to the dining room. Finally, he said, "I can't remember a time when I wasn't a thief."

"You mean as an adult?"

"No, I mean as a person—period."

"Even as a kid?"

He nodded. "My dad was high up in the crime family where I came from. And don't ask, because I won't tell you where that was. Just take my word for it. I grew up learning how to cheat, lie, steal, or even kill anyone who got in my—or my dad's—way."

I sat there with my mouth hanging open. "You mean he brought you up that way?"

"I think it was the only way he knew, to be honest. Before him, his dad was the top pin. Good old Grandpa Jackson. He'd thump you on the back for a job well done, then stab you to make sure you never squealed."

"What about your mom? Didn't she have anything to say about how you were raised?"

Del shook his head and seemed to ponder my question for a moment. "If you knew my dad, you'd know why my mom didn't do anything. She—and everyone else, including me—was terrified of him. I don't think she even wanted to marry him, for that matter, but if he said she was, there wasn't any other option. Do it or die."

"Do it or die?"

"Yeah, cool slogan, huh? I can't begin to tell you how many times I heard my dad say that to me, my mother, his underlings, anyone who was related to or who took orders from him. And he meant it. I remember once when someone told him they wouldn't do something he asked them to do. He asked them to sit down at the table to talk about it, excused himself for a minute, then came back and blew a hole through the guy's head."

My mouth opened, but nothing came out. I was truly at a loss for words. Finally, I managed to croak out, "How old were you?"

Del looked to the ceiling and seemed to be calculating. "I'd say around seven."

"Seven years old? And your dad killed someone in front of you?"

"Yeah, me and my mom, and a couple of older cousins who were at the house that day. The real kicker, though, is that the man he killed was my uncle. My mother's brother. She wasn't even allowed to cry over his death. She had to clean up the mess—and it was quite a mess, as you can imagine—but never once was she allowed to mention to my dad that he'd killed her only brother. She had no doubt, and neither did I, that he'd kill her as easily as he did my uncle. And I learned an important lesson that day. I never once told my dad I wouldn't follow an order he gave me. Not one time."

My heart was pounding so hard it was probably somewhere in my sinuses by then, and I couldn't think of anything remotely appropriate to say to the man in front of me. All I could see was the seven-year-old Delbert, living a hell no one else could fully understand. No wonder he was rough around the edges.

"What finally happened to him, Del?"

"My dad? Ha! This is rich. My mother killed him one night right after supper while he was drinking coffee and having a slice of cake. His favorite—chocolate. She told me later she thought he should have his favorite dessert since it would be his last. I guess she got the last laugh, though, didn't she? Only she used a knife in the back—she told me it was easier to clean up."

I couldn't believe what I was hearing, although I knew full well he said those words. I could hear the little boy in him as he was telling me. He sounded lost, and somehow, jaded. "How old were you, Del, when your father died?"

"Eleven. I'd just had my birthday a couple of weeks before. He wouldn't let my mother buy me a gift because that was too sissified, as he used to say."

I sat there, stunned, while Del drummed his fingers on the arm of the chair. My mind couldn't settle on a question to ask. Why? When? Who? *Why?* I glanced at him, hoping his disclosure hadn't upset him too much. "Del, are you okay?"

He looked over at me with a smile, pointed his finger at me, and said, "Gotcha!"

At first, I didn't comprehend what he was saying. I was still processing the horrible story he'd just told me. But slowly, realization dawned and I figured out he was kidding me.

"Did you just *make that all up?*"

"Yep."

"But why?"

"No reason, except to see if I could pull it off. And I guess I did, didn't I?"

I took a deep breath. I didn't know whether I should hug him in relief or skewer him with the fireplace poker. Since I didn't think he'd like either option, I stuttered instead. "You ... b-b-but why? Why would you tell me that?"

"Well, Pastor, I'm not as dumb as I look. I thought a sad tale from the viewpoint of a kid would tear you up—and it did. Del-1, Pastor-0."

"You've got that right, Del. You got me, okay? Now how about the real story?" I took a drink of tea, set the glass down (on the coaster), and said, "Would you put your glass on that coaster? Mel will kill me if it leaves a ring on the table." I watched as he did as I requested. "Okay, now that you've gotten your practical joke over with and made a fool of me, let's hear what really happened in your childhood."

Del was still grinning. Mel was right; he didn't look all that ugly (*whoops, I'm sorry, Lord*) ... uh, formidable when he smiled. "I was just a regular kid with a dad who was a pickpocket. A highly-skilled pickpocket, I might add. He unknowingly taught me everything he knew, and that led to bigger and bigger things, and here I am now— hunted by the mob and condemned to live in obscurity for the rest of my days."

"Well, I'm sorry you grew up stealing from others, but I'm sure glad your dad wasn't a killer. Your mom too. Speaking of which, what did your mom think about your dad's career?"

"Oh, it wasn't his job. He was a welder. He just loved pulling one over on somebody. Every time I was with him he gave it back and said, 'Sir, I think you dropped this.' And my mom had no idea. She was a school teacher and would've crowned him if she'd known what he was doing—and what he was teaching me."

"He was knowingly teaching you to steal?"

"Naw. He never meant it that way. He was trying to show me how careless people are with their purses, wallets, stuff like that, but in the process, I realized I could make a tidy living with that skill."

"Are your parents alive?"

"Yep. They live in Indiana. Haven't seen them for a while, though. Didn't want them to know how I ended up. I told them I was a realtor. They're so proud." He looked down at the floor. "It'd kill 'em if they knew the truth."

"You know, Del, I'm not sure I can believe you this time either. What's to say you're not making the Indiana story up just to confuse me and make me look like a fool?"

He leaned back in his chair and stretched his legs out. "Sorry about that, Pastor. I didn't mean anything by it. Just thought I'd have a little fun while I was here."

"So making me look like a fool was the best way to have fun?"

"Sure was." He grinned and tried to wiggle his eyebrows. He couldn't.

So there.

Chapter Seventeen

Not long after that little charade, I answered a call from Bristol. I wouldn't have known he was one calling, except Mel programmed my phone to put his picture up when it was him on the line, as if that wasn't weird. Besides, the phone told me it was him ("Call from Bristol.") Talk about creepy. Forget Groucho Marx; let's talk about smart phones.

"Hey, Bristol," I said, hoping to amaze him with my telepathic powers. "What's up?"

"Just got word from Mack that someone's on their way to Virginia."

"Why didn't he call me?"

"He tried earlier, but you must have still been at the cabin. He got busy, then decided to wait until he got more info. He tried you again, no answer, so he gave up and called me. Looks like there's definitely someone—make that two of them—on the move from Florida. He's not sure who it is, but he knows they're from the cartel. Better decide what we're gonna do with Del. Mack says we have about thirteen, maybe fourteen hours until they get here—if this is where they're coming—maybe a bit more if they stop somewhere for the night."

"Great. Any names or descriptions? Are we looking for men? Women? One of each? What are they driving? And where are they coming from? And how on earth did they even find out?"

"Let me get over to your place. I'll fill you in on the little bit I know."

He hung up. "Well, Del, looks like we're going to get some action around this little backwater town. Bristol says there are two people on their way to Virginia. Let's hope they're here for a trip to Colonial Williamsburg. If not, we've got a problem."

"If they're the guys I know, they don't like history. In fact, they don't like much of anything."

Two minutes later, Bristol was standing in the doorway between our dining room and living room—leaning actually and breathing like he'd run four miles in under a minute. "Sorry, guys," he said. "I don't remember the last time I ran so fast."

"Probably back when the drug thugs were here."

"Yeah. Seems to happen a lot around here, doesn't it?" He began breathing normally, and walked over to the couch to flop down. "Okay, Del, we're gonna need as much info as you can give us. Any idea who these guys are?"

"You sure they're guys? There's a woman I wouldn't want to deal with under any circumstances. Looks all homey and nice, when in fact she's the biggest ..." He halted, probably looking for another word for the bad one he was about to say. "... well, let's just say she isn't a nice lady." He looked first at me, then Bristol. "At *all*."

I sat with my elbows on my knees and tapped my clenched hands against my mouth. "Okay, let's assume—for the moment, at least—that she's one of them. With our luck she is, and even if she isn't, it can't hurt to be completely prepared."

"I agree," Bristol said, "but I still wonder how on earth they tracked him to Road's End. Even if they'd spotted him in Richmond, there are several other directions, as well as cities, for him to hide out in. And I can't imagine Mack not noticing a tail if they, the cartel I mean, happened to notice him in Mack's care."

Del spoke up. "Care? You call the way that giant manhandled me as *care*? He all but tore my arm out of my shoulder dragging me everywhere."

"Well, Del," I said. "I hate to be the one to tell you this, but I think you had that coming. Planted or not, you did your share of nasty stuff with the cartel before you turned state's evidence. Besides, relocating you isn't in Mack's job description, and believe me, he has a big ol' bunch of other important stuff he could've been doing. Dislocating your shoulder would probably be a small price to pay for getting you away from the bad guys."

"Well, thanks a lot, *Pastor*."

"You're very welcome, former *bad guy*." I had a flashback to first grade.

"All right, you two. Times'a wastin' and we still haven't figured out anything."

"Wait, Bristol. How did Mack find out any of this?"

"Oh, yeah. Forgot to tell you. There's another undercover agent in there—the cartel, I mean. He managed to type a text to his superior, who then told Mack about it. Mack must've told the guy he had a real interest in keeping this town, and us, safe."

Made sense. But because I'm just so darned good at it, I started to worry, and then out of the blue (or actually in the back door) the day was saved and all our problems were solved. Just kidding. George and Dewey barged into the kitchen through the screen door of the Inn. I knew it was them because one of them hollered, "PIs on the premises. Don't try anything funny. We're armed." Simultaneously, the other one screeched, "That's PVs comin' in, and it won't be funny, 'cause we got us four arms." As usual, all I heard was the cobbled-up version which sounded a lot like "PIscomin'inpremPVsinnfunnyarmsed." Try saying that three times real fast.

Together, the three of us (with six arms) groaned. We didn't sound half-bad and I wondered how we'd sound as a singing trio. But I shook my head vigorously and pitched that thought right out the window when our town's detectives came into the living room. George was crouched, with his arms extended, holding what looked like a cap pistol in both hands, swinging it around in all directions just like he'd seen on countless cop shows. I'm not sure if he was imitating a detective from some TV show or having trouble standing upright. Probably both. Dewey was carrying a big stick I remember tossing into my leaf pile in the side yard, and he managed to trip over it trying to walk and brandish his weapon at the same time. He stumbled in, while George crouched in.

Finally, I thought, Road's End is in good hands. Ha! *Dear Lord, please give me patience, and don't let me beat them with that stick.* I don't know how often the Lord hears those words, but it's pretty common here in Road's End.

"Hi, guys. What's up? Have a seat. Bring in chairs from the dining room if you'd like."

George nodded yes, and he motioned with his pistol that Dewey should do just that. Dewey turned toward the dining room and slapped his stick smack-dab on George's bottom. Needless to say, there were some dirty looks flung between them. When the chairs were in place, Dewey plunked himself down, while George sort of backed into his chair with his head down, and just sat there at a 45-degree angle staring at the floor.

"You okay over there, George?"

He tried to nod but couldn't do it without his chin hitting his stomach, so he just muttered, "Yep. Doin' fine, Hugh."

"Okay then, guys. What brings you here today?"

"Trouble." That was George, the one with his mouth in his belly.

I can believe that, George.

"We have intel there's trouble in town."

You're just now coming to that conclusion?

"What kind of trouble, and what intel are you talking about?"

Dewey beat George to the punch that time, probably because George was trying to breathe with very little air available in his abdominal area. "Not sure yet. But it's comin'."

"Well, any idea at all?"

"Nope. That's fer you to answer." Dewey looked supremely satisfied that he was handling the conversation while George was temporarily incapacitated.

I didn't have time to monkey around with the two people in town who usually cause, or at least exacerbate, trouble. "Me? Why me?"

"We figgered you'd know, bein's that yer the pastor and all."

"Dewey, my being the pastor in town doesn't mean I know when trouble's coming."

Dewey was fresh out of answers, so he just quit talking. After a second or two, George took up the slack. "You knew about that blizzard last year."

"George," I said between gritted teeth, "everyone in the state of Virginia knew there was a blizzard on its way."

"So you admit it?"

"Admit that I knew bad weather was coming when all there was on TV and radio was non-stop information about the blizzard coming our way? Yep, I admit it. And everyone else with a pulse in Virginia would admit to it, as well. You guys knew it too!"

"But we're not talking about everybody else in Virginia, are we? It don't matter if we knew it or not. The question here is whether or not *you* knew about it."

Dewey added his expertise on this matter by saying, "Don't go blamin' ever'body in Virginia, Hugh."

"I'm not blaming everybody else, Dewey. I'm just telling you that … you know what? Never mind. Let's just forget about it. Tell you what. If I hear about any incoming trouble, I'll be sure to let you two know, okay? How's that sound?"

Dewey leaned over as far as he could without toppling headfirst to the floor, trying to look George in the eye. "How's that sound, George?"

"Sounds like he's bein' cagey, that's what it sounds like, but I guess our hands are tied until the warrant arrives."

"What warrant?" That was me, the one who was just about to commit a major crime in my living room.

"Wouldn't you like to know, Hugh? Huh? Wouldn't ya?"

Bristol had had enough. "Shut up, Dewey. You too, George. You two don't know what you're talking about, so just go home, and warm up whatever your wives left for you for dinner. If and when we feel you need to know about any so-called trouble on its way into town, we'll let you know."

Dewey smiled. "Okay. Sounds good, Bristol."

George tried to nod. He couldn't. Instead, he waved an arm in Dewey's direction. Dewey got up and walked over to George, hoisted him up out and out of his chair, and the two of them walked out—one with a view of the floor, and the other tripping over a stick.

Bristol waited until they were out of earshot, and said, "When you die, Hugh, I'm going to see to it they make you a saint."

"Wrong denomination, Bristol. Appreciate the thought, though. Maybe you could visit me in prison?"

"Deal."

Del looked from one to the other of us. I could see his belief in our ability to keep him safe was waning, and his fear of being in this town among people he was either afraid of, didn't respect, or who hated him, was becoming a problem. I feared revolt at best, an escape attempt at worst.

I tried to reassure him. "Del, I know this conversation sounded strange. It was strange. No getting around it. But strange is a relative term—at least around here it is—and relatively speaking, this is about par for the course around Road's End. Believe me, we've seen worse, but I doubt we'll see better."

"Let's get back to the real problem," Bristol said. "Two people—two men or one man and one not very nice woman—are on their way up here from south Florida. With two of them in the car, they could take turns driving rather than staying overnight somewhere. I think we're going to have to assume they're gonna be here in twelve to fourteen hours."

I thought about that for a moment. "Sounds about right, Bristol. Any suggestions where we go from here?"

Del was turning green. "Get me outta here."

"We're going to do our best, Del. In fact, I have some information that might be of real interest to both you and Bristol."

I explained Emma's hiding place and Bristol agreed immediately. Del hadn't yet seen the remoteness of the cabin, and was justifiably leery of it, but eventually he agreed.

"I'm not sure I wanna spend any time with those women, though."

"I understand your misgivings, Del, but it's either take you there and pray they don't find you, stay here and wait for them to arrive, or think of another place to hide. Frankly, I don't have the foggiest notion where to put you here … wait … the tunnel! We could put him in the tunnel!"

"Tunnel? What tunnel? Oh, crud, you mean that one that I was sitting on in that old shed last winter?"

"Technically, Del, Sophie was sitting on it and you were beside her."

"Sophie?"

"Yeah, you remember. Sophie, the camel?"

Del groaned while Bristol punched the air and said, "Why didn't I think of that, Hugh? The tunnel's perfect!"

Del, close to tears, nearly fell out of his chair and blurted, "I hate tunnels! Can't stand to be closed in. Forget it. I'm not doing it." He looked genuinely scared, and frankly, I knew his pain.

"Hey, I know the feeling. I hate being enclosed too, but it boils down to being in the ground and still alive or being underground in your coffin—dead. Either way, you're underground." I hated being that graphic, but he needed to understand—*really* understand—the seriousness of the situation.

Bristol added, "Listen, Del, we have very few choices here. Seems to me you have just three: go underground to the tunnel, go to the cabin and go underground in the root cellar, or stay here, hide behind a dresser, and hope they believe us when we tell them we haven't seen you."

Del looked back and forth between Bristol and me, hoping, I guess, that one of us would come up with something better. Unless we find an invisibility cloak lying around somewhere, he had the three options Bristol had just named from which to choose.

"Del, why don't we give you a few minutes to think this over while Bristol and I put our heads together." I know he heard me because he nodded, but the look on his face was one of fear, regret, and hopelessness. This was a mess he couldn't get out of easily. Some things are like that when bad choices are made. Sometimes you can reverse things. Sometimes not.

In this case, there was no reverse. There was only hide or die.

Deborah Dee Harper

Chapter Eighteen

In the end, we gave in to his fear and decided to take Del to the cabin to (hopefully) keep him out of sight. If he needed to hide, a root cellar probably would be less-claustrophobic than a tunnel, historic or not. I wasn't happy, though, because taking him to the cabin meant we were potentially putting Mel and the ladies in danger if somehow the cartel men figured out he was there. *Lord, please put Your Hand on us all as we try to hide Del from those who would harm him, and probably us if they feel like it. We put our trust in You, and if there's anything I'm doing that You don't want me doing, please let me know. In Your Precious Son's Name, I pray, Amen.*

I had a feeling the Lord didn't want me doing any of what I was doing, but until He told me or gave me a sign that I should stop, I had no choice but to go forward with whatever plan we could cobble together in the next forty-five minutes.

Del grudgingly agreed to the trip to the cabin, but I could almost feel the fear emanating from him when he thought of being with all those women. Frankly, I didn't blame him. They were formidable when they got their dander up, as my dad would say, and being around Delbert T. Jackson has that effect on people.

Del pointed out something I hadn't thought of. We had no idea where the killers were when Mack got word they were on their way, so they could have had four, maybe eight hours under their belts before anyone realized they were coming. I considered calling Mack, but I knew if he had any concrete information, he'd let me know.

I told Bristol and he groaned and slapped his forehead. "How could I have forgotten that detail? Man, I guess I've been out of detective work too long."

"Don't sweat it. The drive to the cabin takes only a couple of hours, so even staying for a few minutes with the women before driving back means we'll be back here in plenty of time to greet our visitors."

"Better get going then."

Del walked in just then. "When are we leaving?"

"We were just talking about that, Del. We think we'd better get going since, as you pointed out, we don't know how far they travelled before anyone noticed they were on their way. I don't know what you'll need at the cabin except clothes and personal items, so go grab them and we'll be on our way."

Bristol bit his lip. He does that when he thinks. "Do you think we should split up? If for some reason they arrive before we get back, there'll only be Perry, the detective duo, and their cohorts. I don't like the idea of leaving them alone."

I nodded. "Good point. Okay, I'll take Del and you keep the home fires burning. I just thought of something. Hang on for a minute." I walked to the bottom of the stairs, cupped my mouth, and yelled, "Del! Can you come to the top of the stairs for a second?" He appeared immediately, and I continued. "Make sure you don't leave anything of yours in that room. And tidy it up, please. If they get aggressive and start looking through homes, we don't want them finding anything of yours or have a room look like it's been occupied."

He nodded and walked back into his room.

"Don't worry, Hugh. I'll make sure that room looks good and that he hasn't left anything behind. You just get him to the cabin, okay?" He looked down and rubbed the back of his neck before looking up and saying, "And here's another thing. Should we take some handguns for the ladies in case it gets bad?"

I must have looked horrified because he tripped over himself to explain. "I'm not thinking of letting all the women know about them or even see 'em, for that matter. I was thinking that both Mel and Grace have level heads and in an absolute emergency, they could at least threaten the bad guys."

I was still trying to get my heartbeat under control. "You know what? Maybe you should go with Del, and I'll stay here. You have the know-how with these kinds of things and I don't. I should be here because I'm sure they'll be searching every room in the Inn and Mel will kill me if they lay a finger on anything. Besides, you're right. They *will* need some weapons aside from Sadie's mouth."

"Hey, I didn't think about Sadie. They're not as helpless as I thought." With a big grin, he walked to the bottom of the stairs, and I followed. "Hey, Del! Are you … oh, sorry, didn't see you coming down. All set? It's time to hit the road."

He turned to me. "Sorry about yelling in your ear, Hugh, but I feel a real urgency to get him outta here."

"Me too, Bristol. You know this, of course, but I'll be praying for both of you every single mile." Del looked sideways at me with a questioning look. "What's up, Del?"

"Nothing. Just never thought you'd pray for me. I got all you guys into this mess in the first place."

"Del, when you're a true Christian, you love everyone, just as Jesus Christ has instructed us to do. You're one of His children or could be if you haven't yet been saved. Think about it. If you want, Bristol here can answer all your questions."

With that, we patted one another on the back, and they walked out to the car.

Please be with them, Lord. Please.

Just before they reached the car, Del turned and yelled, "By the way, there's a flock of chickens in my room. Might wanna get 'em outta there."

I spent the next two hours alternately praying and tidying up—most of the time I prayed *while* I tidied things up. After making sure Del's room was spotless and free of any traces of him or Francine and her chicken thugs having spent time there, there wasn't a lot I could do. I sure didn't want to run into George and Dewey again, and I knew I would if I left the Inn. So, I went into my office and tried to write Sunday's sermon. After twenty minutes, it was obvious it was going be a very short sermon as I'd written precisely nothing. While that might suit some of my parishioners just fine, I felt an obligation to at least open my mouth. Finally, I delved deep and prayed hard enough that the words began to flow.

I hadn't heard from Bristol, but I knew he'd call if he had anything to tell me—if he could even make a connection, that is. Emma knew what she was doing when she bought that land. Perhaps the surface of the moon is a bit more remote, but not by much. I tried to push back my fears that Mel and the others had no way to contact us if trouble erupted, not that we'd be much help, anyway, being two hours away. I knew God had His Hand on them, us, and the entire situation, but it's hard being a human and not acting like one. I had faith in our Lord, but gosh, it was hard to give up the ingrained need to do something about the situation myself. I know He wouldn't want us to just sit back and let the cartel get their hands on Del and maybe in the process hurt the women, so I guessed we were still in His Will. I prayed that He would rein me in if I overstepped my bounds.

All that time I was thinking about the cartel characters and how close they might be. Not knowing for certain they were even coming to Road's End was annoying, but in fact, I had no reason to think otherwise. Unless they were after some other poor soul-turned-state's-evidence, they were aiming for our little village. I guessed all we could do was deny any knowledge of his being in Road's End lately. Of course, they might have easily found out he was here last winter, so to pretend we never heard of him would be a big mistake. We'd acknowledge we knew him but didn't care for him with his bad behavior and poor manners. That should satisfy them. I hope. And sadly, it was the truth.

I could've hugged Bristol when he walked in the back door of the Inn. He had a grim look on his face, and I dreaded hearing what he had to say.

"How'd that go?"

Bristol shook his head. "Fine, I guess. I just have this feeling I'm forgetting something important. I worried all the way back that something wasn't right, that I could've done more to keep them safe."

"I know. I'm worried too, but I can't think of anything else we could do besides staying there ourselves, and that leaves Road's End in the hands of our dandy detectives. We'd come back with the whole town burned down. I wish we had a bird's eye position where we could watch both places at ..."

"That's it!" Bristol slapped his forehead. "I'm such an idiot. I should've thought of this right off the bat." He groaned and plopped himself down on one of the kitchen chairs. "Got any coffee?"

"Nope, but I can make it. So, tell me why you're an idiot."

"The phones!"

"You mean the useless phones we have?"

"No, I'm talking about the pair of satellite phones I have back at my house that I haven't used in quite a while now. Never had a reason to. But you know me, I couldn't toss out anything remotely useful in a bad situation."

The coffee was ready and I grabbed two mugs from the cupboard and a dozen doughnuts we'd spirited out of Sadie's place, put them on the table, and poured us each a cup. "Satellite phones? Don't they bounce off satellites?"

"They sure do. Do you know what that means?"

"Actually, no, I don't. Tell me before I pour this pot of coffee over your head."

"Okay, you know our smartphones won't work with them so far away. They can't get a signal either because they're in the middle of nowhere up there or they haven't experimented to find a place that might give them one. But a satellite phone doesn't need a signal from a tower down here. It bounces off a satellite. That means if we can get one of these phones—after I calibrate them, of course—to the ladies, we *can* communicate!"

He stopped talking to take a gulp of coffee. "Ouch! Hot stuff." He grabbed a doughnut and said, "I wish I'd thought of that before I made the trip. Would've saved a lot of time. Now one of us has to go back there to give it to them."

"Well, I'd go with you, but they'd probably get here before you got back, and I'm not sure the men of this town wouldn't blab their heads off or try to fight them off with a cap pistol and a long stick."

Just then, my phone rang. Up popped Mack's picture. After the usual pleasantries, I said, "Really? How do you know? Do you think we can beat them there?" I mouthed the word 'Mack' to Bristol. "Well, we're gonna try, anyway, so even if they're there when we arrive, we'll do whatever we can to keep Del and the ladies safe. Great. Thanks, Mack. Well, not thanks … but, you know … okay, see you soon."

"What'd Mack have to say?"

"You're not going to believe this, but they have intel of some kind or another that those two are heading for the cabin. Not sure how the cartel figured it out—or how the government found out the cartel knows about the cabin or that they're *going* there, come think of it. Maybe they, the cartel guys, have been on to Del for a while now and did a thorough study of every single one of us here in Road's End. Heck, we didn't know about the cabin, and we see Emma every day of our lives. I guess it doesn't really matter. We'll find out in the end." *If any of us are still alive to ask questions.*

"If they'd done that, they'd know about Sadie. They probably think she's here. No wonder they changed plans. Did he say how close they are?"

"He didn't know precisely, but he thought we could still get there if we left immediately. I can't believe I'm asking you this, but do you have any extra handguns? It goes against everything I'm supposed to be to ask for a gun to shoot someone—not that I'm anti-gun, not by a long shot. Oh gosh, what an awful pun. These are perilous times, though, as someone once said, and we have to take drastic measures. And believe me, my asking you for a gun is the definition of drastic."

Bristol grinned. "It's actually kind of funny with you having spent your career in the military. Yeah, I have extras. I'll meet you back here in ten minutes. Is your car gassed up?"

I nodded. I have this thing about always having to have a full tank, even if I've only driven twenty miles since I last filled up. Mel thinks I'm paranoid, and of course, she's right. But I guess I can hold that over Mel's head when this is all done. Won't she be surprised? The pastor's packin' heat and having a full tank of gas finally paid off!

"Then we'll take your car. Since they're apparently bypassing Road's End, I'm not worried about the men. They'll more than likely fall asleep until morning after eating supper, anyway, so we're good until tomorrow morning, at least."

"Good. I'll be ready to go when you get here."

Bristol stopped just as he was about to jump off the back step. "Hey, Hugh! Bring those doughnuts. And Francine and her friends are in your backyard."

"Again? Don't worry, I'm way ahead of you. You get the guns and ammo. I'll be in charge of the refreshments."

I could hear Bristol chuckling until he reached Rivermanse Lane. I hoped we'd have other opportunities to laugh after all this was over with. Something told me these guys weren't fooling around.

I went outside to chase Francine's flock out of the yard and back into their pen, but there was no sign of them. I didn't have time to look for them, so I left them to their running around. Must be Francine is taking advantage of Sadie being out of town. Or taking charge.

True to his word, we were in the car and heading out of town ten minutes later. Being a pastor and all, I try to obey laws to the best of my ability. Today, though, I made an exception to the rules. I sailed along as fast as I dared, pushing past the speed limits as often as possible. For the most part, we were quiet during the trip. I don't know what Bristol was thinking, but I was coming up with multiple bad-case scenarios ranging from a sandstorm to an invasion by the Chinese, and none of them gave me great confidence in our abilities to survive the visit by the cartel committee. I wished the women would call—despite not having cell service. That was something the Lord was going to have to orchestrate.

And then He did.

I jumped when my phone rang. I saw Mel's beautiful face. "Mel! You got through! How? Oh, my gosh, be careful. Listen, Bristol and I are on our way back up to the cabin. I'll explain more when we get there, but in case we lose the signal, the bad guys are on their way to the cabin. I have no idea how they figured out where he is or how long it'll take for them to get to you. Do whatever you think you need to do to get the ladies ready and organized and I suppose we'd better let them in on why Del's really here. We should be there in …" I looked over at Bristol.

"At this speed, we should be there in just over an hour."

"Did you hear that, hon? Yes, just over an hour. Be careful. I think we're ahead of them, but there's no way to know for certain. Keep your eyes open. I love you, too. See you soon."

"How'd she manage to get a signal?"

"Climbed up on the roof."

"Whoa, great idea. I never thought of that. Well, now we know that works. You've got yourself an exceptional lady, you know."

"I know." *And I want to keep her.*

I sped as fast as I could, but I still felt as though I should jump out of the car and run. As we drove closer to the cabin, I realized I had no idea what they were driving, but that it didn't matter, anyway. No one else knew this cabin even existed, so anyone parked at the access point had to be the bad guys.

We decided to pull off the road and park behind a group of trees that would hopefully hide our presence. It helped that my car was a dark green, so it blended in better than a brighter-colored car would have. We took a couple of minutes to load our guns (I can't believe I just said that), talk a little strategy (and I do mean little), then exited the car and shut the doors as quietly as we could.

We walked a bit farther up the road to the path that would lead us to the cabin. So far, there was no sign of anyone having driven or walked down that direction. All tire tracks and footprints were ours, and we scuffed them as well as we could on the fly, so we were fairly certain they would have no idea where to even find Del. They'd also have no idea a welcoming committee awaited them. Of course, that committee would consist of one man who knew firearms, a pastor who didn't, the pastor's wife and his secretary, and six octogenarian women (with one, maybe two of them certifiably nuts), plus Del, the target, who was probably, at this moment, shivering in his shoes and enduring snide remarks from Sadie.

Just as we reached a shallow dip alongside the road, an ear-piercing whistle split the air.

Chapter Nineteen

I don't know what Bristol was thinking, but I was busy wondering if I should drop to the ground, stand my ground, run across the road like a deer bent on suicide, or shoot something. Turns out Bristol had a fifth option. Smart aleck. He quickly slipped behind a tree and waved at me to do the same. Since my side of the road offered a sapling and a scrubby shrub from which to choose, I belly-crawled through mud, leaves, and slimy sticks to an oak tree with a broad trunk. I looked like Rambo, only Sly Stallone wasn't wearing a golf shirt and the new jeans Mel bought me last week. Too bad I didn't have a bandana to wrap around my head to keep the sweat from my eyes. And believe me, there was sweat. Mel was gonna kill me; I knew I was walking, or slithering, my last mile. By the time I got to the tree and looked for a thumbs-up from Bristol, he was standing in the middle of the road, talking to Hazel Parry. *Hazel Parry?*

Apparently, our rules of engagement had been modified. I tried, with no luck, to brush off the leaves, twigs, and mud from the front of my shirt and pants and walked in their direction, looking as dignified as a muddy, leaf-encrusted, gun-totin' pastor could look.

Hazel looked up and smiled. I wasn't sure if it was joy that her pastor was now in the midst of their little group, or the sight of me looking like a prop in a first graders' production of *A Muddy Tree Named Hugh*.

"You look like a muddy tree, Pastor. Melanie's going to kill you." Well, at least that was settled.

Bristol put his hand on my shoulder and said, "Hazel's an amazing whistler, Hugh." That seemed like an odd observation for him to make considering our dire situation. Then it hit me that he was referring to the sound that had me scurrying like a ground mole around the forest floor.

"That was you, Hazel? Wow."

"Seems the ladies have been working hard on a plan. Hazel volunteered to hide in the woods and whistle when someone drives by."

"You've been in the woods all this time, Hazel?" I might have inhaled some of those dead leaves. "Oh, wait, you mean you came here just a little while ago? That makes more sense." Hazel's smile dimmed, and no doubt her confidence in her pastor dimmed right along with it. "How do they know we're not the bad guys?"

"I whistle once when it's you two, and twice when it's the bad guys."

I whistled—well, next to Hazel's, mine sounded more like the mewling of a dying field mouse—and said, "Wow, Hazel, that's very courageous of you! How do you know they won't come looking for you once they hear the whistle?"

Bristol, who'd been rocking back and forth on his heels in impatience, said, "She whistled like that because she was telling them it was us. She also knows bird calls and she'll use that when they arrive so the cartel won't know it's not a bird native to the area—a loud bird—when she whistles that it's them."

"I have to hand it to you, Hazel. You ladies have been strategizing, haven't you? What made you come up with this idea?"

Hazel brushed away a piece of hair that had escaped from her bun, and said, "Yes, we have. We all sat in the cabin and listed our strengths and weaknesses, so we could best be used to protect Del. We tried to make assignments that wouldn't involve our individual weaknesses. After all, it wouldn't have been prudent to send a woman on a mission to the woods surrounding the cabin who was afraid of bears, for instance." *Or pastors, for that matter.* I couldn't believe there was a woman among them who wasn't afraid of bears, and then I remembered Sadie. *I guess I know where Sadie is.*

Hazel continued, "After we tallied both our strengths and weaknesses, we asked for ideas. My idea was coming out here to let them know who was on their way into the meadow."

"That was great thinking, Hazel."

"Oh, it wasn't me who thought of that. It was God."

I patted her arm. "Yes, I'm sure He's looking out for all of you."

"No, Pastor, I mean God *told* me to come out here. I always wondered what my gift from God was, and now I know. It was my ability to whistle, and it wasn't necessary until now. Isn't He amazing?"

He certainly was. "You mean you heard His voice?"

"Not really. He sent an angel."

If I hadn't been so wired, I'd have passed out on the spot. Given we had a big job ahead of us, though, I put unconsciousness on the back burner. "Wow. Just wow, Hazel. Let's talk more about this later, okay? Right now, I think we'd better get out of the middle of the road and head to the cabin. Those guys could arrive any time now."

"I'll see you gentlemen later then."

"You're not coming with us, Hazel?"

"I can't. The bad guys haven't arrived yet and I have to stay here to warn the others. You go on ahead. I'll be fine."

Every fiber of my being resisted leaving that lovely woman alone out there with the cartel thugs on their way. But when I looked at the determination on her face, I knew she would be fine. I said a quick prayer, smiled at Hazel, and turned to follow Bristol.

We didn't try to hide the noise we made as we practically ran to the cabin. Neither of us said a word, but I for one (and I'm certain Bristol felt the same way) was eternally grateful we'd arrived ahead of the bad guys. We might not have much time, but any amount of time was better than arriving after they did. We reached the edge of the meadow and jogged the rest of the way. When we reached the cabin door, we saw only Ruby Mae.

"Hi, Ruby Mae. Where's everybody else?"

"Well, hello yourself, Pastor. Bristol. Don't you worry none. They're around here. You just can't see 'em."

What is this, I thought, hide and seek? Briefly, I felt impatience at her words, but then thought about what they meant. The women were safe, and either hidden or located someplace where they could be of the most help. "Where's Del?"

"Oh, he's around here somewhere, too, Pastor. Don't you worry 'bout nothin'. We got things under control here. Thanks for stoppin' by, though. Now if you'll excuse me, gentlemen, I have to get into position."

Stopping by? Getting into position?

"Ruby Mae, we're not just stopping by. We're here to fight those men when they come to take Del with them. We can't let them do that, and we thought you ladies might need some help keeping them at bay. Where's Mel?"

"Right here, hon."

I turned around to see my wife standing behind me, pretty as always, with a pistol in the waistband of her jeans. Now that's something I don't see every day. "Yep, there you are, all right."

"You look surprised, Hugh."

"That would be putting it mildly. I could've seen a T-Rex standing there and I'd be less surprised than I am at this moment."

"Are you comparing me with a dinosaur, buster?"

"If I was, you'd be the prettiest dinosaur to have ever lived. But no, it's that gun. Makes you look … I don't know … different."

"Very eloquent, dear. Don't worry, it's not loaded yet. I know I don't normally dress like this. I usually save it for special occasions. You don't know this, but I'm a spy while you're at church, so I'm used to things like guns and … well, spy stuff."

"Well, I've gotta say it looks good on you, but I think I'd prefer you gave up the life of a part-time spy and stick with the innkeeper/pastor's wife side of you."

"It's a deal. Listen, I know we don't have much time, and the Good Lord knows we're out of our element here, but I think we've got a fairly decent plan going."

"We ran into Hazel out on the road, and she told us about taking stock of your individual strengths and weaknesses. Brilliant. What's your strength—besides the obvious plant whisperer side of you, and the others lives I just mentioned?"

"It took me a while to think of one, to be honest. But I couldn't see where my being able to grow plants and trees would come in handy with this scenario, nor would being an innkeeper, so I chose being the pastor's wife."

"Aha."

"Are you a little underwhelmed?"

"No, just confused."

"I decided that between the two of us, we've witnessed and shared with one another everything from drama, death, obstacles, and hard times to new life, Mandy's wedding with the president in attendance, good times, you know… just about everything … and I realized my strength was being adaptable."

"You're right. You *are* adaptable. But how will that help you in these circumstances?"

"I'm not sure yet, hon, but I think God will show me when the time comes. And don't worry, I'll take the gun out of my waistband, load it, and hide it before I talk to any of them— unless I'm pointing it at them—to keep them off-balance and let them think we're just helpless women."

"And then you're going to drop the hammer?"

"Something like that." She put a hand on my chest and said, "I think it's time to take our places, dear."

"Okay, will do. Wait a minute, what places?"

"Okay, quick rundown. Del's in the root cellar behind the fake wall. Ruby's going to be in the meadow picking flowers—I think she's rekindling her love for her hats. Grace will be with her in case, in Grace's words, she needs to kill her to shut her up. If they approach Ruby, she's going to talk to them, and you know how that makes a person feel. They'll be desperate to get away from her, which will give the rest of us a chance to get a leg-up on them. Let's see…. as you know, Hazel's in the brush beside the road …"

"Yeah. She's a good whistler."

"That she is. She'll move into position as soon as she's alerted us. She's going to block their escape."

"But …"

"Don't worry, she'll have a pistol. She grew up on a ranch and knows quite a bit about guns. Martha and Winnie are going to be in here baking some bread." She lifted towels to reveal three pans of rising bread dough. "They're around here somewhere. They'll be the welcoming committee; you know, offering coffee, iced water, etc. Another diversion. Emma's under the bluff along the river somewhere. She'll determine where she can be of the most help. She's armed, too. Brought her own weapon and an extra and ammo for both. And I'm going to drift. I know it sounds hare-brained, hon, but I really feel I should wait until I know where I can be the most valuable."

"Aren't you forgetting someone?"

"I wondered if you'd catch that little omission. She's somewhere around here, also armed, but wouldn't tell us where she was going to be."

"And you're not worried about that?"

"You mean for her or the bad guys?"

"Good point. How about arming Del? Seems he should have a weapon too, since he's the one they're going to kill."

Mel grinned and punched me in the arm. "We're way ahead of you, hon. He's down there with a gun too, so if they should by some weird chance find him, he'll have a fighting chance. And our story is that we're having a ladies' church retreat, so they won't think for a second we're going to give them any trouble."

"Gosh, I guess you didn't need us, after all."

"You're wrong, hon. We were all brave and determined at first, but I know we're all shaking inside now that it's here. Having you and Bristol here is a blessing straight from God."

"Speaking of God, Hazel mentioned a visitation."

"Yep. But we'll talk about that later, okay? Now you two go hide somewhere, and wait for the bird whistle."

I gave her a kiss and a tight hug and went back outside to Bristol.

"Okay, let's get this show on the road, pal. Where should we go?"

Bristol looked around and said, "Good question. I'm assuming they'll have to use the path, once they find it, but for all we know, they could be coming through the woods as we speak, so let's keep that in mind."

"Well, hopefully, Hazel will have a chance to warn us. Mel said Emma's under the bluff by the river. Maybe we should join her. If there's any shooting, the bluff will be good protection and we can change positions without them knowing."

"Let's go, then. They could be here any second."

We ran to the bluff and had no sooner found a way down to the river when two long, shrill, and very loud bird calls sounded. Bristol and I looked at one another.

The game was on.

Chapter Twenty

I slithered down the bank and leaned against the bluff. A soft chuckle greeted me, and I turned to see Emma six inches away from me. "Yikes, I nearly crushed you. I'll be more careful next time I careen down an embankment to get away from thugs." She giggled and I took a deep breath. "So, ready or not, I guess the bad guys are here."

She nodded. "Let's whisper. I'm not sure if this water or the bluff or the breeze might magnify our voices. No sense taking chances, though."

Bristol crab-crawled over and hunkered down beside us. "I'm going to take a peek. I'll stay behind these wildflowers over there. Hopefully they're not scoping out the flora and fauna around here. You guys stay down. If they do happen to see me, there's no sense in letting them know there are three of us."

We both nodded and held our breath as he slowly raised his head above the bluff and behind the clump of wildflowers. He watched for a couple of minutes, then lowered his head and made his way over to us again. "They're using the path, so at least we know where they are. They're walking toward the cabin. Both six feet, one might be maybe an inch or so taller. Wearing the loudest Hawaiian shirts I've ever seen. Guess they weren't worried about hiding from anyone. One guy is bald, and the other has blond hair."

"Well, I sure hope Martha and Winnie can hold it together, maybe even get them to sit down for a cup of coffee."

Bristol whispered back, "I don't think they're the coffee and doughnuts kinda guys, Hugh."

"Who said anything about doughnuts? It's coffee or nothing."

Emma nodded, then said, "I hope Grace saw them go inside. Maybe she can drag Ruby Mae away from her flowers long enough to get to the cabin before they leave. Ruby Mae could talk them to death and we wouldn't have to be sitting here on the wet riverbank."

Bristol doubled over laughing, and I joined in. I had to bury my face in the crook of my arm to keep the sound from drawing their attention to the party going on behind the bluff. Coming from Emma those words took on special meaning; she's one witty woman, along with all the other attributes we're discovering about our town's richest resident.

Once Bristol got himself under control, he motioned to us he was going to take another look. Four long crab-steps took him to the same clump of wildflowers. He didn't take as long as last time before he lowered his head and returned to us.

"Well, I don't see them, so they're either inside the cabin or at least on the front side. I did see Grace dragging her mother toward the cabin, so maybe our troubles will be over quickly."

"What should we do? If they're inside, they can see us approach the cabin from the river."

"No problem there, Hugh," Emma said. "I closed the curtains on the back side of the house for that very purpose. Did you happen to notice if they were still closed, Bristol?"

"Come to think of it, they must have been or I'd have seen them inside the cabin—well, at least movement. Yeah, I think they were closed. Want me to take another look?"

I glanced at Emma. "I think you'd better, Bristol. If they're still open, there's no way we can get up there without being seen, and probably shot."

Emma looked at me, her face set in a scowl. "You mean they'd shoot an old woman?"

"Not sure about that, Emma," Bristol said, "but you're not going, anyway, so it's a moot point."

"Oh yes, I am," she whispered loudly. "I'm not taking the cowardly way out. I'm coming with you and that's final."

Bristol and I locked eyes, daring one another to be the first to tell her she wasn't. Neither of us spoke, so she won by default.

A rumble of thunder growled from the west. For a moment, I thought a motorcycle gang had arrived. *Well, isn't that just dandy.* I realized my mistake when I glanced upward to see black clouds above us, churning like a giant kettle of … burned butter, I guess. I pointed upward. I guess I was so busy thinking and planning, I didn't see the storm approaching. Both Emma and Hugh followed my gaze.

"Could be good news for us," Bristol said. He sat down and rubbed the front of his thighs. "Boy, I hope I never have to walk around like a crab again. My legs are killing me."

"Yeah, me too, Bristol. You look weird. Won't rain make getting around trickier? Traction, vision, all that stuff?"

"Well, it might, but we're not the Three Stooges. We've walked in rain before—I even walked in the rain one time on the *grass*. Talk about tricky! I think we handle it."

"Very funny, Stooge Boy. Okay, you give the word. Wait—what are we doing once we reach the cabin?"

"I'll take the back, and Emma, you go to the right. Hugh, take the left. Are there windows on the sides?"

"Nope, just front and back," Emma said. "Hugh and I should be okay once we reach the sides of the house, but you'll be completely exposed, Bristol. And it would be just like Ruby Mae to open those curtains even though I told all the ladies I was closing them and why."

"I'll be careful, Emma. Now once we get going, stay low, and if you see they're opening those curtains, flatten yourselves in the grass. That might not be enough cover, although that grass or wheat or whatever it's called is pretty high, but it'll be better than nothing. Get down as far and as fast as you can. And don't move until I give the signal."

"What's the signal?"

"Not sure yet, Hugh."

It embarrassed me a little when Emma scrambled up the bluff easier and faster than I did. I tried to make myself feel better by thinking she'd probably done this before. Not the-bad-guys-with-the-guns-in-the-cabin-and-Del-in-the-root-cellar stuff, but since she's been here ... oh, never mind. I followed behind her and Bristol was well on his way to the back of the cabin. I ran as fast as I could, but Emma still made it to her side of the house a few seconds before I did. I sat on my knees. Should I stand instead, or would that make me a bigger target? I decided my head would be too easy to hit if I was sitting, so I stood up slowly. *Thank You, thank You, Lord, for getting us here safely. Please watch over all of us.*

Okay, now what?

That cabin might be old and a bit shabby, but the walls were thick. I couldn't hear a thing going on inside. I hoped Bristol could hear something through one of the windows. Apparently, he could because he came around my side of the cabin. I nearly died on the spot.

"Don't *do* that!"

"Do what? They're in there, all right, and if I'm never proud of Ruby Mae Headley again, the pride I feel right now will make up for it. She's jabbering in there just like she always does. They've got to be going insane."

"Serves 'em right. What'll we do now?"

"I want you to stay right where you are."

I started to object, but Bristol put his hand up. "Forget about it, Hugh. I need a pair of eyes on this side. Emma will do the same thing on her side. I'm the only one moving, got that?"

I had no choice. After all, he was armed and I've seen him shoot. I was armed, too, but that meant nothing. I couldn't hit a beached whale from six inches away. I thought about Mel and where she might be. I knew she was a smart woman, but I couldn't help but worry about her with all these men who knew how to shoot and a husband who couldn't hit a beached whale.

I let Bristol have his way, but I wasn't happy. Right then wasn't the time for a tantrum, so that would have to wait for later. If there was a later.

Bristol gave me a small squeeze on the shoulder, probably to show his confidence in me. I, on the other hand, interpreted it as goodbye-Hugh-see-you-in-Heaven-if-we-don't-make-it-out-of-this-mess-and-if-it's-you-who-doesn't-make-it-because-after-all-you-can't-hit-the-side-of-a-beached-whale-from-six-inches-away-I'll-see-to-it-Mel-is-looked-after.

I can be a baby sometimes.

I watched him disappear around the corner of the house. Just as I turned my head back to the front, I saw movement. It happened so quickly I couldn't make out if it was one of us or one of them. I decided to assume it was them but would make sure before I shot.

I can be so thoughtful sometimes.

I'll be honest. My hands were shaking as I took my gun from its hiding place—my pocket—and took a step forward. I didn't have to wait five seconds before there was more movement, but this time I could make out it was Grace. *Thank You, Lord.* I could hear her talking and it sounded to me, although I couldn't hear everything she said, that she was talking all about their church retreat, and that her mother, the one talking inside, would be happy to tell them all about the Lord and how they could become saved. I don't know if the bad guys had come in aggressively or were playing the same game the women were playing, but so far it didn't sound as though there was any antagonism between them. I closed my eyes and concentrated (as if that would sharpen my hearing) and heard her saying something about a GPS system story she'd heard about a man being led a thousand miles or so off course because his system was on the fritz.

And then I realized what that meant. They were somehow able to track Del with the use of a GPS. I know nothing about those things because I'm a diehard map guy. I don't like someone talking to me from a teensy screen sitting on my dashboard telling me I should get into one of the two right turn lanes. And I know cell phones can be used—somehow or other—for directions, but I have a hard enough time answering it without trusting my life to it. But these guys might be more technically savvy than I am. That wouldn't be difficult. A week-old kitten whose eyes haven't yet opened would probably know more than I do.

Where's a kitten when you need one?

The voices lowered in volume as she talked, and I assumed she was leading them away from the cabin and trying to convince them that they'd tracked Del to our present location because their satellite had gone wacky on them. I must admit she did a good job of sounding like a gentle, kind, and gracious lady. How come I don't get that treatment? I knew she was capable of knocking them unconscious with just a look. I hoped she'd use her secret weapon if necessary.

Since I didn't know if Shiny or Blondie, whichever one she was talking to, was facing in my direction, I didn't dare look. I flattened myself against the cabin as close as I could get. Eventually, their voices faded to nothing. Maybe, just maybe, she'd been successful in getting them to leave quietly.

Nope.

Just then I detected movement from my left—and it wasn't Grace this time. Neither was it Bristol, Emma, Mel, or any of the other good guys. It was Shiny.

And he had his gun pointed right at me.

Chapter Twenty-One

They say your life flashes before your eyes when you think you're going to die. Must be I had a pretty boring life so far because nothing flashed before my eyes except a steely determination that I've never felt before. All I could see was red. I remember it because Shiny looked a lot like that old caricature of the devil. I guess, too, that I was fed up with people messing with the folks of Road's End. We are some of the gentlest, most generous, and earnest, Christ-loving people you can find on the planet, yet we're constantly in the middle of some kind of war—and I don't mean spiritually, although that's no doubt behind all our troubles. The devil (the real one, not Shiny) likes to target the virtuous because he's a cowardly loser who doesn't know when he's defeated, and takes his rage out on the innocents of this world. He knows he can never have us, so he sows seeds of danger and any other disruptive, evil, and cruel thing he can think of to make us miserable, create doubt about ourselves, and limit the good we can do for the Kingdom.

But not on my watch, buddy. Not on my watch.

As if I didn't have enough on my plate with Del hiding in the root cellar, Bristol doing something … dangerous, and all the women scattered around who-knew-where so I had no idea how to protect them, and a bad guy staring down his gun barrel at me, it started to rain. I don't mean drizzle, sprinkle, or even pour. I mean it *rained*—buckets, dump trucks-full, heck, even those planes that drop water on forest fires couldn't compare to the volume of water pouring down from above. Apparently, that kettle of burned butter wasn't butter, after all. It was tons upon tons of water droplets in clouds that sneaked their way across the sky to surprise us with the mother of all rainstorms.

At first, I was annoyed. But a split-second later, I realized what a blessing it was. Talk about a diversion. If I was soaked, that meant

Shiny was too. And no doubt distracted. Before I had a chance to think, I aimed my gun and stalked toward him with a determination I can't describe. God was giving me super-courage. No doubt about that. I hoped He'd also endowed me with a bullet-proof force field. Even as I stepped closer and closer, I thought to myself, "Hugh, what on earth do you think you're doing? You'll die here in the rain, all wet and shot to pieces." But it didn't matter what my brain was telling me. My heart was saying, "I've had it, devil. I'm sick and tired of you interfering with our lives. From now on, I'm the new sheriff in town and you can just get the heck out of Dodge."

At the moment, I would've had to make my decision to shoot or be shot, I detected movement in the trees behind Shiny. While we stood facing one another on a very wet playing field, whatever I'd detected exploded from the woods. Ten seconds later, I was standing and Shiny wasn't. Something arrayed with tree branches, mud, leaves, and a nasty attitude stood staring at me in the rain.

It was Sadie Simms.

As quickly as she appeared, she was gone. She left only Shiny behind, and the big rock she'd used to knock him unconscious. I shook my head just in case it was me who had fallen—dead, shot to smithereens, and lying in the muddy meadow. But no, this wasn't what Heaven was supposed to look like, so I assumed I was still alive, Shiny was out for the count and we had only Blondie to contend with.

I'd have to save my undying gratitude to Sadie for later. As happy as I was that one of the two bad guys was out of commission, I couldn't forget that one of them remained. I couldn't see much beyond the end of my nose, but everyone else out in this stuff would be just as handicapped as I was, so I left Shiny to his nap and returned to my station.

But I couldn't just stand there and hope someone bad came around the corner so I could manhandle him, so I walked to the back edge of the cabin and peeked around the corner to check with Bristol. He wasn't there. I crouched low to pass the windows and peeked around the next corner. No Emma. Had they started the party without me? Were they rounding up Blondie or were they … lying somewhere? I hadn't heard any gunshots and I didn't think the downpour, as heavy as it was, would completely muffle the sound of a gunshot, particularly in such a small area. Well, I thought, I'm not getting any answers just standing here.

I headed for the next corner, the one that would show me the front of the cabin. I stopped for a moment to even out my breathing, say a prayer, and round up the courage to see whatever was around that corner. *Please, Lord, don't let any of the ladies or Bristol be hurt. Watch over us.*

As her husband, I admit I added *especially Mel* after *ladies* in that prayer, but as a pastor, I fervently hoped *none* of them were hurt or worse. Road's End needed every last citizen, every crazy, boisterous, squabbling, stubborn, Christ-loving one of them. They'd become close friends to Mel and I over the time we've been in Road's End and frankly I couldn't stand the thought of any of them in harm's way. Yes, I've dreamed of clobbering at least one of them every day since we arrived in that sleepy little town, but I would never hurt any of them. Lock one (or all) of them in a basement? You bet. Hurt one of them emotionally or physically or allow anyone else to? Not on your life.

Standing in the rain daydreaming about how grateful I was for my fellow residents wasn't getting me anywhere. If I wanted any sort of future that included them, I'd better get moving and see if any of them needed me. I took a deep breath and slowly moved my head so I could take a look. I saw nothing, but just as I was about to withdraw my head, I heard voices.

"I don't have the foggiest notion what you're talking about, young man, and get your hands off me! When's the last time you washed them, anyway?" That was Winnie Wyandotte, who is known for telling folks, particularly Dewey, to wash their hands.

"Oh, Winnie, let the poor man be. After all, it's difficult to stay neat and clean when you're hunting people, isn't it, Mr. …? I just realized I don't know your name."

Mumble, mumble. Must have been Mr. Last Name That Martha Didn't Know, a.k.a. Blondie, because it was a deep, male voice.

"Why, I declare! How can you defend this … this hulking, angry, dirty man? Don't you know he'll turn on you the minute he has a chance?"

"You hush now. Have a seat, sir, and I'll get you some coffee and maybe I can even find something sweet here in our provisions."

"Don't you dare give him any of our food!"

Were they playing Good Cop, Bad Cop?

"How can you be so selfish? We are, after all, on a women's church retreat. The minute we're away from home you show your true colors? Is that it?"

"Why, I declare! We have no idea what this man wants … and he's carrying a gun, no less. How do we know he's not going to rob us?"

"And take what? Our bread? Is that it? Are you afraid he'll take one of your precious loaves of bread? Sir, if you'll hand me your firearm, I'll put it right up here on the chair next to the front door."

"He's not going to give you his gun."

"Why, thank you, sir. I'll just put it here, okay?"

"Wha …"

"What were you saying, dear, before I put this young man's gun on the chair?"

They were! Martha and Winnie, the counterparts to their husbands George and Dewey, were playing Good Cop, Bad Cop. Will wonders never cease? And he gave them his gun? He must have a second one somewhere on his body. Martha was clearly leaving clues to the location of his gun. If I had a clear chance, I could reach in and grab it.

I didn't.

Chapter Twenty-Two

Just as I extended my arm and mentally prepared myself to duck under the kitchen window, then lean in and grab that gun, around the corner, lickety-split, came a very soggy Shiny—although he wasn't as shiny as he was before he hit the muddy deck. Apparently, he's a two-rock kinda guy and Sadie's knock on his noggin needed a bit more clout. As I locked eyes with him, the rage I felt the first time I saw him returned ten-fold.

Suddenly, he embodied all the evil I'd ever had to contend with—from my Air Force years as a chaplain counseling young men and women facing the atrocities of war and others who died after spending time in prayer with me the night before, to the goons of last winter, the tornado that should've flattened Road's End and killed every last one of us, and now to these two thugs threatening the lives of those I held dear.

I looked at those soulless eyes and knew he meant to pull the trigger and blast me straight to Heaven. But I had more to do on this earth and I wasn't about to let him take me out quite yet. If I met Jesus face-to-face in the next five seconds, then Shiny here was going to find himself in a lake of fire. I definitely had less to lose than he did. But I had a feeling he wasn't going to listen to my plea for his salvation. In all honesty, the depth of my rage surprised and frightened me. I had no idea I harbored those hateful emotions and yet, since I'd spent my life worshipping my Lord and Savior and doing my best to destroy the devil and his evil minions, I shouldn't have been shocked. Perhaps this seething anger was righteous. After all, we're all born into a supernatural war against the evils of the dark forces, forces that do nothing but target humans by either wooing them into giving up their souls to everlasting separation from God and unrelenting pain, or discourage, side-track, hurt, and torment those people whose souls they know they will never have. At any rate, this was a moment of truth. Live or die? Kill or not kill?

Before I could act on anything, Shiny went down like a soggy shoestring. I stood there, amazed. Not because Shiny was down for the count for the second time in one day—not having a good one, are you, Shiny?—but rather because of who was on top of him.

My wife. Where did *she* come from?

Mel quickly put her finger to her mouth to shush me. We still had Mr. Last Name That Martha Didn't Know inside the cabin with Martha and Winnie and perhaps even more of the ladies. She, being on the other side of the door, had a better view of the kitchen, and namely the table. She put her fingers to her eyes, then motioned toward the back of the cabin. Apparently, Mr. LNTMDK was sitting with his back toward the door. That must be why he didn't notice his pal slumping to the ground like a Slinky on its way downstairs. We had that much on our side, at least. The two of us were ready to charge in the front door and manhandle Blondie, but we were interrupted.

By a gunshot.

Mel and I both hit the deck on either side of the open doorway when we heard the shot. We looked at one another, our eyes as big as robin's eggs. Where on earth had that come from? Who was shooting? And who was being shot *at*?

We had both Shiny and Blondie with us. Unless one of the ladies or Bristol had shot at another member of our team, there must be at least one more bad guy in the vicinity. *Lord, please have it be another bad guy. Please.* Looking back on it, it seemed to be a strange request of God, but I know He knew it was because I didn't want any of the Road's Enders hurt or worse. Suddenly, we saw him come into view at the opening to the path.

Make that two.

How does this keep happening to us? It's bad enough we're in a battle for our lives. How come it gets worse every minute it drags on? I told myself I'd have time when this was all over with to mope and feel sorry for myself and the others. But at the moment, we had Shiny to tie up and Blondie to disarm. Together, Mel and I grabbed a couple of Shiny's limbs and dragged him inside, fully expecting to be shot or knocked out when we entered the cabin.

To my delight, the ladies had not only clobbered Blondie with his own gun, but also searched him for a second weapon. They found it in the back of his waistband. Winnie insisted on looking for a knife on his ankle, and I'll be darned if she didn't find one. When we got home, I'm going to buy them every season of whatever crime-busting show they want. It was obvious they knew what they were doing, because Martha dragged both of his arms behind him and zip-tied them together. She grinned at me and said, "Zip ties are possibly the greatest invention of all time."

Mel had slammed the door to the cabin just as a bullet whizzed by my ear and straight out the back window. Someone owed Emma a new window. Meanwhile, I helped Martha drag Shiny to the corner of the bedroom and toss him unceremoniously to the floor, and she got busy zipping his hands behind him. All this was done at ground level to avoid being shot.

I crawled over to Mel. "What now?"

Mel said, "Not sure. Any ideas?"

"Well, we should probably take up positions at the front and back of the cabin so we can shoot them if they come at us from either side. Other than that, I can't think of a thing."

Another gun shot, but this one sounded closer. Where were the others?

"Okay, now I'm getting mad. Don't these guys have anything better to do than shoot at us all day?" I knew that was a stupid question, but I was so in the dark, even my words couldn't see what they were doing.

Martha and Winnie sat on the floor, one on each side of Blondie. He groaned and raised his head, but Winnie cracked him on the noggin and he was out again.

"Winnie, I didn't know you had that in you. I'm very proud of you."

"Pastor, are you forgetting who I'm married to?"

I didn't know how to answer that, so I turned to Martha. "Were you two playing Good Cop, Bad Cop?"

"We sure were, Pastor. A body can learn a lot from cop shows, even if they're reruns of shows long gone." She smiled the smile of a vindicated woman.

Maybe, just maybe, I've misjudged most of the residents, at least the women, of Road's End. It was an interesting thought, but there was no time to think it over. My brain was getting frazzled just trying not to die; new thoughts would have to wait and take their turn.

Another shot, this time from the front of the cabin. It didn't come into the cabin, so it must have been shot in another direction. For that, I was exceedingly grateful, but still, I couldn't ignore the fact that shots were being fired. I prayed as hard as I have ever prayed. *Lord, please protect Your children. Don't let evil triumph in this battle. Show the devil Who's the Boss and send him back to wherever he came from.* I moved over to the kitchen window to take a peek.

If I live to be a hundred, I'll never forget what I saw. Sadie Simms was lying face down in the wet grass.

"Lord, no," I cried out. "Please, Lord, don't let her die. No, *no!*" I scrambled to my feet, and grabbed my gun. It was damp, but I prayed it would still fire if I needed it to. "Ladies, stay low."

"Hugh, don't go out there! Please, hon?"

"I have to, Mel. It's Sadie."

Her gasp was as grief-stricken as I felt. I turned back to the door and pulled it open. Someone was running toward her, and it wasn't Bristol. Had this guy just shot Sadie? Was that the last shot we heard? He was closer to her than I was, but I rushed out in her direction and would've made it if Sadie hadn't taken that moment to pull out her gun and shoot Bad Guy in the knee.

The scream that came out of that guy's mouth was loud and … well, unlike anything I've ever heard. I could hear Mel screaming in the cabin and in a split-second she was beside me. "I thought it was you," she sobbed. "I thought it was you. Don't you *ever* do that again! *Ever!* Is Sadie okay? Sadie, are you okay?"

Sadie cackled, "Sure am, Mel, but this guy's not doing so good, are ya, fella? That's what you get for shootin' at an old woman. You won't be runnin' nowhere for quite a while, I'd say."

The relief I felt was indescribable, but we were standing in the open, and despite the heavy downpour, someone was bound to see us. This guy had a partner lurking nearby, and apparently these guys showed no mercy. We needed to get back inside. "Sadie, are you wounded?"

"Naw, just real wet," she said with a grin. "This is kinda fun, isn't it?"

"Oh, Sadie, I can't tell you how happy I am to know you're okay. We'll talk about the fun later. Get back to the cabin now. You, too, Mel. I'll be back as soon as I can."

Mel started to protest, even though she knew she couldn't persuade me to go back to the cabin when there was at least one other man out here with murder and mayhem on his mind. As for me, well, I knew it was time to put my pastor's hat on the table, and fight just as dirty as the devil was. I walked over to the guy on the ground and said, "Sorry, fella, but I can't drag you anywhere right now. Just hang on and we'll get you some help when we can. How many more of you are there? No answer. I tried again. "Listen, guy, you're out of the game and you know it. You'll either die here in the rain or go to prison for a long, long time. So, if you want a doctor, you're going to tell me the truth. How many more are there?"

"Just the one," he said, gritting his teeth and groaning. "Ya gotta help me, mister. That old lady shot me. She *shot* me."

"You got that right. You're lucky that old lady didn't aim a bit higher or shoot you a second time. And you shot at her first, so quit with the victim act. Believe me, you messed with the wrong old lady. So where is this other guy?"

Nothing. I moved my foot toward his knee, which was bleeding all over the place. "Should I try to convince you to tell me what I want to know?"

I couldn't believe I was doing this—threatening to mess with the knee that Sadie just obliterated to get info out of him. But apparently, I was. It just goes to show how thin the line is between playing fair and playing any way you had to play to get the job done.

"No, no!" he yelped. He's down by the river." He gasped. "Gonna clear out anyone down there, then come in from the rear."

I grabbed his gun and wasted no time in pivoting around and running toward the bluff. I had no idea if Emma was there or not, but I couldn't see her anywhere else, so it was as good an idea as anything else. If she was there, she was in mortal danger. I could hear No Knee hollering after me, begging for help. We'd get someone to come and get him after this mess was taken care of, but his pain wasn't my problem at the moment. I reached the bluff in what had to be record time. This time I didn't even bother to slither down the side. I jumped.

Chapter Twenty-Three

And landed right on top of Grace and Hazel and the unfortunate man they were clobbering. We fell to the ground in a tangle of arms and legs—both good and bad. I extricated myself fairly quickly and stood just in time to see Hazel drive her fist right into his nose. He screamed and she and Grace cheered. I'm gonna have to be careful around these women. They're more dangerous than I would've thought possible.

"Where's Emma? Has anyone seen Emma?" I was frantic.

"She's right here, Hugh." I twirled at the voice and saw Emma and Bristol walking side by side atop the bluff.

"Oh, Emma. You too, Bristol. You had me pretty darned scared. Are you both okay?"

"Yep, just tuckered out and wet," Bristol said. "Emma here saw this guy heading for the bluff—remember the clump of wildflowers? They came in quite handy today. Anyway, she saw him coming, and ran down the riverbank to a path that leads upward into the trees. I lost track of what happened after that."

Emma spoke up. "I eventually decided to return to the riverbank when nothing was happening where I was at the cabin. I watched the new guys from behind the flowers, so I ran into the woods. After a few feet, I came across Bristol here aiming his gun at me."

"Sorry about that, Emma. I didn't know it was a good guy—or lady, I guess. I was hiding behind a tree when I saw Sadie go down. I was just about to go get her when I saw that other poor guy with the blasted knee get wiped out—serves the jerk right—then you ran out to Sadie. I was just about ready to head for the cabin to sort out what was happening, when Emma found me and told me the other one was heading for the bluff. So, we started over there, through the woods again and back down to the riverbank when Grace and Hazel jumped him. We saw you jump on top of all of them; I gotta tell you, it was all I could do not to burst out laughing. These guys, all four of 'em, never stood a chance. I didn't fire a shot!"

"Neither did I," I said, "so I guess they didn't need us after all. Hey, where's Ruby Mae?"

Grace spoke up. "Left her in the meadow. Told her to git herself flat as she could on the ground, and she might not get shot. She looked at me like … well, like I'd told her she might get shot. Funniest thing I ever saw."

"Are you sure she's all right?"

"Are you kidding, Pastorman? There's not a bullet in this world that could penetrate that ego of hers. By the way, she's back to making hats. I knew it was too good to be true. She keeps talkin' 'bout Yoo Hoo, though. Gonna be a star, she says. What's that all about?"

"Long story, Grace, but I'll tell you later. Maybe someone should go out to find her and bring her back to the cabin. And we have to call an … what's that noise?"

I looked up to see a helicopter coming over the trees and heading for a landing in the meadow. That got Ruby Mae's attention and she jumped up like a grasshopper, took two steps, fell on her face, and scrambled back up. She ran, with a limp, back to the cabin, while I tried to figure out if the helicopter was good news or just a big bunch of more bad guys. When I saw the lettering on the side of the chopper, I knew they were from the Virginia State Police.

I ran toward them and before I could get there, four troopers met me halfway. Mel jogged after me. I've never been so happy to see anyone in my life.

"Boy, are we glad to see you!" I was practically jumping up and down like a kid waiting for his ice cream cone to be scooped.

One man who appeared to be the highest-ranking, said, "We got word to pick up some wounded at this location. Sorry we couldn't get here any sooner, but that rain prevented us from taking off."

"No, no, don't apologize. We have four wounded here. All bad guys. No Knee over there has a bad leg injury, Shiny's in the cabin, along with Blondie—I think their egos and maybe their heads are hurt. Nothing serious. And River Boy over there with the bloody face is the one being dragged by those two women and Bristol."

"Odd names."

"Odd people," I said with a grin. "I have no idea what their real names are and didn't have a chance to ask them amidst the gunfire. All I know about them is they're from a cartel, and were sent here to ..."

One trooper held his hand out. "Whoa, we were notified on a need-to-know basis, so don't bother giving us the reason they're here. Our job is to make sure you and the others are okay and bring these yahoos in for medical attention and a long time in prison. You can handle the rest, Mr. ..."

"Oh, sorry. I'm Pastor Hugh Foster, and this is my wife, Melanie. The man over there laughing his head off is Bristol Diggs and the women are all on our side from Road's End."

"Never heard of it."

"Don't worry about it. Nobody has."

Medics had already put No Knee on a stretcher and were loading him into the chopper, while one trooper went over to Bristol, the jubilant women, and River Boy, and the second one met Shiny, looking bedraggled, and Blondie, looking like he'd been hit on the head one time too many. Martha and Winnie turned their charges over to the trooper, while Sadie ran around the meadow looking for her warriors-in-arms. A great celebration exploded upon the wet grass of that meadow, and it was a good twenty minutes before anyone could hear anyone above the din of questions, laughter, a little crying in gratefulness, and lots of prayers thanking God. I hugged Mel with a new appreciation of the blessing I'd been given when I met her.

With all their wounded on board, the officer gave us a two-finger salute, jumped into the chopper, and closed the doors. Five seconds later they were airborne. The chopper rose upward, then banked in a graceful U-turn and flew away.

We were alone once again. The clouds dissipated and clear blue skies took their place. Steam could be seen rising from the damp ground, and for a while there, it looked like we might be on the set of a Disney film. We all wandered around, greeting one another, sharing hugs and back-slaps, and in general, celebrating being alive.

I finally remembered Del, still in the root cellar. I ran over, pulled open the door, and let him out of his underground bunker.

"Is it safe now?"

"Sure is, Del. Come on out and meet the heroes who saved your life."

I held the cellar door as he climbed the homemade, but surprisingly sturdy ladder, and out into the world. He squinted against the sunlight—I imagine being underground all that time had made his eyes sensitive to the light.

Soon, though, he was surrounded by his heroes and well-wishers, all clamoring for a chance to congratulate him on not being dead. He looked astounded. The look on his face said it all. I don't believe anyone has ever responded to Del the way my friends and neighbors in Road's End did that day. There was confusion, there was delight (never thought I'd see *that* expression on Del), there was relief. I couldn't tell if he was ecstatic to be out of the root cellar or relieved to be out of danger and in the company of people who were treating him kindly and including him in the celebration. It was probably a combination of every good and thankful expression he could muster.

"Hey, folks," I said when there was a lull in the chatter. "I hate to break up our celebration, but I think we should clean up the mess we've made and get back to Road's End."

"Mess? What mess?" That was Martha Washington. "Heck, Pastor, we cleaned that up before we even brought those two hooligans out of the cabin. Everything's clean as a whistle."

"Speaking of whistles," I said, "I don't think this would have turned out so well if it weren't for Hazel's whistling abilities. Way to go, Hazel!" Everyone cheered and Hazel blushed. "And believe me, every single one of you did a superb job today. I had *no* idea the ladies of Road's End were such fighters, so willing to do what had to be done even when the result would probably be getting shot—or worse. I think when we're all together again, we should have one huge celebration in the streets of Road's End. Maybe a huge barbeque with lots of food that you ladies prepare so well. Does anyone make a mean grilled hamburger or hot dogs or maybe ribs?"

I glanced around at everyone else glancing around. Yep, things were getting back to normal. Just as I was about to tell them we'd figure out the details later, Del stepped forward. I almost passed out. "I used to grill all the time when I was younger. Loved it. I use charcoal, though. Nothing cooks food better than charcoal."

"Well, there we go! Del, you have yourself a job. You're the chief barbeque king of Road's End! Listen, folks, I don't know about you, but talking about food is making me hungry."

Mel chimed in. "I think we'd better let the men get on the road and head for the nearest fast food joint. Right, Hugh?"

"You read my mind, Mel. Aren't you ladies coming back home with us?"

Emma spoke up. "I don't know about the other ladies, but I think I need some rest and relaxation before packing up to leave. I say we stay as long as we planned to stay originally."

"Me too," Sadie yelped. "Chasing and clobbering and shootin' bad guys is good fun and all, but I was kinda looking forward to kickin' back and enjoyin' nature. Livin' in the big city is great, but bein' here in the middle of nowhere is soothin'."

Big city? Maybe someone clobbered her on the head. She seemed to be mixing up Road's End with, oh say… Atlanta.

"Well, ladies, I think we're staying a few more days if everyone else agrees." Mel looked at me. "Is that okay with you, Warrior Man?"

Warrior Man? Well, it's better than Smarty Pants. "It's fine by me, ladies. But I'm surprised, to be honest. Are you sure being out here isn't going to spook you after we leave? After all, this was an unusual and extremely stressful day."

The ladies looked at one another. Finally, Grace spoke up and said, "You know, Pastorman, I think we need this time to be together, exchange stories, and thank the Good Lord we came out of this mess unscathed. Maybe decompress a bit. We might be jumpy, but we can handle that. And we still have the weapons and ammo we brought with us. We'll be fine."

"Do you all agree?" They nodded, one by one. "Okay, then, but please keep in mind that you can call us—be careful on the roof, though." I was staring at Mel. She smiled. "And you can call us day or night or when we're two hours down the road. We'll turn around and be back in a flash." I looked at Mel. "Hey, is that where you were when you jumped Shiny?"

"Where'd you think I came from? Dropped from a drone? Yep, that's where I was. Good thing I listened to the Lord and adapted to the situation, don't you think?"

"Oh boy, do I ever! You and God make a great team, honey."

"Make that everyone here and God make a great team. I felt His Hand upon us all through it."

I snapped my fingers. "Hey, that reminds me. Hazel, you were going to tell me about your visitation!"

"Yep, I was," she said with a grin, "but that can wait for a while. I'm still digesting everything he told me. I can tell you this, though. He said, "Today, the Lord will send a deluge of His blessings upon you. He will cause your enemies to stumble."

I gasped. "Whoa, that's uncanny. If I'm hearing him correctly, that angel was saying God sent that colossal rainstorm to help us out? It was a deluge, all right. And yes, our enemies surely stumbled! Our Father amazes me more and more every day."

"Yes," Mel said, "and what better protection could we have up here than an angel of the Lord?"

Bristol walked up, grinning, and said, "We should get going. The men are likely to have torn down Sadie's place looking for sustenance. I'm sure they're approaching death by starvation by now."

"I'm with you, buddy. I could use some of Sadie's stuff myself right about now. Let's get going."

Five minutes later, we were saying our goodbyes and walking down the path to the car. Del looked relieved to be leaving, but I'm not sure if it was because he was leaving the women behind or if he was just tickled to be alive. Maybe both.

As we drove down that old firebreak road, we ran across both vehicles the cartel guys had used.

"Should we notify someone these are here?"

Bristol said. "Naw, let's just let the cartel wonder what's going on. We can report them to the police later. Right now, I need a greasy cheeseburger, some fries, and a whole lot of something to drink."

That Bristol is a good man.

Two hours later, we were back in Road's End. I parked the car and we all gathered up our fast-food debris and tossed it away. The men came streaming out of their houses like characters in a Stephen King book. We'd been gone eight hours and I swear they'd lost weight. Had we won one battle just to wander into a zombie zone?

"Hey, guys," I said, waving. "We'll be back in just a minute. What do you say we gather at Sadie's for coffee and cookies?" Stupid question. I could almost see them drooling.

After visits to the bathroom, quick showers, and changing into clean clothes, we walked over to Sadie's. They were all there, hanging around the door like a bunch of high schoolers waiting for the window to open so they could buy tickets to some concert. Do they still do that? Probably not.

I unlocked the door and turned on the lights. I went to the kitchen to start the coffee, while Bristol insisted the men sit down and wait. Together, we were able to keep the mob from swarming us. We called out that the coffee was ready, and the stampede that followed rivaled Pamplona's racing of the bulls. Coffee in hand, they wandered back to their tables and watched me put a box of doughnuts on three plates and some cookies on another two. I lined them up on the short countertop Sadie has and stepped out of the way. I've seen piranhas stalk and eat their prey slower than these guys demolished those baked goods. Good thing I saved out a bunch for Bristol and me. Del wasn't here, so I took some for him, too. In less than five minutes, every bit of the baked goods was gone, and the coffee pot was empty.

I was tempted to ask the men, bloated and caffeinated by now, for some help in cleaning the kitchen, but decided I'd be better off leaving a classroom of kindergartners alone with six open gallons of brightly-colored paint. Instead, I sent them home and told them we'd see them in the morning.

"What's the scoop, Pastor?"

"Did ya git those guys?"

"What'dja have to eat?"

"We'll let you in on everything tomorrow, but right now, we're tired and need some rest. Your ladies are all safe, though." I noticed nobody asked about them and so I thought I'd shame them into it. Nope. They wanted to know what we ate.

Another ten minutes passed before we had them all shoved out the door and had the place to ourselves. Del walked in right after the guys left. "Did I miss the party?"

"Believe me, Del, you didn't miss anything except seeing some men eat like one-year-olds in a vat of spaghetti sauce spilled across the floor."

"I believe Hugh is downplaying things, Del, but we saved you some doughnuts and a cookie or two. Coffee's gone, but we can get some at the inn. Ready to go, Hugh?"

"Boy, am I ever. You coming with us to the inn, Bristol?"

"Thanks, but I'm going to hit the hay. I still haven't finished that roof repair project."

"What day is this?" That was me, the befuddled pastor in the room.

"Why?"

"I'm just wondering if I have to give a sermon tomorrow. It's Wednesday, though, isn't it?"

"Yep. You've got a few days. Go home, get some sleep, and I'll see you two in the morning. Del, how are you at fixing roofs?"

"Don't know," he said. "Never done it. Need some help?"

"Yeah, if you don't mind. Our ladder was constructed about the same time the church was built, so it's pretty darned rickety. I just need someone to steady it when I'm on my way up or down."

"No problem."

I gave Bristol a hurt look and said, "I thought I was your ladder-holder."

Bristol laughed out loud. "Hugh, you nearly faint when you get within ten feet of that ladder. Sorry, man, but you've been laid off from your ladder-holder job."

"Fine. I'll go elsewhere to find a job."

"Hugh, you've *got* a job. Several, in fact. You're the pastor and chief financial officer of the Christ Is Lord Church, an innkeeper, mediator, mighty warrior, coffee guy, key holder, and kitchen cleaner."

"What about the baked goods?"

Bristol shook his head. "Sorry, that's my job."

I slapped him on the back. "Go get some sleep."

Just as I was about to walk with Del to the Inn, that chatterbox Leo walked up to us.

"Hey, Leo, what's up?"

He blew out a smoke ring, messed with his pipe a little, put it back in his mouth and began to chatter. "Detectives." He turned and walked toward Frank's place, where I assume he was staying at the moment since his farm was out of town and Heaven forbid any of these men should be separated from one another with the wives out of town.

I looked at Del. "What on earth did he mean by that? We don't have detect … oh, wait a minute. Oh, no! Was he talking about George and Dewey?" I hung my head and tried not to cry. "I can't handle anything else tonight. I just can't. The detectives are on their own 'til morning."

He nodded and we continued our short walk to the Inn.

I slept uneasily, dreaming of guns and gunshots, men pouring out of the forest, running, but not making progress, and being very, very wet. The last thing I wanted was to relive the horrors of the day. I woke up at least five times, thrashing and calling for Mel. The last time, she touched me on the shoulder and said, "I'm right here, hon." I grabbed her hand and opened my eyes.

"Hey, sweetie, what are you doing out of bed?" I sat up abruptly and almost slammed my head into her chin. "Wait! What are you doing here? Are you okay?"

She sat next to me on the bed. "We're fine, just fine. But Hazel remembered the angel telling her one more thing, and since we couldn't get a signal, wouldn't you know, we confiscated the bad guys' cars and drove home."

"You stole their cars?"

"Would you rather we walked instead of stealing the cartel's property?"

I rubbed my eyes. "No, no, honey. It's just that I heard Grace talking to one of them outside the cabin about GPS systems. She was trying to convince him their GPS signal was wrong and there was no one around but the ladies. I remember thinking they must have some sort of tracking system on Del to have found him in such a remote spot. Then all heck broke loose and I forgot all about it until now. I've got to call Bristol." I stood up, then leaned down and gave her a kiss. "It's great to have you home, honey. I'll get dressed and call Bristol. I have a bad feeling about this. I'm so sorry I forgot about that. At the very least, we could've looked for a device on Del or his clothing."

"But, hon, they're all in custody now. They can't hurt us any longer."

"Then why did two extra men show up? What if the second set was checking up on one and two? If that's the case, what's to say they haven't sent a third pair of assassins to check up on three and four?"

I stopped in my tracks and pulled my sweatshirt over my head, thinking.

What if Del still has that tracking device on him? And even if he doesn't, if either of those two cars has one on it, we've brought them straight to our doorstep.

"Honey, I need you to make some phone calls for me."

Chapter Twenty-Four

Twenty minutes later, Bristol, Mel, Del, Hazel and Perry Parry, and Grace sat around our kitchen table. Mel had a fresh pot of coffee on, but alas, there were no doughnuts or cookies. I casually mentioned I had a key to Sadie's, but Mel aimed a glare at me, and I dropped the idea. Besides, Sadie was home, and would've knocked me senseless.

"Thanks, everyone, for coming over here in the middle of the night, but I think we might have trouble on our hands—again. I told Mel when she woke me up a little while ago that I'd forgotten what I overheard when Grace was talking to one of them. It was about a GPS system, right, Grace?"

Grace nodded. "Sure was. He kept tellin' me the GPS told 'em the man they were lookin' for was at the cabin. Didn't seem to care that it was in the middle of nowhere. Fool. He was sure Del had to be there. 'Course he was, but *he* didn't need to know that. I had no way to convince him otherwise, so I told him some story I pretended I'd heard about a faulty GPS system leadin' a man to the east coast instead of the west coast. Musta been some sorta dummy to not notice he wasn't headin' in the right direction. How many road signs does it take some people to convince 'em they're headin' toward Philadelphia instead of San Francisco? Well, I made it up, anyway, so no sense beatin' up some poor guy I conjured up on my own. But bad guy—Blondie, I think, 'cause he had blond hair—was positive their boss wouldn't give 'em a system with a faulty satellite. He seemed to think his boss was the Lord Himself. Crazy idiot."

"Okay, so we know they used some kind of tracking device on Del." I turned to Del. "Do you remember them inserting some kind of chip or ... I don't know anything about this stuff. I'll just make a fool of myself."

Grace laughed out loud. "Wouldn't be the first time, Smarty Pants."

Back to Smarty Pants, are we?

Del saved me. "No, I don't. Unless they knocked me out to do it, they didn't do it at all."

"Had to be in his clothes, Hugh."

"Bristol, are you saying we've led them back here?" I shook my head. What a mess.

"Not necessarily. If they're not looking for him anymore, no harm done."

"But I got to thinking a while ago when Mel surprised me that they sent River Boy and No Knee right behind Shiny and Blondie. How'd they know how to get to the cabin if the first two guys didn't have a tracking device on their car?"

"Good point."

"And if they sent #3 and #4 to check up on #1 and #2, it's not that much of a stretch to think they might have sent #5 and #6 to check up on the second pair, especially because they dropped out of sight. I'm getting confused here. Does anyone follow me?" I looked around the table. Mel gave me a thumbs-up, and Bristol seemed to be thinking. The rest of them were drinking coffee and ignoring me.

"I do, Hugh," Bristol said. "Let's assume they put a tracking device in Del's clothing somewhere. That alone would bring them straight to Road's End—and would have if we hadn't taken him to the cabin. So, we accidentally brought them to the cabin by taking Del up there for safekeeping—and did it again coming back here because we thought the danger was behind us." He shook his head. "This just gets worse and worse. Okay, there's that, but there's also the possibility that the first car was being tracked by the second pair of no-gooders. They found themselves up there along with all the rest of us. I think we have to assume that the kingpin is sending another pair of his henchmen to find out where the others disappeared to. By driving back to Road's End in the two cars the bad guys left, #5 and #6 might be heading here at this very moment."

"Right. But if that's the case, we led them here *first* by bringing Del back with us. Oh, my gosh, what a mess."

"That's assuming a lot, though, isn't it, Hugh?" Melanie looked into my eyes, and I could see the pleading. She wanted this to be over with, she wanted to get back to normal in Road's End, she wanted to cry.

"It is, hon, but I don't think we have any other choice but to prepare for another battle, this time in Road's End. But before we go off the deep end, let's hear from Hazel." I turned to her, and said, "When Mel woke me up a little while ago, she mentioned that you'd remembered more of what the angel told you, Hazel. Can you tell us about that? The whole episode, if you don't mind. As long as I've been a pastor, I've never had an angel appear before me, let alone talk to me."

Hazel looked at Perry, then smiled at the rest of us around the table. "I'd be happy to, Pastor, but I should tell you something I've never admitted to anyone but my husband."

She had me interested; I can tell you that.

"Yes? Go ahead, Hazel. You're among friends."

"Oh, I know that, Pastor, but this is something that's going to surprise you all." She drummed her fingers on the tabletop, then said, "I've been seeing angels now for many years. They don't always talk to me, but when they do, it's always something important."

"I can understand that, Hazel. But why would you keep that a secret? I'd be shouting it from the rooftops!"

"Yes, well, a lot of people don't believe in angels, or God, for that matter, and it always turns into a therapy session with them trying to get me to admit I made it all up. It's just easier not to mention it. But enough of that. I sometimes see the same angel, but occasionally, a different one will appear. This one was one I'd never seen before."

"And you remember more of what he told you?" I tried not to be impatient, but I was anxious not only to hear her story, but to address the cold fingers of imminent danger messing with the back of my neck.

"Oh yes, Pastor. It's hard not to remember when a messenger of the Lord comes to visit. Sometimes it just takes me some time to process it all. After I told you what he said about blessings from the Lord and our enemies stumbling, I gave it more thought and it was just about three, no, more like four hours ago that it hit me. He also said, 'While this battle will not be finished here in the meadow, the Lord will be your stronghold in your times of trouble, and not abandon you. Out of the brightness of His presence bolts of lightning blaze forth.'

"That made me wonder if there would be trouble here in Road's End tonight. We would've called you if we could get a signal, but sadly, even standing on the roof, Mel couldn't get the phone to work. It was then that we decided we had to use the two cars left there by those bad men and drive to Road's End to let you all know."

If my wife is brave enough to stand on a roof, why aren't I?

I rubbed the back of my neck and glanced at Bristol. "What do you think?"

"With this new info from Hazel, I don't think we have a choice. Hazel remembered more of what the angel told her about three, maybe four hours ago. And depending on where they were, if they're coming at all, they've had a good head start on us. I think we need to prepare for another battle."

I was afraid he'd say that.

Chapter Twenty-Five

Being a pastor, I'd certainly heard of angelic visitations, and I have to admit, as I've told the Lord many times in prayer, I am envious of those who have experienced one. I always ask for forgiveness for my envy, and of course, He grants it. I haven't heard of any visitations for quite a while, and Hazel's story awoke in me that need to experience a holy visitation for myself.

But I had no time to think about that now. We had a battle to plan, and we had no idea how long we had to do it. At least what the angel told Hazel was encouraging. We'd definitely need the Lord and an army of His angels if we were going to outwit another batch of bad guys. *Please, Lord, be with us as we fight these men, put a hedge of protection around each one of us, and an army of angels surrounding us to keep evil from inflicting hurt or pain or death on any of us. In Jesus' Name, I pray. Amen.*

As much as we dreaded bringing our Daring Detective Duo into our plan, we had no choice. They were residents of Road's End, after all, and had every right to decide whether to fight or hunker down until it was all over—and I wouldn't blame any of them for doing just that. If I had my druthers, I'd be in my bed with Mel and the covers pulled over our heads.

But that wasn't possible, so we called an emergency meeting at the Inn for 6:00 AM. Grace left our place and told Ruby Mae. Within five minutes, everyone in town knew about the meeting. Apparently, she also dropped a comment that she had sustained a battle injury while at the cabin and would need special accommodations for her grievous impairment. Grace sputtered and complained that the only thing wrong with her mother was a mild sprain of her ankle, and a huge case of "Look at me; I'm special."

Still, Ruby Mae wasn't the kind to take an ankle sprain in stride. She would no doubt try to take center stage at the meeting. I prayed I'd have the patience required not to lock her in the coat closet until the meeting was over.

On the bright side, Sadie, thank goodness, was willing to bring baked goods even at that horrible time of day, and Mel readied our largest coffee maker. We were as ready as we were ever going to be—for the meeting, that is. The jury was still out on our readiness for what we feared was looming before us even as we drank coffee and ate doughnuts.

"Okay, folks, sorry to interrupt our refreshment time, but time is of the essence right now. You've all been brought up to date by either Bristol, Grace, Mel, or me, so let's get to work."

"Who's comin'?" That was George, just asking for an argument.

Dewey obliged him. "Who'd ya think is comin'? Santa Claus? The bad guys! The bad guys are comin', you old fool."

I didn't have time for this. "Guys, if you're going to argue, maybe you should step outside so the rest of us have a chance to work out a plan."

"What? We can't do that. You need us. We're Road's End's premiere Private Investigators/Vestigators."

"George, we know you and Dewey have formed a detective agency, and as much as we'd love to talk about it here, we need to decide how to fight off the men coming toward us. Are you with us?" I can't recall ever being that direct with George and Dewey, but I'd had a bad day and a very sleep-deprived night. In short, I wasn't in a very good mood.

"You bet we're with ya, Hugh!"

"Couldn't keep us away!"

"Great! Now I'm going to open the floor to anyone who has some ideas on how to protect Road's End and its residents—namely us."

Bristol stood before anyone else had a chance to, thank goodness.

"Hugh, I think we should divide up into teams, then place teams around town in specific places. It will be the responsibility of each team, if possible, to keep the bad guys from harming the home or business assigned to them—or any of us, for that matter. Of course, our main purpose is to keep them from getting to Del."

"Yes, you're right, Bristol. Del ... where's Del?"

"Behind you, Hugh." I turned to see a very nervous Delbert T. Jackson.

"I hate to tell you this, but the only way we can protect you is to put you in the tunnel for the duration of the fight. I know you hate small spaces, and I do too, but you'll have to put that aside for a little while. Deal?"

"I told ya before, Pastor—I meant it then and I mean it now. I will *not* go into that tunnel by myself. If I hafta climb a tree and hide up there, I will, but not the tunnel."

I was afraid of that. "You said you wouldn't go down there alone. If someone went with you, would you do it? Remember, this might very well, no, probably *will* save your life."

"How many others?"

I looked over at Grace and smiled. Because that woman can tell me what I'll want for breakfast three weeks from Thursday, I knew she knew my intent and was on board with my idea. She gave a slight nod. Okay then. "At least one. Maybe two. And you'll have light, of course, and all the doughnuts and cookies we can get for you to munch on down there."

Del glared at me, and I felt that familiar feeling of flames licking my face. I'd nearly forgotten how cantankerous he could be; for a while there, he acted like a regular human being. I didn't flinch, though, and stood my ground—well, my eyes' ground, at least, and after around twenty minutes, although it might have been more like five seconds, he relented. "You know I'm going to hate it, don't you?"

"Yes, I do, and I know exactly how you feel. I'm claustrophobic, too, and I wouldn't want to go down there either. But it's the only way, and I'm so happy you'll do it. Way to go, man."

We each had a coffee refill and a second infusion of sugar, while we fine-tuned a situation we had no idea was even going to occur, let alone succeed at it. But we had no choice. If they came after Del, and reason told us they would, we had to be prepared to do whatever it took to make sure those thugs didn't find Del, as well as keep them from hurting any of us along the way. I kept this to myself, but I had a feeling neither of these two men, and maybe more, coming into town gave a hoot about our welfare. I felt those cold fingers of danger crawling up my spine and into my hairline, and it was all I could do to keep from shuddering. But I knew those cold fingers were coming from the devil and his twisted, ugly, and evil minions. I wouldn't give them the satisfaction of being fearful.

Besides, we had the Lord and His angels on our side. What did we have to fear?

Turns out (me being King Worrier and all) we had lots to fear, but none of it included the bad guys, the devil, or his minions.

I didn't think about it at the time, but George and Dewey were unusually quiet during the meeting. Sadly, it wasn't because their mouths were full of baked goods, although they were, but for reasons that wouldn't occur to the majority of sane people—which left out most of the residents of Road's End. I wish I'd figured it out earlier.

Before adjourning the meeting, we decided who would guard what home or business. Hazel and Perry Parry, along with Leo, chose to man the church. I would check in periodically by phone or in person to be sure they were kept safe. I just hoped Leo wouldn't talk them into a coma. Sadie chose to guard the Bake House, a plan I heartily endorsed, although I'd have felt better if she had a man with her. But then I remembered who I was thinking about and realized I had no reason to worry. Martha decided to join Winnie in defending the Wyandotte's home, since Martha and George's place was out-of-town, and in no danger. Their husbands would be, as usual, nowhere to be found, but they were accustomed to them being out of the house most days, anyway. Mel and I would guard the inn until I was called away, which I knew I would be, sooner or later. Emma would be joined by Joe Rich at Rivermanse, and Rudy Wallenberg would cruise the downtown area, all four stores, to forestall any damage. Grace was in charge of getting Ruby Mae to the inn, and Bristol would float. Frank, of course, was in charge of sleeping.

Bristol and I spent the next hour drawing up plans to thwart the enemy, but with no idea of how many of them were coming, or *if* they were coming, in truth it was just a way to make us feel good. At least dawn was breaking, and we wouldn't have to face them in the dark.

Mel came down from cleaning up Del's room so they wouldn't know anyone had been sleeping there. "More coffee, gentlemen? I think I could use a cup or two myself."

"Thanks, hon. I know I do. Bristol?" He nodded and she turned her attention to brewing it.

"I'm wondering if we need a guard outside of town to let us know when they arrive and just how many of them there are."

"Good idea, Bristol."

Mel deposited two mugs of coffee in front of us, and sat down with her own. I took a sip. "I can go down a few miles, hide my car, and …"

Bristol held up his hand. "No, Hugh. We need you here. Tell you what. I'll go down a couple of miles from town and report back to you what I find. Then I'll hoof it back here and join up with you or wherever else you think needs some reinforcement."

"Sounds great, Bristol, but are you sure? I'll be happy to go."

"I'm sure. It makes no sense to leave Mel here to argue with those yahoos by herself. When are you putting Del in the tunnel?"

"As soon as Ruby Mae arrives."

"Why?"

"Because Ruby Mae, who has the grievous wound from our earlier battle, won't be of any help to us topside, so we'll put her in the tunnel to babysit Del. It's Grace's job to persuade her to do it, but she planned to appeal to Ruby Mae's vanity—wouldn't want the bad guys to get a peek at the beautiful project of God's, would we?" I took a sip of coffee. "He'll hate us for it, but it's the best place for both of them— and it relieves us of some worry, too. I'm thinking we should put Frank down there with them, as well. He won't be a great conversationalist, but I'd rather he slept in the tunnel and was safe, than at the garage and maybe get hurt."

"Wow! You've got that planned to perfection! Does Frank know?"

"Last I knew, he was still sleeping. I'll wake him just before it's time to go underground. He won't remember any of it, anyway."

"I've got a picnic basket packed with food and drinks for them," Mel said. "Oh, and one of your powerful flashlights, too. I don't blame them for wanting to be able to see. I know I sure would."

"Where's Del?" I looked around as though I'd find him under the table.

Mel stood to get us refills and said, "Haven't seen him lately. I just came from his room, and he wasn't upstairs, so maybe he's in the living room."

"Think he ran away?"

"Naw, I think what's gonna be outside is scarier than what's inside the tunnel."

"Probably right. Well, I'm going to go take a look around. I'm not quite sure when to take off down the road. I'll make sure anyone with a gun has ammo to protect themselves, at least, and see if I can locate our local detectives."

I groaned. "Oh, criminy, I keep forgetting about those two. You don't think they're going to do something stupid, do you?"

Both Mel and Bristol looked at me as if I'd said, "I'm just curious. Do you think the sun is hot?"

I grinned. "Right. Sorry about that. Lost my mind for a moment there."

We waited the whole day, and no one arrived. Poor Bristol spent a good eight hours a couple of miles outside of town in his car, and finally came back to grab a bite to eat with us.

"Well, there goes our daylight advantage," I said, as I dug into a bowl of chili and a huge slab of cornbread. I like to make Mel feel appreciated, so I try to eat a lot of whatever she serves. Thoughtful of me, isn't it? Pretty soon, my whole day will consist of nothing more than eating and running around the town in my jogging pants to burn the calories I just consumed. But I'll make that sacrifice if it means I get to eat her chili.

Bristol reached with his knife for butter to put on his cornbread. "That might be their plan. Actually, if I were them, I'd wait until dark too. It just makes more sense. Maybe we're wrong about this whole thing. Are we just acting with an abundance of caution?"

"I'd agree, Bristol, but that doesn't explain what the angel said. If the battle isn't over and we've mistakenly brought him back here while they're tracking him, then they're coming. No doubt about it. There will be a second battle. I feel it in my gut."

"Me too," Mel added. "I haven't seen an angel, but I have this overpowering sense that we still have to face our enemies—or rather, Del's enemies that we've inherited. By the way, have you two checked his clothes for that device?"

Bristol and I looked at one another. His eyes looked big enough to toss a basketball through. I'm sure mine looked the same. "Oh, my gosh, we forgot all about that. It won't necessarily stop them, but it might confuse them a little." I shook my head at my stupidity. How could I have forgotten about that? I jumped up and ran to the foot of the stairs. "Del! Are you up there?" Before my words reached up the stairway, he appeared. "Hey, Del, you're missing some good chili and cornbread down here."

"I wondered what smelled so good. I'm on my way now."

Ten seconds later, we were seated again. Mel gestured for him to help himself from the tureen in the center of the table, and passed the platter of cornbread. "Here, let me take that towel off for you, Del. It helps to keep the cornbread warm. Help yourself. There's plenty."

Del smiled. Yep, he sure did. I thought at first it might be a trick of the light or another as-yet-unseen variation of a sneer. But no, it was a smile. *Thank You, Lord.*

"I wonder if there's a way, assuming we even find a device, to attach it to something moving. Maybe we could redirect them—or maybe misdirect is the right word—them far, far away."

Del swallowed, then said, "No need. I found the darned thing in my belt. I dug it out and flushed it down the toilet. If we're lucky, it'll lead them to some sewer treatment plant."

Bristol almost cheered. "Del, that is genius, pure genius. Your belt, eh? Good choice, I guess. Most men don't change their belt every time they change their clothes, so the worst that could happen would be that they'd trace you to the last place you wore your belt."

"Well, it's gone now," Del said before taking another bite of chili, "but they're gettin' me a new belt if I have to take it out of someone's hide. You just don't mess with a man's belt."

He sounded so affronted, the rest of us couldn't help but laugh. He looked around and said, "What?" and then grinned. "I got the last laugh, though."

Mel stood to clear away the mugs. "Something's been bugging me. When this is all over with, who's to say the cartel won't hold it against us when they can't find him, even though their GPS led them here? I mean they're going to figure we somehow kept them from getting their hands on Del. Maybe they'll hold a grudge, and attack us some time in the future when we least expect it?"

"Good point," I said. I stood and hugged her. "Remember we've got one of the most valuable assets we could have in Mack. He'll make sure, somehow, that nothing happens to us. And if we can make them believe their GPS system was off, they won't give Road's End a second thought. Besides, hon, God sent an angel."

"If those cartel people have a collective brain the size of a gnat, they won't *ever* come back. Road's End seems to do that to people," Bristol said.

"I'm not so sure about that," I said. "Del wasn't coming back and here he is, the president is planning some kind of peace conference here and he's already been here once. If he still wants to come back after that tornado and an assassination attempt, I'd say the power to repel folks from here is rather weak."

"I never thought about it that way." Bristol stood up, his chair screeching across the brick floor. "Thanks for a wonderful meal, Melanie. I'm going to catch a quick nap before I go back out there. I have a feeling they'll be here some time tonight. Let me know if I'm wrong and they arrive in the next couple of hours."

"Good idea. I'll go out and watch for them so you can get some rest. When this is all over, we're going to sleep for a week."

"What about that barbeque you were planning?"

"Hm-m-m-m. Well, first the barbeque and then we'll sleep for a week."

"Who's going to clean up after the barbeque?" That was Mel, the stick in the mud.

Bristol and Del and I looked at one another and shrugged.

"Just as I thought," she said.

Chapter Twenty-Six

I spent two of the longest hours of my life sitting in my car behind a grove of trees and waited for the bad guys to arrive. I have no idea how Bristol did it for eight hours. I'd be bonkers by then. Just as I was turning the key to start the car, I noticed the sky in the west. Where the sun should be setting was an inky-black darkness approaching Road's End, and it wasn't the impending nighttime. It was a storm, and from the looks of it, it was going to be a doozy. In my preparations for a second battle, I'd forgotten to turn on the radio and listen to WEND, Road's End's own radio station. The forecast would have been wrong, no doubt, but I might have at least looked at the sky. It was apparent we were in for a storm. Why is it always storming when we least need it to be—every single time? Frankly, it was starting to annoy me.

Ten minutes later, I walked in the back door to find George and Dewey holding Del … well, hostage.

"Hi guys. What's going on here?"

"What's it look like, Hugh?" That was George, the one I wanted to pop in the nose.

Dewey piped up, "We're 'terrogatin' this suspect, Hugh. That's what 'vestigators do. We 'terrogate."

"That's *in*terrogating, Dewey. And it's *in*vestigators. We've been over this before."

"We sure have, George. And it's still 'terrogating, not interrogating."

"Guys! Guys! Cut it out, will you? I've had a horrible few hours and I'm not in the mood for your arguments. Now somebody tell me what you're doing at my kitchen table interrogating Del."

"That's 'terrog …"

I shook my finger at Dewey and fairly shouted, "Don't you dare!" He shut his mouth and turned away from me like a six-year-old who thought if he couldn't see someone, they couldn't see him either.

"Touchy, are we, Hugh? 'Fraid your guest will be found guilty? Huh? Is that it?"

"George, I don't want to argue with you. Just please tell me what's going on. I'm tired and hungry and sick to death of fighting off bad guys."

Silence. Had they fallen deaf? Come under a spell? Died? They'd *better* not be dead. Frankly, I don't have the time or energy or inclination to conduct two funerals at the moment.

Finally, Del broke the silence and said, "These men think I know who's after us. I told them all I know—which is *I don't know*. It could be an army, could be just one man, could be a fighter jet for all I know." (Great. Now I had something more to worry about. What were we supposed to do with a fighter jet—throw stones at it?) Del continued, "Could be one man and one woman, which I *really* don't want it to be." He threw up his hands and said, "I just don't *know!"*

I pulled out a chair and plunked down. I noticed the napkin holder was askew, which added even more trauma to my already tormented mind. I straightened it and glared my disapproval at George and Dewey for their part in my table's blatant disarray. I took a deep breath. A long one. "Okay, I'm sorry, guys. Let's start this conversation over, with just one caveat. I'm exhausted, ornery, and not in the mood for petty arguing. Deal?"

George reached over and patted my shoulder. "Now, now, Hugh. We know you had a rough time at the cabin. And we understand 'bout all the petty arguin'. In fact, I'm goin' up to Emma's place right now 'n' tell her to tell the women to stop with all the fussin' goin' on. It's not seemly, and it's drivin' you crazy. 'Course, you ain't never been quite right, anyway. Still, that's no reason for the womenfolk 'round here to add to your mental illness. You're unbalanced as 'tis."

I didn't know whether to laugh or cry. I opened my mouth to explain but swallowed my words because I knew it wouldn't make any difference. Besides, maybe he was right. Maybe I *am* unbalanced. I brushed that thought aside and said, "Thank you, George. I appreciate your concern." George nodded, and Dewey said, "How's just one caviar gonna help us?

I never did find out why they were interrogating Del or why they felt it was okay to invade my personal residence. I suggested that George and Dewey go back to Dewey's house to help the women protect the Wyandotte's house. "Guys, listen. They didn't show up today. That leads me to believe there's a good chance it'll happen tonight when it's dark. And it's getting ready to storm—again. Please be careful out there." They nodded their heads, but I knew they weren't listening to me. At the moment, I didn't give a rip. They were out of my house, and I couldn't control what those two old men did, anyway. I prayed the Lord would keep watch over them and the rest of His children and forgive me for losing patience with them.

I turned to Del. "Listen, Del, I appreciate you going in the tunnel and for putting up with George and Dewey."

"That's nice, but don't go getting used to it."

"Deal. By the way, have you seen Mel?"

"Not for an hour or so. I think she was going to check on the folks around here." He stood and carefully put his chair under the table. "Listen, Hugh, I know I'm the reason you're exhausted, and the town is gearin' up for another fight. I don't know how you put up with those two old men. I'da shot 'em years ago, but bein' a pastor, I guess that's not somethin' you could pull off. I guess I'm tryin' to say thanks."

"That means a lot to me. Really. And no, I can't shoot people— unless they're bad guys, of course—but that doesn't mean I haven't thought about it with George and Dewey. I think God brought Mel and me here to teach me patience."

"So, God's mad at you?"

I chuckled. "You mean Road's End would be a good punishment? As true as that may be, the answer to your question is no. He's not a vengeful God. Just the opposite. God is love."

"Yeah, I've heard that, but …"

"No, Del, I mean God IS love. He is *literally* love. There should be a picture of Him in the dictionary next to the word 'love', except we can't see the face of God." Del looked very confused and he could be thinking I'd lost my mind. He might've been right about that.

"Long story, Del, and one I'd love to tell you as soon as we know we're all going to survive."

"Okay." *Okay? As in maybe he'd actually listen to me?* Already my day was looking up.

But of course, that couldn't last.

When Mel didn't come home in the next five minutes, I went out looking for her. As I suspected, she'd gone to Rivermanse to check on Emma. I caught up with her and Emma chatting in the front yard, and as I approached them, I pointed to the stormy western skies. Already, a brisk wind performed an opening act—a wildly-choreographed dance of fallen leaves garbed in the gemstone colors of autumn—to announce the imminent arrival of the main attraction. I missed my peaceful fall weather. Maybe when this was all over, I'd be able to rake some more leaves and pretend we lived in a town full of sane, normal folks.

"Looks like we're in for a storm, ladies. But then when *isn't* Road's End in the middle of a natural disaster at the same time important or horrible things are happening? Must be some sort of meteorological phenomenon that defies logic."

Emma chuckled and patted my arm. "You've had a rough couple of days, haven't you, Hugh? But then when *don't* you have rough days living in this town? Perhaps the Lord is sending a storm to help us out like He did at the cabin!"

I sighed. "Maybe. He's big on water lately, isn't He?"

She grinned and nodded. "Sure seems to be, Hugh."

"But at least it's not like the first time He used water. No need for an ark. No rounding up two of every animal. All we have to do is convince a couple of thugs to leave town and never come back." That was Mel, my beautiful, calming wife who always looks on the bright side.

"Well, when you put it that way, I guess we're a lot better off than anyone on Earth who wasn't an immediate family member of Noah's. At least we have cars to get away if we have to get to higher ground." Something clicked just then, but I lost it before it could materialize completely in my brain. I hate it when that happens.

I put that thought on the back burner (which was getting mighty crowded), asked Emma if she needed anything, and she said Joe was already in the house making sure no windows were opened. Joe walked out onto the front porch at that moment and said, "Hey there, Pastor, Melanie. Emma, you're all checked out and things look good. No one's gettin' in here tonight 'less they use a batterin' ram." He grinned that charming smile of his and said, "Snug as a bug in a carpet."

I cringed. *It's rug, Joe. Rug! Not carpet. Doesn't make any sense to say carpet. It's supposed to rhyme.* Sadly, I could've gone on for years, but we had a battle to fight, thank goodness, or I'd be worrying about that 'rug vs. carpet' travesty the whole night.

After thanking Joe for helping Emma, I gave him a look that said, "Please look after her." He nodded slightly, and I forgave him for that carpet remark. I took Mel's hand and we walked, then jogged, then ran full-out as the clouds overhead dropped their load of water. I've often wondered what precipitates that first raindrop. (Pretty good pun, wouldn't you say?) Is there one droplet that tips the scales and out it all comes? Another time-consuming and fairly useless train of thought considering we had at least two thugs or one thug and a thugette on their way into town bent on killing Del and probably taking as many Road's Enders as they could along with him.

We dashed inside the back door of the Inn just as a clap of thunder rolled across the sky, followed by lightning bolts on the horizon. Just what we needed—lots of noise, water, and electricity. At this rate we wouldn't have to wait for the cartel characters to arrive; we could die right now by drowning or electrocution and save them the trip.

"Good grief, Hugh, where did that come from?"

"I would imagine it came from the sky, hon."

"Very funny, buddy. Just for that, you can get your own towel. Any more word on when and if we're having guests?"

"None. That reminds me, I'd better call Bristol. I hate to interrupt his nap, but it won't matter that he's well-rested if they shoot him in his sleep."

"Now that's a pleasant thought, Pastor." She snapped her wet towel at me and caught me across the back.

"Hey, that's not fair. I don't even have a towel!"

"Why do you need a towel? Are you saying you'd hit a woman? Your wife, no less?"

"Only in self-defense—like when I get snapped to death with a wet towel."

"Just how many deaths-by-wet-towel have you heard about?"

"Quit changing the subject, hon. Right now, I don't have time to give you all the examples. We'll talk about this some other time, okay? Say... oh, fall 2050?"

I walked out of the kitchen and heard the snap of a wet towel behind me. Close, but not deadly. I pulled out my phone—I hate this thing—and pushed on Bristol's face to call him. His phone rang. He must have his volume set on high because I was sure I could hear it ringing.

"Right behind you, Hugh."

"Hey, Bristol. You're awake. Good."

"Right behind you, Hugh."

I felt a tap on my shoulder, turned around and there he was, right behind me. "Why didn't you tell me you were here?"

"I did. Two times. You're a bit thick-headed today, aren't you, Hugh? You need a nap."

"I won't argue with you on that." I put my phone and Bristol's face in my back pocket and got down to business. "You know, I'm glad we have everyone safe, but I feel as though we're just taking a defensive stance. We should go on the offensive. Any ideas?"

"Actually, I do. I didn't do a lot of sleeping—it's hard to sleep when you know your town's going to be attacked any minute. We need an early warning system but sending someone down the road to warn us just doesn't make much sense. For one thing, it's putting someone in danger needlessly. There must be some other way."

And just like that, our problem was solved. George and Dewey walked in the back door, yelled "Hello" to Melanie, and marched themselves right into the living room.

"Hey, George. Hey, Dewey. How's it going?"

"Great."

"Not so good."

As always, I got a mash-up of their answers. "Grenotsogoot." And as always, I ignored it. They'd speak up sooner or later. This time it was sooner.

"We've got a problem, Hugh. Bristol, you can hear this too."

"Yes, I expect we do," I said, a bit more sarcastically than was necessary. "We have thugs from the cartel on their way. Do you have another problem I'm not aware of?"

I could almost see my sarcasm flying over the heads. This time they both said, "Nope." I heard "Nonope."

"Well, let's hear it, gentlemen. You're soaking wet. Let me get you a towel."

"On my way, Hugh." Mel walked into the room and handed a towel to each of them. "Would you men mind talking in the kitchen on the brick floor? This wood is taking a beating with all this water dripping on it.

"Oh, Mel, I'm sorry," I said. "I never gave that a thought. Come on, guys, let's get back to the kitchen."

"Yesep!" Guess who that was.

Ten seconds later we arrived. "George, Dewey, let's hear about your problem."

"Not really our problem," George said. "It's more like everyone's. 'Specially Del's."

"Okay," I said, "let me hear it."

"Right. Well, near as me and Dewey can tell, it's raining out there."

I nodded. "Yep. I'm following you so far. Go ahead."

"Well, it'll be dark soon."

"Go ahead."

"That's it. It's raining and getting dark. Pretty soon, we won't be able to see anything."

You guys should consider opening a detective agency.

"You're right, guys. Thanks for the info."

"Don't be in such a hurry, Hugh. There's more."

"I'm sorry, George. I didn't realize that. I thought you said … never mind. What is it?"

"The bad guys are at the village limits."

"Village limits? How do you know that?"

"Our early warnin' system. We set it up while you guys was sleepin' and gabbin'. Seemed the least we could do seein' as you two and the women got beat all to pieces up at the cabin."

"Well, it was mostly the bad guys who got beat up, Dewey, but thanks for the thought. We don't have any time to mess around. What's your system?"

"It's complicated, Hugh. We call it our Early Warnin' System or KEN."

"Why KEN?"

George sighed, as if he'd had it with me. "KEN stands for early warnin' system, Hugh. For obvious reasons, EWS didn't make any sense, so we say KEN instead so folks'll understand what we're sayin'."

I hate to break this to you right now, George, but folks never know what you're saying. KEN will be of no help.

"Nifty, huh? It's a top-secret method we investigators 'round the world use when we're doing detective work."

"Okay, that's good, but what is it and how can you be sure they're that close to us right now?"

"'Cause KEN went off." Dewey looked at George and twirled his index finger next to his head in a not very subtle way of telling him I was crazy.

I decided to mess with that later, and said, "Okay. This is it, guys. I'm takin' Del downstairs right now." I hollered for Mel, "Hey, hon, where are Grace and Ruby Mae?"

"Just walked in the door."

She ushered the ladies inside and said, "You take Ruby Mae and I'll go to get Del. I overheard you talking. Please be careful, everyone."

But Del surprised us by coming downstairs on the fly. I guess knowing someone was in town looking to kill you does that to a person.

"Del, my man, let's get going." I grabbed him by the arm and signaled to Bristol to do something with George and Dewey—tie them up, knock them out, whatever he had to do to get them out of the way. We dashed into the kitchen; the pantry door was already open, and I could hear Ruby Mae talking. "Honestly, this is no place for a lady of my stature. Grace, what got into you to put me down here? After all, I'm a wounded veteran."

"Shut up, Mama. I'm tryin' to save yer life. Now git down there and we'll talk later." She looked up. "Del, you're next. Hurry up! Is Frank in there already?"

I nodded. "Yep. Leo brought him over about a half hour ago." I peeked into the cramped area at the bottom of the primitive ladder to the basement that led them to the tunnel. "I'm sure he's fast asleep." I turned to Del. "Listen, Del, I know you don't want to go down there. I don't blame you, but you'll be safe, and we'll come to get you as soon as we can."

Del looked horrified, but I'm not sure if it was the men coming to kill him that terrified him or the fact that he was going to spend a sizable chunk of time locked in a tunnel with Ruby Mae. Personally, I think it was the second, but that's not very nice of me.

I relieved Grace of holding the heavy door that covered the route to the basement while she scampered down and pulled open the second door in a room off the main part of the basement. I held it open for Del and motioned him to move in front of me and turn to reach that first rung on the ladder.

"Del, listen to me. There's another door that Grace is holding open right now in another small room. You can't miss it. Get down into the tunnel as quickly as you can. Don't worry. There's lots of light, food, and well, people down there. Frank will no doubt be sleeping, but Ruby Mae will keep you company."

He gave me one of his face-melting glares, then turned slowly so he could go down the ladder. I waited until he was in the tunnel and Grace was back in the pantry with me before I lowered the door and placed the rug over it. I ran my hand over my face to make sure it hadn't melted into my neck.

I followed Grace from the pantry to the kitchen. She turned to me, and said, "Boy, oh boy, is she ever gonna be in a mood when this is all over."

"Well, you know, Grace, she *is* a wounded veteran." (My apologies to all *true* wounded veterans.)

"Oh yeah, right. I've gotten worse sprains sleeping in my bed. She's not wounded, but she sure thinks she is. I can't change her mind, so I'm putting her in time-out."

"Ha! Does she know it's a time out?"

"Are you kiddin' me, Pastorman? Fact is, I'm thinkin' that if the bad guys won't give up, we might threaten to bring her upstairs and let her jabber at them until they run, sobbin' their heads off, straight out of Road's End."

I couldn't help smiling. "I shouldn't be talking about your mother like this, Grace. I'm a pastor and I know better, but this stress is really getting to me."

"It's been a couple of rough days, I'll grant you that—even by Road's End standards." She turned to leave and said, "Be careful, Pastorman. I don't feel like breakin' in a new pastor just yet." That was practically a proposal of marriage from Grace. Usually she'd have turned on her heel, called me bald, and hidden the half-and-half for a week.

"I don't want you to either, Grace. Well, I guess I'd better get out there and figure out what George and Dewey were trying to tell me. They said their early warning system had gone off. I have no idea what they're talking about."

Grace stopped in her tracks, turned to me, and said, "I wonder if it was the bell I heard ringin' while I was draggin' Ruby Mae over here."

"What bell?"

"You don't know 'bout the bell? Geesh, where have you been?"

"On Air Force bases around the world for the most part. What's so special about this bell?"

"Back in the day, round 'bout the Revolutionary War days, the town put up a bell just outside the village limits. Ain't you never seen that?" When she's stressed, Grace reverts to her southern roots.

I shook my head. "Nope."

"Well, it's probably a bit hard to see now since the bushes are overgrown. Anyway, they used it to alert the townspeople of British soldiers, Indian attacks, fire, stuff like that. We don't use it at all nowadays since we've got Ruby Mae to tell the world our business. But I bet George and Dewey remembered it was there and they're probably using it somehow to warn us." She shook her head. "Can't believe those two are smart enough to do that."

I had to agree with her but hated to put it into words since I'd been so cranky lately; it was time to turn over a new leaf and become the pastor I was just two days ago. *Lord, forgive me for my flippant attitude, and my disregard of the love You feel for all Your children. Please keep my loved ones and friends safe from the evil that would hurt us if it can. Please, God, help me be more patient and loving. In Jesus' Name, I pray. Amen.*

I felt better, although I knew I'd be facing more stressful situations before the night was over, and I hoped I'd behave better than I had lately.

"Well, maybe we've all just misjudged them, Grace. Happens all the time."

"Yep. Well, I'd better get back to the house. Boy, would I love to put a big sign on the front porch that says, 'Free hats! Take all you want,' but Ruby Mae would have a stroke and I'd feel bad."

"I'm sure you would, Grace. After all, Ruby Mae's your mother."

"What? Oh, … well, you're right—that too—but I was talkin' 'bout feelin' bad 'bout not bein' able to put that sign on the porch."

Okay then. Looks like there are two of us who need our attitudes adjusted and brought back in line with the will of our Father. As much as I would've loved to stay put and continue in prayer with God, I knew we had a battle on our hands, and I'd better get to it.

I walked out the back door and guess who I ran into? Yep, Dick Tracy and Joe Friday. Standing in the rain. Just like me.

"I'm tellin' you, George, this is the best spot for it."

"I'm not so sure. Look at all this yard. Not even any trees 'round this part. How do we know they'll even come over here?"

"George, it's the back door! Do you think they're gonna come to the front door?"

"Yeah, Dewey, I do. If they're half as smart as a dead canary, they'll be all nicey-nice'n come to the front door just like any other guest would do. They ain't gonna trot around the yard and come to the back door. Now, if they show up guns a'blazin', then you're right."

Dewey was dumbstruck. He looked at me, then back at George. Back to me. "Didja hear that, Hugh?"

"Yes, Dewey, I did. And I agree with George. You're right. But I am a little concerned we haven't seen or heard from them and it's been at least thirty minutes since you said your early war …"

"KEN, Hugh. It's KEN."

"That's right, George. Thank you. Where are they? Shouldn't they be comin' in, guns a'blazin', as Dewey said, or at least pretending to be nice guys? I haven't heard from anyone that they've seen them."

"Well, that's because they've got four flat tires 'bout now." George's chest stuck out so far, I was afraid he'd break every last rib.

"How?" That was me, the very wet pastor with all the questions and none of the answers.

"'Cause we planned it that way. At first, we tried to rig up a rope connected to the bell that would ring when they were about two miles outta town. Didn't work, so we rigged up this deal. We got warned by the bell, they got flat tires, can't get outta town, and they'll be at our mercy."

"Wow, guys. You've really been working on this, haven't you?"

Dewey sighed. "Hugh, you can be slow sometimes, ya know? Now I ain't sayin' you don't know *some* things, like givin' sermons, funerals, stuff like that, but when it comes to common sense, well, you musta gone inside instead of going through the drive-through like ever'body else when they handed out common sense."

My head hurt trying to figure out what he was saying, but it amounted to me being dumb. *I couldn't agree more, Dewey.*

"Well, we *are* the premier private investigatin' firm in Road's End, ya know. We ain't just …

"That's 'vestigatin', George."

"Shut up, Dewey. … some backwater town clowns pretendin' to be detectives. We're the real deal."

"You sure are. I've gotta think they're pretty teed off about now, and I don't think they're even going to pretend to be nice guys. They'll know we did this deliberately and come looking for us."

"That's the plan, Hugh. You jest watch'n see."

"George, I hope you two are right. I really do." I thought for a minute while water dripped off my head and down my nearly-melted face into my shirt. "Listen, Del told me that one of them might be a woman, and she's a particularly nasty one. Looks and acts nice on the outside, he says, but meaner than a snake inside. Be on the lookout for her and don't fall for any sweet talk. Spread the word if you see any of the others around, okay?"

"Four-ten …"

"That's ten-four, Dewey."

"'Tis not."

"'Tis."

"'Tis not. Don't make no sense being ten-four. Four's a smaller number than ten. Didn't your mother teach you anything?"

"You leave my mother outta this, Dewey."

They wandered off, oblivious. I wished I could be.

I was soaked, so it didn't matter where I went. I headed for the church. It was the first building the bad guys would come to once they entered the city proper. Well, teensy village proper, I guess. I wanted to make sure they didn't take out their frustration and anger on the Parrys who were guarding the church. The storm raged on and an occasional flash of lightning lit the western sky, which was quickly becoming our overhead sky. *Just what we need, Lord. Are you trying to help us or allowing the devil to send this storm? How can we use it to our advantage?*

No answer. God works in mysterious ways, so I put my hope and faith into the Lord to get us through this mess. And it was getting messier by the minute.

Chapter Twenty-Seven

I walked up the church steps and through the wall water pouring over me, I could make out four—oh, great, four of them—figures gesturing and screaming at one another. I couldn't hear their voices, but they were obviously not in good moods. In this case, the rain worked in my favor. If I was as indistinct to them as they were to me, there would be no reason for them to wonder why I didn't come to help them.

I pulled open the big oak door and stepped inside, careful to stay on the carpet to prevent water damage to our historic floors. I'd have to remind them to keep the doors locked after I left.

"Stay off the floors!"

"Grace?" What was she doing here?

She walked out from her office in a huff. "Are you stalkin' me again, Pastorman? I thought I told you to cut that out."

"No, Grace, I'm not stalking you. I'm just surprised you're here instead of at home." I almost didn't recognize her in her casual clothes and boots.

"Well, Ruby Mae's in the tunnel, and there's nothin' inside that house but hundreds of stupid hats, so I figure I can do more good here at the church. They won't even bother with the house. And if they do, they won't stay long."

"Well, be careful, Grace. They're just down the road a ways and George and Dewey tell me they have four flat tires now. Don't know how they did it, but they managed to rig up a system that would ring that bell *and* flatten their tires. Pretty ingenious, I'd say. Since this is the first building they'll come to, they might be testy."

"Testy, huh? Is that what you call it when hired guns come into a town to kill someone and git flat tires on the way? Testy? I'd say more like maniacal."

"I bow to your knowledge, Grace."

"Don't bow to me in the Lord's House, Pastorman. He gets all the glory 'round here, 'member?"

"You're right, Grace. You know, sometimes so much happens in this church other than worshipping the Lord, that I forget it's a sacred place. We are indeed in the Lord's house, and any bowing I do will be to our Lord and Savior."

"Good, Pastorman. Real good."

Just then the big door opened to reveal three dripping-wet men and one sopping woman.

"Well, hello there, folks! Come in, come in."

"Stay on the rug! And keep off the floors. I mean that." That was Grace, my 'equal opportunity to get screeched at' secretary.

I turned back to them and said, "She's very protective of our church, and these floors in particular. How can we help you? How did you find your way here? I'll bet you're lost. This town is pretty much off the grid!"

They scowled. And dripped.

Finally, the woman spoke up. "Gosh, it's nice to get out of the storm. If I could use your restroom, maybe I could make myself more presentable." Yep, this one was Witch Lady.

I pointed in the direction of our teensy half-bath. "It's over there. There should be some towels in there."

"Shoes off, ma'am. Can't have water drippin' everywhere."

The woman looked at Grace and gave her a wan smile that was so close to a smirk you couldn't have slipped oxygen between them. The woman slipped off her shoes and padded toward the bathroom. She shut the door a bit harder—make that a lot harder—than necessary.

"Careful with that door!"

I could feel the waves of anger emanating from under the bathroom door. Grace has that effect sometimes, particularly with bad people. She is the quintessential bossy lady and doesn't take any backtalk.

I exchanged a glance with Grace that said, "Please, please, please don't make them any angrier than they already are."

She looked back. Her gaze said, "Hey, they're already mad. I'm just not gonna show a lot of respect to people I know are rotten to the core."

I used my voice this time. "Grace, weren't you going to the Inn? Mel probably has supper ready. Remember you were going to join us since your mother is out of town?"

She gave me a "I'm on to you" look but walked into her office and returned with an umbrella.

"I'll be over as soon as I'm finished with our visitors, okay?"

"Yep." She opened the door and walked into the rain. A roll of thunder rippled over the town. At least I think it was thunder. Might've been Grace.

"Well, gentlemen, you must be lost. Need some directions?" I smiled my best 'I'm just a harmless backwoods pastor' smile and waited for them to answer.

Finally, one of them, a tall, broad-shouldered guy with a ponytail and tiny goatee said, "We're not lost. We're lookin' for someone."

"Well, unless it's someone who lives in town, I'm afraid I can't help you."

Ponytail said, "Name's Delbert Jackson. Ugly guy."

I pretended to shudder. "Delbert T. Jackson? Well, he's not here now and I don't think he ever will be again. We met him last winter during a blizzard when he got stuck down the road. Meanest guy I ever ran across. I hate to say it, being a pastor and all, but that is one man we will never again let into town."

The second guy stepped forward. He was short. Short and skinny and didn't look like a thug at all. He looked more like a sixth-grader who just discovered wife-beaters and wore his with pride. I doubted if he could overpower Pewter, the church cat. He frowned and stood like some kind of superhero with his fists on his waist. It was all I could do to ask what his superpower was, but I figured being that small and with the cartel, he probably carried a gun. A little one. "We'll take a look."

"Excuse me? I just told you he's not in town. And even if he'd come here earlier, you'd have seen him on his way out of town because there's no way anyone in town would welcome his presence. There's one road in and the same road takes you out. No, Delbert T. Jackson is definitely not walking the streets of Road's End. *He's under the streets of Road's End, but let's not put too fine a point on it.*

The third guy had a patch over one eye and a scar running down the cheek of the other eye. If he'd been Johnny Depp, he still wouldn't have looked like a pirate. He just looked … well, like a guy with a patch over his eye and a scar on his cheek. Some guys look fine in a patch; he was not among them.

"If you don't mind, we'll look for ourselves."

"Why would you bother? I just told you he's not here. What makes you think he's here, anyway?"

"We have our ways." I looked to my right. It was Witch Lady. She wiped off the sneer and grinned. "I just mean we're good at what we do, and we think we've located Mr. Jackson in this town."

"Well, you'll just have to take my word for it, folks. Everyone in town is hunkered down during this storm and Delbert Jackson is not one of them."

Without a word, they walked out the door. Witch Lady had a little trouble getting her shoes back on, but eventually she too walked out. I didn't know what to do except call Mel and Bristol. I punched Bristol's face and waited. On the third ring, he answered.

"They're here, Bristol. And they're not a happy looking bunch. Witch Lady's with them."

"I know. I'm standing outside the church. They can't see me, but I can see them. Looks like they're trying to figure out where to go."

"Well, I was adamant with them that Del wasn't here, but they don't believe me. Maybe I don't lie convincingly."

"You don't. But it wouldn't matter if you did. Their GPS brought them here, and they're bound and determined to find him. We'll just have to take them down. Maybe one by one. Gotta go."

The line went dead and I walked into my office and nearly passed out when someone stood up. "It's me, Hugh. Hazel Parry. Perry and I thought it best that we stay out of it as long as you were here to deal with them. They're not very cheerful, are they?"

"No, Hazel, they aren't. I'm glad you stayed away. Not letting them know anyone's here might come in handy later. Stay low. Perry, are you in here too?

"Yep, right here, Hugh. I turned and saw him standing behind the door.

"Hey, pretty clever, Perry. Take care, please. I'd better go meet up with Bristol. Oh, I almost forgot. Is Leo okay? Where is he?"

"He was in the sanctuary, but now that those people are gone, he's in Grace's office with the door closed. He thought he might be able to see something through the rain and warn us." He took a step toward me and patted my shoulder. "God be with you, Hugh."

"Thank you, Perry. God be with you and Hazel and Leo, as well."

Bristol was as good as his word. I turned to the right toward our cemetery and walked around the corner. Bristol was standing there under the eaves with water pouring down him. "You look a lot like a fountain, Bristol. Kind of a nice touch to the cemetery."

"Thanks, Hugh. I'll add that to my list of unpaid duties." He grinned his huge grin and continued. "I think they're on their way to the Inn."

My heart dropped to my knees. I knew it was inevitable, but I kept hoping something would forestall a visit to the Inn by the bad guys. We talked for another minute or two, then we split up. I couldn't wait to get to Mel.

I ran as fast as I could through the rain and puddles and came in the back door. I could see Mel talking to the four of them in the foyer. Grace was right next to her, and I noticed all four of them were standing in their stocking feet. Witch Lady wasn't smiling, but she wasn't shooting at us, either, so I took that as a good sign. But I could almost see the noxious tension in the room between Grace and WW. I hoped no one lit a match.

"Well, hello again," I said. I removed my shoes and walked toward them. "Hi, hon. Hey there, Grace. I see you made it here without drowning. Whatever you're making for supper smells delicious, Mel."

"Thanks, dear. It's chicken noodle soup, salad, and muffins—blueberry. I take it you've met our visitors? They're looking for Delbert Jackson. Remember that disagreeable man during the blizzard last year? I told them he's not here, and if I'm perfectly honest, I hope he won't ever be."

"Yes, we met at the church earlier. I told them the same thing—Delbert Jackson wore out his welcome in a big hurry the last time he was here. He won't *ever* return to town. I'm sure of that." I walked over to Ponytail and said, "I don't believe I introduced myself over at the church. I'm Pastor Hugh Foster, and the lady you met over there is my secretary, Grace. She's the one who keeps the church ticking along." I pointed toward her, then moved over to Mel and put my arm around her waist. "This beautiful lady is my wife, Melanie."

Nothing. Not a peep out of them. "Well, I suppose you'll want to be on your way with this storm and all. It'll be good to get to your hotel—I hope you're staying the night somewhere. There's a nice place down on the main highway about sixty miles west of here. It's a good night for staying inside."

SuperShrimp spoke up and said, "Isn't this place an inn? Why can't we stay here?"

I looked at Mel and she smiled. "If you had a reservation, you could. We'd be glad to have you, but we have a wedding party coming in tomorrow and I'm still putting the finishing touches on their rooms. Maybe some other time."

SuperShrimp flexed his little muscles and said, "I betcha got room for us for just the one night."

"No," Mel said, shaking her head. "No, we don't."

Witch Woman stuck her nose in and said, "Oh, please? It's pretty nasty out there and I'm really scared of storms."

Mel shook her head. "I'm really sorry."

Witch Woman's face morphed into a look most demons would covet. "That's too bad, missy, 'cause we're stayin' whether you want us to or not."

"I beg your pardon? I just told you we don't have room. That means we *don't have room.* Now, please put your shoes on and leave."

"My little friend here says otherwise," Ponytail said.

I glanced over at SuperShrimp and got a nasty look for my trouble. Ponytail waved a gun in my direction to get my attention. "Not him. *This.*"

"Now wait just a minute," I said. "Put that gun down. *Now.* I'm sorry you can't stay here and I'm sorry you haven't been able to find your friend, but that's not our problem. My wife has been working on these rooms for weeks now. She will *not* have you stay in those rooms, and neither will I. So please leave. Now."

"Find room for us, or else." That was Ponytail.

Bristol walked into the foyer just then (*Thank You, Lord*) and evened up the playing field. "I wouldn't be so sure about that, big guy.

The pastor asked you to leave and that's what you're going to do." He raised his arm and, thank goodness, a gun was attached to his hand.

"We can't. Our car's not working."

"We'll push it out of town then." Bristol wasn't making himself very popular with them.

"Can't." That was SS.

"Yes, we can, little guy." *Calm down, Bristol.*

"We have four flat tires."

"How on earth did you get four flat tires? I've never heard of that happening. Have you, Hugh?"

I shook my head. "Nope. Must be some stroke of bad luck you're having, folks."

Pirate Wannabe went to pull out his gun, and Bristol beat him to the punch. "Drop it, matey. *Now!* Grace, will you please pick up that gun?"

Grace walked over, picked up the gun, pointed it at Witch Woman, and moved toward her. "When the pastor and his wife say you're not stayin' here, you're .... *not ... stayin' ... here.*" She used the barrel of the gun to poke WW in the chest.

Good grief, we're going to get ourselves killed right in the foyer. Mel will have a fit.

WW was fuming, SS was embarrassed, Pirate Wannabe was just itching to get to his gun, and Ponytail's ponytail was coming out of its rubberband.

"You might wanna fix yer hair when ya leave, buddy," Grace said. "You're losin' your bun there."

I could see Ponytail's hands fisted and flexing. He would give just about anything to get his hands on one of us.

"Listen, folks, we seem to have gotten off to a bad start ... and end, for that matter. You said you're looking for Delbert Jackson. We know of him because he was here last winter, but we will never let him into town again. As you can see, this is a tiny little place; if Delbert Jackson was here, we'd know about it. We don't have a room for you to stay overnight, so you'll have to leave, and I'm sorry about that, but that's all there is to it. Now, you have four flat tires, and again I'm sorry. Maybe we can call for a wrecker. That's all I can tell you."

Mel spoke up. "We're sorry you had to drive so far out of your way just to find that Mr. Jackson isn't here, but if you'd called ahead of time, we could have saved you a long trip and four flat tires. Now, if you don't mind, I'd appreciate it if you'd put on your shoes and leave."

WW was turning the color of spaghetti sauce. I was afraid she might explode all over our wood floors, and then Mel would really be disgusted. Fortunately, WW was merely angry and not in any immediate danger of detonating body parts across our foyer.

Pirate Wannabe burst out, "Just what are we supposed to do then?"

"I'm not sure I can make that decision for you, matey," Bristol said. "You might have been invited to a meal of some of Melanie's delicious food if you hadn't pulled a gun in their house. I guess you're going to have to get hold of a wrecker service and have them haul you out of here."

"Forget it."

"Whatever you say, but if you have a spare, I'd put it on. It won't help the rims on the other three, but it might get you a little way down the road." Bristol wasn't making any lifelong friends in this group, but then in their line of work, their lives probably wouldn't be too long anyway.

I walked to the front door and opened it. The rain was still pouring down and puddles were forming in the yard.

"Watch your step, folks. It's wet out there."

One by one, they walked out the door and into the dark, wet night. I shut the door, locked it, turned the deadbolt, and turned to Grace, Mel, and Bristol. "You know they're going to separate, don't you?"

"Countin' on it, Hugh."

Chapter Twenty-Eight

I was glad Bristol had a plan because I didn't have a clue. It was dark, slippery, electrifying, and windy out there. Reminded me a little of Mandy's wedding night. I didn't see how them separating and going in four different directions was going to help us, but I knew Bristol knew what he was doing.

"Okay, spill the beans, buddy. How's their separating going to help us?"

Bristol wiggled his eyebrows (not as well as I do, though) in a "wouldn't you like to know" look, then said, "Because when we take 'em down, we're only fighting one of them. We tie that one up and go looking for the next one."

"Okay, that makes sense, but how do we know which directions they're going?"

"Simple. We follow them."

"And if one of the others runs across us trying to take down one of their buddies, what'll we do?"

Bristol thought for a moment. "Well, I'm not sure any of them are best buddies to begin with, but since they have no way to get out of town, they might be a little more inclined to keep their numbers up. I guess we either tackle the second one or if we have to, we shoot 'em."

Grace raised her hand and said, "I volunteer to shoot the woman."

"Don't like her, do you, Grace?" I couldn't help smiling. "She might be able to pull off her sweet little woman act on some folks, but not our Grace."

"Well, she didn't have to pull it off for long," Mel said. "She turned pretty nasty almost immediately."

Grace nodded. "Guess the nasty in her was just achin' to get out. I have a feelin' if she comes lookin' for trouble, it'll be me she's lookin' for."

"I agree," I said. "Maybe you should stay right here with Mel instead of going out in that stuff, no matter how much you dislike her, Grace. You did enough at the cabin. Why don't you sit this one out?"

"Yeah, right, Pastorman. I'm gonna let an armed woman—she has to be armed with a mouth like that on her—get the upper hand over me? Not likely. 'Sides, are you forgettin' the beatin' I gave Mack?"

"No, Grace, I'm not. In fact, I don't ever think I'll forget that. And I don't think Mack will either." We smiled at one another over the memory of her wailing on the biggest man I'd ever seen after he pinned me to my desk thinking I was threatening him. "Nope, never gonna forget that. But I still don't think you ought to go out there."

"I'm goin', Pastorman, and that's that. You can try to stop me, but I'd hate to hurt a pastor—even if he does leave the half-and-half out of the fridge most of the time."

"Hugh, are you still doing that?" That was Mel, Grace's partner in guarding half-and-half with their lives.

"You know what, guys? We gotta get going. I think at least two of us should stick together, so why don't Grace and I team up? Hugh, you watch the fort unless I call you, okay?"

I wasn't keen on staying inside when they were going out into that nasty weather to face even nastier bad guys, but I understood his logic. No sense in all of us wandering around. I'd stay good and ready to go wherever he told me to go when the time came.

"Okay. I don't like it, but I get your drift. But don't hesitate to call at the first hint you'll need help. Let's just keep in touch with our phones all the time, though. The more we know about who's where, the better off we'll be."

"Roger that, Hugh. Now go eat some soup and muffins for me. See you soon."

They went out the back door and it was all I could do not to follow them. But Bristol was right, and I knew his experience as a big city detective overruled my small-town pastor expertise in catching villains.

"Come and sit down, Hugh. No sense in not eating. You're going to need your strength if you end up out there."

I sat down at the table, waited until she'd put a plate of muffins on the table and a bowl of steaming soup in front of each of us, and prayed. "Heavenly Father, we are in dire straits, and we need You more than mere words can express. I know you know all about it and have a plan. Please don't let me miss any directions you give to me, and please protect Grace and Bristol, as well as all the other people in Road's End. Thank You for Mel's delicious food. In Jesus' Name, I pray. Amen."

"Hon, I know you're worried about them, but Bristol will take good care of Grace. I think he's sweet on her, and I *know* she's in love with him. Eat your food and rest up a little."

Before they left, Bristol made sure Grace's weapon, formerly owned by Ponytail, his own gun, and mine were all loaded and ready to go. He gave both of us extra ammunition, and I sincerely hoped I wouldn't have to shoot so many times that I needed to reload, but that wasn't my call. We were as ready as we'd ever be.

I answered, "I hope George and Dewey did as I asked and went to meet up with Winnie and Martha. We don't need those two wandering around in harm's way. I know they mean well, and their plan to warn us and flatten those tires was genius, but still, they're old and this weather won't do them any good. Besides, I don't think they have a gun—oh Good Lord, please don't let them have guns—so they'll be sitting ducks."

Bristol's phone call came right after I finished my last spoonful of soup. "How's it going?" I said, foregoing any pleasantries. I listened as he quietly and quickly told me they were on SuperShrimp's tail and would probably be able to take him down, tie him up, and wait for me to come out, grab him, and stick him somewhere out of the way.

"Got it, Bristol. Be there soon."

Mel looked at me with tears in her eyes. "Hugh, I know we're supposed to act with Christ's love toward everyone, but is Del really worth getting shot for?"

I thought about that for a second. "Yes, hon." I thought some more, then nodded my head. "Yeah, he is." A second later, "Hon, I almost forgot. Would you call the Wyandottes, Emma, Sadie, Frank—wait, forget Frank, he's in the tunnel—and the Parrys and Leo at the church and anyone else you can think of, and let them know that the cartel has separated and gone in four different directions. They need to make sure doors and windows are locked, curtains closed, not to answer the door unless they're positive it's one of us, and to stay away from windows. Lay low if they hear gunshots or suspect someone's in their yard. No sense giving the bad guys an easy target. I have no idea where George and Dewey are. I hope they're with their wives, but if they're not, text me and let me know, will you?"

She gave me a weak smile, stood to give me a hug and a kiss, and turned away. I walked over to the coat hooks on the wall, grabbed the darkest one I had, and put it on. "Be sure to lock this door behind me, Mel. I love you."

She turned and said, "I love you, too, Hugh. Be careful."

I walked out the door and shut it as quietly as I could. Outside it was as bad as it looked from the inside. We'd decided we wouldn't use flashlights as they would only draw the attention, so I was walking blindly, rain running down my face, and wind whipping around the corners. *Why is it always bad weather when we have trouble in this town?* I was getting a headache and I hadn't walked four feet from my porch.

Bristol told me he had SuperShrimp in sight over by Frank's Garage and Convenience Store ("Where you're always guaranteed to get gas.") Frank's garage consists of several smaller buildings cobbled together to make one big mess of … well, cobbled-together buildings. That's about the only way to describe it. Apparently, before my time in Road's End, Frank felt the need to expand. His idea of adding-on was to use wooden planks to connect the ramshackle buildings. He changed oil in one building, took engines out in another, and did tire changes, etc. in a third. The fourth and largest of those buildings contained his office, convenience store, and his home on the top floor.

This bunch of buildings suited Frank's purposes, but they created havoc for good guys chasing bad guys on a dark, rainy night. I had nowhere to start, so I began creeping along the outside walls and peeking around corners. My heart pounded so hard it hurt.

I was about halfway around the third building before I caught sight of SuperShrimp crouching beside a rain barrel filled to overflowing. If he was trying to stay out of the rain, he picked the wrong building. He was sitting between a rapidly-filling puddle and an overflowing rain barrel.

I worried about a lightning strike, but realized he'd never know what happened. For a moment, I felt sorry for him until I saw him raise his gun and take aim at someone moving along the outside wall Frank's office.

At just the right moment, lightning crackled across the sky in a display of the brightest light I've ever seen. It momentarily blinded him, and I took the opportunity to pull my gun out of my coat and point it at him.

I tried not to quiver as I yelled, "Put it down, buddy! Right now. I said *now* or I'll shoot!" He didn't, and there was a shot, a scream, and SS was down. It all happened in about four seconds. *How on earth did that happen? I haven't even touched the trigger.*

I looked up to see Bristol walk over to SS, grab his arm, and yank him upward.

"Hey, that hurts!" That had to be SS, since he was the one who got himself shot for not following orders. I bet he'll think next time.

"I'm sure it does, Shrimp. I coulda killed you but decided I'd rather you rot in prison for the rest of your life."

"Hugh, take this bag of garbage and stuff him somewhere, would you? He's bleeding from his arm, and he might need a bandage, but he'll live." Before he turned him over to me, though, Bristol looked him right in the eye and said, "Where are the others? *Now*, buddy. You know how impatient I am. Tell me *now*."

Just for grins, Bristol gave him another shake and the guy whimpered. "Hey, cut it out. How'm I s'posed to know?" Another shake, this time harder. "Ouch! I don't know fer sure." A rather violent shake followed, and suddenly Shrimp's memory returned. "Okay, okay. Wanda went lookin' for that woman, Jake went up there." He pointed to Emma's place. "And Patch went over there." He pointed at Sadie's place. If Patch was Pirate Wannabe, and that made sense, then Jake must be Ponytail.

One last shake, and Bristol dragged him in my direction. I met them halfway, and Bristol said, "I'll take Emma's. You catch up with Grace—she's over there." He pointed to the same place he'd appeared from just a minute or so before. "Wait, I'll send her to you. Then you two go over to Sadie's, after you've deposited Shrimp boy someplace."

"Okay. Consider it done."

Bristol mouthed, "Hurry," and I nodded. Both Emma and Sadie were forces to be reckoned with, but not even those two could out-talk, insult, or put to shame a gun. I latched onto Shrimp and started to walk him back to the Inn. I heard Bristol say, "Watch your back."

Mel unlocked the door when we arrived and held it wide open. I shoved Shrimp into the kitchen. "He's got an arm wound, hon. You might want to grab a towel. Bristol doesn't think it's very bad, but he might make a mess."

"Are you alright? The phone's been ringing off the hook since we heard the shot."

"Yeah, I'm wet, but okay. I'm on my way to Sadie's now. Would you grab one of our folding chairs from the pantry? I'll duct tape him to it for the time being. The towel and tape should stop that bleeding for now." Mel found the chair and I plunked Shrimp down into it. While I taped, she found a towel to put around his wound. I slapped some tape on his mouth. He wasn't going anywhere unless he walked out with that chair attached to him.

I pointed to the junk drawer. "Get me a zip tie, would you, hon?" She brought it back, and I tied it around his wrists behind him. It certainly wasn't comfortable, but he should've thought of that when he chose a life of crime.

"Okay, give me a call—no, you'd better text me—if he gets out of hand, although I think you could take him all by yourself." I turned to Shrimp and put my finger in his face. "If you so much as *think* a bad word in my wife's direction, I'll let Bristol manhandle you again. Got that?"

He nodded.

I kissed Mel again and went out into the rain via the back door. No sense dripping water all over the house just to go out the front. Besides, the less SS knew about where I was, the better. I couldn't imagine how he could communicate with his buddies, but no sense giving him a roadmap.

Grace was at the door when I went back outside. I'd made sure all our porch lights were off and I noticed everyone else in town had done the same. It made it harder for us, but it was worse for the bad guys because they didn't know the lay of the land. We crouched to make ourselves as small as possible, and in ten seconds we were at the front of the Inn. Sadie had a light on inside her house. No doubt she was baking up a storm, regardless of villains running loose on the streets of Road's End.

Misjudge

As we scuttled across Gloucester Street, one at a time, I couldn't help but wonder what life would've been like if Mel and I hadn't run across The Inn at Road's End on one of our lengthy drives around Virginia. We wouldn't be running around in the rain chasing bad guys with guns, that's for sure. But on the flip side, we wouldn't have made the acquaintance of all the residents—crochety, cranky, obstinate, opinionated, and nuts as they could be—or Grace, Bristol, and Emma, the three normal folks in town. All in all, I was glad we were here, but nights like this were exhausting.

We reached Sadie's house with only Grace taking a spill and landing knees first in a puddle. I managed to stay upright, miraculously. Her spill probably just cemented her determination to find and capture the cartel people. Grace isn't a particularly patient woman when it comes to killers. Just a funny quirk of hers.

I motioned we should go around the house and knock on the back door. It wasn't as easy as I thought it would be. The yard on that side of the house was filled with rose bushes that were breathtaking in bloom, but difficult to plow through in the dark. But we made it with only a few scratches and walked up the three steps. Grace knocked lightly, and the door opened inward.

A gun pointed right at us.

Chapter Twenty-Nine

I don't know about you, but whenever I see a gun aimed at me, I get jittery. Maybe it's because I'm a pastor, or a big chicken, or maybe, just maybe, I'm being smart. Simultaneously, Grace and I plunged to either side of the old porch. I don't know about Grace, but I was bushed and throwing myself all over the place wasn't helping my overall health or mood.

"State your name, rank, and serial number."

I recognized George's voice. "It's us, George. Let us in. It's wet out here."

"Cain't do that until you state your name, rank, and serial number."

"George, it's me. You know it's me, and you're going to be in big trouble if you don't open that door this instant."

"Cain't do it, Pas …"

Grace leaped up the steps and slammed the door open, pinning George behind it.

"Ouch! Who did that?"

Grace peeked around the door and said, "I did, George. Any questions?" I'd scrambled inside by then and shut and locked the door behind me.

"What's gotten into you, George? You knew it was me and yet you still insisted on playing those crazy games of yours."

"Wouldn'ta done it if I'd known Grace was with ya."

I guess I know where I stand in terms of my ferocious reputation in these parts.

"Okay, let's leave this 'til later. Is Dewey with you? And Sadie? Is everyone all right?"

"Yeah, we're fine!" Sadie appeared from behind the refrigerator door and continued. "Both yahoos are with me. I did as Mel asked. Locked up tight as can be, closed the curtains, no porchlights, and stayin' away from the windows. 'Cept for that bozo over there." She pointed straight at the bozo, Dewey, who was standing in front of the window peeking between the drawn curtains as if no one could see him standing there—backlit—looking like a little kid waiting for Santa to stop by with loads of presents.

"Hey, I ain't no bozo," Dewey complained.

"Get away from that window, Dewey. *Now!*" My patience was about as thin as my temper was at the moment, which was about a tenth the diameter of a spiderweb.

Dewey moved to the side and walked toward us. "Hey, you don't need to go yellin' at me, Hugh. I'm just ..."

A shot splintered Sadie's window into glass dust and buried itself just below the edge of the kitchen counter. Everyone hit the deck and screamed in a variety of pitches. It'll be a miracle if I'm not deaf by morning.

"What on earth?" My chin hurt from banging it on the counter when I went down. "Everyone okay? Stay *down* for crying out loud. Dewey, you could've been killed!" I think I got murmurs and nods that they were all okay, but it was dark as pitch inside the house and my ears were ringing. "Grace, make sure they're all okay."

She did and they were.

Sadie stood up, untied her apron, threw it on the counter, rolled up her sleeves, and started forward. I grabbed her by the arm before she could march outside and deck whoever broke her window. "Hold on there, Sadie. They have guns."

She held up a nasty looking firearm, and said, "So do I."

"But they know how to use theirs, Sadie. Please?"

"And so do I." She jerked her arm from my grasp and before I could stop her, she stalked to the front door. She peeked around the corner of the window, which was now letting in rain and wind all over her living room, stuck that gun out the window, took aim, and pulled the trigger.

Someone screamed.

Is this night ever going to end? I pulled out my phone, punched Bristol in the face, and while I waited for him to answer, I said through gritted teeth, "Sadie, you get yourself back here right this minute!" Surprisingly, she followed my order. She walked back, set the gun down, picked up her apron, put it on, and pulled a cookie sheet of fresh cookies out of the oven.

He answered on the second ring. "Bristol? Did you hear that shot? Yeah, it was Sadie. She hit someone; hope it wasn't you. They're in the front of her house. Probably in the street. From the sound of that scream, she might have shot another kneecap to bits."

I waited for Bristol to stop laughing. It took forever. "Done now? Dewey, George, Sadie, Grace, and I are at Sadie's house. Someone—whoever sent that bullet through her front window and into her kitchen counter—is gonna replace that glass pronto. What have you come across?"

I listened for a couple minutes more, said goodbye, and turned to address my four compadres. Make that two. George and Dewey were nowhere in sight, and the backdoor curtains were still swaying from the wind that rustled them when those two left the house.

I tried to stay calm, but this wasn't a cozy kind of night. It was a miserable, wet, gun-totin', window-blasting, kneecap-shattering, windy kind of night. And I'd had it.

I told Grace to stay with Sadie and make sure no one leaped into that window, unless it was me or Bristol. I didn't mention George or Dewey because I knew they'd never in a million years get themselves hoisted up there before the weekend and by then it would be all over and we'd either have won or died.

"You goin' back out there, Pastorman? You sure you don't want me to go with you?"

"No, Grace, thanks just the same. Unless Wanda's the one Sadie shot, she's still out there looking for you. It's bad enough that we have this gaping window to worry about." I turned to Sadie. "Do you mind if I push that big armoire in front of the window?" It was where Sadie kept her extra pot of coffee, spoons, napkins, and such for her customers at the bake house.

"Heck, no, Hugh. Never did like that thing. My husband's mother foisted it on us years ago and I've hated the stupid thing ever since. Can we write a note on the back that says, "Shoot this critter to pieces?"

I chuckled despite my bad mood but didn't have time for frivolity. "Probably wouldn't be a good idea, Sadie, but I'll push it in front of the window just the same. Grace joined me and together, we manhandled that sucker—boy, was it heavy—in front of what used to be a window. I looked around to see if I could find anything else that might keep them safe. If we moved the couch in front of the door, that would block it, but then if Bristol or I needed to get inside, we'd be out of luck. "Listen, ladies. Stay low, okay? If you're gonna bake, Sadie, do it in the dark. Any little bit of light gives them an advantage, and I think by now they're probably getting a little desperate, and they're not about to fight fair."

I slipped out the back door after reminding Grace to lock it behind me. She gave me that "don't you go tellin' me what to do" look, then quietly said, "Be careful out there. Call if you need me, okay?" I nodded, smiled, and turned to be greeted by a barrel or so of cold water thrown in my face. I wiped my eyes, walked around the side of the house, and stood behind a tree along Gloucester Street. I wondered how Mel was doing and looked up and down the street. Pirate Wannabe was around here somewhere, let alone Witch Woman and Ponytail. I couldn't afford to slip up.

On the other hand, George and Dewey were wandering around out here somewhere, too, and as always, those two managed to complicate matters—particularly in the rain, wind, snow, and dark of night. The nastier the weather, the better. I hoped they'd gone back to Dewey's house, but that wasn't likely. No, they were still wandering around out there somewhere, no doubt hoping to be of help, but more than likely putting themselves and the rest of us good guys in danger.

I prayed for everyone's safety and called Bristol. He whispered into the phone. "What?"

"Well, hello to you, too! Whatcha doing?"

"I'm in the middle of saving the free world. What are you doing?"

"Well, I'm hiding behind a tree by Sadie's house, hoping I won't be found, shot, or have a heart attack. Thanks for asking. Any luck with

Ponytail? Hey, listen, I haven't found Patch, but there's a lump of something writhing in the middle of the road. I'll bet that's one of them. I'm going over there now to see who it is. Stay on the line, will you? I'm not scared—just, you know, petrified." I heard him chuckle as I took another look up and down the street, as if I could spot them because of the reflective tape they were wearing just for me. No such luck. It was just me and Lumpie in the middle of the road.

I had my gun out and aimed right at whoever it was. I could hear moaning, then a few swear words which firmed up my resolve to get this guy put away. I walked up to him, and said, "Throw your gun to the grass in front of you, and if you dare to move, aim, snarl, or swear, I'll send you to hell via a bullet to … well, somewhere it'll hurt a whole bunch." Maybe I should work on my tough guy persona.

Patch looked up, but still couldn't see me because of his bad eye, so I walked around behind him, and said it again. "*Now,* Pirate Boy. Toss your gun over there. Three, two …" What was I going to do if I got to one? I should've started at ten. Thankfully, he tossed the gun to the grass in front of Sadie's. "That's better. Now get up."

"Are you nuts? I can't get up. Someone shot me." If he'd left it at that, he might have been okay. But of course, he didn't. He started in with his swearing, and I'd had just about enough of these mouthy, gun-wielding, ill-mannered characters, so I took aim and put a bullet into the road right next to his head. That got his attention. He screamed, I jumped, and Bristol screeched through the phone, "*Are you okay?*"

"Yep, but Patch is a little shook-up. He's whining over here. I have his gun, so I think I'll just leave him here for the moment. It's doubtful he'll get run over, but if he does, it'll serve him right."

"I'll turn you into a detective yet, Hugh."

"No thanks, Bristol. I think I'll just retire to a nice little Virginia backwater town, maybe buy an inn … Listen, I have no idea where Witch Woman or Ponytail are, so watch your step, okay?"

He agreed, we hung up, and I stood around looking indecisive, which of course, I was. And wet, and muddy, and out of breath, and angry, and sore, and tired, and hungry. I had one more thing to hold against them.

I decided to head over to the inn to be sure Mel was okay, then check in at the church. I gave Mel a call as I ran to the backdoor. "Hon,

I'm coming in the back, but don't open it until you hear my voice, okay?"

She agreed and ten seconds later, she was as good as her word. I knocked, identified myself as her loving husband, and she opened the door. I scooted in as quickly as possible, and she lunged at me and almost smothered me with a giant hug. "Hugh, you have to stop this messing around. You're scaring me with all those gunshots. Who got shot?"

"Patch. Sadie shot him. She's getting pretty good. We may have to rein her in when this is all over. That last shot was me giving Patch a piece of my mind. Nasty-mouthed heathen." I took a look around. SuperShrimp, still gagged, tied, and taped, was sitting at our kitchen table, and I could see where Mel had been sitting by the open Bible lying on the table. I looked at her in amazement and she shrugged.

"Sometimes we have to get innovative, dear. He's been the perfect student."

"I should hope so, hon. Any other activity?"

"No, although I thought I saw a shadow pass the dining room window a few minutes ago."

I motioned for her to follow me into the living room. I didn't want SS to hear anything more than necessary. "It might have been Witch Woman or Ponytail. SS in there told us Patch went to Sadie's and Ponytail went to Emma's. I have no idea where Witch Woman could be. Bristol's at Emma's now, so I imagine we'll have a third one captured soon. Grace is with Sadie, and so were Dewey and George until they flew the coop. They could be in Toledo by now." I thought for a moment, "Hey, don't those shutters on the inside of our windows close?"

She looked at me in amazement. "Why didn't I think of that? Of course, they do. We might smush the draperies a bit locking them into place, but that'll be a small price to pay."

I tiptoed back into the dining room and peeked into the kitchen. SS was still sitting there, looking dejected. I returned to Mel. "Okay, let's do that right now, and then I'll go out and see what other mischief I can get into."

"If that was supposed to be funny, it wasn't, Hugh. Not in the least."

"I'm sorry, hon, but if I don't have some fun with this, it'll turn into nothing more than a night of horrid weather and gunshots. We don't want that, do we?"

She smiled and together we closed the ones in the dining room, living room, and my office. I ran upstairs to close those in the bedrooms while she resumed preaching to her captive audience. In five minutes, I was downstairs, checked the front door to be sure it was locked good and tight, kissed Mel, and went back out into the storm.

I'd moved about two steps beyond the porch on my way to the church when I was slammed from behind and thrown to the ground.

Chapter Thirty

I was getting real sick and tired of being shoved around and having guns pointed at me. Face-planting into the soggy grass of my backyard only added to my misery. Besides, I didn't know who had shoved me, so maybe I had even more to worry about.

A split second later, I discovered I wasn't going to die—at least not at that instant—but I *was* going to do some head-knocking of a couple of old men.

George spoke first. "Get up slowly with yer hands behind yer head."

"George, it's me."

"Hands behind yer head, buddy."

"George, cut it out. It's me."

"Don't make me shoot ya, fella."

"George, for the last time, it's *me!*" I stood up and faced him.

"Well, fer cryin' out loud, Hugh, why didn't ya tell me it was you?"

Maybe it's not such a bad idea for them to be out here. Sorry, Father. I didn't really mean that. Forgive me.

"Guys," I said shaking my head and turning my Air Force chaplain glare between the two of them, "why on earth are you out here?"

Dewey said, "Well, from the look'a things, we're out here savin' you, Hugh."

"What?"

George piped up. "That's right, Hugh. We saved ya from bein' shot by those no-goodigans."

No-goodigans? "Why? Have you seen them? Are they close by?"

George looked over at Dewey and they both shrugged. "Beats us, Hugh."

"Seems ta me yer the one that oughtta be lookin' fer 'em, Hugh. Ain't we done enough by savin' ya?" That was Dewey, the one whose funeral I was planning in my head, as if I didn't have enough other things to occupy my mind.

"Guys, thank you for … saving me from … something, but you've got to stop treating me like I'm your enemy. I'm on your side, remember?"

"Gee whiz, Hugh. Do you think we're dumb?"

Don't think it, Hugh. Don't think it.

"Of course not, George. It's just that I'm worried about you two getting hurt. Why don't you go home …"

"Can't, Hugh. I live outta town. Seems ta me you coulda 'membered that, me bein' one of your flockers 'n all."

I hung my head. "George, of course I remember where you live, but I wasn't talking about your house. I was talking about Dewey's house. You and Martha are staying there tonight, aren't you?"

"Where'd ya hear that? Gossip? Is that it? I thought pastors weren't s'posed to gossip. Shame on ya, Hugh. Just … (hanging his head in misery) … shame on ya."

"It wasn't gossip, George. You told me yourself."

"You callin' me a liar?"

No, George, I'm not calling you a liar. I'm calling you a … forgive me again, Father. These two really drive me nuts. Why was I standing in the pouring rain, lightning bolts skewering this and that, arguing with two crazier-than-a-hoot-owl men when there are still two armed villains willing to shoot us and burn the town down to get Del?

I grabbed both of them by their arms. "George, Dewey, we've got to get out of here. They could be anywhere." I looked around. Nothing. Well, not exactly nothing. There was mud, slippery grass, wind, lots of high-voltage electricity, and two octogenarians I would just as soon store in a shed. But no bad guys. I wasn't sure if I was blessed or if God was reprimanding me for my lack of grace toward the men. Could go either way.

For once, they listened to me and we hightailed it toward the church. We had almost reached Rivermanse Lane, the two-track that leads to Emma's house when I caught a glimpse of something moving. I didn't trust my eyes in this rain, so I motioned to George and Dewey to squat down (forgetting for the moment just what I was asking of two old men) in the trees, and they did their best to obey my command. I crept closer to the lane. Whatever I saw was either my imagination, aware of my presence and stalking me as I stalked them, or one of the good guys. I wasn't about to ask if they were good or bad, so I stood for a moment and looked in every direction. Nothing. Must have been my imagination.

I motioned to the men they could get up (which they couldn't) and five minutes later they'd reached my position next to the lane—a journey of about four feet. We looked every which way before crossing, then scooted into the trees on the other side of the lane. Just as I started to make the trek across the grass to the church, I saw something again. It couldn't be wildlife—it was too tall, even for a deer. Whatever it was, man or beast, it moved quietly as I hadn't heard it all before catching that glimpse. Was he, or maybe she, following us? Bristol, maybe? Or Ponytail or Wanda? Those were the only three, besides George, Dewey, and I, who were outside in this mess. I decided to give Bristol a call.

He answered immediately. "Hugh, no luck up here. Where are you?"

"On the west side of the lane standing in the trees. George and Dewey are with me. I thought I saw something a couple of times, but I can't make out enough in this rain to make sure it isn't you."

"It's not me. I'm inside Emma's place right now. I think you've got to assume it's Ponytail or Wanda."

"I agree, but I can't leave these two out here by themselves. I was taking them to the church, but if I do that, I'll lose whoever's out here with us."

"Let me think." Five seconds later, "Okay, George and Dewey have been out there for a while now. A little longer won't hurt them. Leave them where they are, and I'll come down to get them. You go over to the church and check up on them. Be careful, though. They probably know they're two down and mad as all-get- out."

"Okay, that makes sense. I won't be there long. Be careful."

We hung up, I whispered the plan to George and Dewey, they nodded, and after checking the area again, I made a beeline for the church. After I tapped out the secret knock we'd agreed on earlier, Perry promptly opened the door, and I scooted inside quickly.

"Thanks, Perry. Anything new?"

"I'm not sure, Hugh. I thought I heard voices outside the church, but of course I couldn't make out what they were saying. It sounded

like a man and a woman arguing. I didn't dare look out a window for
fear they'd notice me somehow. Besides that, it's been quiet."

"That was probably Ponytail and Witch Woman."

"Odd names."

"Odd people, Perry. How long ago was that?"

He thought for a few seconds. "I'd say it was maybe twenty
minutes ago. I'm not sure exactly sure. Sorry, Hugh."

"Don't be sorry, Pastor. You're doing fine. Are Hazel and Leo
okay?"

"Oh yes. Leo's as quiet as ever, and Hazel is watching for her
angel."

"We've got to talk some more about that when this is all over,
Perry. In the meantime, though, continue being quiet and keep the
lights out. Don't even let Leo's pipe glow be seen. Have him sit with
his back to the window."

"He already thought of that, Hugh."

"Good. You three are doing a great job, but please be careful.
Don't let anyone in who doesn't use that special knock, okay?"

He nodded and I stepped back outside. I had no idea where that
person or mirage or heck, Bigfoot, for all I know, could be. I stepped
from the porch as quietly as I could, hunched over, and hurried to the
shrubbery on the east side of the church. It wasn't much as far as cover
goes, but it was better than nothing. I squatted down ... *I'm so sorry,
George and Dewey* ... and groaned. I keep forgetting I'm not seven
years old anymore. I kept an eye out for movement, but aside from the
rain, nothing seemed to be stirring.

And then I saw it.

It was a man and a woman coming out from the trees and sloshing
through the squishy grass next to and behind the church. The woman
seemed to be having a hard time staying upright. *Serves you right,
Witch Woman.* They were heading west about a hundred feet in front of
me. They were either heading towards Molly, Bristol's house, or
looking for a back way into the church. Either way, it was bad news.

I didn't think Bristol was home—he'd been at Emma's just a few minutes ago when we talked, but he might've picked up George and Dewey and stashed them at his house. He loved that place. It had been a wreck before the church members offered it as payment for his work on the church. He spruced that little place up so well it was hard to imagine it had ever fallen into such disrepair. Before and after pictures were the only proof of his handiwork. If he put George and Dewey in there, and Ponytail and Witch Woman were looking for a place to hide, Molly would've been ideal. And that wouldn't sit well with Bristol.

I sat there in that squat until I realized if I didn't get up right then, I was never going to. My thighs burned as I slowly forced my legs to work. Once I was standing, I took a moment to let my blood circulate and try to figure out what to do next. It was at that exact moment in time when a brilliant flash of lightning lit the scene and I could see, even through the rain, that the man wasn't walking beside the woman, but rather pulling her. It wasn't Witch Woman, after all. He had a gun to her head.

Ponytail had Mel.

Chapter Thirty-One

I couldn't breathe. I couldn't think. My stomach lurched and my guts twisted. I wanted to rip his head off, do something, *anything*, to end this nightmare. I could only watch. If I made a move to stop him, he'd shoot her and I had no doubt he wouldn't give it a second thought. I've never felt more helpless in my life. I put one hand on the rough brick of the church and threw up. I wiped my mouth with my hand, wet from the rain, then spit, and wiped it again. I sank to my knees again and breathed in great gulps. I needed air. I needed strength. I needed a plan. But first, I needed God.

Lord, I know you knew this was coming. I know that in some way You'll make something good of this, but for the life of me I can't figure out what it could be. Please send angels to watch over Mel, over the rest of us, and over Road's End. Please lead me to what You want me to do to stop the devil in his tracks. Just tell me, and I'll do it. PLEASE, Lord, please just tell me. Don't let them take Mel from me. Keep her from harm, Father. We need Your Glory, Lord. We need to defeat the devil and show once more that Your Glory, Your Strength, Your Holiness are more than sufficient for all our needs. In Jesus' precious Name, I pray. Amen.

Those few seconds gave me time to catch my breath, slow down my heartbeat, and calm me enough that I could begin to plan. I started by calling Bristol.

The moment he answered, I blurted, "They've got Mel."

"How? How on earth? ..."

"I don't know, but I saw him dragging her in Molly's direction. He has a gun to her head." I tried to remain calm and gathered my thoughts. "If he hurts her, God help him."

"Where are you?"

"On the east side of the church behind that shrubbery."

"Okay. Stay there, I'm coming."

He arrived just two minutes later, but it was enough time for me to realize it must have been my fault they were able to get to Mel. I racked my brain trying to remember locking the backdoor after I left her at the table reading the Bible to Shrimp. I remembered making sure the front door was locked, but I couldn't remember locking the back. If she hadn't gotten up and locked it, then I'd left the door open—and gave Ponytail his chance to grab my wife. Any last-minute thought of locking the door would've been lost when George and Dewey tackled me.

I was the reason she had a gun to her head. It was my fault. I stood and waited for Bristol. I didn't hear him approaching, but suddenly he was in front of me. "Hey, you okay?"

I looked at him. "I will be—just as soon as we get her away from him."

"We will, Hugh. We will. If I don't ever do another thing in my life, I'll make good and sure we get Mel back safe and sound, and that those four get caught and sent to prison for the rest of their miserable, drug-dealing, murdering lives. I promise you that."

I knew he meant it, and I thanked God for my friend. It's funny that I never thought of Bristol as my best friend, but he is. He's as close as a brother could be, never thought twice about helping, advising, calming me down, playing jokes on me, or like now, carrying out impossible promises.

We stood there for a few minutes, thinking, and finally formulated a plan. We decided to go to the inn to see if SS was gone and if there was any clue as to where they were taking her or what they were planning to do with her. After looking around, we slipped out from behind the shrubbery ("Remind me I need to trim these shrubs, Hugh.") and across Rivermanse Lane to the inn. As I suspected, the back door was unlocked. I started to enter, but Bristol held me back. "Let me," he whispered. He stepped up the stairs and slowly opened the screen door. The back door wasn't latched, so all he had to do was push it open with the barrel of his gun. I followed closely behind, making sure no one was sneaking up on us.

I shut the door behind me as we entered the kitchen. The candle Mel was using to read the Bible by was still flickering. But there was no Mel, no Shrimp. I moved to the kitchen table and there, under the napkin holder next to a butcher knife he must have used to free Shrimp, was a note on the back of a convenience store/gas station receipt. "Let's make a deal."

They wanted to trade Melanie for Del.

For as awful as they looked physically, I had to admit they were smart. They knew a man would do anything for his wife, and that I'd have no choice but to turn Del over to them to get Mel back safe and sound. But even if we did there was still no guarantee they wouldn't kill her or come back at a later date and obliterate the entire town. We had to dig out the cancer—all it. All four of them. And soon.

Bristol motioned to me he was going to search the rest of the house, and I nodded. I looked around. No Grace. I'm sure they didn't take her with them because there's no way she'd go without shooting at least one of them. She must have left the inn for some reason before they came in and took Mel. Everything looked dull and drab—and it wasn't the absence of lighting that caused it. It was the absence of the love of my life. I dropped into the chair she had been sitting in before Ponytail or Witch Woman or both of them walked in and destroyed my life. I looked at the Bible she'd been reading from—the one I'd given her on our first anniversary—and smiled. She had editions of at least ten different translations, but this was always her go-to Bible, filled with handwritten notes along the edges, highlighted areas, and bits of paper or photos here and there she was using as bookmarks. The binding was so frayed and worn I wondered how it stayed together.

It was opened to 2 Samuel 22:13. "Out of the brightness of His presence bolts of lightning blazed forth."

I thought about that for a minute. Although I'd read that verse dozens of times, this time it hit home in a distinctly personal way—two ways, in fact. First of all, I knew I'd recognized those words when Hazel told me what the angel had imparted to her. He was quoting Scripture. Secondly, either Mel had deliberately read that passage to SuperShrimp, which seemed unlikely as that seemed like a strange verse to begin teaching to a non-believer, or I was being given a clue by God through His Word. Could my fear be affecting my thought process?

No, I was certain God was using the Bible Mel left behind to give me comfort, and perhaps a clue. But while I was definitely comforted, I had no idea what clue might be found in those words.

Bristol came down just then. "Nothing," he said, as he pulled out a chair and sat. "I don't know how they got in, but nothing else seems disturbed, and there's no one hiding here. Where's Grace? I thought you said she stayed with Mel."

"I don't know about Grace. I must have misspoken because she was at Sadie's when I left the bakehouse, but I wouldn't be surprised if she came here to check on Mel and poke Super Shrimp in the arm. So honestly, I have no idea where she is. But I can tell you how they got in. I left Mel and Shrimp here in the kitchen after I came home to check up on her. She and I closed the inside shutters on the windows both upstairs and down, then I checked to be sure the front door was locked and headed out the back. Normally I would have locked it behind me, but I guess I didn't this time. Right after that, George and Dewey tackled me, and any chance of my remembering to lock it was lost. If Mel didn't get up and lock it, then the door was open to anyone who checked to see if it was locked." I looked at Bristol and shook my head. "Any other time, my OCD would've compelled me to do it. I just got distracted. What have I done, Bristol?"

"You haven't done anything, Hugh. You're a human being who can't handle two hundred things at once. It just isn't possible. Besides, now that we know they have her we can begin to rescue her—and take them down in the process."

"I wish I had your enthusiasm and optimism, Bristol. I really do."

"Are you kidding me? Where do you think I learned to be enthusiastic and optimistic? Don't sell yourself short, Hugh. We can do this."

"No, Bristol," I said. "We *will* do this."

We had no one except ourselves to help unless we called in reinforcements. Perry, Leo, Frank (in the tunnel), Rudy and Joe were all occupied in other important ways. I didn't even want to think about bringing in George and Dewey at this point. Bristol told me he had to leave them to their own devices when he got my call about Mel, so who knew where they were. That left Grace.

"Should we?" It seemed like an awful thing to ask of my secretary.

"Well, if we don't, I'm not the one who has to tell her why we didn't."

"You've got a point. I'll give her a call."

Five minutes later, Grace stood dripping in the kitchen. "Let's go git these no-good thugs," she said. "Come on, time's a'wastin'."

"You're right, Grace," Bristol said, "but Mel's okay for now. They won't harm the only person they have to barter with."

I was frantic with worry. I prayed over and over that God would deliver her out of their hands, that the devil would be not only repelled, but sent scuttling away in utter defeat. We gave Grace the outline of our thrown-together plan, went back out into the storm (deliberating leaving the door unlocked in case we needed to get back inside in a hurry), and headed toward Molly.

We were there in under five minutes. No lights were on, but then we didn't imagine they'd welcome us with the porch light on and the living room lit up. Also, being dark inside the house gave them an advantage we didn't have—they didn't have to worry about lightning illuminating the yard and exposing them. We did. But so far, so good. We stopped at a stand of three ancient oak trees in Bristol's side yard that afforded us protection and concealed us from their view.

Molly is a small house built sometime in the late 18th century, shortly after the Revolutionary War. When Bristol renovated her, he was careful to keep the integrity of the house intact, and aside from some cosmetic touches that held to its former construction era and adding plumbing and electricity, the house looked much like it would have when it was originally built. I know that secondary to Mel's safety, he had to be worried the thugs would trash his home. I pity the man or woman who did, though.

We stood behind those trees for a minute or so trying to figure out if they were inside, while making sure they weren't sneaking up on us from another angle. The rain still made it difficult to see any farther than about two feet, so spotting someone would be more of a fluke than any particularly keen eyesight on our part.

Bristol motioned he would go around the back of the house to see if he could detect any movement inside, while Grace and I kept watch outside. Two windows that matched those on the front of the house were in the back, so he'd have to be careful he wasn't seen while checking things out. Two minutes later, he returned to us and said, "Nothing. I don't think anyone's been here since I left after my so-called nap. Everything looks the same as it did when I left. I doubt they'd have found the ladder to the attic, since I lean it against one wall in my bathroom when I don't need it to keep from tripping over it every time I walk past. It's nowhere in sight, so it must be in its usual spot, which means they're not hiding upstairs."

I didn't know whether to cry in relief or anguish. Finding Mel here would've been faster but trying to get to them would've caused serious damage to Molly, and I hated to have that happen. Bristol would've shot me on the spot if he knew what I was thinking, but I know how much pride he takes in his little home. But that left us with a problem. Where was Mel?

The only other logical destination was the church. The rear entrance was seldom used. In fact, I can't remember using it in the last six months, but that didn't mean the cartel guys wouldn't. Since the vandalism that occurred during that miserable blizzard we had last winter, Bristol had installed a new lock, so unless they found a way to break in through the back, they were out of luck. They'd have to use the front door. I hoped Perry remembered to listen for the secret knock (I felt like a third grader with his treehouse gang). Both Leo and Hazel had been given the secret knock, as well, so I was pretty sure no one had come in through the front either. That left us with … nothing.

We sneaked through the cemetery to get to the front door to check on the Parrys and Leo before we took off for parts truly unknown. They were all fine, and Perry didn't have any more reports of shadows or voices. We were at a standstill.

"I don't get it," I said. "I know I saw them. I know it was Mel, and he was holding a gun to her head." That last part was hard to say. "If they're not at Molly or here at the church, where else could they have gone?"

Grace spoke up. "Their car?"

"But they have four flat tires, Grace. What did they think they were going to do with that useless car? Levitate?"

There was silence for a moment, until Grace snapped her fingers and said, "But they have phones, I'll bet. They're going to hold her at the car until someone drives out here to get her."

I looked at Bristol, then Grace, then back to Bristol.

"She's right, Hugh. We can look around at other places across the street from the church, like's Grace's house, and the Wyandotte's, but I'd lay good money that she's right. It doesn't matter if they have four flat tires. They have reinforcements coming—probably from Richmond—to pick them up when they're done here, and to take Mel with them if they don't get Del."

It wasn't good news, but at least we had a starting point.

Chapter Thirty-Two

Grace volunteered to check out the other houses on the short street across from the church, among them the house she shared with Ruby Mae. She was back in ten minutes and said, "Nope. No one in sight, and when I stopped at a couple of the houses, they said they hadn't seen or heard anything. I think it has to be the car."

Bristol put his hand on my shoulder and said, "At least we know what we're doing now, Hugh. There are lots of overgrown trees and bushes along that stretch and we can easily sneak up on them if we don't use any flashlights or make any noise."

"Or better yet," Grace said, "we can go cross lots behind those houses"—she pointed to the street she'd just come from—"and bypass that stretch of road altogether. I'd want to warn the folks I just talked to 'bout what we're doin' so they don't go takin' a shot at us, but I think it'd be easier and faster. What do you think?"

"Whatever will get us to Mel the fastest and quietest is fine by me," I said. I was itching to get going, to do something, *anything*.

"I think Grace is right." He turned to her. "Do you want to go tell those people not to kill us, and we'll follow you? Both of you have your guns and ammo? Do you need to reload? Got your phones in case we get separated? Remember, volume muted and cover the light from the phone if you get or send a text."

We nodded. I think Bristol knew we already had done everything he was asking about and we were as prepared as we could be under the lousy circumstances, but he wanted to make sure—it was his way of settling his nerves. Yes, he'd covered a lot of cases in his life as a detective in the big city, but those didn't include the welfare of his friend's wife. I knew Bristol would do anything he could to save Mel. The three of us had become fast friends and he wasn't about to let her get hurt. But there was always that one thing that could trip us up. The one thing we couldn't see, hear, or predict.

But God could. It was all in His capable Hands now.

Grace took the lead, while Bristol and I checked out the street and yards just to be sure no one was lurking around. She talked to the residents—there were only four, in addition to her and Ruby Mae—and I didn't know any of them personally. They weren't churchgoers and I vowed then that I'd do what I'd put off for too long and talk to them one of these days about the state of their salvation. They were senior citizens like most all Road's End and while the Lord had allowed them to live long lives, that meant their death—and their eternity—were closer than ever.

We met up with Grace in the backyard of the house farthest down the street to begin our trek across the back lots which amounted to nothing more than woods. Overgrown woods, at that—small, medium, and large trees, saplings, bushes, fallen branches, weeds, you name it. I tried not to think about the snakes and spiders that were out and about. I hoped the rain would keep them at bay, but just in case, I tucked my pantlegs into my socks.

Bristol noticed and said, "Great idea, Hugh." He did the same thing. Grace was wearing jeans with boots, so she was all set.

"You know, Hugh, this would be a good time for the troops to show up. What exactly did Mack say about that?"

"Well, he's not supposed to be doing anything, but the president is behind him—and us—all the way. Far as I know, Mack has notified the Virginia State Police again—they must think we're nuts—and they'll send someone a.s.a.p. But with this weather, I don't know. I guess we're on our own for a while, at least."

Bristol nodded, looked at Grace, then me, and said, "Well, let's get to it then."

We began to walk. Bristol took the lead, followed by Grace, and I brought up the rear. At first it was just a matter of not getting smacked in the face by branches and vines that were snapping back from Bristol and Grace passing through them before me—not easy in the dark. A few minutes in, though, the deep pockets of mud and water appeared, and we were literally sloshing our way through them. How that much water penetrated the solid wall of vegetation is beyond my understanding, but it was there and there was nothing I could do about it but continue to slosh.

I was looking down and not watching where I was going. After all, forward was the only direction I could go, anyway, and putting my feet into the holes left by Grace was the best way to do it. I didn't notice that Bristol had stopped, and I slammed into Grace.

"Oh, gosh, I'm sorry, Grace," I whispered. "Why did we stop?"

Bristol turned around, put his finger to his lips, and I shut up. He hunkered down and Grace and I did the same, although I couldn't help but wonder if I was just asking for a snake bite on my rear end. Bristol motioned ahead, then held up his hand for silence.

I was running on adrenaline and knew I'd be out for the count when this was all behind us. I like to consider myself healthy and fit, even though I devour food like a piranha, but these last few hours—the whole day and the previous one, in fact—were beyond my physical capabilities. The only thing holding me up was my clothes. That and Mel. I'd want to collapse after I found Mel and took her home safe and sound. I prayed continually.

After five minutes, Bristol motioned us forward. While standing upright was certainly a relief, I knew we still had a hundred yards or so to go if my recollection of the land around that area was correct. I'd never had any reason to know before that. Ruby Mae and Grace were the only people I ever visited on that street, and the jungle of tangled, overgrown, and out-of-control vegetation was never on my radar. I doubted I would ever forget it after this.

Bristol slowed the pace gradually as we neared where we thought their car was stranded with its four flat tires. As we nearly tiptoed our way toward what we hoped was the edge of the road, I could hear voices. Both Bristol and Grace turned to me with fingers to their mouths. They must think I'm a blabbermouth. I nodded.

Another step. Voices. Another step. Louder voices. We listened. Ponytail seemed to be ripping someone—probably SuperShrimp—up and down for getting himself captured and taken out of the game. SS wasn't taking it well and we heard a slap, a sharp one at that.

"Hey, you keep your hands off me, Jake. Who made you the boss, anyway?"

"*I* did, you little runt! Now get over there, sit down, and shut your mouth. If you're lucky, I won't tell Mugs all about your stupidity."

Mugs ... now that's an original name for a thug. Why not Bonnie and Clyde?

"Me? Why me? I got a flesh wound, but Patch is layin' down in the middle of that road down there, just a 'bleedin' everywhere. Now *he's* the stupid one!"

"Forget Patch. If we're lucky, he'll bleed out and we won't ever have to look at his ugly face again."

"What're we gonna do with that woman?" That was Wanda.

"Not sure. I'll leave it up to Mugs. In the meantime, we keep her here where no one can git to her and we rip this rinky-dink, hole-in-the-wall town apart until we find Jackson. I don't care how we get him, dead or alive, but I *want* him."

"How long before Mugs ..."

"I have no idea, Wanda, but you'll be the second to know when he does. How's that for an answer?"

"Shut up, Jake. You always were a jerk."

"Oh yeah? Well, you're a ..."

And then I heard the sweetest sound in the world—Mel's voice. "Hey, you guys. You might not care if you go to hell, but I don't have to hear your filthy mouths while you're getting there. And believe me, that's exactly where you're heading. Just remember that the next time you draw a gun, because sooner or later you're going to be at the other end of that barrel—and hello, lake of fire."

"What's she yammering about?" That was Jake.

"Whatever you do, don't ask her. She'll make you listen to Bible stories all night. She's relentless."

Wanda piped up. "Let me at her. I'll shut her up."

"Wanda, I don't know what happened in your life to make you so calloused, but please listen when I tell you your soul is in mortal danger." That was my sweet wife, always trying to save souls. "But if you ever try to shut me up, I'll tear your hair from your scalp and rip your nose off your face. Just so you know."

Bristol and Grace looked at me with their mouths hanging open. Apparently, they'd never seen the warrior side of Mel. It was impressive.

There was silence for a moment. I was afraid she might have pushed her hand too far, but Wanda answered, "Yeah, yeah, missy. I've heard all about your Bible stories and I'm not buyin' a word of it."

"Well, if you ever want to talk, I'll be happy to answer any questions."

"Okay, okay, enough chit-chat, ladies. We need to get back to work. Runt, do you think you can keep it together long enough to get back to work?"

"Don't call me Runt."

"What? You want me to use your real name? Huh, Claudius?"

"Shut up, Jake."

Well then, I guess we knew they weren't best buddies. And SuperShrimp's real name is Claudius.

"Wanda, you stay here with Bible lady. Call if you run into any trouble, but I think you can take her easy enough if she gives you too many commandments." He laughed, slapped someone on the back, and the two men must have wandered off.

We waited until their voices drifted away. I wanted to charge in and get Mel right off the bat, but Bristol held up his hand, and we waited some more.

It's a good thing we waited. In less than a minute, Jake was back—he must have sent Shrimp on alone—and said, "I got a better idea. Let's keep her with us. They might think twice before shooting if they think she'll get hit." He walked over to the car, yanked open the door, and said, "Hey, Bible lady, you're comin' with us."

"Okay, Jake. Whatever you say."

"Cut it out, lady. No one's polite when they're ordered around."

"Obviously you're wrong, Jake, or at least you're running around with the wrong crowd. Some people are polite regardless of the circumstances."

"Well, if you think it's gonna get you any brownie points, you can jest forget it. I'd shoot you as soon as I would a rattlesnake."

"Well, I sure *hope* you'd shoot a rattlesnake! I hate snakes. I sure hope there aren't any in Heaven, or if there are, that I lose my fear of them." Mel was doing a good job of confusing the dickens out of Jake.

"Quit your yammerin', woman. Get out here and don't do anything fishy. Remember, I'm the one with the gun."

"True, Jake," she said, "but I'm the one with the Lord. I don't think we're evenly matched."

He swore, grabbed her arm, and jerked her forward. "Let's go."

As I inched forward, I caught a quick glimpse of who I assumed was her as she passed by our hiding place. It was all I could do to keep from trying to get to her, but I wouldn't have made it six inches before I was so tangled up I couldn't move.

After a minute or so, Bristol said, "Actually, this is a good thing. Since we don't know when Mugs—who names these guys, anyway?—is arriving to take her away, this gives us a chance to get her before the others even get here." He started to move forward, then said, "I'm not too sure we're going to get out this way. I thought I saw a clear spot to our left on the way here. Maybe we can spot it again and get out of this brush. It'll be on our right."

Fifteen minutes later we stood in the middle of a small grassy, wet, muddy area that, for whatever reason, didn't have any trees or other vegetation on it. "Probably the landing site of some alien craft that left radiation so nothing could grow here," Bristol joked.

"That's good to hear, Bristol. We have a witness stashed in our historic tunnel so thugs won't kill him, so now they're trying to kill us, two old men running around trying to be helpful heroes, Lumpy bleeding all over our historic bricked street—maybe I shouldn't have shot a hole in it, come to think of it—one embarrassed and shot-up little guy who wants to prove himself, more thugs on the way, a rainstorm that just won't quit, one Ponytail guy, along with an armed and crazy witch with a grudge against other women, dragging my wife around with them, and now we're going have radiation poisoning."

"Don't forget the aliens, Hugh. If they landed here, they've probably colonized and could appear at any moment. And who knows if they're friendly or hostile. It would explain an awful lot about this town, wouldn't it?"

"Gee, Bristol, you're such a Pollyanna, always trying to make me feel good."

"I do my best, Hugh. I do my best."

"Shut up, you two. I haven't eaten since around six this morning, so I'm starvin', and you know how I get when I'm starvin'."

"That's right, Grace. We need to get this wrapped up in time for supper. Well, suppertime actually passed around three hours ago, but we'll eat a late one just this once. Can your tummy wait that long?"

Grace punched Bristol who almost knocked me down while dodging her. We were turning into a vaudeville act. Might have been the hunger, panic, or fatigue. Probably the radiation.

"Okay, since we don't have to be quiet, let's blast out of this mess, and go get Mel."

"I'm with you, Bristol."

"Will you guys jest shut up and *move*? I'm hungry!"

Deborah Dee Harper

Chapter Thirty-Three

Fifteen minutes later we were out of the jungle and back in the yard of the house where we originally began our journey. Grace went to the door to tell them we were finished and if they heard or saw anything else, to give us a call. She came back and said, "Okay, they know Mel's with them, so they'll be careful. No shooting."

We resumed our slinking from tree to tree and house to house until we were back to Gloucester Street. Since we had no way of knowing where they were, we had to assume they were everywhere. I wanted to go back to the church, but I knew Perry would be sure not to let them in, so we decided to skip the church for now and split up to try to catch sight of them.

"Listen," Bristol told us, "I'm not sure if they're still together or not. They might have realized splitting up wasn't such a great idea and are staying together this time. But that means there are four people or five if Runt's with them, and that makes a big bunch of people to keep hidden, particularly since Mel will be working against them at every move. Grace, I think you should go with Hugh. It makes sense they'd go to places they haven't been to yet, so I think we can rule out Frank's place, and the inn."

"Remember, I left that door unlocked, Bristol, so we could get back in if we needed to. They might have gone back inside if for no other reason than to make Mel fix them something to eat."

"That's right. In fact, if I were one of them, I'd be hungry too. And they did catch a whiff of what Mel made for supper when they first came to the Inn." He looked around. "Okay, I'm open to suggestions."

"They might stay away from Sadie's because they know someone in there can shoot and shoot very well. If they knew who it was, they'd leave town in a heartbeat. We haven't been to the Wyandotte's place yet, so maybe we should look there. Why don't Grace and I head over there and talk to Winnie and Martha. It would be nice if George and Dewey were there, too, but I'm not counting on it."

Bristol nodded. "I think you're right, Hugh, and that makes it extra hard because we can't just assume that a body or shadow we see is a bad guy. Could be them."

"Well, if anyone runs across them, we'll just call the others so we're all on the same page. Grace and I will check out the Wyandotte place and Sadie's, just in case someone wants payback for Patch's nasty wound. None of us are going to be able to look into the inn because Mel and I shut the inside shutters both upstairs and down, thinking we were doing the right thing. Boy, will I be glad when this night is over. I thought we were so clever, and now I've kept us from being able to see inside the inn ourselves."

"Don't beat yourself up, Hugh. You had no way of knowing and I'd have done the same thing."

"Guys," Grace inserted, "have you forgotten I'm hungry?"

"No, we haven't, Grace, but remember to use your powers for good." Bristol tried to dodge her punch but didn't quite make it. "Ouch! You pack quite a wallop."

"You oughta see what I can do when I'm not weak from hunger."

"I can vouch for that, Bristol. She can be ferocious. You know, I wonder what's keeping the police. I called Mack an hour ago, and he said he'd let them know something was happening and to get here as quick as they could."

Bristol nodded. "Yeah, but this storm is a big one and the lightning is fierce. It'd be hard to bring a chopper in under those circumstances, and let's face it—if they're driving here, they've got a long way to come. We're way out here in the sticks."

"True. I'm just anxious. Let's get to it, guys. God bless us all, watch your backs, and let's get my Mel back and end this miserable night."

Grace and Bristol nodded their heads and gave me a thumbs-up. Bristol headed for the inn to look into some of the outbuildings, while Grace and I went to the Wyandotte house.

I could see the curtains move just a smidge before Winnie opened the door a crack when I knocked. "Is that you, Pastor? Grace? Are you alone?"

"We sure are, Winnie. Can we come in for a minute?"

"Why, of course you can. Come in, come in. How does some hot coffee sound?"

"Sounds great, Winnie, but the bad guys captured Mel and we don't have time right now. Can we get a raincheck?"

Both ladies gasped and put their hands to their mouths. "Oh no, not Melanie. Where did they take her?"

"Not quite sure, but that's what Bristol, Grace, and I are going to find out. We just wanted to make sure you ladies were all right. Everything locked up and closed? Lights out?" I looked around—pitch black. "Well, I guess you've got that one covered. Any idea where your husbands are?"

"The last I knew they were heading out to finish their work on their ... what did they call that, Martha?"

Martha looked off into space for a moment, then said with a snap of her fingers, "Oh, you mean that thing they were going to work on? Let's see. It had something to do with fighting or winning or hurting somebody." She shrugged. "I'm sorry, Pastor, I can't remember anything else. Oh, wait! I do *too* know something. They called it Roy! Yes, Roy. That should help you!" She beamed, pleased as punch at her brilliance.

"Yes, Martha. Yes, that does help. Thanks so much. Well, ladies, if you see your husbands, please make them stay here and not wander around out there. They could easily get hurt, and even though I know they're trying to help, we don't them to become innocent victims."

"No, no, we don't," Winnie said, sadly, before brightening up and saying. "Well, if you change your mind, come on back and we'll make you some coffee. We have some doughnuts, too!"

We sneaked out the front door and hid behind a large maple tree that was dropping leaves like mad with all the rain. "Well, at least it wasn't KEN," I said.

"Who's Ken?"

"Sorry, Grace, I thought you knew. KEN is their early warning system, and ..." I held my hand up to stop her. " ... before you ask, I have no idea why they call it KEN. And therefore, I have no idea why they call this ... this ... whatever it is, ROY."

"Odd people live in this town, Pastorman."

"Odd people visiting this town, too."

"Well, ya certainly got that right."

We stood under a tree dripping both water and leaves. Grace said, "Where to now?"

I looked over at the inn and said, "I just have a feeling about the inn, Grace. Even if we can't see inside, maybe we can see something, or someone, outside. Maybe we can hear something. There shouldn't be a soul in there, so if we hear voices, we'll know there's someone hiding out, even if we don't know who."

"Sounds good, Pastorman."

For once, I was glad Road's End had only one working streetlight, and even that one had begun to flicker lately. Wouldn't be long before the whole town was in the dark all the time, much the way I feel most every day. Since the kitchen was the most likely spot to hear voices, and there were only curtains across the kitchen windows, not shutters, we slithered our way beside the house until we reached that window. The rain was still coming down which made it difficult, but we agreed we couldn't make out any voices or movement.

"Should we go inside?"

"I wish I knew, Grace. If one or both of them are in there and we just can't hear them and get caught, then Bristol's left out here all by his lonesome to face these guys. I think we'd better leave the inn for now and get back to the church. Sound okay to you?"

"You're the boss—except when we're at work, of course."

"Of course. That goes without saying, Grace." I smiled. Some things never change.

We followed the same path I'd used with George and Dewey just a couple of hours before. Once we reached the first stand of trees, we stopped to listen. Rain. All I could hear was rain. I was just about to cross the lane when Grace grabbed my coat by the sleeve, put her finger to her mouth, then pointed upward. She mouthed, "Voices."

I strained to hear. Nothing. I gave her a questioning look; afterwards I wondered why I bothered. We couldn't see an inch in front of our noses. Just as I was ready to resume our journey, I heard something.

And then the cold, dark lump in my stomach started to tumble.

"Dagnabit, Dewey, git that thing outta my face."

"Sorry, George, jest tryin' to git it tied."

George and Dewey? George and Dewey *in a tree*? Could this night get any worse? Now we had thugs—with more on their way—holding my wife at gunpoint, incessant rain, and two old men in a tree above our heads with lightning dancing here, there, and everywhere.

I whispered as loudly as I could without blowing my vocal chords forever, "George! Dewey! Get down here this *minute*. Don't you know lightning could strike that tree any second now?"

"Did you hear someone, George?"

"Just the rain, Dewey. Just the rain."

"Get down here right now!"

"Okay," George said, "I heard that. I'll bet it's one of them bad guys tryin' to keep us from our sworn duty."

"Yer right, George. Private 'vesti .... Okay, okay. P.I.s don't never let anythin' git in their way of their never-endin' battle for truth and justice!"

They're quoting from the Superman show?

"Watch it, Dewey. You almost fell outta the tree. Now concentrate."

"I am, I am, George. It's just hard to handle this wire in the rain. It's gettin' slippery. 'Sides, I can't see the darned thing. Wish lightning would come and light us up for a minute."

I groaned, which isn't easy when you're whispering. *Wire in a tree in the rain with lightning all around? You just might get yourself lit up, Dewey. What next?*

And then it came.

"Here, Dewey, hold it up high, like this. It's easier to handle when it's pointed straight up as far as you can get it."

I'd had enough. I had no idea what they were up to. ROY, I guess. Standing beneath a tree in a thunderstorm was stupid enough, but Grace and I had little choice in the matter. Those two, though, were going to get charbroiled if they didn't get out of that tree immediately.

I started to climb. "Hugh! You'll git yourself killed too!" Grace grabbed onto my boot, but it was wet and muddy, and she had no chance of holding on.

"I'll have to take that chance, Grace. Tell Mel I love her. And if these two should happen to survive, tell them they're idiots." I groped for another branch, then another. I felt something pelting me, but I mistook it for small branches snapping this way and that. Nope, it was Dewey beating me on the head with his wire.

"Stop it, you idiot!" That was me, the kind and compassionate pastor acting out his Christian beliefs. I couldn't have gotten much farther away from the way I should be acting if I'd taken up residence on Betelgeuse. I apologized to the Lord and asked for protection from the storm, the bad guys, the lightning, and perhaps the worst of all, my temper. I took a deep breath and almost sucked in a quart of water through my nostrils. Two more branches and I was eye-to-eye with a very surprised Dewey.

"Hey, George! Look who came to visit!"

George looked over his shoulder. "Hugh, what on earth are you doing up here when you should be looking for bad guys? There'll be plenty a'time to play treehouse or whatever it is you're doin' up here when things're back to normal. Shame on you."

I discarded my pastor persona for a moment to grit my teeth, fry their eyeballs with a scorching look, and say, "Get outta this tree this very minute, you two id ….uh, men. You're gonna get electrocuted up here. Don't you know anything about trees and lightning and dying?"

"Whatcha mean 'dyin',' pastor?"

"You're going to die if you don't get out of the tree this instant! I mean it, and drop that wire … "

"It's ROY, Hugh. We call it ROY."

"Drop ROY then, and get down and away from this tree before you get struck."

"You mean by God?!"

"No, George. I mean by lightning." (*Or me, whichever comes first.*) "Now get down here!"

I could hear them muttering to each other about how grumpy their pastor was these past few days and how they'd have to investigate ("That's 'vestigate, George.") me when this was all over with and make their report to the Lions Club, who apparently held some power over me as a pastor. Dewey argued it should be the Rotary Club because his brother-in-law, now dead, bless his soul, used to be president of a chapter in the early 60s, but since we had neither the Lions Club nor Rotary Club in Road's End, they'd have to start their own chapter and maybe that should be their next project or they could make up their own club and not let me in—and they were off and running in all directions—except down the tree. Just listening to them made me short of breath. Don't they ever stop to expel carbon dioxide and take in some oxygen?

I tried to calm myself, which isn't all that easy when you're living from one second to the next, always wondering if you're going to see a great light and then see *another* great Light after the first great light killed you. *Lord, help me, I'm starting to sound like them.*

"Come on, guys. We can settle all that later. Right now, let's just get out of this tree, okay? And when this is all done and the bad guys are captured and Mel is back with us, we can all sit down and talk about expelling me from your treehouse club over doughnuts and coffee at Sadie's."

"Now that's what I'm talkin' 'bout, George! He's finally talkin' common sense. He oughta hang out with us more often."

By the time I got them out of the tree, the guys from Richmond could've driven here, built a house, added a sunroom, and died of old age.

"Guys, listen. I'm sorry I sounded so grumpy up there but being under a tree during a storm is bad enough. Being *in* a tree, with wire, no less, is suicidal. I was worried. You could've been killed. How on earth did you get up there in the first place?"

"How'd *you* git up there, Hugh?" That was George, the inquisitive one.

"He musta flown up, George." And that was Dewey, the one with all the answers.

And this was me, the one who was going to throttle both of them, then have a heart attack from the stress I've been under. "Men, I climbed up, just like you apparently did. But we're all okay now, so let's get back to rescuing Mel, okay?"

"Mel?"

"You know, George, Hugh's wife Mel? Pretty with light brown hair? Lives in the inn with Hugh."

"I know who Mel is, you ninny. I meant why are we rescuing Mel?"

"Because the bad guys have her," I said. "And I want her back."

"Don't blame ya there, Hugh. Mel makes a darned good cup of coffee. Not as good as Sadie does, mind you, but still passable."

I turned to Grace. She grabbed them both by their coats, jerked them toward her and said, "Shut up."

They shut up.

Well, things were looking up. We knew where George and Dewey were—underfoot—and no one died. I called Bristol and as quickly and quietly as I could, told him the story of their stu … bravery. Bristol seemed to be finding a lot of humor in this whole situation. This was the second time in one evening I'd had to wait for him to stop laughing.

"I'm done, Hugh. Wait a minute while I wipe my eyes. Your life should be a sitcom."

"Or maybe one of those investigative shows where people disappear and nobody ever finds them stashed in an historic tunnel by a deranged pastor."

"Yeah, but I like the sitcom idea better."

"I'm glad you're having such a good time, buddy."

"I am too. Where are you off to now?"

"I think I'll check back with Perry, and make sure the bad guys haven't somehow gotten inside the church. I kinda hope they have. At least I'd know where Mel was."

"Listen, Hugh, I know you're worried about Mel. I am too. But she's a smart lady and if I know her, she's giving them more trouble than she's worth to them. They might just drop her off somewhere and leave town."

"Don't I wish. But I'll bet the bigwig at the cartel has quite a bounty on Del, and these guys and Witch Woman are going to do everything in their power to get it. I think we can keep them from Del, but I want her back before we accomplish anything else."

"I know, Hugh. I know. Don't worry, we will. I looked in all the outbuildings and no one's there, so I'm going to see if anyone's up at Emma's place. We have to find them sooner or later; we're running out of places to look. Good thing we don't live in a big city. You head over to the church with the gang—maybe you should stash George and Dewey there—and check things out. I'll be around. If I hear or see anything, you'll know pronto."

"Sounds good. Same here. Careful."

I stood there for a moment and prayed that the Lord would protect us against the evil roaming the streets of Road's End—with my wife, no less. And that included Francine and her chicken cohorts who happened to pass between Grace and me, just looking for trouble on a stormy night. *Wait until Sadie find out what you've been up to, Francine. You just wait.* I turned to tell Grace, George, and Dewey we were going to head to the church.

But I couldn't. Dewey and George were gone—again. Maybe they joined Francine's gang.

I couldn't believe it. "Where the heck did they go this time?"

"Who? Oh no, those two?" Grace whipped around in a circle. No men. "For being so old'n all, they're pretty nimble."

We looked in all directions, even up, but saw no one. No bad guys, no Mel, no Detective Duo. Just a flock of chicken escapees. So much for stashing George and Dewey at the church. I shrugged and said, "I can't wait any longer. We have to check things out over there and if we find them on the way, great. If we don't, we're no worse off than we were a while ago."

Two minutes later, we were on the church grounds. Before going to the front door to knock, though, I wanted to check out the yard. It was getting soggier by the minute and that made it slicker and harder to traverse without falling, which I did twice, and Grace did once. We were just turning the corner to the back of the building when I saw a flash of light. But it wasn't lightning this time.

It was headlights. The reinforcements had arrived.

But not ours. Theirs.

Chapter Thirty-Four

"Do you see what I saw, Grace?"

She nodded. "This night couldn't get any worse."

"Don't say that. It just might." I thought for a few seconds. "Okay, I'm letting Bristol know …"

"Never mind, Hugh. I'm right behind you."

I whirled around. "Boy, I'm glad to see you. Everything okay up at Emma's?"

"Yep. I told 'em we were looking for Mel and not to shoot. The grounds looked clear, so I decided to hook up with you guys down here."

"The reinforcements are here. Hope there aren't any more than four. That would be bad enough, but any more than that and we're doomed."

Grace smacked me on the arm and said, "Pastor, we aren't ever doomed with the Lord on our side. Remember, 'The Lord is my light and my salvation—whom shall I fear?' and 'The Lord is the stronghold of my life—of whom shall I be afraid?' Right?"

I smiled as I realized immediately that Grace was quoting Scripture—the first verse of Psalm 27, to be precise. I'm blessed to have such a woman as a secretary. She keeps me on the straight and narrow at work, and Mel does a fine job of it at home. I'm a twice-blessed and much looked-after man.

"I know you're right, Grace. I'm just tired. And wet and dirty and frantic. I need to find Mel and know she's all right."

"We will, Pastorman. We will. I don't care if they've brought a dozen yahoos with 'em, we're gonna be victorious because God is walking before us."

Bristol, the more practical one among us, spoke up. "True, Grace, but we still need to hide in the shrubs." After we settled into the wet, prickly bushes, he said, "We need a plan. Now."

Frantically, I searched my mind for an idea. We still didn't know if anyone was inside the building, so we had to assume someone *was,* just as we had to assume someone was in every other building in town.

What a mess. I needed to focus and so much was going on, I had no idea where to go or what to do first. Just then a flash of lightning illuminated the yard and the façade of the church.

That's when I saw it.

In the window just above Bristol's head was a hymnal propped up against the glass. It was a miracle the sky lit up just as I was looking at that window. I would never have seen it through this driving rain. The glass is original to the church, making it around 250 years old, and I allow only candles on the sills. Only on Christmas, Easter, and weddings do I make an exception for wreathes and flower arrangements. Only three people in the world know how much I hate anyone using the windowsills of that historic church, and two of them were with me, sitting in the pouring rain in the middle of a bunch of thick, scratchy bushes. The third one was Mel. There was no reason whatsoever for that hymnal to be there—unless Mel set it there. She knew if I saw it, I'd understand what it meant.

And what it meant, thank the Lord, was that Mel was inside the church.

"This is it, guys. She's here. There's the proof." I pointed to the hymnal, although they had more trouble seeing it than I did.

"If Mel didn't put that there, someone's in big trouble," Grace said. "Big trouble. I pity that poor creature."

"How do you know Witch Woman or Ponytail didn't put it there?"

"Bristol, my man, can you honestly see either of those two picking up a church hymnal, leafing through it, then putting it on the windowsill?"

He grinned. "You've got a point. So, we know she's in there, which means that Ponytail and WW are in there too. And maybe Runt, too, but he's no problem."

I added, "And Hazel, Perry, and Leo. I hope they're unharmed. I don't know what I'd do if any of them were hurt. Where do we go from here?"

"Well, I think the first thing we should do is find out how many of their friends just arrived. You two stay here and I'll take a peek."

"Careful, Hugh."

"Yeah, watch yourself, Pastorman."

"Guys, I'm only moving five feet."

"True," Grace said in her caring way, "but you're not the most graceful guy around. You could break your leg sittin' in your chair."

"I'll watch it, Grace. Thanks for your concern." I crawled (so as not to break my leg by standing on it) the five feet to the front edge of the church, then slowly peeked around the corner. I saw four men; at least I hoped they were men. The women in that cartel seem to be extra prickly. They were standing around in the rain inspecting four flat tires as if their being there might change the situation. It didn't.

I crawled back and whispered, "Four guys. Not too bright, either. Standing in the rain looking at flat tires." Of course, I was kneeling in the rain watching them standing in the rain looking at flat tires, so I guess I couldn't say much. "What next? Should we simply confront them? I don't know if any of our guns will even shoot in this rain. Bristol, you're the expert. What do you think?"

"I don't think we should confront them right now. We have bigger problems to handle at the moment."

"What pr ..." I followed his finger as he pointed toward the intersection of Rivermanse Lane and Gloucester Street. "Oh no, no. Please, someone tell me I'm seeing things."

No one answered. They were too busy watching George, Dewey, Martha, and Winnie marching down the street, weapons in hand, heading straight for the four newly-arrived, not very bright, but well-armed men from the cartel.

It was going to be a massacre.

Chapter Thirty-Five

I hung my head in misery. Those people were going to die before my eyes unless I did something immediately. But what? What could I possibly do to stop the inevitable? I was frozen to the muddy ground, helpless to prevent what I knew was going to happen.

"Hugh, I'm going around the back to the other side of the church. Grace is coming with me. Hugh! Are you with me?"

I turned my head and looked at Bristol. "Uh, yes, I'm with you, Bristol. I just can't believe what I'm seeing."

Grace touched my arm and whispered, "What you're seeing is a bunch of people who, despite their being nuts most of the time—okay, all the time—love Mel and you and this itty-bitty town they call home. And you know what I think? I think they're sick and tired of bad guys makin' themselves at home and shootin' and explodin' and kidnappin' and talkin' nasty. I think they're takin' their town back."

I looked at her and grinned. She could be so wise sometimes. "You're right, Grace, and they can want to take their town back all they want, but these guys aren't about to listen to four senior citizens." Grace pointed to the road.

George had moved out in front of the group, still holding his gun, which still looked like a cap gun. *Oh, Lord, protect him ... them ... all of us.*

Then Dewey stepped out with his trusty stick and joined George. They just stood there looking at the bad guys who were, in turn, laughing their heads off. One of them slapped another on the chest with the back of his hand. "Hey, Mugs, think we can handle it?" Mugs had dirty blond, or maybe just dirty, hair and was wearing a wife-beater tee shirt. *Mugs must be the fashion idol SuperShrimp worships.*

As if on cue, Martha and Winnie stepped out from behind their husbands and took their place beside their respective mate. Martha held a rolling pin, and Winnie carried a cast iron frying pan. The cartel guys laughed harder.

I turned to say something to Grace and Bristol, but they were gone. Must've gone to the other side as they'd planned. That left me not knowing what to do. I decided staying put and doing my best to protect the four senior citizens was the best thing I could do at the moment. There was just one thing wrong with that plan. I'm not a great shot, and I'm sure the bad guys were—or were at least comfortable with their guns. I'd feel more comfortable hauling around a tank in my pocket that I planned to throw with deadly accuracy at the bad guys and stop 'em in their tracks.

Well, I knew that wasn't going to happen so I'd have to rely on my skills with a gun—namely, none—and do the best I could. But what if my best wasn't good enough? Then I remembered what Grace had said just a few minutes before. I bowed my head and asked the Lord for forgiveness. I had let the enemy plant fear in my heart, and forgot, momentarily, that our Heavenly Father was with us—all of us—during this mess.

"Okay, devil, you just watch what happens next." I had no idea what that would be, but God did and that was good enough for me. The four of my friends lined up in the street walked as one toward the bad guys who were slapping one another on the back in glee at the sight of four senior citizens trying to defend their town with what amounted to a toy, a long stick, and kitchen utensils.

Closer and closer they walked. Harder and harder the other guys laughed. My heart beat faster than Sadie's cookies disappear on a Saturday morning. Speaking of Sadie, where was she? I should've been relieved that our star shooter wasn't with them, but that wasn't like her. I had an awful feeling in the pit of my stomach, and it wasn't hunger. Well, part of it was—okay, most of it was—but not this latest feeling. This was different. This was that "cold bacon grease mixed with lemonade" feeling deep in the pit of my stomach. The fierce foursome walked closer, the bad guys … wait, the bad guys weren't laughing quite as hard. Why would four obviously well-armed guys stop laughing at four old people? Maybe they wondered what was going on. Later on, I decided it was because the four were so obviously low on weapons, but high on guts, that the cartel guys began to wonder what made them so confident—or stupid, as the case may be.

And just like that, the bulb turned on.

Well, not exactly a bulb, but even better. The lightning bolt that split the sky and hit something terribly close to us, lit the scene as if it were noon on a sunny Virginia day. It lasted only a millisecond, but in that instant, I could see Joe, Rudy, Emma, and Sadie sneaking up behind them—behind the cars, in fact. They must have travelled nearly the same path cross-lots that the three of us had just a while before. With the bad guys occupied by the ludicrous sight of pretty much unarmed senior citizens, the other four could walk the short distance up the road and hide behind the car the reinforcements arrived in.

Well, that evened things up a little, but both Emma and Sadie, while formidable in the word department, were nevertheless pretty lame in the fighting-battles-with-really-nasty-men department. But again, I misjudged my friends. *What are you trying to teach me, Lord?*

Sadie gave no warning shot. She told me later they didn't deserve one. I saw her stand up, move to the side of the car with the flat tires, aim her gun, and pull the trigger. A guy wearing a red jacket screamed, grabbed his right thigh, and fell to the ground. Before the others could react, Joe stood, aimed, and shot another one wearing a denim jacket in *his* thigh. Another scream. Another one down.

With both Red and Denim hurt, the other two finally figured out they were being shot at from behind. They turned, guns drawn, and the Fearsome Foursome advanced toward the un-shot men who had their backs to them. And the battle began in earnest. My phone rang, I pulled it from my shirt pocket, slapped Bristol in the face, and answered, "Yeah?"

"What the heck is going on?"

"I think God is leading us into a mighty battle."

"With senior citizens?"

"Yep, you and I haven't even pulled the trigger. I might just go home and get some soup, as soon as we find Mel."

"I'll be right behind you. Watch yourself, Hugh. The others are still inside with Mel. They're bound to make a move soon, and Mel might be in the line of fire."

"I know. Boy, I wish this day would end."

"Me too, buddy, me too."

I sat in the bushes for a few more seconds. I felt foolish and useless. I couldn't see what was going on. There were so many people involved that only an aerial view would give me the full picture.

And that's when it hit me. I remembered speaking the words 'higher ground,' a while ago, and for some reason that stuck in my mind as if I'd need them later. And I did. Only I wished I didn't.

But there was no way out of it. I was going to have to climb to the roof, and get a bird's eye view of the battle. *If You're trying to relieve me of my fear of heights, Father, this seems like an odd time to do it. But Your will, not mine.*

Fortunately, Bristol had left the ladder leaning against my side of the church. It was still older than dirt, and now soaking wet and no doubt rotting before my eyes, but it was the only way I had of climbing up there, other than levitating, and I was pretty sure I wasn't going to do that. I walked to the ladder, grabbed it on both sides, asked the Lord for protection, and put my foot on the first rung. This ladder is so old it doesn't have nails in it. There are holes dug, not drilled, mind you, but *dug* into the vertical sides of the ladder to accommodate each rung—one hole on each side. Periodically I've heard Bristol yelping when he's tumbled to the ground because one of them fell out.

I quickly surveyed the rungs. They all seemed to be in their proper holes, so I put my other foot on the rung and began my journey to the roof. I knew time was of the essence, so something—my Heavenly Father, I'm sure—gave me the courage to complete my upward trek to the roof. I felt as though I were climbing Mt. Everest, minus the snow, cold, rocks, Sherpas, ice, and a Yeti. When I reached the peak, instead of shrieking with joy to be off that ladder, I actually climbed up the incline to the back of the steeple, and took my position high above the battle below.

It was pure bedlam. Both Red and Denim were lying on the ground moaning, bleeding, and useless, thank goodness. The other two looked confused, furious, and beat-up on. Both Martha and Winnie were making full use of their kitchen utensils to beat the living daylights out of Mugs and #4, who I dubbed Clyde. Don't ask me why. He just looked like a Clyde. At least the top of his head did. Thank goodness, he must have left Bonnie at home.

Misjudge

I could see Bristol and Grace getting into position to take down Ponytail and Witch Woman when they exited the church. I knew they'd have Mel and I couldn't stand the thought of her getting hurt. Not my Mel. Not the woman I married 25 years ago, who bore my children, travelled the world beside me wherever my Air Force duties took us, and to this day helps me tell others the good news of Jesus. Runt has no idea how lucky he was to get shot and bound, hand and foot, in the kitchen at the Inn with my beautiful wife, Bible in hand, ready to try to save the soul of a man who came to hurt and kill.

"Not on my watch, devil. Just you watch. You and your minions are gonna be running with your tails tucked between your legs and scooting out of this town so quickly you won't know what happened. But I'll *tell* you what happened: God led us into this battle, knowing full well our inadequacies and our strengths, and He's helping us win. And we *will* win. You can't seem to get it through your thick skull that you've lost, devil. You're defeated. You're headed for the lake of fire."

And before I forget, thank You, Lord.

I took stock of the situation below me. Mugs looked like Winnie might have gotten in a good swat to his forehead, which was bleeding and even from this height, when the lightning came, I could see it was swelling. Speaking of lightning, I wondered how smart it was to be on the roof, but figured if God was leading this battle, and He was, He wouldn't let me get electrocuted atop His house of worship.

Martha had it easier with her rolling pin (honestly, have you ever tried to swing a cast iron pan?), and was making full use of her weapon. Both of the men were getting swatted on the back, arms, front backs of their knees (good thinking, Martha!), and shoulders. They worked as a team. Martha whacked them with the rolling pin, and when they crouched to get away from her, Winnie clobbered them with the frying pan. They wouldn't be moving any part of their body for days.

Sadie, Emma, Joe, and Rudy were conversing among themselves, and if Sadie had any input, were probably wondering if they could do some target practice in the direction of the bad guys. Apparently, they'd voted her suggestion down, so she walked around the second car shooting out tires. She looked like she was having the time of her life.

At the moment, Sadie's gang didn't have a role to play—aside from destroying other people's property, of course—but that changed instantly. I saw something moving behind Rudy. It was a car, no doubt another big bunch of bad boys, coming our way at about 80 miles per hour. I was glad I didn't own that car. Their shocks were gonna be as worn out as the killers were. And how many people do they *have*, for crying out loud? Shouldn't they be running out of assassins or cars pretty soon? I shouted a warning to my friends below, but they were having too much fun to stop.

I was perched, standing, behind the steeple, but could lean over and see more clearly what was transpiring below me. I saw the church doors open; I knew it would be just seconds before Ponytail, Witch Woman, and Mel would come out. Someone—either Hazel, Perry, or Leo—turned on the church lights which gave us at least a less dim and murky view of the chaos. The last working streetlight happened to be right over us, too, which was both a blessing and curse, although it presented the same, both good and bad, to the cartel.

And then they emerged from the church. This time it was Witch Woman who held a gun to Mel's head. I could almost hear Grace's rage and I knew she was going to get WW if it was the last thing she did. I fought the urge to scream, but I couldn't give away my location, although for the life of me I couldn't figure out what I could do aside from watch or maybe warn someone. Then, I heard that still, small Voice inside me that said, "You can jump." *Jump? Did I hear You right, Holy Spirit?* I waited for an answer and hoped it would be something along the lines of, "Just kidding, Hugh. Go ahead and shoot 'em in the head." That didn't sound remotely like anything the Holy Spirit would say, so I wasn't surprised when I heard that Voice again. "Yes, you did. Now jump!"

I'm in the habit of doing whatever Holy Spirit tells me and this time would be no exception. I knew full well this would be the last thing I ever did on this planet because I would surely die jumping from this height in the dark and pouring rain. Grace thought five feet on my hands and knees was treacherous. What would she say now? I waited for my moment. I didn't care about Ponytail. The others could handle him. I was going to get Witch Woman and free Mel. If WW got hurt in the process, well, that's what happens when you align yourself with the devil. Besides, WW had a date with Grace, and I had a feeling it wasn't for coffee. If I didn't take her down completely, I knew I had back-up in my "don't-you-dare-hurt-my-pastor's-wife-you-nasty-drug-dealing-murdering-dirty-mouthed-thug" secretary. Grace is a woman of many talents, and one of them is pounding the daylights out of people.

I uttered a short prayer for protection, waited for the right moment to jump, and before I knew it, I was airborne—but not under my own power. I was picked up from that roof, flown to Witch Woman, and deposited forcefully on her shoulders. It happened so quickly I had no idea how I got where I was. WW probably wondered too. The force of my landing smack-dab on top of her knocked her to the ground taking me along with her, and in the process her gun went sailing, and Mel broke free. Once we landed on the ground, I wrestled to keep her from throwing me off and reaching for her gun.

I needn't have worried. Grace was standing in front of me with Witch Woman's gun in her hand.

"Hello, Wanda," she said. "We meet again."

Wanda let out with a string of profanity the demons would envy if they weren't busy getting themselves away from this holy ground. God was surely in our midst, and had sent Hazel's angel to help us out.

"Get off me, you big lout."

"Gladly, Wanda," I said breathlessly. Jumping, or rather flying, from a roof and wrestling with the meanest woman in the world takes a lot out of you. "You need to find another occupation. Maybe making license plates or sewing inmate uniforms? Maybe working in the laundry?"

She swore again. I had the biggest urge to call my mom and tell her to get herself to Road's End that very minute and wash out Wanda's mouth. She'd do it, too.

"Shut up, Wanda." That was Grace, the one with the gun.

I hauled Wanda up from the ground, handed her over to Grace, then turned to find Mel. She was standing beside the steps looking at me with that beautiful smile of hers. I ran to her—which was about three feet, but felt like three miles—and gave her the tightest hug she'd ever gotten.

"Hon, you're breaking my ribs!"

"Whoops! I'm sorry, hon." I had my hands on her shoulders, stepped back a foot and looked her over. "Are you hurt? Do you need to go to the hospital? Anything broken or cut or sprained or whatever else could've happened while you were out of my sight?"

She laughed. "No, I'm fine, but I think you might want to take a look at Ponytail's face. I sort of scratched him … hard … and well, deep. He's not happy with me at the moment, but maybe my witnessing to the two of them inside the church will mellow him out when he has a chance to think about it. Oh, and Wanda has a big bruise on her left arm and the back of her right leg, but she'll heal eventually."

In my joy at finding Mel, I nearly forgot the car barreling toward us. I shouted at Bristol a few feet away. "Hey! More of them on their way. Car coming down the road lickety-split. They should be here in under a minute. Tell Rudy and Joe!"

Bristol flashed me a thumbs-up, ran to Sadie's gang over by the cars and delivered his message just as the car skidded to a stop midst splashes of water and mud, and deposited another four nasty-looking men to the road. They had some mighty lethal-looking weapons, and my heart sank. I guess they weren't insurance salesmen or trying to sell us some nice plasticware, unless those folks carry weapons with them on their travels nowadays. Nope, they were just another batch of bad guys.

And they looked mean. Really mean.

Emma, Sadie, Joe, and Rudy all raised their guns, and I waited for the annihilation of four of my brave friends. I needn't have worried, though. George and Dewey, conspicuously absent after marching up to the bad guys, walked up just then, walked between Sadie's gang—one between Emma and Sadie, the other between Joe and Rudy. They strode over to the newcomers, and raised their weapons against the stunned men who probably thought the two of them were daft, which of course, is correct. (Even bad guys can be right some of the time.)

And then George and Dewey fired. Their weapons, spray bottles which may have held window or sink or bathroom/kitchen cleaner at one time, hit their targets in the face, and in the eyes, specifically. Both George and Dewey fired again, this time against the other two, who by then had raised their own weapons. My guys were relentless; squirt after squirt of something that stung like crazy, maybe homemade pepper spray, found their targets. The men dropped their weapons to cover their heads and faces, and to protect their eyes—which by now must be burning like all get-out. Bristol ran over, grabbed the guns as they fell with a thud and a splash, and took them back with him.

Joe and Rudy rushed over and manhandled two of the men whose eyes were streaming with tears into a position on their knees. They had zip ties with them—probably got them from Martha—and tied them hand and foot. My men moved to the other two men, still wiping their eyes and staggering around helplessly. They joined their cohorts on the muddy ground and were soon as incapacitated as the others.

I looked around. Two of the first four men of the back-up team to Ponytail and friends were shot and down for the count. The other two of that team had been beaten with the rolling pin and frying pan until they were lying on their backs on the ground trying to fend off the women without sustaining further injury to their arms. The four back-up men (to the first bunch of back-up men) were sitting on their knees in a mud puddle. One of them face-planted into the mud in front of him, and rolled around like a pig enjoying a good mud bath until Joe reached over to yank him back to his knees. So, by my calculations, the four who came to town to back up Ponytail and friends, and the four back-up men to *them* were defeated. Lumpy was probably still lying in the road between the Inn and Sadie's Bake House. Witch Woman was getting what-for from Grace, and … wait a minute. Where were SS and Ponytail?

And then I knew.

Ponytail came up to Grace and grabbed her from behind, restraining her with a chokehold. That freed Witch Woman who immediately turned on Grace and tried to slap her. But even in a chokehold, Grace held her ground and holding on to Ponytail's arms, she viciously kicked with both of her legs at WW's knees. She fell like a sack of potatoes dropped from an airplane, groaning, cussing, and promising revenge.

SuperShrimp arrived on the scene with our towel still taped to his wounded arm, and tried to take out Bristol who had just become aware of Grace's problem. Sadly for him, he was unsuccessful. Bristol swatted him away like a mosquito, then punched him in his wounded arm. There was a scream, and just like that, another one went down.

Only Ponytail was left, and he wasn't going to go down easily. "Everybody get back or I shoot her in the head. I mean it. Drop your weapons. Go on! Kick them away, and get back. Get *back!*" A volley of thuds sounded as everyone did as they were told. We were now unarmed. He waved his gun around wildly; I guess he was trying to threaten everyone with his smooth move, the "gun wave." In my opinion, all it did was keep his arm busy.

He had to know there was nothing he could do at this point. He was defeated, but like the devil, he didn't want to accept that. He started to move toward the cars, taking one slow step at a time, still waving that darned gun around. While he knew about the flat tires on the first car, he didn't know about the second car's tires that Sadie had shot out. He side-stepped his way to the third car hoping, I'm sure, to make his getaway. He looked down at the tires and cursed. In the bedlam surrounding us, Sadie had shot out those four tires, as well. Sadie cackled and said, "Whatcha gonna do now, fella? Got yerself four more flat tires, don'tcha?"

Ponytail turned as quickly as possible considering he had another human being attached to him. He aimed his gun toward Sadie and I shut my eyes. I couldn't bear seeing her hurt. There was a shot and another scream, but it wasn't Sadie's. I opened my eyes to see Ponytail holding his rear end. He'd been shot, but by who? In a flash I surveyed the townspeople. Everyone's weapon was lying on the ground. Then who shot Ponytail? A movement from my right caught my eye—and I knew who our rescuer was.

There stood Delbert T. Jackson.

Chapter Thirty-Six

I was in shock. Last I knew, Del was tucked away in the tunnel far away from the action and danger. "Del, what are you doing here?"

"I'll tell you more, Pastor, after we get these no-good creeps out of our sight. Why don't you call the police or your friend, the giant, and see if they'd be interested in taking these losers off our hands?"

"Good idea, Del. Great idea, in fact."

I made a call to Mack, told him as briefly as I could about what we'd been through, and waited for him to stop laughing. I might have to take on a side job as a stand-up comic. After a while, he settled down and assured me they'd have someone there as soon as possible. He reassured me they had plenty of back-up on the way, as well, in the form of a parade of Virginia State Police patrol cars—enough to transport the bruised ones, and the chopper would take care of the wounded ones.

The rain stopped, wouldn't you know it, just at that moment, and while it was still dark, damp, and muddy, it was a welcome relief. By the time a chopper arrived, we had the eight back-up guys, and Ponytail, Witch Woman, and SuperShrimp lined up and waiting. Lumpy was still lying in the middle of the road like some kind of huge speed bump. Twelve guys. Well, eleven guys and the meanest woman in the world. A chopper, perhaps the same one from yesterday, landed in the intersection of Gloucester and Rivermanse, and an officer jumped out and walked toward me. I waited as he approached, and when he reached me, he said with a smile, "You've had a busy couple of days, Pastor! You have eleven lined up here—boy, they look beat up. Where's the 12th?"

"Well, that's a funny story, but he's lying in the middle of the road with a gunshot wound to the knee. I call him Lumpy. Red, Denim, and Ponytail also have gunshot wounds, while the others have bruises, contusions, and a big case of embarrassment."

"More odd names, I see."

"More odd people, officer." We both grinned.

"Pastor, I wish I could hear more about this—it's certainly intriguing—but we're here on a need-to-know basis again, so I'd better not hear anything else. Have you ever thought about making a sitcom out of your town?"

"No, it's hard enough living through it the first time." I smiled. "But it's good material, I admit that! I'll keep that in mind if God ever kicks me out of the pastoring business."

"Not on your life, buster!" That was Mel, the one who keeps me in line at home.

"Never gonna happen, Pastorman." That was Grace, the one who keeps me in line at work.

I looked at the officer. "Guess it's never gonna happen, officer. Thanks for the great idea, though."

The officer, my next-to-best friend, said, "I had no idea you had so many perps out here. I know back-up is on the way. But we'll stay here until they arrive. We might have to recruit your town citizens to a special task force." He looked around at the wet, muddy, and victorious senior citizens around him and shook his head. I thanked him and we shook hands, while his men gathered up the bloody, muddy, and wet prisoners, and two of them walked over to Lumpy and put him on a gurney. I could hear him groaning from where I stood. He'd be okay, but not for a while. A couple of medics looked over the ones who sat on their knees as they awaited transportation to the hospital, and then directly to jail where they wouldn't be collecting their $200.

An hour later, all the prisoners traveling in squad cars had been transported to the hospital in the company of ten or so officers sent to escort them. Road's End's population spiked, then dropped back down to normal (read: teensy) after they left.

It was time for the chopper to leave. I gave the officer a two-finger salute when he boarded after everyone else had, and for the second time in as many days, I watched that chopper rise, then bank in a graceful U-turn, and fly into the night.

I looked at my friends, neighbors, and "flockers." All of us were at least as muddy and wet as the bad guys were, but thank the Lord none of us were shot or even harmed, aside from some minor bumps and bruises. And if they were anything like me, they were *starving*.

Everyone agreed they should go home, shower, eat some supper, and if they felt like it, return to the Inn to discuss the day's events. At the last moment, Mel spoke up and said, "Listen, friends, even if we don't want to admit it, I think we're pretty well tuckered-out. We've fought two battles in two days, vanquished a lot of bad guys, and we can be very proud of ourselves, and thankful to the Lord that He was with us the whole way. But instead of gathering tonight, why don't we plan to meet at the Inn tomorrow afternoon around 4:00 and we'll have a great big potluck. And if everyone's in agreement, maybe we can have the barbeque that Hugh mentioned earlier ... was that today? Yesterday? Seems like three weeks ago. Anyway, is everybody in favor of this alternate idea?"

Everyone who had enough energy to raise their hand did so. The rest just nodded their heads. Ruby Mae, rescued from the tunnel, made several references to her wound, and after the fourth time, Grace slapped her hand and said, "Mama, cut it out. Everyone else here has wounds far worse than yours, so just forget about it, okay?"

Ruby Mae looked at her for a long time. I expected tears and theatrics, but Ruby Mae surprised me, along with Grace and most of Road's End, and instead said, "You know, I forgot about that, Gracey girl, and you're right. My apologies to all you fellow wounded veterans. We should form a club or something!"

I don't think anyone in Road's End had ever heard Ruby Mae speak when she wasn't saying something narcissistic or drawing attention to her hats, her expertise at making hats, or the fact that she felt she was God's special project. They all looked shell-shocked, and I have to admit I admired this new version of Ruby Mae. I hoped it held, but tomorrow's another day and when it comes to Ruby Mae, anything could happen.

We parted ways, each of us walking slower and groaning more than we do on days when we don't fight battles with drug cartel thugs in two different locations, in the pouring rain, no less, and mere hours apart. Mel showered first, and by the time I was finished with my shower, she was fast asleep in bed. I went downstairs just down long enough to check the doors and turn out the lights. Mel's candle on the table had long since extinguished itself, and I couldn't help but smile at the bravery and ingenuity of my beautiful wife.

After the doors were checked and the lights turned off, I pulled myself up the stairs by the handrail, turned off the bedside lamp on my side, and slowly lowered myself to the mattress. I don't believe a bed has ever felt as good as that one did that night. I remember thinking that I couldn't remember what I was thinking … and didn't open my eyes again until 9:00 a.m. the following morning.

I slept the sleep of the "I can't believe I'm not dead," and woke up ravenous. Mel and I hadn't even eaten supper the night before, so 12 or 13 cups of coffee and as many doughnuts sounded real good about then. Mel, as usual, was already up and I found her downstairs peeling potatoes. "Morning, hon. Potato salad, I hope?"

"Hugh! You're up. Feeling any better? And yes, it's potato salad."

"Good!" I love her potato salad. "Actually, I find this hard to believe, but I think I feel a little worse."

"Same here. I think our bodies are paying us back for what we did to them the past couple of days."

I grabbed a mug from the cupboard and poured a cup of coffee. "Want some, hon?"

"In a minute, hon. Go ahead and sit down. I went over to Sadie's a while ago and got you some doughnuts."

I reached over to the bag sitting on the table. "You read my mind!"

"Well, I hate to be the one to tell you this, but your mind is not all that hard to read."

I took a bite, swallowed, and turned my attention toward my coffee. "You mean I'm not mysterious, brooding, an enigma?"

She didn't have a chance to answer. George and Dewey walked in the back door in the middle of my sentence, and George pointed to the table. "There they are, Dewey! Mornin', Mel. Hugh. Sadie told us ya bought doughnuts and her next batch wouldn't be done for ten minutes, so she said to come over here in the meantime."

Thanks, Sadie. There go my doughnuts. You guys couldn't wait ten minutes?

Mel probably read my mind, and said with a warm smile, "Well, have a seat, gentlemen. Would you like some coffee?"

Dewey nodded, and elbowed George, who looked up in disgust, no doubt because his doughnut grazing had been interrupted. "Hey, you want coffee, George?"

George glanced at Dewey in surprise. "When have I *not* wanted coffee, ya nincompoop?"

Dewey turned to Mel and said, "That means yes, Mel."

"Comin' right up, men." She found two more mugs, filled them, and put one in front of each man. "Help yourselves to the dough ... oh, I see you found them. Well, good. Cream and sugar's on the table."

My chance for a few uninterrupted moments with my wife flew out the window, much like my daydream of tossing the two old guys at the table with me into the front yard. But then I remembered how brave they'd been the day before and my heart softened. "Take all the doughnuts you want, men. We can always get more."

They didn't need another nudge. They stuffed the doughnut they were currently working on in their mouths for safekeeping and dived into the bag. Both of them emerged with three more. We were down eight doughnuts and I hadn't even finished my first. It was going to be a rough day in Road's End, Virginia.

They might as well have not even been there because they were so busy gobbling down doughnuts they didn't speak a word. Mel and I looked at one another and smiled. There would be time to talk to one another when George and Dewey wandered over to Sadie's, which I knew would any time now because it had been nine minutes since they barged in the backdoor.

George nudged Dewey. "Better get a move-on, Dewey. Don't want to miss those doughnuts."

Dewey nodded, swallowed, and managed to squeak out a thank you to Mel. "You're a good woman, Mel," he said. "Thanks for the doughnuts."

"You bet, guys. We'll see you later this afternoon."

I walked the men to the front door, more to make sure they really left than any act of chivalry on my part. Just as I was about to shut the door, I heard Dewey say, "Why do you think Hugh thinks he's an enema?"

I did as much as I could around the house, including opening all those shutters, then wandered down to the battlefield site. It was a mess, all right, but just churned-up mud, tire tracks, and a few stray puddles that I knew would probably be gone by tomorrow. We could probably just rake it out. No bodies.

But Mel wanted to hold the barbeque outside at the inn, rather than in the church yard, because she'd need access to a refrigerator larger than the "first-ever-made" model we had at the church, which was about the size of your average photo album, so it made no difference what the road looked like anyway. But that meant I should locate some folding chairs to bring back to the Inn.

I walked into the church, and heard Grace singing in her office. I walked to her doorway, and said, "What on earth are you doing here?"

"Well, let me think on that for a moment." She pretended to ponder the question, then snapped her fingers and pointed at me. "Singin'. I was singin'. Why? You stalkin' me again, Pastorman?"

"Nope. Just came for some folding chairs for the potluck this afternoon. How are you and your mom doing?"

"We're both sore. Me from fightin' that evil witch last night, and her for sittin' in that tunnel all that time. But we'll be better soon. How 'bout you and Mel? Did they hurt her at all? 'Cause if they did, I'll go right to Richmond and kick their heads to Chicago."

I was sure she would, too. "Thanks, Grace. We're sore, but doing fine, and no, they didn't hurt her at all. In fact, it was just the opposite. I haven't heard the details yet, but she left her mark on Ponytail's face and Witch Woman has some rather large bruises on her body, inflicted, I assume, by Mel. Then she witnessed to both of them."

Grace laughed until she couldn't breathe. "That's our Mel," she said, grabbing a couple of tissues to stem the flow of tears running down her cheeks. "If anyone can get a person saved, it'd be Melanie."

"What about Martha and Winnie and your mom and the rest of the ladies in town? They did a pretty good job last winter witnessing to those thugs."

"Yes, but they're the 'let's-hold-'em-hostage-'til-they-can't-stand-it-no-longer-and-repent-just-to-get-out-of-listenin'-to-us-anymore' kinda witnessers."

Witnessers? Is that a word?

She continued. "Mel's more patient and lovin'. I'll bet she's never belted someone 'cross the back of their head because they got the names of the four gospels wrong."

"You're probably right, Grace, but I'm not with her 100% of the time. Maybe she does that kind of stuff when no one's looking."

"You can be an idiot, Pastorman."

"Yes, Grace, I can. I finally got that down pat, but still, I try to be modest. Are you and your mom coming this afternoon or don't you feel up to it?"

"Are you kiddin' me? I wouldn't miss that for all the world. Just one thing, though. Don't eat the tuna casserole. You can mess it up with a spoon, dig holes in it, whatever you want to do to make it look like someone's been eatin' on it, but *don't* git yerself killed the day after the cartel tried to do it."

I gave her a thumbs-up. "Got it, Grace. Thanks for the info. Are those chairs and tables still in the basement?"

"Far as I know, but I haven't done my daily folding-chair-and-table-check yet today. I don't generally do that until around 1:00 p.m., but if you want me to change my schedule 'round, I can work it in earlier jest for you, Pastorman."

I tried to keep a straight face. "No, that won't be necessary, Grace. I'll do it myself this time. Carry on." I turned to go to the basement, and out of habit—which is whenever I say something stupid in front of Grace—I ducked. She just missed hitting me in the back of the head with that legal pad.

It was a glorious autumn day. White puffy clouds floated in a deep blue sky, the sun warmed the nip in the air, a slight breeze ruffled the trees and released hundreds of ruby-, topaz,- orange citrine-, and chocolate diamond-colored leaves. (I know those gem colors from Christmas shopping for Mel. See? It just goes to show you can learn something doing just about anything!) I brought the chairs, four at a time, from the church to the Inn and set them in the yard. I left the tables until Bristol could help me. I wasn't sure I could climb another set of stairs, let alone drag a table behind me.

When I was finished with that chore, I went inside to ask Mel if she could use my help. "Hey, hon, anything I can do for you? Test that potato salad, eat one of those brownies, drink some of that iced tea?" I take my husbandly duties in the kitchen very seriously. She gave me that 'I'm on to you' look and pointed to the table. I sat, while she reached into the fridge and brought out a plate full of food and a glass of iced tea. While I prayed, I thanked God for the blessing of a wife who not only loved Him, but me as well, and showed that love in so many ways.

She sat down beside me with a glass of iced tea. "No lunch for you, Mel?"

"I've had my lunch in a little bite here, another little bite there… so I think I'll just have some tea now."

"It's delicious, as always."

"Thanks, hon. You know, I don't think I tell you enough how much I appreciate you appreciating me. I know that came out funny, but it's true. The fact that you're so happy with everything I do, and tell me that you are, is a real treasure. Just like you."

"Just like me, huh? I'll have to mention that to Grace. She seems to think I'm an idiot."

"Yep."

"Yep, what?"

She ignored me.

We sat like that for a few minutes, then Mel said, "Are your bones and muscles feeling any better now?"

I moved my shoulders and neck and thought about it. "Yeah, they are. Must be they just needed to be loosened up a bit. We're gonna hurt for days, but in the end, we'll be back to normal."

The front door opened, and I almost dropped my head into my potato salad. I looked at Mel and mouthed, "Please don't let it be those two again."

Misjudge

It wasn't, thank goodness. Mel waved and said, "Come on over, Del. We're just having some lunch. Sit down and I'll fix you a plate. Iced tea?"

"Sounds great, Melanie. I'll just wash up first." He headed for our half-bath down the hallway. I said, "Where's he been?"

"He's getting our grill ready for barbequing. It's …" she consulted her watch "… two o'clock, hon, and he says he likes to get his coals burning just right and then put the ribs on to cook slowly. Doesn't that sound wonderful?"

"Sure does. Even stuffed like I am now, it sounds great."

Del walked in behind me, pulled out a chair and sat. Mel said, "Do you like potato salad? Chicken salad?" He nodded to both. "Good, because this is going to be a salad-sample-sort-of lunch. Here's your tea."

Del dove into his lunch with more gusto than I've seen him eat before. Yes, he gobbled his food down other times, but with less finesse and fewer manners than he displayed now. He was still such a mystery to me, but before I could even think about whether or not I should ask him some questions, he spoke.

"Listen, Melanie, Hugh, I … I … well, I want you to know how much I appreciated what you and the rest of the town did for me. I mean that was unbelievable. Two ferocious battles, both in the pouring rain just a day apart. Both men and women fought. *Old* men and women. Not you, Mel, or even you, Hugh, although you look kinda ragged today, but the rest of this town is darned old. And they did it for a no-good thug like me. Did anyone get hurt?"

"Well, if you're talking about the bad guys, I'd say every last one of them got hurt, but as for us and the rest of the town, maybe a scratch or scrape somewhere, but absolutely nothing that even needed medical attention. I'd say we were lucky or else very good at fighting off villains, but that wouldn't be true." I took a deep breath, because I knew he was going to buck me on this. I dived in. "The truth is, Del, the Lord was with us last night. He led us into battle, and He got us through it. No doubt about it."

"I thought maybe that was the case."

I had to grab the table to keep from pitching face first to the brick floor. "You did?"

"Yeah, hard to believe, huh? But I knew there was no way men and women in their 80s were gonna fight off guys with guns—guys that have no respect for human life, whether an infant, old person, or somewhere in-between. That would have been a slaughter yesterday if you hadn't had help."

I looked at Mel, back to Del, then Mel. Mel, Del. Mel, Del, Mel, Del. I had to close my eyes and concentrate to keep my brain from repeating that the entire day. "Does this mean, Del, that you're open to a conversation about this when things get back to normal?"

"I want to give it more thought, Hugh, but maybe."

I slapped him on the back and said, "Well, I'll take maybe."

"You know, there's a lot of stuff I'm wondering about that happened yesterday 'cause I was hidin' out the whole time for both battles—well, except for the tail end of the last one. How'd you end up with so many of 'em? Take out an ad? I mean, there were eleven of 'em last night when I got there …"

"Actually, there were twelve. Lumpy was lying in the street right over there with a gunshot wound to his knee."

"Whoa … way to go, Hugh!"

I shook my head. "Wasn't me, Del. Sadie did it."

He grinned, but then said, "I can see that happening. So, there were twelve last night, and a total of four at the cabin, right?"

I nodded. "Yep. Shiny, Blondie, River Boy, and No-Knee were at the cabin. Ponytail, SuperShrimp, Patch (or Lumpy as I call him now), and Wanda the Witch Woman got here first, followed by Red, Denim, Mugs, and Clyde."

"Odd names, Hugh."

"Odd people, Del."

"What'd you name the last four?"

"Didn't. I didn't get to know them well enough to know their names."

"Good point."

We sat there for a few more minutes before Del stood up and said, "I'd better get those ribs on. Melanie, thanks for a really delicious lunch. Can I reach into your fridge for a minute to grab those ribs?"

"You bet. They're right in front."

A minute later, he had his ribs and was out the front door again. I turned to Mel. "Did I die last night, or did I really hear Del say he'd consider letting me talk with him about the Lord?"

She pinched my arm. Hard. I yelped. "Nope, you're alive. And yes, you heard him correctly. Will wonders never cease? Maybe, just maybe, Hugh, the Lord isn't finished with our little town quite yet." She winked, got up, cleared away the dishes, and sent me on my way.

An hour later, our friends began arriving—with food! Each of those women has a specialty they're famous for baking, cooking, poaching, frying, sautéing, simmering, broiling, or blanching (and no, I have no idea what most of those terms mean), and in my experience as a starving pastor, there's no better sight in the world on the day after you defeat cartel thugs bent on killing you than to see women streaming from their homes with dishes of food in their hands. Kind of like zombies. Only with food.

Between lunch and their arrival, Bristol and I hauled six long tables from the church to the Inn, set them up on the lawn in the sunshine and set the chairs around five of them. The sixth one was dedicated to the food. Mel had draped tablecloths over them (how on earth did we accumulate all those tablecloths?), put out plates, bowls, cups, glasses, and silverware, and before long we were ready to eat. Del stood close by with his grill and ribs, along with an assortment of hamburgers and brats. I came close to snatching one off the grill when he wasn't looking ("Look, Del, a bald eagle chasing a Sasquatch!"), but figured I'd burn myself and not be able to eat anything else.

When everyone was seated, I stood and asked for their attention. As per usual, they ignored me. Mel stood up, and the crowd hushed immediately. I must be doing something wrong. At any rate, we had their attention, and I thanked them for all they did the previous day and congratulated them on their victory. There was so much to discuss, I proposed we eat first and talk later.

"Would you bow your heads? Dear Lord, we don't know where to begin to thank You for not only the many blessings we enjoy every single day, but also for what happened yesterday and the day before when we were attacked by men and one woman with evil intentions. You marched before us, and our enemies were defeated. You sent the rain and our enemies stumbled and eventually fell. You sent an angel to

Hazel to give us hope and encouragement; You sent an angel, perhaps the same one, to me when I was on top of the church. You sent the lightning so I could gain valuable information I needed to continue our fight. Thank You, also, Lord, for providing this beautiful meal that the wonderful ladies of Road's End have prepared for us—even after two days spent fighting evil. In Jesus' name, we pray. Amen."

"Let's eat folks," Mel said, pointing to the table. "Tableware's on the far right, then breads, main dishes, desserts, and finally drinks. Enjoy! And don't forget the best part—Del's barbequed ribs, hamburgers, and brats at the far right."

It didn't take any urging for George and Dewey to elbow their wives and everyone else aside to reach Del and the table first. They knocked their chairs backwards in their flight to sustenance (finally!) and were at the front of the line and back with their food in under thirty seconds. Being first gave them two advantages: the first was obvious, they were able to dig in before they died of starvation since it had probably been an hour or so since they stole something from their refrigerators at home. And second, if they were first to get their food, that meant they'd be first to get seconds. It made perfect sense to them, and frankly, I admired their ambition, if not their manners.

Sadie had done her usual bang-up job with the desserts and everyone took advantage of our friend's obvious baking talents. All the other ladies had made their specialties, which were all crowd favorites. I happened to be in the kitchen getting another pitcher of iced tea from the fridge when I walked in on Grace shoveling great gobs of tuna casserole down the garbage disposal. "If you tell a soul, other than Mel, what I'm doing, I swear I'll have a hit put out on you."

I held my hands in front of me, palms-out. "Whoa. Why don't you just do it yourself and save yourself some money? Don't worry, Grace, your secret is safe with me, but is it really that bad?"

"Have you ever tasted raw fish mixed with homemade noodles—Ruby Mae's noodles, no less—mixed in with some off-brand slimy cream of mushroom soup, and thrown into the oven for five hours?"

"Uh, no. But why five hours?"

"Well, first off, if you ever do taste that, you'll be eating like a king compared to what I'm shovin' down this disposal." She turned on the faucet to facilitate the annihilation of the offending casserole. "She says it takes that long for the flavors to blend—sorta like takin' a few days for road kill to stink."

"She makes her own homemade noodles? That sounds good."

"Well, if you'd like to try some I'll shred some cardboard at the office, soak it in vegetable oil for four or five days, boil it for another day, and bring you a plate."

I was laughing so hard by then I could hardly stand. "You wouldn't find it so funny, Pastorman, if you had to eat the stuff she calls food. I live there, remember? It's a wonder I'm not out in the cemetery next to Roscoe ... "

"And he was a mean one, right?"

"Darn tootin' he was a mean one, but even him bein' mean'n all, I wouldn't feed this stuff to him. Wouldn't be fair, dead or not. No man should have to eat it. Or woman, for that matter. So, I'm doing a public service here, and let's just leave it at that, okay?"

"Your secret's safe with me, Grace. But won't this just encourage her to continue making tuna casserole every time we have a potluck?"

"Maybe so, but I can only worry 'bout one poisonin' at a time, Pastorman."

"Fair enough, Grace."

I walked outside again with a fresh pitcher of iced tea, and Grace left the kitchen with a casserole dish nearly empty.

"Grace, honey," Ruby Mae said when she ran into Grace, "what're you doin' with the casserole?"

"Jest warmin' it up, Mama. Jest warmin' it up."

Chapter Thirty-Seven

The leisurely meal ended and the ladies put away the rest of the food, leaving the desserts and drinks out, of course, while the men moved the tables before we settled back to discuss the events of the day before. I felt we needed an opportunity to ask questions of one another, since so much was going on, and no one could be everywhere at once.

"Hey, everyone," I started, assuming I'd have to ask Mel or maybe that squirrel over there to stand up and gain their attention without saying a word. But they hushed immediately. Sometimes I think the Lord has fun playing with me and keeping me on my toes. I continued. "Well, folks, we made it. We fought four guys at the cabin and 12 last night, all sent by the drug cartel, saved Del from their clutches, and came through unscathed except for some minor bumps, bruises, sprains, stuff like that."

"Hey, don't forget my front window!" That was Sadie, Road's End's crack-shot and baker extraordinaire. "And Emma's! One of those idiots shot out a window at the cabin!"

There were murmurs of agreement all around the table, and a lot of head-bobbing and comments "Someone oughta shoot their lights out—and I'm not talkin' lamps." Sadie again. I made a mental note never to break one of her windows. While they commiserated with Sadie and Emma, I looked around at my friends and "flockers" sitting there in their "Sunday casual" outfits, looking full of fine food, floating in iced tea and lemonade, nodding and smiling at one another.

"Should we talk among ourselves or give details and ask questions one at a time?"

Del stood up from the far corner of the four tables we'd moved into a square so everyone could see everyone else. "Hugh, if you don't mind, I'd like to talk to you guys first."

"That's fine by me, Del. The floor, or rather the grass and some weeds here and there, is yours."

"You've gotta work on your jokes, Hugh," he said, smiling. I smiled back. I hear that a lot.

He cleared his throat, pursed his lips, and looked around at the men and women sitting at the table. "Folks, I think you all remember me from last winter." Groans, heads nodding, and a comment from George, "Yep, you sure were miserable, Del," And then good old Dewey, ever the peacemaker spoke up. "That's not what you told me, George. You told me he was a no-good, lousy, ugly snake-in-the-grass."

George looked around the table. "Who said that?"

"Me, you dimwit. I'm sittin' right next to you."

George turned his head and looked surprised to find him there as if Dewey wasn't glued to his side every minute of every daylight hour of every single day. "I did not."

"Did too."

"Not."

"Too.

Slap. Slap. Winnie and Martha saved the day by stepping in as they often do to shut their husbands up.

"Okay then, folks. George and Dewey, I'd have to agree to everything you said about me back then—or even when I showed up on Hugh and Mel's doorstep a few days ago. I was an unpleasant, mean, mouthy mug, and I thought you folks were all prissy, stuck-up, holier-than-thou snobs."

Okay then, this was getting off to a great start. If anyone forgot they hated Del, their memories were all refreshed by now.

He continued. "But as ornery as I was, and as adamant as I was about not returning to Road's End, well, here I am. Believe me, no one was more surprised than me to find out I was returning to the same little town I swore I'd never step foot in again. And I'm sure you folks felt the same way."

"You betcha!" *Slap.*

"Ya got that right!" *Slap.*

"Go on, Del. I think we're all eager to hear what you have to say." That was Emma, without a doubt the nicest person, next to Mel, in town.

"Thanks, Emma. I won't go into detail about what I did to end up here again, but it was something I had no control over. I've made some bad mistakes, horrible decisions, and hurt a lot of people." He looked at

Misjudge

each person around that table—eye to eye. "You people were some that I hurt. When I returned here, I was surly—I think Hugh and Melanie can attest to that—and I certainly didn't deserve one iota of courtesy, let alone kindness. And I'll admit, at first, I was trying to be decent just to keep from gettin' myself killed. But as the days and events wore on, I realized I was being nice because I just felt like being nice. Believe me, I was as astounded as you must be. Being nice or friendly or helpful just wasn't *me*. I've tried to take a good long look at myself to figure out why I'm that way, and I think I'm making some progress.

"Yesterday and the day before were the best days of my life. I'll bet you're thinking that's easy for me to say. I was behind a false wall at the cabin and in the tunnel here during both battles. I missed the rain storms, the lightning, the gunshots, injuries, kidnapping, worry, fear, rage, danger, bruises, and the fighting you folks did on *my behalf*. Can you understand how strange that was to me? Not so much that I missed out on all that stuff—not until the very end, at least—because I've done my share of fighting. I know what it's like. But, no offense, you folks are kind of gettin' up there in age, and knowing you put your lives on the line for *me* is unbelievable."

He took a breath. "Please bear with me. I know I'm going on and on. The reason they were the best days of my life is because you were fighting for the least worthy of any of you in town, an enemy of yours from the git-go. You took on twelve of the meanest, bad-to-the-bone people to ever live on Earth just last night, and four at the cabin the previous day. And you beat them. You not only beat them at their own game, you literally *beat them*. I can honestly swear to you that none of those sixteen rotten people have ever had decent people band together against them. I'm sure they're flabbergasted, hurting like crazy, and embarrassed right now, and I don't know about you, but that brings me great pleasure."

Del took a deep breath and looked up. "I owe every single one of you an apology for my treatment of you last winter, and for the trouble I brought to you and your town. You know, it's funny, but as much as I thought I hated this little hole-in-the-wall town, it's started to grow on me. With your permission, I'd like to visit again if I ever get out of the trouble I'm in. And last, but most importantly, I ask each of you for forgiveness for my nastiness, and to thank you all for putting your own lives on the line for me. I know I didn't fight in this battle, but I did get to shoot Ponytail, and believe me, he's been a pain in my rear for a long time. I thought it was time I returned the favor. So …. thanks, folks."

There was total silence. Not a word was said, not a sniff, cough, sneeze, or breath taken. And then Emma stood up, then Grace, Bristol, Perry, Hazel, and before long, every last one of us was standing and clapping. Del looked astounded. I think this was the very first time he ever felt he belonged. But I'd do it all over again (except for that kidnapping of Mel part, of course) to have him know what it feels like to be cared for and appreciated.

Sadie jumped up next and jumped right in. "You know how it went down at the cabin. Everybody fought against those two gun-slingers, and then two more, and then we had to do it all over again here in town with 12 more of those idiots. I didn't want to limit myself to just one spot at the cabin, so I sorta freelanced it as I went. My favorite part of the whole day was surprising that yahoo and shootin' him in the knee, and then I got to do it again here in town to another idiot! Boy, did those two dummies look surprised. Man, that was fun."

She shook her head with a great big grin on her face as if blasting away cartilage, bone, and tissue from the knees of two separate men in two days' time was as good as being visited by Publisher's Clearinghouse with an oversized check in their hands. Then she turned serious. "But I also noticed somethin' else. Normally, the people in this town are snipin' at one another. I try not to be in that camp, bein' a more easy-going, friendly type of person, but there are some in this town that don't think that way. It's a shame, but that's the way it is. We all have our failin's, and when I find mine, I'll let you know what it is. Anyway, to make a long story a little less long, I was proud of Road's End and those of us who live in it. We fought together and 'nihilated those critters. And speaking of critters, I've got a buffet with a couple of gunshot holes in it that I don't want no longer. Anyone who wants to cart it away can have it for free. You can do what you want with it—fix it, use it, carve it up to make caskets, whatever you feel like. And you don't hafta thank me. I'm just bein' my normal, generous self. Guess that's all, 'cept I'm proud of us all."

Sadie Simms, the most/least humble person I've ever met. "Thank you, Sadie. Who wants to be next?"

Nothing. Mel was in the house, so I was prepared to call on the squirrel when Hazel Parry stood. "Hazel. Yes, I'm sure we have some questions for you! Do you want to say something before we hound you with questions?"

Hazel was usually a quiet, nearly invisible woman, and knowing she'd held this secret within for so many years because others made fun of her made me sad. She was the perfect pastor's wife—loving, kind, generous, and pious. She's always stood by Perry's side, and just knowing that God saw fit to send angels to her on occasion made my heart swell with joy.

"I guess, Hugh," she started, "I want to echo Sadie's words, minus the knee-shooting part, because of course I didn't have a chance to do any of that. I'm proud of us individually and as a town. So, ask away, friends."

I raised my hand to speak first. I'd been waiting to talk to her about this for what seemed like a year but was only about 24 hours. "Hazel, are you sure you're okay with revealing this to everyone? I don't want to cause you any discomfort."

"Oh, Hugh, don't you worry 'bout that. These are my friends, and I haven't told them simply because it hasn't occurred to me, and certainly not because I didn't want them to know. The people I referred to yesterday are some family members and old friends who don't know the Lord, so of course, they're skeptical." She took a deep breath. "Well, friends, most of you probably already know this because of what happened over the last day, but I see angels. They visit me sometimes. I catch them watching over me at night, or I might see them smiling at me when I'm doing the laundry or making lunch. I gotta say I've been startled out of my apron a few times! Now, they don't usually speak. It's as if they simply want me to know of their presence, and if they do speak, it's because Perry and I are facing a crisis. But the one who spoke to me at the cabin was there to give me—us—a message from the Lord."

There were gasps, smiles, clapping, and somewhere in there, I heard Frank snoring. *Good. We remembered to get him out of the tunnel.*

"Thank you, friends. You have no idea how grateful I am to our Father for allowing His angels to visit me. The one who came the day before yesterday was one I hadn't seen before. He was magnificent—at least eight, maybe nine feet tall, I'd say—and I remember thinking I wished the bad guys could catch a glimpse. They'd have high-tailed it out of there pronto! He told me "Today, the Lord will send a deluge of His blessings upon you. He will cause your enemies to stumble." And that, of course, came true when it rained so hard in the meadow. Our enemies did indeed stumble. But what I didn't remember at the moment because—as you can well imagine—seeing an angel of the Lord sends your heart and brain spinnin' out of control, was what he said next. Sometimes it takes me days to remember all that he said or did or what he looked like. Fortunately, I thought of it later that night and the ladies and I decided to come home immediately to tell Hugh and the others what else the angel said."

"What was it, Hazel?"

"Don't go holdin' out on us, Hazel." *Slap. Slap!*

"Yeah, we deserve to know." *Slap. SLAP!* One of those ladies had really had it.

"Folks, how about if everyone just quiets down and lets her speak? She'll tell us when she gets to it." That was me, the impatient pastor scolding people who wanted the same thing I did. Nothing hypocritical here, folks.

"Thanks, Hugh. I know you're all anxious to hear what else the angel told me, so here it is. He said 'While this battle will not be finished here in the meadow, the Lord will be your stronghold in your times of trouble, and not abandon you. Out of the brightness of His presence bolts of lightning blaze forth.' I don't know about you folks, but that means something to me. Something that describes the battle here in Road's End."

She sat and I stood. "Hazel, thank you for telling us your glorious story. I am so happy for you, and if truth be told, a little envious. I want to mention quickly, before I tell you something of interest to all of us, that the Lord did indeed send bolts of lightning to light up the landscape just when we needed it. I didn't realize it at the time because there was too much going on, but I've had a little time to go over it in my head, and I realized a while ago that He had led the way through His bolts of lightning."

I stopped for a moment to think and have a sip of tea. "Okay, most of you know how scared I am of heights, tunnels, spiders, snakes, the list goes on, and Bristol teases me about not being able to get to the second rung of a ladder. He's right. I freeze right up. But last night when I was crouching next to the church and Bristol and Grace had gone around to the other side, I was feeling helpless. I didn't know what to do to help out my friends, and I was afraid you'd all die at the hands of those men."

I stopped to breathe. Another sip of my iced tea. "At that moment, I knew, really *knew* I'd have to climb to the roof of the church. It was something God put in me that I couldn't deny. So, despite the fact that Bristol uses a ladder that was already old when this country was founded, I somehow found the courage to climb it to the roof. Actually, I didn't find the courage; God provided it. So, I was up there. What next? I stood behind the steeple and had a better view of things, but still didn't know how I'd be of much help up there way above everyone. That's when Holy Spirit said, 'You can jump.' My first thought was, 'No, I can't.' I thought He was joking, but He wasn't. He told me again, 'Jump.'

"Now I always obey Holy Spirit, so I knew I was going to jump. I readied myself and waited for just the right moment to spend my last seconds on Earth in mid-air. I thought I'd surely die. Just as I was about to take the leap, I felt two strong hands grab me under my arms and *fly* me down to the top of Witch Woman's shoulders. I hit hard, and knocked her to the ground. I don't know who was more surprised—me, Witch Woman, or Mel, who was suddenly free. I didn't see him, and we'll never know if it was the same angel that gave Hazel the message, but I'll go to my grave with the feeling of those strong hands holding me."

Joe, Rudy, and Emma each said something to fill in the holes of yesterday, Leo puffed out a squiggle, and Frank put in his two cents by snorting—his version of talking, I guess.

I looked to Mel. "Want to say anything, hon?"

She smiled and stood. "There really isn't much to tell, everyone. As you know, Ponytail managed to get inside the Inn because I forgot to lock the back door when Hugh left to go back out into that horrible weather. He slit the tape and zip ties wrapped every which way around

Shrimp, grabbed me, and then scribbled a note and left it for Hugh. He was a little rough at first, but I reminded him that I was the wife of a pastor, and I didn't think the Lord would look kindly upon someone harming one of His children. I don't know if he believed me or not, but he stopped holding my arm so tight, and that was a relief.

"Eventually, we ended up at the church. I was hoping he couldn't get in, but somehow, he knew the secret knock—probably lurking in the bushes when Hugh used it—and of course, Perry did the right thing and answered the door. Ponytail pushed me inside, and told Hazel, Perry, and Leo to sit in the pews and keep quiet. I was able to get a hymnal to place in the window. You all know how protective Hugh is of those historic windows, so I knew he'd know I was inside if he saw it there. I remember thinking to myself that it was a useless gesture because the rain and dark would surely keep Hugh from seeing it. But he tells me he saw it in a bright flash of lightning. Isn't our God good?

"Then things got a little crazy. The other four men arrived, and Ponytail and Wanda went outdoors. Wanda held me with a gun to my head, and I have to admit I wasn't fond of her at that moment. But Hugh appeared out of nowhere, knocked her to the ground, and suddenly I was free."

Mel sat, and Grace stood. "I don't know if I can contribute anythin' more than what you already know, but I'll give you my story. The cabin was pretty straightforward. I tried to persuade one of them that their GPS was flawed, and that's how we figured out they'd probably put some kind of tracer on Del. It's gone now, floating somewhere in the sewer pipes. The next night back here at home, we were all over town and it rained every single minute. When Hugh flew down from the church roof, Wanda dropped her gun and I grabbed it and then her. I had a few choice things to tell her. I'm not ashamed to say I hated that witch, but that's not Christian of me, so I won't say it. Things looked pretty good until Ponytail grabbed me, but eventually Del showed up and shot 'im in the rear end. That tickled me. That's about it."

"Thanks, Grace. Anyone else?"

I knew this was coming. "Me next!" and "Pick me," which sounded a little like first graders picking out T-ball team members. Of course, I heard "Mickexme." George jumped up first; Dewey followed close behind.

"On behalf of Road's End's premier Private Investigating office, I have the following to report..."

"George, that's ..."

"Shut up, Dewey. You can call it what you want when it's your turn."

Apparently, Dewey didn't know what to say. He looked like he was thinking "I'm going to get a turn?"

"Anyway, me and Dewey ... don't say it, Dewey ... put our early warning system, KEN for short, in place and sure enough, those guys ran right over the spikes we put in the road, flattened all their tires, and rang the warnin' bell. I'd say we were instrumental ... and no, Dewey, it's not 'strumental... in fightin' off the cartel."

I couldn't help myself. "Your wives told us that you and Dewey were working on something you called ROY. What was that?"

George scratched the back of his neck, and finally said, "ROY didn't work out. We was settin' up this trap thing where the bad guys was gonna run into it and it'd scoop them up and keep 'em trapped 'til we got there to 'rest 'em. That was what we were tryin' to do when you interrupted our top-secret plan and hauled us out of the tree."

"Well, what happened to it? ROY, I mean."

"Nuthin'. We couldn't figure out a way to steer 'em in the direction we needed 'em to go, so 'ventually we just gave it up and went to get our back-up weapon."

Dewey piped up. "My turn now, George. ROY woulda worked if they'd run where we told 'em to. I guess it was kinda like the lightnin' bug thing. Couldn't git 'em to go where they was supposed to go." He thought for a minute. "But then we thought of our top-secret blindin' spray we developed for jobs just like this one. We used window cleaner with a little vinegar mixed in, and a ... oh, whatcha call it? ... well, never mind ... stuff that kills germs 'n' added some vinegar and bleach to it, and whamo! we had a top-secret spray. George took one 'n I took one and set out to restore peace and justice to Road's End. We're gonna market it 'round the world to other detective agencies like ours. We're gonna get a Patton on it." *Patent?*

George added, "We're gonna call it the 'World-Famous Blindin' Spray for Secret Agents 'Round the World to Restore Peace and Justice Wherever They Need It.' Catchy, huh?"

I stood. "Sure is, George. Men, thanks for a great report and for your part in stopping the cartel and taking out so many of them so quickly. Wow. We are a very ingenious community, and we can be very proud of what we've accomplished."

"Can we get more dessert?" That was George, the Empty Stomach Man.

"Hey, how 'bout some more of that fish noodle stuff?" That was Dewey, the one who was going to need his stomach pumped shortly.

I looked around at the ladies. "Is that okay with all of you?" Everyone nodded, so I said, "Well, what are we waiting for?"

Two hours later, everyone but Del and Bristol had gone home, the tables and chairs were back in the church basement, and the four of us sat down in the living room to relax a bit before we turned in for the night. Del entertained us with wild stories from his cartel days and how he eventually was discovered to be an inside man. He made a frantic phone call to his supervisor who tried to get hold of another undercover agent, but he was so deep into his covert role he couldn't help get Del out of danger. But he did know someone he could call and that happened to be Mack.

"And the rest is history," Del said. "I wasn't exactly enamored of the giant who rescued me, but I think I've changed my mind about him."

I cocked my head and looked at him. He was a different man from the one Mack dropped off. Without his scowl, his scars weren't as apparent, and when he smiled, he looked downright pleasant. "You know, Del, I'd say the whole town of Road's End has changed its mind about you, as well."

"I agree wholeheartedly," Mel said.

Bristol brought up the rear. "I second or third, whatever, that too, Del. Do I still have a roof repair partner?"

"Sure do," Del said.

A few minutes later, we turned out the lights, Bristol went home to his little house, and Del retired to his room. Mel touched up the kitchen while I locked the doors. Ten minutes later, we were tucked into bed. It felt good going to bed knowing there weren't bad guys out there ready to kill anyone in their way.

But, of course, that wasn't true.

Chapter Thirty-Eight

The call came at 4:10 AM. What is it about 4:00 AM that makes Mack feel obligated to wake me up?

"Hey, Mack, what's up?"

"Trouble, Hugh. Sorry, but there's more trouble."

"I assume it's them again. Just how many bad guys does that cartel have, anyway?"

"You don't want to know, Hugh. But this time, the big man himself is on his way to Road's End. He must really be upset with Del. He's about ten hours away from you. The only reason we're not picking him up now is that they want to swoop in and grab him in the act. So, you'll have to prepare yourselves for another confrontation. But if all goes well, they'll finally get him and take this whole cartel down for good."

I was wide awake by now and sitting by the side of the bed. "You're saying that we have to fight another battle with these yahoos so you guys can pick him up? Mack, you know it's a miracle we survived the last two battles with no serious injuries or deaths. I told you that when I called you yesterday. I don't know if putting these old people in danger again is a good idea. Sure, they're feisty, but frankly, they're exhausted. And come to think of it, so am I."

"I know, Hugh. I know. And just to set the record straight—I'm in this unofficially. There's no part of my job description that says I should be involved, but I feel an obligation to you and the town. After all, I got you into this by dropping off Del. Assuming the president doesn't have to go somewhere today, I'll let him know where'll I be and why. He's on board with whatever we have to do to protect you and the town. I'll head over there when I can. I'm sure he'll do all he can, as well, to make sure you're protected."

I sighed. "But ... okay, I get why whoever is trying to grab him wants to catch him in the act. Why can't they just be here when he arrives?"

"They might be, Hugh. In fact, I asked them specifically to send men to surround Road's End and keep a close watch in case things get hairy. I think they'll honor that request, especially considering what you and the rest of the town have been through. But I can't guarantee it. If all goes well, they'll be in place when the big guy arrives and they'll step in as soon as they feel they can do so without putting you guys in harm's way. If they can't catch him red-handed in trying to hurt one of you or setting fire to the town, they've still got enough on him to put him away for 200 years."

"They'd *better* be in place. This town and these old folks have just about had it. They've proven their worth and their mettle and I don't think they should have to take on more bad guys."

"Hugh, I agree 100% with you. They've done the country a huge favor already, and to do it again would mean they're extraordinarily brave, patriotic people who should certainly be recognized. I'll make sure of it. Listen, I'm really sorry about this. Seems like I'm always having to apologize for doing something awful to you and Mel and the rest of the town. I'll make it up to you somehow, okay?"

"Mack, I'm not blaming you. You don't want to be a part of this any more than we do. You got dragged into this just like we did. Let me call a meeting and see what they say, okay? I'll get back with you as soon as I can. You said ten hours, so that means around two o'clock? Well, at least it'll be daylight and the rain is gone. Tell whoever's coming to circle the town that I'll send Grace after them if they let just one of us get hurt."

"Ouch. Will do, Hugh."

We hung up and I headed for the shower. I had a feeling this was going to be another stressful day. I finished my shower, dressed, and went downstairs to make coffee. Mel came down about five minutes later.

"Good grief, Hugh. It's 4:45. Why are you making coffee at this time of day, well … night, and why are you even awake?"

I turned to her after pushing the button on the coffeemaker. "Mack called."

Mel reached for a chair, hung on, and said, "Not at 4:30. What did he want? I'll sit because I presume it's not good news?"

I put my hands on the back of the chair across from her and said, "You're right, hon. He says the big daddy of drug dealers is on his way to Road's End to get Del, I imagine. He's either run out of bad guys to do it for him, or he's just going to make sure it happens. He should be here around two o'clock. He, meaning Mack, tells me we'll have back-up surrounding the town to save us if things fall apart. I told Mack they'd better step in or I'll send Grace after them."

"Ouch."

"Same thing Mack said." We shared a smile over the time Mack first met Grace.

Mel reached for the cup of coffee I handed to her. "I've got to say I'm sick to darned death of people coming into our town and shooting at us."

"I think your feeling is unanimous around these parts. I don't understand how this one teensy little town attracts so much drama but thank goodness we have our Lord to watch over us. And He's been doing a darned good job, hasn't He?"

"He sure has, but Hugh, do you really think the residents are going to want to do it all over again? I mean George and Dewey might, and maybe even Sadie if she can find a knee to blow up, but the rest of them are liable to say forget it."

"And I wouldn't blame them. I told Mack I'd let him know what they say after a meeting with them. It's at Sadie's place—well, if Sadie agrees." I stood, gave her a kiss on the top of her head, and headed over to Bristol's house. I'd need him with me when I went to Sadie's to break the news to the rest of the town.

"Are you *kidding* me? Really? He wants us to do it all over again? Heck, I'm still sore from the first fight at the cabin. I don't know if I have enough fight left in me for a third go-around." That was Bristol, the man who didn't appreciate being awakened at 5:00 AM and told he was going to get shot at again. He's weird that way.

"I wish I was kidding, but sadly, I'm not. Whatever this guy's name is—I'm calling him Bigwig—will be here around two this afternoon if the calculations are correct. I'm not sure what we can do to prepare for him except make sure our guns are in working order after that monsoon we had, and that we have enough ammo. I'll check in with Winnie and Martha to make sure their rolling pin and cast-iron pan will be available."

That last statement coaxed a grin out of Bristol. "Sad, isn't it, when two of our most effective weapons turned out to be kitchen utensils? I've got to say those two have guts—and strong arms and wrists. I don't think those guys will ever step foot in a kitchen again."

"I'm sure you're right. Want to come with me over to Sadie's in about a half hour? I might as well let the men know so they can begin blabbing. Oh, I almost forgot. I should call Grace and have her mom call around. We should have this town notified and ready to get prepared in about 45 minutes, tops."

He agreed to meet me over there, and I went over to the church. I meant to leave a note for Grace on her desk, but she was already there.

"What on Earth, Grace! It's 5:15 in the morning. What are you doing here? Have you moved into the church?"

"No, but that's a good idea, Pastorman. But the real reason is I needed some time to myself to ask the Lord if I'm doin' the right thing by encouragin' Ruby Mae to try to sell her hats. By the way, I talked her out of YooHoo."

"Oh, you did? Good. I don't know why I came up with that idea— it was just one of throw-away things we toss into conversations once in a while when we can't think of anything else to say. How'd you talk her out of it?"

"Told her the lighting on YooHoo was horrid and would make her look orange and her hats all creepy lookin' and she wouldn't sell a thing if that's what customers had to look at."

"Smart thinking, Grace. So, you think she should try to sell them through a website?"

"Well, that's what I was askin' the Lord when you interrupted me. Good thing the Lord is patient."

"Whoops. Sorry, Grace. I'll get out of your hair now and let you get back with the Lord."

"Good thing it's not the other way around, Pastorman."

I was halfway home before it hit me what she was saying. You're slipping, Hugh. You're slipping.

Chapter Thirty-Nine

The men at Sadie's were just as noisy as they always are. Sadie, however, didn't seem to care. No screeching, name-calling, towel-snapping. In fact, if I didn't know better, I'd say she wasn't there at all.

Bristol was already seated with a "I know something you don't know" look on his face. I pulled out a chair, sat down, and within five seconds, I knew what Bristol knew. Sadie was dressed in a bright yellow dress with a perky little apron covered in cherries, her hair just so, and worst of all, a great big smile on her face.

"She had another rough night losing her mind, didn't she?"

Bristol nodded. "Appears so. I haven't heard her raise her voice once since I've been here, and on a normal day she would've lambasted everyone at least once, maybe twice by now."

"How long have you been here?"

"Around thirty seconds. But she never goes this long without shuttin' someone up or threatening to knock their block off."

I nodded. "You're right, Bristol. Think this is another case for the premier private investigators in town?"

He almost spit his coffee out. "Heck, no. We won't recover from the last one for a year or so. Let's let them come up with something else stupid before we go reliving their past projects."

"Four-ten, Bristol."

"Four-ten? What's that all about?"

"Believe me, you don't want to know."

After a couple of doughnuts and two cups of coffee, I felt fortified enough to approach the topic of Act 3 of our battle. I stood and literally yelled at the men two tables over.

After three attempts, I hollered, "Come on, guys. Listen to me."

I felt a hand on my arm, and there stood Little Happy Sunshine Girl. "Hugh, let me try."

"Men ..."

They shut up and glued their eyeballs to her. She gave a coy little smile and turned to me. "It's not that hard, Hugh. You just have to use the right tone of voice."

I thanked her and turned to address the men whose mouths were all open and drooling. Literally. They looked like a nest of baby robins and Sadie was their worm. Don't tell Sadie I said that. Not exactly flattering.

"Okay, guys, now that Sadie's helped me out, I have something important to tell you. When I'm finished here, you might want to run home and start making preparations."

"What? The president's comin' again?"

Smoke squiggle.

Snore.

"We havin' another one of those potlicks?" *Potlicks?*

"That's potluck, Dewey, not potlick. You idiot."

Snore.

Squiggle.

"'Tis not, George."

"'Tis too."

Another squiggle. I wish Leo would shut up.

Before we could get on that merry-go-round, I dived right in. "Nope to all that. No president, no potlick, no potluck. Mack called me this morning to tell me that the top guy of that drug cartel is on his way to Road's End. He'll be here around two o'clock."

"Well, he's not gettin' none of our potlick food! 'Specially that fish noodle stuff. Man, that was good."

"No, guys, he's not coming for food. Not even the fish noodle stuff, Dewey. He's coming to get Del."

"Does Del need a ride?"

"Too bad. I was just gettin' to like that guy. I'll be sad to see 'im leave."

"No, men," I said, trying not to reach over and grab George and Dewey by their collective total of seven hairs and shake them until some sense spilled out of them, but then I realized there wasn't any to spill, so I might as well just let that little fantasy go. "He's coming to shoot Del."

"Doesn't he know that's already been done?"

I sighed and hung my head. Why am I always the one hanging my head? I'm not the dumb one; I'm the pastor who has his head on straight, the guy with some common sense, the one whose life expectancy drops alarmingly every single time I talk to these guys.

I looked up. "Yeah, I imagine he does know it's been done, but no one killed or captured Del, and he really wants that to happen, so he's coming here to do it himself. And you know what that means."

"Yeah. He's gonna wanna be in on the potlick afterwards. Greedy guy."

Finally, Bristol came to my rescue. "Guys! Listen up. First of all, quit giving Hugh such a hard time. You all act like kindergartners around him. Secondly, *stop* acting like kindergartners. Right now. And forever. And most importantly, that guy is coming to kill Del, so we're going to have to fight another battle with him and whoever he brings with him. Is that clear enough?"

"What's their names?"

"Whose names?"

"The guys who're comin', Bristol. Yer gettin' kinda slow lately."

"I don't know what their names are. How would I know?"

"Well, you knew last time. Ya called 'em Ponytail and Red and Denim and all other kindsa names. All I wanna know is what their names are. Is that so hard? You holdin' out on us, Bristol?" George turned to the other men. "Been hangin' 'round that Hugh too long."

Bristol had had it. "For the last time, that man is coming here to kill Del, and *us, too,* if we aren't careful, so stop acting so doggoned dumb. Now get it together, men. Go home, tell your wives, and get ready for another battle. We're meeting at the Inn at noon. And no, there will be no refreshments, no potlick, no potluck. None of that. Just a meeting. Got that? Just a meeting."

"I'm not sure I wanna go to a meetin' if there's no 'freshments."

"What's the point? Heck, they could just tell us what's up. But, oh no, those two have to have a meetin' and make it all complicated 'n' such so we don't know *what* to believe."

Bristol sat down. "Listen, Hugh, I think we ought to grab Del, Mel, Emma, Sadie, and Grace, and beat feet out of town. Let these idiots deal with the cartel. They'll drive Bigwig nuts, and we won't ever have to worry about seeing them again."

"What about Perry and Hazel?"

"Okay, they can come too."

"Think we can get out of here before two o'clock?"

Bristol grinned. "Don't I wish."

It occurred to me that I hadn't told Del his old boss was on his way to kill him. That might be something he'd be interested in. When I walked in the back door, he was sitting at the kitchen table and Mel was just setting a plate of bacon, eggs, and hashbrowns in front of him.

"Hey, hon. Hungry?"

For the first time in my life, I wasn't. "You know, hon, I'm not at the moment. I'll have a cup of coffee, though, if you're pouring."

"Are you sick?"

"No, just worried. I realized over at Sadie's that I hadn't told Del that Bigwig was on his way to town." I turned to Del, who had half a slice of bacon just about in his mouth. "Del, your old boss is on his way to town. I guess he wants to get the job done himself. Sorry I forgot to mention it to you right away. He—Mack, not Bigwig—called a little after 4:00 this morning. I talked to Mel about it, then Bristol, and by then Sadie's was open and I went to tell the men."

"How'd they take it?" That was Del, the oddly-relaxed man whose head was on the line.

"About how you'd think they'd take it. They asked a bunch of dumb questions, insulted me, and got all huffy when Bristol told them there would be a meeting here at noon with no refreshments. You'd have thought I told them the world had run out of oxygen and they'd all have to start breathing sulphur fumes for the rest of their lives."

"Do they understand the danger we're in, hon? I mean, they're goofy, but when push comes to shove, they usually come through. Barely, and in ridiculous ways, of course, but for the most part, things turn out okay. Don't they?" Her look said, "Please let me be right."

I recognized the barely-disguised fear Mel was exhibiting. She'd been strong the other night when Ponytail grabbed her, but I wondered if the gravity of her situation would hit her sooner or later. "Hon, you're right. It's just that those men simply don't respect me. They'll listen to Sadie—by the way, she lost her mind again last night—but you'd think I was a great big jellybean for all the attention they pay to me."

Del laughed. "Hugh, if you were a jellybean, you can bet your bottom dollar they'd pay attention to you."

"I guess that was a bad example, wasn't it?" I grinned, and the tension in the room dispersed.

"I'm not sure how many of them will show up at the meeting. They never come to hear what it is we have to tell them, anyway. They come for the refreshments. We'll probably have the Parrys, Grace and Ruby Mae, Emma, and Sadie, and that's it. But just maybe they'll decide it's in their best interests to be in on the plan."

Del set his coffee cup down and said, "What *is* the plan?"

I couldn't lie to him. It was bad enough I'd forgotten to tell him. I looked at him and said, "No clue."

Chapter Forty

"Tell me again just why the authorities want him to come to town, instead of nabbing him somewhere between Miami and Road's End?" Del was surprisingly in control of his emotions. Clearly, he was more confident about us than I was.

"They want to catch him in the act of whatever he's planning to do. I hope it isn't blowing up the town. Maybe they'll have a better case against him if he's allowed to go as far as they can let him go, without killing someone? Maybe they're waiting to see if there are any more of his gang members who tag along behind him by an hour or two, just to make sure they nab as many of them as they can. Mack assures me they'll be in the vicinity if things start to go downhill. I don't know what Bigwig's driving or how many other men he has with him. As usual, we're in the dark, but fortunately, we have the Lord leading the charge."

Mel patted me on the arm. "You're right, Hugh, and I'm so sorry for being uptight about all this. I guess I'm just tired—tired of running, and worrying, and ...," she waved her hand as if to grab her thought, "... being under fire all the time. We're just a peaceful little village. Heck, the last gunshot this town heard *should've* been during the Civil War!"

"It's okay, hon. I don't blame you for wondering if we can pull this off a third time. I have my doubts too." I turned to Del and said, "Del, Bristol will be over in a few minutes and the three of us will figure out what we're going to do. No sense involving the others in the planning stages. Who knows what they'll come up with. We'll figure it out and tell them at noon. I want to be ready ahead of time in case they make incredibly good time and arrive earlier."

Del nodded. "Sounds good to me, Hugh. I hope you know I'm not planning to go underground for this one. No, no ..." He held his hand up. "No, now I mean it. This isn't about being afraid of being enclosed. Granted, I'm not crazy about it and probably never will be, but I think it's more a matter of not wanting to be talked to death than any fear of small spaces I have."

He smiled. "I think you know who I'm talking about, and I know she's a good woman, but criminy, can that woman talk! But the *real* reason I want to stay topside this time is that I've already caused you folks enough trouble to last the next 100 years. I'm going to be *involved* in this one. This time it's special, it's personal, and I'm going to help bring him down." He paused for a moment, looked down at his hands clasped in front of him, then back at me. "Hugh, I don't mean to be dramatic, but I'd die for this town. That's how grateful I am for all that's been done for me, and how determined I am to end this once and for all."

I glanced over at Mel. She looked at me and shrugged her shoulders. "Well, Hugh, I guess he has a point. If it's more than just not being caught, if it means that much to him, then maybe we should have him above ground and figure out what he can do and not get killed."

I thought about it for a couple of minutes. "Okay, Del, you've got a deal, but expect to get some flak from Bristol. I know he won't be in favor of it, but you're persuasive. You can convince him. I guess what we need to figure out is whether we are going to assume they're violent when they get here or act innocent? Bigwig knows about Road's End and what happened to his men, so he knows we've been through two battles already, and I think if we act as though we aren't the least bit suspicious of them, he won't fall for it."

"Exactly, Hugh," Del said. "Tito—that's his real name or at least I think it is— may be rotten to the core, but he's not stupid, and he knows by now that the folks of Road's End aren't stupid either. We either have to have an entirely unique approach to this or just begin shooting the minute they drive past the village limit sign."

Mel stood up and said, "Why don't you two get comfortable in the living room, and I'll send Bristol in when he gets here. I want to get these dishes done and the house picked up before we start beating the dickens out of mobsters and shooting people in the rear end." Mel is nothing if not neat and clean and always prepared to entertain. Even when it calls for gunfire.

We did as she suggested and five minutes later Bristol walked in. Mel followed him with a pitcher of lemonade and three glasses. "I know battle-planning is thirsty work."

"Thanks, hon." I poured some for each of us and we began to talk. When we finally came to an agreement, we were sure we were going to get clobbered. "Should we just surrender right now, so we don't have to get all messed up?"

"Naw, let's give 'em a run for their money," Bristol said. He drained his glass, set it on the tray, and excused himself. "I'd better get going and do my part. If I'm not back by noon, good luck with the meeting. I wouldn't want to be in your shoes, but heck, I'm not that crazy about being in mine."

The meeting at noon went as well as could be expected, and I was happily surprised to see everyone there. I'd be hearing from the peanut gallery (emphasis on "nut") for the rest of my life regarding my no-refreshments stand, but some things can't be helped—things like drug thugs in Road's End and my stance on brownies at meetings.

I also was sure this would be my last day on earth. If the drug dealers didn't get me, George and Dewey would. My funeral loomed before me. I shook my head to clear the thoughts regarding my demise from taking over. But those thoughts had led to something I'm sure Holy Spirit planted in my head. I motioned for Bristol to come over, and we stepped into the kitchen. I told him my idea and he agreed.

"That's brilliant, Hugh! How'd you ever think of it?"

I held out my hands, palms out, and said, "Don't look at *me*. I don't deserve any of the credit. Holy Spirit came up with that idea Himself and passed it along to me. Do you really think it'll work?"

"If Holy Spirit thinks it'll work, it'll work, Hugh. You realize, don't you, that we're going to have to let them know Del was here, because I don't think Bigwig is going to believe us if we say we haven't seen him. Besides, Del shot Ponytail in the rear—and we don't know for sure whether or not Ponytail used his one phone call to call Bigwig—so they not only know Del's here, but that we've been denying it all along. You know, Hugh, we're just a big pack of liars. We deserve to be shot." He shrugged, then said, "Let's tell the yahoos out there."

"What about the non-yahoos? Can we tell them too?"

"Yeah, we probably should. Can't give all our attention to the nuts among us."

"Right you are." I led the charge and we walked back to the dining room, filled everyone in on the plan, cautioned them to remember what we told them, said a prayer—a fervent one. Then I told them to be back at the Inn no later than 1:00 PM and everyone scattered to their respective homes.

I'm sure George and Dewey will expect refreshments at our 1:00 PM gathering. My head hurt.

One hour later, we gathered once more in the dining room of the inn. I complimented them on their preparations and after privately consulting with Sadie, promised them a nice array of refreshments after this was behind us. I know that was pretty darned optimistic, but I knew the Lord was in our midst, and I was fully confident He would like us to have post-battle snacks. I sent them on their way. Mel and I walked to the church holding hands.

As we got closer to the crowd, I couldn't help overhearing Joe and Rudy talking about cleaning up the ambulance later that afternoon. Before we arrived, Road's End had purchased, third-hand, an ambulance with no working siren and no lights. Of course, they didn't have to worry about traffic getting in their way, and it was cheap, most of its parts worked, and the last time they used it was when Bill Manning, Winnie's brother, died at home surrounded by peas and greasy chicken.

Joe said to Rudy, "Maybe we'll luck out and have some shot-up people and we can crank that baby up today."

Rudy responded, "Yep, but 'member, it's my turn to be the doctor."

"What d'you know about gunshot wounds?"

"Nuthin.' What do you know?"

"Nuthin'. Heck, we might have to let 'em die."

You know, there are moments when I truly love and appreciate our neighbors and parishioners or "flockers," as George calls them. This wasn't one of them.

I went into my office to pray. "Lord, I know we're going to be out-gunned this afternoon. Please give us the strength, courage, and wisdom it will take to be victorious. And please be in our midst, leading the battle against the evil that doesn't seem to want to leave our town. In Your Son's name, I pray. Amen."

I opened my eyes and looked out the window. A large black car was just pulling up to the crowd gathered in front. *Please, Lord, make this work.* The windows were tinted so heavily I couldn't make out how many men it held, but six could easily fit in there. Hopefully, Tito had wanted to make the trip by himself. Not likely. The driver (forgot about him) jumped out and opened the passenger door and out came a couple of brutes and an older brute. I wondered if that was Tito. The driver then went to the back door and released another two men. Okay, we have a driver, Tito, and probably four bodyguards.

I walked outside and called to my neighbors. "Friends, if you'll come inside, we'll get the service started." They looked up at me from their conversations with one another and began to slowly make their way to the front door of the church. I walked over to the car, held out my hand, and said, "Hello. I'm Pastor Hugh Foster. Were you folks friends of Delbert's? I'm sorry for your loss, but happy you've come to the service. Road's End is hard enough to find when you live here. Coming from someplace to this town usually happens by mistake!" I smiled my innocent, gracious pastor smile, and swung my arm in an inviting manner to lead them to the church. "Feel free to sit wherever you want. I'm sorry, I forgot to ask your names."

Tito sputtered, "T-T-T-Thomas. Thomas ... uh, Jefferson."

"Well, Mr. Jefferson, you'll be happy to know that one of your compatriots, George Washington, lives here and is in attendance. Have a seat. I'd better get the service started."

I left them there and walked to the front of the church. When I looked up, Tito, a.k.a. Thomas Jefferson, was sitting in the back row, but his men flanked the back door of the sanctuary, two on each side.

"Friends, neighbors, and guests ..." I pointed to TJ and his friends, "... we're here today to say goodbye to Delbert T. Jackson. Although,

Del wasn't a resident of Road's End, and he, in fact, hated the town and all of us, he nevertheless died here. The fact that we fought two miserable battles with men who were apparently trying to find him, and we kept telling them he wasn't here, might give us pause to attending to this final event of his life. Little did we know that he *was* here and we just didn't realize it. So just as he gave us trouble the first time he was here, the last time he came to town he brought trouble *with* him. So, we're giving him a burial because we're Christ-followers and He would want us to treat Del's ashes with dignity and love."

I glanced at Tito/Thomas. He looked perplexed.

"I've been told by many of you that you'd like to say something at this service, so I'll turn the podium over to anyone who would like to speak."

Sadie's hand shot up and her body right behind it. She bounded up the two steps to the raised platform and pushed me aside so she could get to the podium. "Listen up, everybody. I hated Delbert T. Jackson and I'm not at all sorry he died. Too bad he died in Road's End because now we have to find someplace to put his ashes. I vote we stuff them in a trash bag and take 'im to the dump next time Joe and Rudy make their trash run. That's all I've gotta say about him. Good riddance."

I pretended to be shell-shocked at her in-your-face comments, then asked if anyone else wanted to speak. Hazel and Perry rose and walked to the front. Hazel spoke first. "Pastor is right that we're doing this out of Christian love for others. Personally, I don't think Delbert really knew how to be a good man. Just not in him. I hope he's not in hell, but he probably is." Next Perry spoke. "Well, as a former pastor, I should try to ignore the bad and concentrate on the good. Trouble is, there didn't seem to be any good in Delbert. Thank you."

Martha and Winnie came up together. "Whenever I think of Delbert Jackson, I remember that night we dragged him around face first in the snow and then shoved him into the shed with Sophie, the camel," Winnie said.

"Yep," Martha interjected. "Those were good times. But he's dead now." They walked back to their seats.

George and Dewey were up next. George started. "I don't know what to think 'bout Jackson. I know he didn't do nuthin' when we were battlin' those drug idiots last winter in that blizzard—just sat there tied up in the shed with that camel—so I guess I'd say he was lazy."

Dewey added, "Yeah, lazy and had no manners. First class slob."

They sat. Mel got up and walked to the podium. "I hate to say bad things about a person, especially at their funeral, but I have to say Delbert Jackson was the sloppiest man I've ever met. And ungrateful and crude and bad-mannered and loud and just plain nasty."

Joe and Rudy were last, as Emma couldn't bring herself to say what she really thought about Del previous to his latest visit.

Rudy said, "Never met the man 'til he was dead as a doornail."

Joe added, "He was cheap. Got an ambulance ride to Thirteen Colonies Antiques and Mortuary and never paid the bill. It's crooks like him that take the glamour out of a good ambulance run."

I walked back to the pulpit. "Mr. Jefferson, is there anything else you'd like to say? I don't know how close you two were, but to come all the way to Road's End, you must have some feelings toward him. Do you want to share those with us this afternoon?"

TJ shook his head and stood up, apparently to leave. "Oh no, Mr. Jefferson, please don't go yet. We're giving everyone a chance to walk past the urn one last time before we … uh, dispose of him for good. Please come on down. If you're in a hurry, we'll let you go first. You and your fellow travelers, that is."

I motioned them down. He looked like a mouse with a hawk three inches from his head. He started to shake his head but thought better of it and walked toward me. "Please feel free to linger as long as you wish with Del—well, what's left of Del—before you leave. I know these are sensitive times. Please don't rush on our account."

TJ walked up to the urn (an old vase that Ruby Mae had placed a cap of aluminum foil over as if she were keeping some beans warm, then wrapped a pink ribbon around it) and glared at what he thought were Del's ashes. I hoped he didn't wonder where on earth Del was cremated. I'd have to tell him it was at Thirteen Colonies Antiques and Mortuary, but no one in their right mind would believe me. In truth, it was Bristol's job to burn some leaves and twigs and scoop up the ashes to dump into the vase. They were still warm, in fact. But I guess we could say that's proof he's in hell.

Fortunately, that didn't cross TJ's mind. He muttered something like "rot in …" and I didn't catch the end but could pretty well figure out what he was saying. He turned to go, and I rushed behind him to shake his hand. "Thank you so much for coming, Mr. Jefferson. As you probably noticed, folks around these parts weren't exactly enamored of Mr. Jackson, but wouldn't want to miss an opportunity for a good funeral and potluck afterwards. You're welcome to join us."

"No, no," he said. He turned his head at his men, flicked his hand toward the door, and they were gone in ten seconds. I heard car doors slam, the engine roared to life, and then some gravel being kicked up by tires that probably cost more than Road's Ends' entire yearly budget. Of course, we don't have a budget, so they wouldn't have to be particularly expensive tires. I didn't care, though. Those tires rolled those five men and a driver out of Road's End forever and that raised their value in my eyes.

Mack told me later that they'd set up a roadblock about sixty miles down our road—at the intersection with the main highway—and taken all six men into custody. He said they'd make sure TJ and his buddies knew it wasn't connected in any way with our town. They'd be assured that Del was dead and would have no reason to send anyone else to town. The guys who were shot and beaten up by us would be in prison for a good share of the rest of their lives.

It was official. Delbert T. Jackson was dead to the mob and free to do whatever he wanted to do with the rest of his life. He might want to change his name, and the WPP had probably done that for him already, so he's a free man. It seemed ironic that the tunnel beneath the yard at the inn was once again used to free someone from their past. Of course, the slaves had a far worthier cause than Del did, but I was willing to give him the benefit of the doubt.

"Folks, as soon as we're sure they're out of town for good, we'll meet over at the inn for our promised refreshments. Maybe we can convince Del to do a little more barbequing for us later on tonight. That is if you ladies think you'll have enough time to cook up your specialties."

"Potlick, here we come!"

"Potluck, Dewey. I ain't gonna tell you again."

Life as we know it in Road's End was back to normal.

Chapter Forty-One

Later that evening, Del manned the grill he'd been warming up since we left his funeral and I deemed it safe for him to come outside and prepared some more ribs, hamburgers, and hot dogs. We were out of brats. Darn. The ladies came through once more, and prepared their favorite recipes, even though some of them (Ruby Mae's fish noodles, for instance) took a while longer. So, it was nearly dark by the time we settled down at the same five tables we'd eaten on the day before. Mel and I set candles and lanterns out, and frankly, the yard looked intimate and festive.

Just as we were finishing up our meal and anticipating dessert, Emma tapped me on the shoulder and asked for a moment of my time. We walked a few steps into the shadows beneath the giant, ancient oaks. She turned to me and said, "Hugh, I wanted to run this by you to get your opinion before I asked Del."

"Okay, Emma. I'm game. What's up?"

"Well, I noticed in Del's talk to all of us yesterday that he'd like to visit Road's End again. Since he's sort of footloose at the moment, as far as work and a home are concerned, would you object, or do you think anyone else in town would object, to my asking Del if he'd stay in one of my spare bedrooms as part of his pay—the Lord knows I have more rooms than I know what to do with—like the church does for Bristol, although I admit he doesn't get paid anything else. Del could do my yardwork and other maintenance jobs around Rivermanse. That should keep him busy for years! That would free up Bristol, who, sweet man that he is, has been trying to cram it all into his already busy schedule. And it would give Del a place to live in a town he's already said he's fond of, and a job to give him a sense of worth. What's your take on this?"

I looked at Emma in the dim light and saw a precious woman, a friend, a sister in Christ, and one of the gentlest people I've ever met. "Emma, I think you already know what my take is on that idea. It's a wonderful and perfect gesture on your part, and though he hasn't yet given you an answer, or heard about it, for that matter, I have no doubt he'll accept with a joyous heart. Let me know what he says!"

"Oh, don't worry, Hugh. I will." She turned to go, then stopped and looked back at me. "You know, Hugh, it appears to me that we've misjudged Del all this time, much like I misjudged all the kind, loving, and somewhat insane people of Road's End for so long."

I laughed and walked over to her for a hug. "You know, Emma, I've come to that conclusion too—not about you, but about the way I saw the crazy ones in this town. Deep down, they're brave, loyal, and will do anything for anyone, even risk their lives, as we saw them do. You did, too, Emma. You fought right alongside the rest of us and before that, offered safety and security to Del up at the cabin. If they hadn't had that tracer on his clothing, they'd never have found him. You're a brave, fine woman, Emma, and we are so lucky to have you in Road's End."

"Thanks, Hugh," she said with a smile. "You too, you know. You too."

It was late that night when I had a chance to talk to Del. He told me about Emma's offer and said he'd decided to accept her generous gesture. I told him he'd made the right choice, and that we were genuinely pleased he'd be staying in our little village.

"Do you think the quiet will wear on you, Del?"

"Quiet? What quiet? I've never seen this town when it wasn't in the middle of a blizzard or a horrendous thunderstorm, with gunplay, no less. You mean I can actually look forward to some quiet once in a while?"

I nodded. "Yep, and even better than that, you'll be privy to all the ridiculous stunts that George and Dewey pull off and all the other excitement around here. Are you sure you're up for all this nightlife and revelry every day?"

He pretended to think about that. "Yeah, I think I'm up to it, Hugh. But there's one thing I want to confess to you, and it has nothing to do with the cartel."

"Go ahead. I'm anxious to hear."

"It's about that time I told you about my background and my dad killing people and my mom killing my dad."

"Okay," I said. "What about it?"

"I told you I was lying just to create a little fun, but it was the truth. The cold, hard, ugly truth."

"Oh, Del, I'm so sorry. That had to be the hardest childhood I've ever heard about."

"Yeah, thanks, Hugh. It was tough, all right. But I told you that story to gauge your reaction."

"And …?"

"I thought you'd toss me out on my head, knowing I came from such crappy parents, but you didn't. You were genuinely sad to hear my story. You cared. You heard all the bad I had to tell you, and you accepted me as I was—a sad combination of being rotten to the core and an innocent victim of my upbringing. I guess I just wanna say thanks for seeing past the ugliness and looking for the Del I could've been if I hadn't had such a bad start."

I couldn't say anything for a minute. "Del, I don't know what to say. When I heard the pain of the little boy you once were in the voice of a full-grown man, I knew you were a victim of your home life, your circumstances, and the path your dad chose, as well as the act your mother felt was necessary. It broke my heart to hear your truth, even though you claimed it wasn't true. Frankly, Del, you're not all that good at lying. And as far as not becoming the man you could've been, well, you know, it's never too late. You've taken some giant steps just lately."

Just then Mel came in with fresh coffee (decaf, thank goodness) and some of Sadie's cookies and doughnuts she'd spirited away before they were unveiled to the hungry horde.

"May I join you two handsome gentlemen?"

"You certainly may, my dear, but I'm afraid you'll have to excuse this handsome gentleman while he gets a handkerchief. I have something in my eye. Both eyes, that is."

Chapter Forty-Two

An hour later, Del excused himself to go to bed for his last night in The Inn at Road's End. He planned to take up residence at Emma's Rivermanse the following day. Melanie and I were resting in bed and taking some time to be together without a crowd of residents or drug dealers surrounding us.

Mel spoke first. "That was a generous offer Emma made to Del, wasn't it?"

"Mel, that woman amazes me. Instead of being afraid to have Del in her house as many others in society would feel, she thinks the best of him and then offers what is best for him to get him started in his new life. I have a feeling we have a new, long-term resident in Road's End."

"And he's sane, too! That evens up the playing field a bit, doesn't it?"

I smiled and took her soft hand. "Yep, sure does. If we can just find a few more racketeer-turned-good guys to move in, we might be evenly matched. Gives us something to shoot for, doesn't it?"

"Yes, it does, hon. But please don't refer to shooting." She angled herself to get a better look at me. "I'm looking forward to learning more about this new Del we have. His past was horrible, and he fell victim to darkness as he grew older. But I really think he's turned a corner and we're going to see a much happier Delbert T. Jackson than the one who first came to town. And speaking of the first time we met him, why is it he sounds and acts so much friendlier, so much more educated and cultured and even more intelligent this time around? Yes, he was sullen and crabby at first when Mack brought him here but look at the difference in him in just a few days."

"You know, Mel, I've wondered about that too. Personally, and this is just my uneducated guess, but I think he acted and sounded the way he had to in order to fit into the society he was in. I think the boost of self-confidence he got here gave him a reason to behave and act better all the way around. He seems to be a highly-intelligent man with a good grasp of the English language and grammar *and* a conscience.

When you think about it, he had no reason to act better or to display any intelligence while he was living a life of crime."

"Makes sense. What's going to happen with him with the charges that've accumulated against him?"

"Not sure, but Mack indicated when I spoke to him this afternoon, that he'd put in a good word for Del for his willingness to let TJ take another crack at him, and for his work as an inside man in the cartel. I think he'll come out of all that just fine."

"How'd Mack take it when you told him TJ didn't do a thing while he was in town? After all, they were counting on being able to nab him in the act. That didn't happen with our scheme, although it certainly got them to leave Road's End in a hurry. Was he upset?"

"Naw, they've got plenty of other stuff they can pin on him, which frankly, weakens their case to let him get as far as Road's End in the first place. I don't know why they needed any more bad stuff on him, but that's above my pay grade. But Mack thought our idea was brilliant. Now TJ thinks Del is dead, and will never, ever want to come to Road's End again. It's a win-win. Del will still have to officially change his name and we might have to get used to calling him a different name if strangers ever come to town …"

"But why?"

"Why call him a different name?"

"No, why would strangers ever want to come to town?"

"Good point, hon. Good point."

"What do you hear from Sadie and Ruby Mae and their problems?"

"Well, I asked Sadie just before we came in for the night and she said she'd found a whole new reason for living—not that I was ever aware she needed one. It's easy to forget that Sadie, crabby and independent as she is, also has a vulnerable side. Obviously, she has a crush on Leo, but only time will tell us if it's for real or just a passing fancy. I suspect it's a little of both. She's been crabby for a long, long time now, and maybe tapping into the softer side of her was nothing more than a welcome relief. We'll see. And Ruby Mae … well, I haven't talked directly to her, but Grace tells me she's weighing her options—selling her hats online, giving up making new hats per Grace's ultimatum, or becoming a YooHoo star."

"I thought Grace told her she'd look orange."

"She did, but Ruby Mae thinks the Lord might want her to die her hair orange—it's the latest trend, you know—to blend in better with the rest of her."

"Oh, good grief, Hugh. If she dies her hair orange and YooHoo makes her look orange to begin with, what will her hair end up looking like?"

I put my hand on her shoulder and said, "Hon, calm down. Remember Grace wasn't exactly truthful when she said YooHoo made people look orange. For that matter, *I* wasn't exactly truthful when I didn't correct her mangling the name of YouTube. Besides, there is no YooHoo, except that drink I loved as a kid and if we're lucky, she'll never find out the truth. Grace will tell her it went out of business or something. At the very least, it'll be interesting to see what happens next with her and her hats."

"Okay, good. It's been a rough few days, but we've done a lot of good stuff." She ticked off the points on her fingers. "The ladies had a wonderful time at the cabin and will be looking forward to visiting again, the men didn't die of starvation, we fought valiantly and our Lord led us in battle both times. Nobody, aside from the bad guys, was hurt, Hazel saw her angel, an angel visited you, we gave the old Del a rather unusual send-off, and we welcomed the new and improved version of Delbert T. Jackson into our hearts and homes." She took a breath. "Emma now has a protector and handyman up at her house, Del has a place to live and a way to make a living with his head held high, Bristol's workload is lessened, Mack no longer has to feel bad about dumping Del off with us, TJ will never darken our town's village limits again, Sadie's got a new reason to live, George and Dewey didn't kill anyone or get killed themselves by being detectives ..."

"Sorry to interrupt, hon, but you look like you need some air. That's all true, but Ruby Mae is going to continue to make her fishy noodles for every potlick because Dewey won't be quiet about them, and I still haven't seen an angel."

"Are you happy now that you've found the downside?" She elbowed me and grinned. "Besides, an angel carried you down from the church roof. That was a real miracle."

"Oh, hon, I know that and I'm very grateful, and yes, it was a miracle, but I'd just like to see the angel who helped me ... well, not die, I guess. I was certain I'd be facing Jesus in just a few seconds, but He saved me from death. And as for seeing an angel, maybe I will someday. I'll just keep asking God."

"Yes, do that, Hugh, but the Lord will decide when, where, or never. Now let's get some sleep."

"Okay, hon." I gave her a kiss and turned out the light, snuggling up against her, and thanking the Lord for my beautiful, kind, gentle, and wise Melanie.

Four hours later, I awoke to realize I'd forgotten to use the bathroom before going to sleep. I was still wrapped around Mel and had to untangle myself. She roused a little and turned over. "Sorry, sweetie. I have to visit the bathroom. I'll leave the light out, okay?"

"Um-m-m-m-m."

I wasn't sure if that was an "okay," "don't you dare," or "why don't you go *before* we crawl into bed? It's been 25 years now." I chose to believe she was saying, "Of course, my love, go right ahead. I'll be right here waiting for you to come back to bed, and it's no interruption at all." I can read a lot into "um-m-m-m-m." It's a gift.

I turned over, tossed back the covers, fumbled around for my slippers and then gave up, walked barefoot in the pitch dark to where I thought the door probably was, missed and tried again, and on the third try found it, stubbed my toe, then minced my way along the wall to the bathroom. Five minutes later I was on my way back to bed. I heard a "cluck, cluck" from downstairs, but I didn't give a rip. If Francine wanted to roam around the inn at night, more power to her. I needed sleep.

There was a welcome glow emanating from our bedroom that lit my way back to the bedroom. *Mel must have turned on the light. What a sweetie.* I walked back into the room with a lot more confidence and fewer little accidents than I had leaving it, and walked over to the bed. Mel was in the same position as when I'd left her. I reached over to turn off the light. The room lit up. *Wait. This light wasn't on. I just turned it on. Maybe Mel's side? Yeah, that makes more sense.* I leaned over Mel to the lamp on her nightstand, and turned that light off. Again, the room lit up. *What's going on here? Did I fall asleep in the bathroom and I'm dreaming?*

I heard a soft chuckle, and startled, I looked in the direction it came from—behind the bedroom door. Slowly, the glow became a full-blown radiance I've never experienced before and moved away from the wall slowly. Once my eyes adjusted, at least partially, to the light, the mystery of the blinding glow was solved.

There in the corner of the bedroom stood an angel, resplendent (and very tall) in his tunic of white belted linen. He held a mammoth sword in his right hand. He glowed with a light that defies description by mere humans and it was all I could do stop myself from falling to my knees—not in worship, but because my legs wouldn't hold me up any longer.

Instead, I sat on the edge of the bed with a 'thunk' and a bounce, and stared, open-mouthed at one of God's majestic and mighty angels not two feet from me. I wanted to say something—anything at all—to thank him for coming, and for carrying me down safely from the church roof (because I somehow *knew* he was that angel), or for giving Hazel the warnings, but my heart pounded so fiercely, it was all I could do to keep up with the blood pumping through my veins, let alone put together a coherent sentence. I think, though, he knew what I wanted to say from the look on my face. I don't know how long I sat there mesmerized by his magnificence and the great blessing God had bestowed upon me. When it was time for him to go, he smiled, lowered his head in a sign of recognition and farewell, and disappeared.

The glow remained for five minutes or so—after all, a light of that brilliance doesn't fade away in an instant—and when it had finally disappeared, I sat there on the edge of the bed in the dark. *Thank You, my Lord and Savior. Thank You.*

For the longest time, I sat there in shock and wonder, contemplating the awesomeness of the Lord's mighty angel and our Father's sweet love in answering my prayers.

And then … I wept.

3333333333333333

Dear Reader,

I hope you enjoyed *Misjudge*—Book #3 in the Road's End series—and if you haven't read Books 1 and 2, *Misstep* and *Mistrust* (formerly *Faux Pas*), I invite you to do so. *Misfits* (#4) and *Misfire* (#5) will be coming soon! Same crazy people, same little town, but different adventures for the fine and funny folks of historic Road's End. Lots of humor, inspiration, and adventure for readers of all ages with no bad words, sexual content, or violence.

Spend some time in the presence of retired Air Force chaplain, Colonel Hugh Foster, his loving wife, Melanie, and the other crazy/loyal/funny/stubborn/devout/and just plain weird residents of the tiny and historic village. The Fosters bought the Inn at Road's End to relax and enjoy their retirement. Too bad they didn't get it.

I love to hear from my readers. Please feel welcome to contact me at deborahdeetales@gmail.com.

I hope you've accepted Jesus Christ as your Lord and Savior. He loves you, you know. Enough to die for you. Please don't die without Him.

"But may the righteous be glad and rejoice before God;
may they be happy and joyful."
(Psalms 68:3 NIV)

Remember to always Laugh with the Lord!

Deb

About the Author

Deborah Dee Harper writes from Murfreesboro, Tennessee, and specializes in humorous, inspirational Christian books for both children and adults. Her novel, *Misstep,* is the first of five novels in her Road's End series.

Deb has three grown children—Derek (married to Renee), Dennae (married to Richie), and Darice. Between them, they've given her five lively grandsons—Dustin, Hunter, Cannon, Tyler, and Adam, and one beautiful granddaughter, Molly. Deb took an early retirement and began writing seriously, including two newspaper columns, feature columns, greeting cards, essays, articles, poetry, and had stories published in multiple anthologies including *Chicken Soup for the Soul.* She was a member of the Jerry B. Jenkins Christian Writers Guild. Her manuscript for *Misstep* was a finalist in their 2009 Operation First Novel competition.

Deb finds humor everywhere and believes God deliberately gave us a sense of humor to enjoy the truly funny, joyous, unbelievable, or downright silly things in life. Humor not only gives us joy, it often changes our opinion of others (or ourselves) and helps bridge the gap between people of differing opinions. When she's not writing, Deb enjoys photography, herb gardening, astronomy, and chasing the occasional grizzly bear for a picture.

Visit her website at
www.deborahdeeharper.com

Follow her on Facebook:
https://www.facebook.com/authoredeborahdeeharper

Follow her on Amazon:
http://amazon.com/Deborah-Dee-Harper/e/B005D2HS6Y

Other Books by the Author

Now Available on Amazon

Coming Soon!

Deborah Dee Harper

Thank you for purchasing my book.
If you enjoyed reading Misstep, please tell your
friends, and provide a brief review online to help
others discover my work.
I appreciate your help.

Deb

www.ingramcontent.com/pod-product-compliance
Lightning Source LLC
Chambersburg PA
CBHW070632260626
47161CB00007B/2670